1-6-16.

Alexa Anne Kempson (signature)

The Tiger Door

Second in the Manawassa Springs Series

Alexa Anne Kempson

D1522157

Cover Illustration: The Tiger Door by Alexa Anne Kempson
ISBN-13: 978-1512265255
ISBN-10: 151226525X

ALEXA ANNE KEMPSON

13.02

DEDICATION

I dedicate this book to old friends from Workman Junior High and Pensacola High School who enjoyed reading my stories and comics such as they were.

CONTENTS

CONTENTS (CONT.)

A note from the author

Dear Reader,

    A number of characters and situations which were introduced in "The Lady With The Lantern" insinuate themselves to a small degree into "The Tiger Door." It is best to have read the former story in order to understand fully the mystery here. Even so, whether the reader is familiar with the first Manawassa Springs book or not, a list of important characters from the first book can only be of help. The list is appended at the end. I hope it proves to be a handy reference.

    Alexa Anne Kempson

PART I
THE LAMB, THE LION AND THE TIGER

The Lamb
William Blake

Little Lamb who made thee
Dost thou know who made thee
Gave thee life & bid thee feed.
By the stream & o'er the mead;
Gave thee clothing of delight,
Softest clothing wooly bright;
Gave thee such a tender voice,
Making all the vales rejoice!
Little Lamb who made thee
Dost thou know who made thee

Little Lamb I'll tell thee,
Little Lamb I'll tell thee!
He is called by thy name,
For he calls himself a Lamb:
He is meek & he is mild,
He became a little child:
I a child & thou a lamb,
We are called by his name.
Little Lamb God bless thee.
Little Lamb God bless thee.

CHAPTER ONE
THE INHABITANTS OF MAISON LEMOYNE

Calla Lily Martin
March, 1906

Calla Lily Martin lay perfectly still. She had no energy to do otherwise. Consumption would have its way. At least that was what Dr. Jefferson Landry said. He said that her task was to remain as still as possible and to breathe evenly and slowly, even if it hurt. She was not to gasp or breathe too deeply because that was when the blood came.

Outside her window the azaleas were in bloom. The whole yard was a riot of whites and pinks and purples. She half lay, half sat propped up high on a pile of fluffy goose down pillows so that she could see them. Dr. Landry had ordered it. "Azaleas," he had said, "are the perfect flower for you, little Calla. You see, God made them so beautiful that they do not need a scent like roses or honeysuckle. You don't have to be near them to know all their glory. Little Princess Calla can enjoy all their beauty from her tower and without overextending herself."

Calla liked Dr. Landry very much. Maman had brought him from New Orleans to care for her. He told her so many stories about New Orleans. He promised her a trip there when she was well. Even when Calla felt very weak and very tired, and when she didn't even want Nurse there, she welcomed Dr. Landry's visits. He was not at all like that *other* doctor – the young one with slits for eyes and too many teeth for his mouth. It's true that Dr. Landry was old, forty, if he was a day. But he had only a little silver, right at his temples, in his sleek black hair. Calla loved that his hazel eyes sparkled whenever he talked to her. He always took his time with her. He didn't just stride in with a sour face like Dr. Caldwell, and without a word, grab her wrist to check her pulse, tapping his foot like he had some place more important to go. She was glad Maman had dismissed Dr. Caldwell for her family's physician from New Orleans. Calla told Nurse that this was the right thing to do because now the impatient young doctor could spend more time caring for Mrs. Bellingham who was very ill, too. Now Dr. Landry came often and stayed – long, cheerful visits as if Calla were his only patient.

"Then the matter is settled." Calla thought, "When I get well I will learn proper manners like Maman, as well as all the duties of running a household. Then perhaps I shall be a suitable match for Dr. Landry." She made a quick calculation using her hands (although her tutor had told her repeatedly that 10 year old girls must not use their fingers when they are doing sums). "Yes." She said triumphantly. "When I am 17 I will be ready for the responsibilities and joys of marriage." That was the phrase Maman had used for her sister when Aurélie wed. Calla understood the responsibility part, but what were the joys? She would find out. "Then I shall marry Dr. Landry. He will be close to fifty." Calla strained to think of someone who was fifty, and who was still handsome.

Mr. Atkins the blacksmith was "just past the half century mark" she well knew. She had heard as much when Edna the maid and Nettie the occasional help snuck out for a cigarette and were talking beneath her window. They often hid in the shrubs beneath her to gossip. This location had two advantages. For the servants it was protected from view and earshot of the public rooms. For the confined inhabitant of the second floor room it was a "sweet spot" for eavesdropping on conversations. Calla would never tell Maman that they met there because she gathered the most interesting news of Manawassa Springs in this way. Nettie, who was an Old Maid at thirty-two, had said that Mr. Atkins was suitable for "a girl who had been overlooked by a younger generation of men." Mr. Atkins might be suitable for Nettie, but was not adequate for a well-born lady like herself. Besides Calla thought he smelled like horses and smoke.

There was "the Advocate" as Maman referred to Mr. Grimm the lawyer. He might be fifty, but he looked older, not much hair except a bushy mustache. Just like his name he was mournful and sour. Carl Phillips, thrice married, twice widowed, was two score and eight (so said the hapless Nettie). That was close to fifty. His new wife Gwendolyn was very, very young. "Finally he will have a wife to provide him with the sons he needs to carry on the family business." opined Nettie. Calla's mind reviewed a number of other candidates whose age hovered around fifty. She came to the conclusion that Dr. Landry would surpass them all in the ability to retain his youthful looks and vigor. "That settles it. I will wed Jefferson Landry in seven years." She declared this aloud, but barely above a whisper being exhausted from her mental exercise. Her head sank deeply into her pillow mountain. Exhausted, she dropped into a sleep as deep as the Gulf of Mexico.

The Lion
Alexa Anne Kempson

Tawny fur and mane of gold
Hide a heart that's dark and cold.
Sphinx-like sits and suns by day,
But night, impelled, must seek its prey.

For self is center and not denied
Spurred by instinct, lust and pride
To seek what suits its purpose best
The Lion forsakes the death of rest.

Léonie Mathilde Lemoyne De Bienville-Martin
April, 1906

The sun was setting and just visible through the tall azaleas that invaded the bay window of the small back parlor at Maison LeMoyne. Léonie sat looking peacefully composed, as straight-backed as the Victorian chair that her form graced. She possessed a beauty in which the majesty of aristocratic French Creole imposed itself on what many considered a less noble ancestry, a subject never broached by the family. Nevertheless, silent evidence of indiscretions among the noblesse oblige cropped up in generations from time to time. Léonie reflected this evidence: jet black hair that curled tight around her face and skin that appeared to be kissed by the southern sun. Never resentful of that aspect of her heritage which many rejected, instead she gloried in it. Her father considered it a liability and had exiled her to Manawassa Springs as the wife of a weak and ineffectual man. It had not been long after their wedding that Léonie had risen to ascendency in all things over her husband, including business affairs. Now she sat awaiting what any mother would consider to be the worst of reports.

Without looking behind her at the dying light she mused that the beautiful display there would linger a little longer, and then it would be gone as would Liliane Aimée. She steeled her mother's heart against emotion. John Martin quietly opened then closed the door as he entered. He dutifully seated himself next to the inanimate form of his wife. Grim faced and disheveled, he presented a stark contrast to Léonie. It was as if all the heated emotion of grief which the wife ought to have felt had fled into her husband – driven out by her own coldness. John Martin rocked in his chair and mopped his brow, not daring to attempt to comfort or draw comfort from Léonie. He did not even glance in her direction. Dr. Landry entered and from the look on his face the couple knew that the news was what they had expected.

The doctor took a seat opposite the odd couple and drew a deep breath. Involuntarily John reached a hand to his wife's arm. Her recoil was instantaneous and not unnoticed by the doctor. Clearing his throat he spoke in a forthright, but compassionate manner.

"I wish I could bring you a better report, but I am afraid that I cannot."

He paused to let this sink in. His eyes moved from husband to wife. How different the reaction of each. He, like the sunset behind him burning itself out as it must at each day's end, wore a face fiery with despair at the approaching end. She bore a countenance as smooth and cool as the waters of Lake Manawassa. He quivered with fear and dread. She sat wooden like her chair, looking as unconcerned as the dog asleep at her feet.

"The delay in sending her to a sanitarium has proven to be a great mistake," he concluded gravely.

With this pronouncement a stifled cry escaped John Martin. After a moment of silence John replied in a halting voice "I know you questioned my wife's…our decision (his eyes momentarily darted to the mannequin beside him), but we thought it would facilitate her recovery for her to remain here at home with those who love her."

"You should make her comfortable and cheer her as much as possible, but the end is not far off."

"I…we will do everything possible to accommodate Calla… Liliane Aimée and… and…" his voice trailed into oblivion.

"Thank you, Dr. Landry. Please accept our appreciation for all that you have been able to do. Do not distress yourself. With consumption, her demise was inevitable." Léonie's voice scattered a hard frost throughout the room.

Repulsed, the doctor turned to the agonized father. "I am truly sorry, Mr. Martin, that I could not do more." He turned to Léonie. "*Je suis très désolé, Madame.*"

Léonie's green eyes met his. "*Merci. Je suis vraiment reconnaissant, Docteur.*"

***

John Mosley Martin
May, 1906

John Martin was not known as an adamant man. Quite the opposite, he was widely noted for his amicable compliance in all matters. Everyone who had social acquaintance with him recognized this as an asset and conversed easily with him. All who had business dealings with him saw it as a weakness and took advantage of it. From the beginning of his marriage his wife had done the latter. The servants, at first, contrasted his "good nature" with her "sour disposition" and preferred the master to the mistress a dozen times over. However, after four or five years of service, their opinions altered considerably. It wasn't that they grew to like their mistress any better, but that they grew to despise their master for his pusillanimity. He was incapable of making a decision. Consequently, all matters, domestic and business alike, fell to his wife. He consistently let everyone down. He always did it with soft words and jest, but the effect was the same: you were left at the mercy of the Lion Warrior (for that is what Léonie Mathilde meant according to an educated maid who lasted only two months at the Martin household.)

So it was that John Martin had all the appearance of authority over LeMoyne, but none of the substance. The first battleground was the name of the abode itself. John had planned their home as a surprise to please his bride. At the suggestion of Léonie's father John acquired an architect, one Monsieur Pasquier, a native of New Orleans. The esteemed architect designed a house that was apropos to his wife's home city. The landscaping was another matter. Bougainvillea and Oleander were both very fine, but John Martin loved azaleas. It may have been the last thing he was in charge of, but he insisted that his favorite shrub be planted everywhere: the foundation of the house, in large drifts around the yard and at the back border of the property. Every color known to the azalea color spectrum of the era was planted. The home itself was painted a hue of primrose that befitted both the native wild azalea and the finer homes of New Orleans. The color contrasted appealingly with the typical colors of the cultivated azalea kingdom. Certain that his young bride would approve, John Martin dubbed their home "Azalea Cottage." After a honeymoon in Paris (for which John cared not a whit) he brought his bride to her new abode which was fully ablaze with azalea blossoms. She expressed approval of the New Orleans architecture and color by remarking, "Maison LeMoyne will be a suitable residence. Thank you." The name officially became Maison LeMoyne.

John sat in his cramped study exhaling occasional clouds of smoke from his pipe. Here, and here alone, he was himself. Here he gave free reign to both thought and manner. Over twenty years of matrimony had instructed him well in keeping his place. His place was the dark paneled study that was situated at the back of the house, not far from the kitchen. As the wind prevailed from the opposite direction, his sanctum sanctorum was relegated to the only place in the house where the odor of his habits, whether pipe or cigar, would not offend. John made no protest, but settled in as comfortably as he could.

He was not much of a husband, not much of a businessman, not much of a father. He winced at this last thought and puffed. Harry was dead because he, John Martin, would not countermand his wife's plan to send the young man to South America. She could not see how ill-equipped Harry was. "Henri must go. It is settled. It will make him a man." Léonie told him. "And if it doesn't?" He had retorted. "Then it will break him." She stated this flatly and without emotion. A mother should have emotion where her children were concerned. She had been correct, though it was the less preferable of the two alternatives that befell Harry. He had died of a fever without accomplishing a thing. Aurélie, beautiful and senseless, had been forced into an arranged marriage with a wealthy, but philandering husband. John knew his character and had he spoken up, she might now be with a suitable common man, poorer but happier. Instead, she had lost her own babies and, unable to endure her husband's dalliances, killed herself. In arranging that marriage, his wife had not been concerned about her daughter's future; she cared only for the right of access across the Peyton scrub land. The spur to the lumber mill would increase Bienville-Martin profits.

Then there was Calla Lily. She had been born before her time. As long as her survival remained in question, her mother thought it best not to name her. She was kept isolated from everyone except the nurse Marthe. Léonie's life was also threatened by the untimely birth and she spent some weeks in recuperation. One would think an unbreakable bond would have been forged between the two of them. To survive danger together ought to create a bond. Yet as soon as old Dr. Guthrie had declared that the child would live, the mother had resumed her duties and ignored her newborn. John himself did not see the tiny infant for six weeks. When he was finally granted entry to the nursery and held the tiny form in his arms, he had called her Amy, his beloved little girl. When the time had come for the naming of the child he had brought up the name Amy, but the mother had simply said: Liliane. In a rare burst of rebellion, John insisted on "Amy" and, after being amended by Léonie to the French form, the child was baptized Liliane Aimée. Nevertheless, it fell out that the entire household, including John, called her Calla Lily because she was as pale and delicate as the flower often used to adorn the caskets of the departed. Calla Lily reminded everyone of the fragility of life and the inevitability of death. All, however, were careful to avoid this designation in the presence of Léonie because they feared the mistress's wrath. In front of the mistress she was always called Liliane or Liliane Aimée. The child seemed to understand and accept this dichotomy with magnanimous grace. John reflected sadly on Calla Lily. Soon she, too, would be gone. Death would take her away and leave him no comfort at all at Azalea Cottage. Even if John were a strong man, he could not contend with consumption. He could have saved his other two children, but not Calla. He resigned himself to this fate; indeed, he knew no other course of action. Resignation was a way of life for John Martin.

Even in their love-life John was the resigned partner. To use the word love was an abomination. He shuddered at their recent conjugal encounter. Unexpectedly he was commanded to appear, to disrobe, to perform his duty and was instructed to do all this with as little pretense at enjoyment as possible. The latter was not difficult for it was a revolting encounter, at the end of which Léonie said, "Now that Liliane Aimée is to leave me, one can only hope this will finally produce a Bienville heir and need no repetition." John was physically sick upon his return to his room. Other men would not have stood for it. Other men would have lovers to comfort them. Other men would have beat Léonie senseless or killed her. But John was not a man.

John leaned back in his chair and watched the smoke rise to the ceiling in hazy circles. Léonie was soon to depart for New Orleans. The weeks that followed this would be a time of blessing for him and the household. He could come out of hiding. John hoped that her brother's June nuptials, the ostensible occasion his wife's trip to New Orleans, would be compounded with a great deal of business which might keep her in the city for some time. While there she might discover she was carrying a child. John snorted with disgust. Léonie's father had grown increasingly irritated by the fact that she had produced no heir, male or female. Harry and Aurélie were dead, now Calla would soon join them. John staunched the grief that welled up inside him. A few weeks without Léonie's presence would lift the pall over Azalea Cottage despite little Calla's illness. It always did, but inevitably upon her return the darkness would descend heavier than ever and smother the unhappy household.

***

NURSE'S SONG

From *Songs of Experience*

William Blake

When voices of children are heard on the green,
And whisperings are in the dale,
The days of my youth rise fresh in my mind,
My face turns green and pale.

Then come home, my children, the sun is gone down,
And the dews of night arise;
Your spring and your day are wasted in play,
And your winter and night in disguise.

Nurse Emily Louise Sattherwhite
May, 1906

Emily sat at her evening toilet. She had let her chestnut hair down and was brushing it the usual quantity of nightly strokes. A silver thread showed itself shining against the red-brown causing her to cease her activity and pluck the offending strand. "No longer in the flush of first youth," Emily mused, "nor even the second," she thought bitterly. She heaved a sigh and resumed her routine. "Yet, I have enjoyed nursing. It has given me a measure of independence and freedom. Had I been a man perhaps I would have become a physician." Emily paused again and toyed with the brush in her hands. She traced the oval shape of its head and its silver handle with her long fingers. She looked lovingly at the enameled back inset with mother of pearl. A gift from someone special. She resumed her ritual and her reflections.

She had begun as a hospital nurse driven not by choice, but by necessity. Emily sadly reminded herself that she had been born into money in New Orleans. She never expected to descend to the station in which she now found herself. A blissful childhood had passed playing games with her sister Nan and brother Freddie, but her most cherished time was spent with her father. She especially enjoyed the occasions he took her along to the docks where he inspected various imports and discussed business with tradesmen for his shipping concerns. Such comings and goings and danger were found there. This excited little Emily. She was sure to be a world traveler one day or in business like her father. Charles Sattherwhite was a big jovial man, sincere and honest to the core, a rarity for the turbulent decades after the War Between the States. He doted on his eldest daughter and, to the shock of many, rebuffed the scornful glances or comments that accompanied his treating a mere girl as though she were a son.

For the most part her education was happy. Emily enjoyed the benefits of a less than structured education (hence her trips to the docks), but without sacrificing the excellence one would expect under this informal tutelage. The finest private secular tutors, as well as the Ursulines from the Catholic school, were provided for her and her siblings. Her mother Annette touted her daughter as a fair young girl destined for a fortunate marriage. She waxed romantically to Emily about the availability of wealthy bachelors. Knowing Emily's thoughts, her father would wink at her and whisper in her ear, "You are bound for far greater things than a marriage to some dolt. I will see to that." She was known not only for her beauty, but for her wit which she never suppressed in public as a genteel lady ought to have done. "A more loving daughter no man can have. Nor a cleverer one." her father often told her. "What about Nan, Father?" He would laugh and only say, "Nan has her charms, to be sure, but cleverness cannot be counted among them."

Nevertheless, her vain and greedy mother was determined to connect Emily to a great family – European royalty would have best suited Annette's interests. So upon reaching fifteen and, despite the protests of both her father and herself, Emily was sent to finishing school in France. The sadness of leaving her Father's home was eventually balanced by the enjoyments she experienced in touring the continent as a part of her curriculum. Nevertheless, she longed to return to New Orleans and at each year's end could think of nothing else than the extended holiday with her father and siblings.

Her final year was nearing its close and she eagerly looked forward to remaining in New Orleans now that she was suitably "finished." She had not met royalty, much less married one, and so she knew when she was ensconced at home her mother would have endless designs to find her a wealthy spouse. Her mission was to escape her mother's designees of suitability and find a husband of her own liking and in her own time. Upon what ought to have been a joyous return, the tragedy of her Father's death wiped out all her happy anticipation. Before the normal stages of grief could effect a recovery to Emily's broken heart, her mother had married again. He was a well-known gigolo, a thoroughly worthless man named Marcel DuBois.

So short a period occurred between her father's death and her mother's remarriage that it had taken Emily's breath away. Her mother had hardly donned her mourning weeds when Marcel appeared on the scene. There was some trumped up excuse of conveying condolences from a long forgotten cousin. He spent an entire afternoon conveying these condolences and Emily remembered grinding her teeth and blushing with shame at the new widow's demeanor. Annette should hardly have been able to muster a weak smile at this point. Yet, there she sat with Marcel laughing and sipping coffee. Marcel was more than ten years her mother's junior and clearly a scoundrel, but her mother had been captivated by his charming attentiveness and flatteries in her time of need. The subsequent, swift marriage afforded Annette the luxury of boasting about her conquest of an exquisitely handsome and elusive bachelor. It simultaneously gave Marcel the funds to gamble away his wife's newly inherited fortune, drink heavily and carouse with women of questionable reputation. Annette spent many hours in her room, too ill for any society but Marcel's when he deigned to appear. Most often he could be found secretly admitting some loose woman to his quarters. Emily who was frequently an unwilling witness to this debauchery tried her best to persuade Annette to turn Marcel out of the house. Her mother would hear nothing against him. Eventually Nan was packed off to finishing school in France. Emily herself was to be turned out of the house altogether with a small stake which was to be used to embark on a life of her own.

Freddie was spared, God knows what, by dying six months after the wedding. He was barely fourteen at the time. The history of his demise was rather pathetic. Dear Freddie, being so like his father, an extremely curious naturalist, could never be found indoors; rather, wandering woods and fields at all hours day was his delight. His father accompanied him on many of these explorations, especially the ones fraught with risks. His mother paid little attention to their adventures. After Charles' death and Annette's remarriage, any notice of Freddie's activity was non-existent. He was never to be seen at home and when he returned from his excursions, evidence of the dangers he encountered could be seen on his person. Without a loving father to caution him, his adventures increased in frequency, danger and injury.

It was in comforting Freddie during the lingering days of his septicemia that her future was determined. She resolved on nursing, but the money allotted her had proven too small to satisfy her intentions. Nothing less than blackmailing the scurrilous Marcel allowed her to secure the necessary money to cover her fees and board at Bellevue Nursing Hospital in New York City for the duration of her stay. Her stepfather was only too willing to cooperate in order to be rid of Emily whom he considered a serious threat to his newly acquired lifestyle. An obligatory kiss deposited on her mother's cheek closed the door on her childhood and her family.

The nursing regimen and curriculum at Bellevue was rigorous, but rewarding. It was after the completion of her training in New York and subsequent employment at Bellevue that Emily stumbled upon the opportunity to return south to New Orleans. M. Georges Henri LeMoyne de Bienville of Bienville Conglomeration, New Orleans, Louisiana had fallen seriously ill after a ruptured appendix. He was an elderly gentleman entrenched in his prejudices, one of which was all things "Yankee." His business trips to New York were a necessary trial that he had to endure two or three times a year. Though it was a Yankee doctor who saved his life, he refused the ministrations of any nurse who had the misfortune to be born on the wrong side of the Mason Dixon Line. This left the hospital staff with few options to comply with his directive of having a *Southern* nurse. In fact, there were but two whose lineage would suffice. Melanie Tucker had only lately arrived from Mississippi and therefore did not have the necessary experience. The selection naturally defaulted to Emily Sattherwhite. She was doubly suitable as not only being from the South, but specifically from New Orleans. There was no cause for rejection in her appearance either, for she was young, shapely and handsome with beautiful chestnut hair which no nurse's cap could contain completely. For M. de Bienville it was a more than acceptable solution, so much so, that when he recovered, he arranged for her to have a position at St. Mary's Hospital in New Orleans. Nurse Sattherwhite made no objections and gladly returned to her birth city.

Once there Emily made no plans to reconnect with her mother. Annette had fallen so deeply into debt that her nerves were spent and her always delicate health was severely compromised. Marcel disappeared as soon as the money did. With both her father and brother dead, Emily, after moving to New York, had thought to rely on her sister as a source of information regarding their mother. There was not much to be gleaned from Nan who now lived in England. She had the good fortune to meet a respectable Englishman while on holiday from her school in France. For all her silliness even Nan understood that soon there would be no money left for her at all. So she married Henry Huxtible, a merchant of comfortable means with whom she had made an acquaintance when her class was touring the Lake Country. Annette had no inclination to correspond with either daughter and so Emily learned of her mother's welfare from rumor and gossip.

Emily built a career in nursing, first at St. Mary's and then as a private nurse. M. de Bienville had been so good as to boast about her skills so often to his friends and relatives that she and St. Mary's parted ways. This allowed her to pursue a more interesting and profitable path.

With great detail could Emily recall her first full charge, a Mrs. Lundquist. Here was a most remarkable woman. She had not reached forty when the cancer was discovered, far advanced and incurable. Her husband was a man of means and spared no amount of money on his wife's care. "It shouldn't be long until she departs this world." he mournfully confided in the young nurse. "The doctor says the tumors are throughout her whole body." The devoted husband had broken into tears. Whether it was Emily's therapeutic skill in nursing, the physician's medicines or Mrs. Lundquist's stubborn refusal to die, the gracious lady lived another five years. She had spells of moderate activity and spells of languishing near death, but throughout them all she remained gay and positive, and lucid to the end. Lydia Lundquist was well educated, well-traveled, well spoken. Her blue eyes would sparkle like sapphires in her pale face as she and Emily spent hours in lively and interesting conversation.

Emily was fortunate to have begun with such a patient, since the next ten years brought an array of moderately satisfactory to completely unsatisfactory charges into her life. There were nasty old men, too ill to function but who leered excessively at their pretty young nurse or who stole an inappropriate touch whenever possible. Their saving grace was that most of them died soon after becoming her patients. There were old women who for some reason did not deteriorate as rapidly as her male charges. As a rule the old men she nursed lived solitary lives, while the old spinsters and widows seemed to find other suitable old women as companions. The company of these companions seemed to have fostered the refusal to die in her old lady patients.

Emily put her brush down and mused on this. Perhaps it was companionship that aided or extended life. Perhaps it gave the old women something to live for. Women liked superintending things around themselves. She thought of how most of the old women had still run their households even from their deathbeds and had run their companions, too. Something to live for. Emily looked into the image in the mirror again. Despite the dimness of the light the lines on her face were plainly marked. Her age revealed itself even at night. Would she end up as an old woman issuing orders to her nurse and her companion? She sighed heavily. She had never had a companion. One who might have been, but she had been cast off despite her pleas. She picked up her comb to disentangle a small matted area of hair at the nape of her neck.

The name Margaretta Chase popped into her mind. Emily smiled at the thought of her. Emily was hired to nurse both her and her newborn child. At the insistence of the patient's husband, Emily was to indulge every whim of his wife, and whims she had in abundance. If her husband were correctly informed of their nature, he might not have been so insistent that Emily indulge them. For Margaretta, by way of the excuse of needing much solitude, often slipped out, known to Emily, but unknown to her husband, and dallied with unsuitable men. Emily remembered peering through the curtains of the nursery in the wee hours of the morning as she calmed the colicky child only to see Margaretta disappear into the night with some stable hand. Emily thoroughly despised her mistress, not only for her intrigues and infidelities, but for the rough treatment she herself suffered from Margaretta's whims. The abuse ranged from shouting to throwing objects and, on one occasion, wrenching her arm. That was the last straw. Emily confronted her patient with the things she had seen. Margaretta demanded of her husband that Emily be dismissed claiming she was now perfectly fine. As Emily packed that night, Margaretta died in her sleep.

A succession of faces rambled across her mind's eye: young boys and girls with consumption, assorted persons with malaria, quite a few with influenza, a military officer with both legs and an arm amputated. She nursed some to life and some to death, always plying her skill to the utmost of her ability and as compassionately as possible. She had begun to tire of her profession, of her ever-changing situations and of her life when an elderly man named Mr. Chilton Beauvais summoned her to his mansion. M. de Bienville had recommended Emily to him as the finest and most competent nurse in New Orleans. Since no one refused a summons from Chilton Beauvais, she went.

Upon arriving she was escorted into an enormous columned room – all gilt and mirrors. Mr. Beauvais, a withered and bent old man with wild gray hair and drooping face entered. He graciously greeted Nurse Sattherwhite then poured out his sad story. With tearful passion he told her of Hamlet Beauvais who was but fifteen and suffered agonizing abdominal pain and digestive disorders. No doctor had been the least useful in discovering and treating the ailment. Mr. Beauvais was adamant that if nothing was to be done for Hamlet, then he would have the best nursing secured for him. M. Georges Henri de Bienville had recommended Nurse Sattherwhite.

He had led her up two flights of an enormous staircase as wide as a city lane. At the top and to the left was a room which can only be described as being secured by two full liveried menservants. Mr. Beauvais gingerly opened the door so as not to disturb poor Hamlet. The velvet drapes were closed tightly. The room was so darkened by their closure and their thickness that seeing anything more than the tip of your nose was impossible. Emily let her eyes acclimate to the murky interior of the sick room but still had a difficult time making out the figure on the canopied bed. The odor was horrific. The pair quietly approached the bed and Mr. Chilton Beauvais cooed softly in a fatherly voice: "There now Hamlet, I have brought you an angel of mercy." The old man stepped aside so that Emily could approach the stricken boy. She bent closer to the bed as a huge deformed head reared itself from the pillow. A stench of warm breath assaulted Emily's face. She gagged as she saw an enormous tongue dangle from Hamlet's mouth; saliva dripped all over the bedcovers. Emily leapt back, both startled and relieved, for Hamlet was a Great Dane. Indignation buried deep within her for years, now boiled to the surface and overtook her speech. "Money be damned, reputation be damned. Hamlet be damned. You be damned." She spoke in her firmest voice: "I do NOT nurse pets." With that Nurse Emily Sattherwhite swirled about and left Chilton Beauvais in complete desolation.

Somehow this incident left Emily in a fine humor. Her former mood of darkness and dissatisfaction was temporarily dispelled. Shortly thereafter she was summoned again, by someone she trusted, at least up until the incident with Mr. Beauvais. M. de Bienville apologized for the episode declaring that he had had no idea that Hamlet was the intended patient. He had assumed it was Beauvais' gout that she was to tend to. He had more pressing matters which was why he had asked her to come. De Bienville's own son John Langlais[1] had just returned from South America where he had contracted a fever. He fell ill on the voyage home and now lay upstairs in a bad state. The doctors gave him excellent chances for

---

[1] The reader should know from the beginning that Langlais is pronounced Lang'-lee.

recovery, but recommended constant nursing to help restore him to health.

At the thought of Jean Langlais Emily lay down her comb and stared in the mirror. She ran her hand over her face: her eyes, her nose, her lips. He had been so frail looking the first time she saw him. A deathlike pallor had replaced what once must have been the vigor of young manhood. She had never met M. de Bienville's son before his illness since he had been sent overseas at a young age to oversee family interests. His profile was as handsome and chiseled as any Greek statue. Were it not for the hair, which in healthier times would have been spilling in long black curls over his perfect brow, but which now lay wet and lank from feverous throes, Jean Langlais could have been Adonis. When she looked upon him for the first time he breathed in long labored inhalations, his nostrils flaring rhythmically. His lips were parted slightly, full and sensuous lips. Despite his illness he exuded life. Emily clutched her apron and sat down on the chair next to the bed. She was overcome. She was captivated. She was in love.

The subsequent months of nursing Jean Langlais to health were all joy and brought new youth to Emily. Jean Langlais was charming without being insincere; educated without being patronizing. They held wonderful conversations on every topic, she being enriched daily by both his education, his experiences and his travels. He found her his equal on many topics of the arts and his better on all things scientific. He was ten years her junior, but the difference in age and in station of life meant nothing to either of them. M. de Bienville was at first pleased with the rapidity of his son's recovery. It recalled to him Emily's competent ministrations that had set him right so many years prior. As his son's convalescence progressed he grew cautious, then alarmed, at the change in the relationship between nurse and patient. Then there came the day when Emily was called to M. de Bienville's office, coldly thanked for her service, paid handsomely and dismissed. As she left Maison Bienville she glanced up to the top of the staircase at Jean Langlais. She was desperately trying to decipher the look on his face, when he turned and disappeared into the shadows of the second floor.

Now the tears, held back for many months, fell unrestrained. Emily recalled how she had wandered around New Orleans in a daze and ended up in Audubon Park. She sat upon a bench to soak up the fresh spring air and contemplate her future. Her world had changed irrevocably and forever. A man of middle age, attractive enough, though somewhat enervated in demeanor, had approached her and began an inquiry. She could recall the whole conversation without difficulty, for than man was John Martin.

***

"Good afternoon, Nurse. I hope I am not imposing upon your solitude." She looked up at the well-dressed gentleman.

"No, indeed, you are not, sir."

"Your uniform has given you away or I would not have been so bold to initiate a conversation. I believe I have seen you at Maison Bienville. You are nurse to my brother-in-law Jean Langlais de Bienville.'

"I was. He no longer needs my services." Emily now recognized the man as Léonie's husband whom she had seen on occasion at the mansion.

"I am glad. I don't mean that as it sounds. What I am trying to say is that I am glad he is well enough not to need you. I, however, am in need of a nurse. You, perhaps, could advise me of how to go about this in the most efficient way possible. I am not much for finding out how to do things, especially here in New Orleans. I rely on, on others very often."

There was something about his reticence and self-abasement that amused Emily and distracted her from current woes. He clearly wanted to ask if her skills were available, but was hesitant to ask her directly. The corner of her mouth twitched, but maintaining her professional decorum she replied to her questioner. "You seem perfectly sound, sir, and quite a figure of health. I am grieved that you are in need of nursing services."

He blushed. Emily could hardly believe it, but he did. She was enjoying herself immensely. Only his next words, so heart wrenching, deflated the playful nature of her side of the conversation.

"It is not for me." He swallowed hard and continued. "It is my little daughter, Calla Lily. She has consumption. I, we, that is, have recently learned of the severity of her condition and her imminent demise. The doctor advised us to make her as comfortable as, as…"

John choked on the last words and Emily came to his rescue. "I am so sorry to hear it, sir."

John Martin seated himself next to Emily and looked searchingly into her eyes. He was clearly desperate.

"The employment would not be here, I am sorry to say. It may be difficult to secure someone who would be willing to go so far. My wife Léonie and I live in a small town in Florida – Manawassa Springs. My wife, that is, I am here conducting business for her family, the de Bienville family as you know. I took the afternoon away from business. I saw you leave and thought I could catch you. You see, it occurred to me that an experienced nurse was far more likely to be found here than in…"

"Yes. I can come." She replied with no hesitation. To be near even a sister of Jean Langlais's would give her solace.

"You? I didn't mean to presume. I only thought you would know someone. I am sure there are many experienced nurses…"

"I will come and care for your daughter. I am a private nurse with quite extensive training and experience. Since I am currently between charges it is fortunate you followed me. When should I be ready to leave?

***

Emily snapped back to the present. John. He cared so for his little Calla. She had done all she could for the sick child. If only it were Léonie lying in bed feverish, consumptive and at death's door. "Oh," Emily uttered a sharp cry of pain. She had violently combed out the knot in her hair. A clump of chestnut with a few coarse silver strands lodged in her comb. She set to pulling the mess from its teeth. "Judgment for my evil thoughts," she said aloud and lay down her comb.

Emily knew John was weak. He was a broken man, but in her short time at LeMoyne she had come to care about him. She assumed he had no such feeling for her. His capacity for both desire and love had been utterly incinerated by Léonie. John was nothing but ashes inside. He had needed a strong woman, but not like Léonie. Not a woman who would devour him. Léonie was not strong, she was brutal. Once Emily had seen a hawk, in anticipation of its next meal, swoop down on an unsuspecting puppy. From nowhere the mother had leapt to do battle with the predator. The puppy had suffered some talon wounds, but thanks to its protectress, now lived. John needed a protectress. Perhaps Léonie would never return from her upcoming business trip.

***

The World of Kipling According To Calla
May, 1906

"I have always been extremely fond of Kipling." Calla reclined in her bed and toyed with Hermione the doll given to her by her father. "If I could be transported to another world I would go to the jungles of India. Not actually *inside* the jungle, that would be too dangerous, but *next* to the jungle. I would reside in a great white house with minarets all decorated with heathen symbols and gods and goddesses. It would be like the Taj Mahal only not so grand." Her imaginary world was interrupted by a fit of coughing. Nurse tended her patient and sadly noted to herself that the Taj Mahal was a tomb.

"I wouldn't believe in the gods and goddesses, but I would permit them because of their native beauty. God would not mind that. Don't you think so Nurse?"

"Surely not." Nurse Sattherwhite replied softly. During her monologue Calla had begun to sit more upright as her imaginations animated her. "I think you need to lie back a little." The competent nurse fluffed the pillows and the pale girl settled back into them again and continued her musings.

"My house would be long and low and take at least twenty minutes to traverse. I would have every kind of domestic servant. There would be ayahs and bearers and compound guards. My house would have to be in a compound for protection against animals and bandits and insurrectionists. I would have been married for some time to a colonel, I should think, a British one, not an American. We met when, when he was a dashing lieutenant and I was the ward of the British Governor. At first the Governor didn't approve of our plans to marry because Jeffery, I mean Lt. Jeffries which is my Lieutenant's name, had a great-grandmother who was a Hindu. But the Governor overcame his objections when Preston (that's his first name) saved me from being crushed by a rampaging elephant!"

Calla's narration was interrupted again by a cough spasm, a light one considering the current stage of her illness. Nurse Sattherwhite raised her to a sitting position, rubbed her back and dabbed her mouth with a cool, damp cloth. She laid the frail girl back on her pillows and soothed her brow with a clean cloth. Calla resumed her fantasy.

"We would have two children," she began softly and with gasps punctuating her monologue continued haltingly, "Nigel and Theodora, eleven and eight years old respectively. Their ayah would be as dark as the night and have a jewel in her nose and dangly earrings. Her robes would be white and flaming like the sunset. She would teach them all sorts of Indian words and customs, but I wouldn't object. It would be natural for them to learn of the culture over which they ruled.

"I would be able to see the entire jungle from my verandah where I would take tea, fresh Indian tea and it would taste so very superior to the tea that is shipped back to England or America. Don't you think so, Nurse?"

"Naturally it would," smiled Nurse Sattherwhite. Calla smiled wanly in return at this affirmation and continued.

"I would laugh at all the antics of the monkeys. They are so mischievous." She paused at length and closed her eyes. "Oh how I wish I could see Mr. Bellingham's monkeys and all the wild animals in his conservatory, even if they are from South America and not India. I imagine that is because South America is so much closer. I am sure if he had been able to import his creatures from India he would have done so. Indian animals are so superior."

Nurse Sattherwhite nodded her head and only managed to refrain from laughing by remembering the seriousness with which Calla conducted her narration and the nature of her illness.

"Exotic birds would flit from tree to tree and I would know all their names in English *and* in Hindi. There would be giant snakes, but I would avert my eyes from them. I don't like snakes. We have rattlesnakes here. They don't have them in India, do they?"

"I believe not."

Again Calla was seized with an involuntary spasm, worse this time. Nurse leaned over and caught the bloody sputum issuing from Calla's mouth and nose. As the wave passed, Nurse Sattherwhite hushed the sick girl compassionately.

"You need to rest now, my little Calla Lily. You are far too animated. Remember Dr. Landry's orders."

The girl leaned back into her fluffy head rest and drew her doll closer to her aching chest. Despite Nurse's admonition and after only a brief respite, she plunged forward with her jungle story with renewed strength.

"But the most intriguing animal would be deep in the jungle, mysterious and dangerous, just as in Kipling. The menacing Bengal tiger would have a growl terrifying all who hear it. He would have burning green eyes that continually watched for prey to devour. He would be satisfied only by death. That is why Preston and I would make sure that our compound was adequately protected so that little Nigel and Felicity…"

"…Theodora," interrupted the Nurse.

"Oh, yes. Theodora. That means "gift of God." Felicity means "happy." She cast large and sorrowful eyes towards the nurse. "I much prefer to be a gift of God and sad, than to be happy." Calla bit her lip at her own words knowing in her deepest heart that she would very much prefer to be gay and active, to run and play and dance and sing as she had before the ravages of consumption. Unable to bear these thoughts she plunged again into the world of her own making.

"To live there surrounded by love amidst beauty and danger, but completely protected and free all the same, I could…I would…die happy when the time came."

***

Into The Lion's Lair
June, 1906

Léonie sat at her ornate gilt secretary looking over accounts. The room about her suited her cold personality. "The Artic" is the name Marthe had given it. Léonie eschewed the wall-coverings that could be obtained in America. She thought them heavy and oppressive. Instead, she had ordered hers from Paris. They were a frosty blue with a *Fleur De Lis* pattern in the palest of gold. The drapes were pure golden silk from the Orient, via New Orleans, and the furnishings from Provence. A rich Louis XV rug adorned the floor.

"Who is it?" At the sound of someone knocking Léonie's sharp, but disinterested, voice pierced the thick wooden door.

"Nurse Sattherwhite, Madame." It was by royal command that everyone referred to the mistress of the house by the French form of address.

"Come in, Nurse." The tone of the voice shifted to annoyance.

Nurse entered the parlor where the mistress spent most of her waking hours conducting business.

"Excuse me, Madame. I have come to you about Ca… Liliane Aimée." She quickly corrected the heretical version of the child's name.

"You are stating the obvious, Nurse. What other reason would lead a nurse to distract me from my duties."

"Calla is not a precious daughter, but only a "reason" to this cold woman," thought the Nurse. Aloud she said. "She seems much weaker. Progressively her mind embarks upon her fantasies. They seem to offer her comfort. They distract and amuse her. She derives such childish pleasure from them. In particular…"

"To the point, if you please."

"She would love to see tropical things, exotic flora and fauna. She is taken with Kipling, India…"

"Are you suggesting we export her to India in her condition?" Léonie tapped her pen impatiently.

The sarcasm was lost on the Nurse. "No, Madame! I was wondering, Madame, if it were possible… we being in such close proximity and all…I don't think it would be presumptuous, but Madame is better suited to decide whether…"

"Nurse, if you are unable to articulate your point, I suggest that you retire to your room and draft a proposal for me. You can submit it whenever you are finished." Léonie turned her attention once again to the ledger before her.

"The conservatory at Belle Magnolia. If Calla could just pay a short visit. Mrs. Bellingham has offered numerous times…"

The words "Belle Magnolia" and "Mrs. Bellingham" froze Léonie mid pen-stroke.

The unobservant nurse blundered on unrestrainedly. Her love for the doomed child outweighed all caution that normally was applied in Léonie's presence. "I know that Mrs. Bellingham is recuperating, but Miss Bellingham and Miss Victoria have repeated the offer on her behalf. I am sure the child could be gently carried there, and perhaps a bath chair used to propel her about the conservatory for a brief, very brief tour. I know that Mr. Martin would have no objection, he is so fond of Calla Lily." (Her grievous error in nomenclature escaped her at this point.) "I would be at hand, of course, in case I was needed. Or perhaps Dr. Landry. That would be preferable. He is very fond of her and listens quite patiently to all her imaginative chatter. A tour of the conservatory would be so wholesome a venture before…." She let the next words go unspoken. "Do you think it possible, Madame?"

The nurse's request was met with icy silence. This did not

discourage Nurse Sattherwhite.

"Mrs. Bellingham is so young and kind and generous. We have all been grateful for her sick visits to Calla Lily, before she lost her own child and became so ill herself. I know that she cannot see Calla now, but her attentions have continued through Eudora and Victoria." The latter name she intonated with a sniff of disapproval. Though Mrs. Bellingham has none of her own, her concern for children is well known. The orphanage…"

Without looking up, and once again setting her pen to the ledger, Léonie interrupted the nurse's stream of praise for Mrs. Bellingham's benefaction. "That will be all."

"Yes, Madame." A flushed and angry Emily Sattherwhite left the room, glad that her mistress could not see her face.

"And Nurse Sattherwhite." Léonie halted the retreat of the angry woman. She turned to face her. "The child's name is Liliane Aimée." With that Nurse Sattherwhite closed the door behind her.

Léonie stopped writing and turned her eyes to the window. Aloud as if to the massive azaleas which bent their petalled ears to catch her words she said, "She is so very ill we dare not indulge every whim the child has." She resumed her accounting.

The azaleas trembled shaken by sudden spring breeze. Were it possible to translate their actions into words, the reply would have been, "Heartless woman."

***

Nurse Sattherwhite was not to be put off. She made the decision to approach John Martin after his wife had left for New Orleans. She was certain her pleas would not fall upon deaf ears. The father loved his little girl and would do whatever he could for her.

Léonie entered the carriage to go to the train depot where she would catch the train to New Orleans. John Martin was in his retreat reveling in a cigar when a faint rapping distracted his pleasure.

"Yes. Come in." He was puzzled. No one ever approached him here, or anywhere for that matter. He was all anticipation to see what would spur someone to knock on his study door. As the door opened and the form of Nurse Sattherwhite filled the doorway, his heart sank. His Calla Lily was dead.

"May I interrupt you, sir?" Her calm words reassured him that his daughter lived. Without waiting for a reply she stepped into the room.

"By all means." John pulled up a chair for the nurse. His admiration for her had grown during the weeks she had cared for Calla. Nurse Sattherwhite seated herself and straightened the crisp blue and white uniform. He looked at her as if for the first time. She was not young, but she was a remarkably pretty woman. Had her circumstances been different; had his choice in brides been different. He left the thought incomplete.

"Thank you, sir. I must speak to you about Calla Lily." Her compassionate brown eyes glistened with concern. Lovely brown eyes. "Er, certainly, Nurse. What can I do?"

Together they concocted a plan.

***

The intervening days of Léonie's absence were a blessing for everyone. Cook had begun singing her tunes again, bellowing loudly due to her deafness. No one minded. Edna became more negligent in her dusting, sloppy in her bed-making, and it paid not to look too closely at the rugs. Not a comment was made. No one cared. Nettie, who was perpetually lax and inefficient in whatever she was asked to do, supplemented her usual truancies with more frequent visits to Frank's shed.

The most marked change was in the Master. He almost deserved the title again. He, not Léonie issued orders, though they consisted mostly of affirming whatever the help told him ought to be done. If he felt like delaying dinner, it was postponed. If he wished to eat in his room, it was so. If he cared to smoke in the front parlor, the drapes were flung wide and the windows thrown open. Edna once caught him whistling. Nurse Sattherwhite was as cheerful as she could be as the nurse of so sick a child. She consulted rather than ordered the staff. A pleasant and casual manner sprang up between the Master and the Nurse. They were often seen in each other's company outside the sickroom.

The household fantasized that Léonie would never return. After her brother's wedding, perhaps she would remain in New Orleans. Her father was ailing, her brother away now on a honeymoon and business affairs had been cascading upon her as of late. Were it not for the sad aura cast by little Calla Lily's decline, LeMoyne would have been Azalea Cottage again, as cheerful and delightful a place as one could wish.

"Tap, tap…tap, tap." sounded at Emily's door.

She fetched her robe from the back of the chair and gathered it around her as she walked to open her door.

"John."

"May I come in, Emily?"

Without a word she opened the door fully to admit her visitor. Silently, John Martin closed it behind him.

***

THE TYGER

By William Blake

Tyger! Tyger! burning bright
In the forests of the night,
What immortal hand or eye
Could frame thy fearful symmetry?
In what distant deeps or skies
Burnt the fire of thine eyes?
On what wings dare he aspire?
What the hand dare seize the fire?

And what shoulder, & what art.
Could twist the sinews of thy heart?
And when thy heart began to beat,
What dread hand? & what dread feet?

What the hammer? what the chain?
In what furnace was thy brain?
What the anvil? what dread grasp
Dare its deadly terrors clasp?

When the stars threw down their spears,
And watered heaven with their tears,
Did he smile his work to see?
Did he who made the Lamb make thee?

Tyger! Tyger! burning bright
In the forests of the night,
What immortal hand or eye
Dare frame thy fearful symmetry?

CHAPTER II
THE TIGER DOOR

A Surprise Awaits
July, 1906

Léonie's brother's wedding was over and, unfortunately for the household of LeMoyne, there was not sufficient business to detain her in New Orleans any longer. She returned a day early from her trip. The house was not thoroughly prepared for her arrival. Léonie was agitated at the staff for the state of LeMoyne, as if prescience ought to have been an inherent ability of servants. "*Les incompétents.*" She muttered under her breath, but spoke openly nothing of what she felt. She didn't have to; the staff was too well acquainted with her body language not to comprehend her displeasure. She knew, rather than suspected, that something was amiss. She had hoped the child would die while she was away, thus sparing her. This had not occurred. Yet she knew whatever was going on involved the dying girl. Something had transpired during the month she was away. She patiently awaited the denouement of the mystery. Nothing could remain hidden from her for long.

Dinner passed without a word or a surprise. Neither she nor John was inclined to talk. His initial inquiry of her stay in New Orleans had elicited a succinct reply that it had proven successful. Nothing followed upon that remark. The dinner things were cleared away and John withdrew to his hideaway. Tired from her journey Léonie chose to turn in early. Before retiring Léonie made her evening rounds of the house. She was perplexed to see Nurse Sattherwhite, tray in hand, heading for the summer porch.

Her sharp call of "Nurse" arrested the woman's movement.

"Where are you going with that tray?"

All color drained from the nurse's face. "To the summer porch, Madame."

"In the middle of the night?" Léonie asked incredulously.

"Yes, Madame." And without waiting for further discourse the nurse vanished in to the depths of the hallway.

***

The absurdity of Nurse carrying a tray of food to the summer porch in the dead of night, tempted Léonie to assemble the household and interrogate them all. This was rejected in favor of sleep. Her condition was an annoyance. A wave of distaste rolled over her mind then receded into the gulf of oblivion. It had been necessary. Now Léonie was too tired to pursue the matter tonight; all would come to the surface in the morning.

The next morning at breakfast Léonie questioned her husband as to the housekeeping while she was away. Her inquiries were met with terse replies. Nothing he said shed light on the mystery of Nurse's behavior the previous night. It was clear that the household, including her husband, were conspirators in some matter that would displease her.

"How is the child?"

"Slight improvement in your absence." John had wanted to say "because of your absence," but restrained himself.

"I see. I shall pay a visit then." Apathy and boredom strove with reluctance in her reply.

No announcement could have been so unwelcome. John knew a visit was inevitable. Then his wife would discover what the household was striving to conceal. He had hoped to see a succession of five or six days before that happened. The time for reckoning had come.

"After breakfast I am sure dear Calla, er, Liliane Aimée will welcome a visit from you."

"Very well. I shall see to it that the sick room is prepared for me to come."

"Yes, well. You see, My Dear, ah… Cal…, Liliane Aimée, is no longer in the sick room."

"I beg your pardon? Where is she then? Have you sent her to a sanitarium?" Her anger grew with each question. "You moved her without asking me, her mother?" She answered her own question. "But that can't be!"

A boldness previously unknown to John infused the words that followed. "Yes, we *have* moved her, but not to a sanitarium."

"Then where?"

"To the summer porch." John folded his paper, slammed it on the table and stalked out of the room.

***

Edna, is the child awake?" The parlor maid was tidying up the tea things, except they were actually coffee things. The Madame eschewed tea in preference for bitter coffee.

"I believe so, Madame."

"Will you see to it that Nurse Sattherwhite prepares her for my visit?"

"Yes, Madame." The parlor maid replied knowing that nothing ever prepared Calla for her mother's visits. She gathered up her tray and turned her back to her mistress. In a fit of concealed independence Edna stuck out her tongue to no one in particular.

Sharply, her mistress addressed the retreating figure. "And Edna, mind yourself!" The panic stricken girl froze in her tracks, her mouth agape in horror. She whirled to face her mistress. All blood drained from her face and the china tottered perilously on the salver. "Maintain proper decorum." The terrified Edna was about to drop the tray altogether when her mistress continued, "Your cap is askew. Straighten it when you are relieved of your tray."

"Yes, Madame." Edna fled the room rattling the china as little as possible.

***

"Leave us, Nurse." The neat form of Nurse Sattherwhite retreated silently.

Léonie looked down at the pale figure asleep on the bed. In only months consumption had wasted the frame of the once plump girl. Liliane's bed was her world, and she looked but an insignificant speck of humanity upon it. Except for the flaming spots on her cheeks, her color was barely indistinguishable from the sheets. Any pity for the tiny thing before her was immediately swallowed up by anger. How dare she die? How dare she? Pity was reserved for weaklings. Léonie would have none of it. At her age Léonie Mathilde LeMoyne de Bienville-Martin still had not produced a viable heir to carry on the de Bienville name and dynasty. Another hope lay dying before her. "*Petits enfants ne sont pas fiables!*" She thought of Henri and Aurélie. She had been disappointed with her husband and their progeny, but she would not give in. There was still a chance.

Léonie swept her eyes around the porch taking in the transformation that had been accomplished in her absence. Potted plants crowded much of the area leaving room for the child's bed, a gaudy blue table and the chair used by her nurse. Sweeping panels of gauzy mosquito netting and flowing linen hung about the porch. They floated now and again carried by an occasional breeze from the back yard. The lush vegetation in the yard beyond the curtains peeped through in shifting greens and reds and yellows. Altogether it produced the effect of a tropical oasis.

The tiny form moved listlessly on the bed. A soft groan escaped her lips. Calla opened first one eye then another.

"Maman, you have come home," she murmured. "*Je suis content de te voir.*"

Home. As if Manawassa Springs would ever be her home. "Yes, child." She replied softly.

"Do you like my jungle that Father made?"

Resentment vied with self-pity in Léonie's breast. She knew she would never be loved by her child as John was loved. "It is unique." She spoke coldly.

"I was wrong." Her whispered words came haltingly and were punctuated by coughing.

A strange curiosity came over Léonie. She could not refrain from drawing closer to the dying girl. "Wrong? About what, Child?"

"The Bengal tiger, Shere Khan." She gasped. "That is what I have named him since he looks so fierce, but he isn't dangerous. He is a redeemed tiger, you see. He protects me from...." Blood from her mouth spattered her sheets as she coughed uncontrollably. Léonie drew back in disgust as the sick little girl continued. "My Shere Khan will reveal his true self. He will not relent until he sets things aright. Maman, do you think it possible that people can be mistaken about the nature of someone who frightens them? Perhaps it is that this person is not quite as awful as one imagines. Perhaps there is a reason. My Shere Khan has shown me many things to come." As if her pronouncement drained all energy from her, she closed her eyes and fell back upon her pillows.

Leonie did not understand these words; nevertheless, they struck a fearful chord in her. She stood erect and surveyed the room for her daughter's protector. There was no representation of a tiger to be seen. She was about to add this to Liliane's other imaginations when a sudden breeze agitated the linens that swathed the porch. Beyond the porch the azaleas and trees remained perfectly still. "How odd!" Léonie thought. Another gust, once again localized to the summer porch, whipped the

hangings into a frenzy. The hair stood up on Léonie's neck and she caught her breath. Her heart began to pound wildly.

Intensifying her search, she finally caught a glimpse of splashes of bright colors, not from the yard, but on the porch itself amid the sterile white that dominated. Hesitantly Léonie began to walk toward them. The gauze lifted and swirled around the kaleidoscope of color depriving her of the ability to see its origin. Boldly she stepped toward the spot and parted the linen panels with one fierce stroke. It was a solid wooden door, a carved door, an elaborately painted door, a hideous door. She tried to avert her eyes from it, but could not. She was mesmerized. Painted all over in gaudy hues of green and yellow and blue and red and brown were monkeys, tropical birds, serpents and other jungle inhabitants. The creatures cavorted as if ready to escape, but they were unable to move beyond the borders of the door. They tried to look amused and carefree, but Léonie knew they were afraid. They must be, for the figure in the middle kept them confined to their door-cage. In the center, what hypnotized and terrified Léonie, was the creature that kept all others in its grasp. A life-size Bengal tiger stalked towards her with its head lowered. Its eyes burned like green poison. A thick pink tongue slid across the fangs of its whiskered mouth. Then it spoke to her.

Léonie stepped back in horror and her hands flew to her face. She did something that she had never done in her life. She screamed hysterically. Her screams brought the entire household staff running to the porch in anticipation of the tragic end of little Calla Lily. When they arrived and saw the little girl's bed they were relieved to see her, very much alive, alert even, sitting up and pointing across the room. Following the line of her gesture their eyes beheld a sight that alarmed them more than if they had found the girl dead. Curled in a heap on the floor among the plants with her knees drawn to her chest, her head buried beneath her arms, rocking back and forth was Léonie Mathilde LeMoyne de Bienville-Martin. The Tiger had conquered the Lioness. Noises of the jungle were emanating uncontrollably from her throat at a rapid pace: monkey gibberish, parrot chatter, elephant trumpeting, snake hisses.

Edna, cap askew, Nettie, mouth open, and Mrs. Pond the cook, spoon in hand, stood stock still without a clue as to what should be done. While they gaped at the remarkable sight John Martin, followed closely by Nurse Sattherwhite, strode up behind them. A sigh of relief escaped him when he saw his precious Calla Lily alive, but relief was soon replaced by shock. The proud Léonie had begun to crawl about the porch floor on her hands and knees growling and roaring.

"Get her up, NOW!" the sharp command issued from John.

Although totally unaccustomed to hearing their master give any order at all, they promptly obeyed. Edna and Nettie half coaxed, half lifted the gibbering woman up off the floor, but it was useless. Even with the ample Mrs. Pond assisting them, Léonie resisted fiercely and her snarling began to be accompanied by scratching and biting. The cook and the maids dropped her to tend their wounds. At last, Cephas roused from one of his assignations with tobacco, arrived. He gently wrapped strong arms around his witless mistress. She continued to thrash and jibber while Cephas spirited the once sedate Léonie off the porch.

"Edna, get Marthe to tend to her immediately."

"Pardon, Sir, but today is Marthe's day off."

"Then see to it yourself, Girl!" John barked at the trembling maid.

During the fracas Nurse Sattherwhite rushed to Calla's side. The child had lowered her arm, but remained sitting upright. A strange look of passive amusement played across the child's face. Directing an unearthly gaze at her father she spoke with conviction:

"All will be well, Father. Shere Khan will take care of everything. I have told him to be vigilant. He will not let go until everything is set to right. There will be no secrets. We will be a real family one day, all of us together."

Like a deflated balloon Calla collapsed into a deep sleep, one from which she seldom awoke.

***

John Martin sent a succinct wire immediately to his father-in-law.

Léonie suffering from severe case of nerves. Needs to recuperate at best sanitarium available. Please advise.

Arrangements were made for Léonie to travel to New Orleans to St. Dymphna's Sanitarium for Nerve Disorders. She was accompanied by her faithful companions Marthe and Cephas. Her stay would be of undetermined length.

***

Where Will I Go?
July, 1906

"No one misses Léonie," thought Emily. "That is not accurate. Everyone revels her absence with great relief and joy. I among them. John's kindness has been of comfort to me. His attentions have been welcome. Soon little Callie will be gone."

The next few weeks saw Calla Lily spend more time asleep than awake. Nevertheless John felt that she needed continual watching. He promoted Nettie to full time and gave her residence in a small attic room there. This was a great relief for Emily who had become so attached to her patient that a few hours at her bedside eroded her stamina more than usual. With Nettie taking turns sitting by Calla, John and Emily spent a great deal of time together away from their long spells at the dying child's bedside. They sat in his study or the parlor. On pleasant days they strolled together in the gardens. In unguarded moments John's hand would brush Emily's and linger. Several times they both reached at the same time to soothe the child's coughing spasm and found their hands locked together. Neither was aware of being observed. Neither would have cared. Each found comfort in the other's company, a kind of comfort neither had had in some time. The focus was their love for Calla and it forged a bond. All else was tangential to the grim reality that she was not long for this world.

Calla's periods of rest and sleep grew in length; her alert times dwindled. When the little girl rallied awake Emily read to her. The odd thing was that although Calla was weaker than ever, she seemed to be more cheerful than ever. One evening Calla lay in a deep sleep, laboring with each breath. She had been in this state much of the afternoon. Nurse had just closed all the white drapery on the porch and was preparing to get Nettie to watch the child while she ate supper. A small voice startled the nurse who drew quickly to her patient's bedside.

"Read to me your song again," said the child referring to Blake's poem *The Nurse's Song*. Calla Lily was seldom awake for long spells and reading Kipling had fallen by the wayside. In these latter times Nurse Emily took to reading short, comforting poems to the child. Currently she was reading selections from Blake's *Songs of Innocence*. "Next to Kipling, it is what cheers me the most," the little girl told her nurse.

So Emily read to the child who could do none of the things in the poem. She could only lie there, still and quiet with her eyes closed, imagining herself with the carefree children.

When the voices of children are heard on the green,
And laughing is heard on the hill,
My heart is at rest within my breast,
And everything else is still.
"Then come home, my children, the sun is gone down,
And the dews of night arise;
Come, come, leave off play, and let us away,
Till the morning appears in the skies."

"No, no, let us play, for it is yet day,
And we cannot go to sleep;
Besides, in the sky the little birds fly,
And the hills are all covered with sheep."
"Well, well, go and play till the light fades away,
And then go home to bed."
The little ones leaped, and shouted, and laughed,
And all the hills echoed.[2]

Calla's eyes flew open and she began to laugh and say, "See, Nurse, I am playing upon the hills. The light is not yet fading." Her head tilted back and forth. "I am dancing." She picked imaginary flowers and gave them to Nurse who struggled to hold back her tears. All at once the child's animation gave way.

The nurse, through long experience, attributed these outbursts to the type of euphoria that often preceded the death of those who were destined for a happy Eternity. Little Calla would be numbered among the saints, no doubt. Perhaps in a way she was already there. Emily hoped as much. Watching a patient in anguish was the part of her nursing duties that was most difficult, especially when it involved one she had come to

---

[2] Blake wrote two poems entitled "Nurse's Song." The first was written in 1789. It became a part of the collection: *Songs of Innocence.* The second quoted above in the introduction to Nurse Emily was written later and is from *Songs of Experience.* The two collections were published in one volume in 1794 as: *The Songs of Innocence and Experience: Showing the Two Contrary States of the Human Soul.*

like and even love.

She looked at the tormented little girl and then at the snarling tiger in the door. Calla's lingering and suffering tore at Emily's emotions the way a tiger' teeth and claws tore at its victims. A quick death was more merciful. Emily had on occasions guiltily contemplated how simple it would be to shorten a patient's suffering and by doing so, her own. But she believed that these moments of suffering were times of Divine communication. Patients, she supposed, might have the opportunity to repent of sins from their past. Yet, in these little ones there could be no need of such repentance. Perhaps they were seeing the fringes of Heaven when they closed their eyes. Her contemplation was interrupted by Calla who had gathered strength once again to speak.

"Draw the curtain fully aside, from the door please, Nurse."

The gauzy linens were almost always drawn aside during the day so that the patient could see the "Tiger Door" as she called it. She had already dubbed the central figure "Shere Khan" and, like Adam in the Bible, proceeded to bestow a name on each of the figures that cavorted around it. The parrot was Calliope because he could talk and produce poetry equal to the Muse herself. She named the monkey after Curioso, Mr. Bellingham's monkey who had lately disappeared. The Python was Kaa and was her secret confident when Nurse and Papa were away. So on and so on she would name the creatures often forgetting one day what she had called an animal the day before and giving it an entirely new designation, all except the tiger Shere Khan.

***

Kipling, the porch, the Tiger Door had become Calla's whole world now. Emily was grateful to John for indulging the child. Emily remembered how this wonder world was created for the dying girl.

One day Calla had spent entirely asleep on her mound of pillows upstairs in her room. As the sun began to set she woke and struggled to sit up. Fearing a coughing spasm, Emily prepared to catch the bloody mucus. Instead the little girl looked at her nurse with large fearful eyes and said, "I am not long for this world. Where will I go?" She fell back on her pillow, alive but barely breathing. Nurse was troubled by the fear she had seen in Calla. She had failed to persuade Léonie to let the child see the Bellingham's jungle creatures. After her departure Nurse Sattherwhite knew how to comfort the child and she brought her idea to John. He had brought the child's Kipling world into being. She vividly recalled the day that Calla was brought down from upstairs to the summer porch.

***

"You may open your eyes now." The kind nurse whispered to the little girl.

Calla who was being carried in her father's arms opened her eyes and raised her head in anticipation. Gently she was conveyed into the room.

"Oh, Father! How wonderful it is." Her eyes swept around the porch. It had been transformed. The finest of gauzy linens encased the porch. In front of them and crowding each other out were pots of tropical shrubs and flowers: ferns, palms, bromeliads, orchids, philodendrons. Vines festooned the upper reaches near the ceiling. To one side stood a low bed piled with gaudy colored pillows, a small table and chair to one side.

Emily plumped and fluffed the bedding as John carefully laid his frail burden down on the bed. She drew in a sharp breath and began to cough. In anticipation Nurse grabbed a basin and some wet cheesecloth.

John sat next to his daughter. "This is all for you."

"You cannot go to Kipling, so we have brought Kipling to you." The nurse gently stroked the child's face.

"Did you send to India for all this?" Her eyes grew wide with amazement.

"No." smiled John. "Our kind neighbor, Mrs. Bellingham has sent it. She herself is too ill to visit."

"You must thank her for me, Father."

He touched his forehead to her pale brow. "I will most certainly do that."

The little girl craned her neck and bit her lip. Her perplexed look prompted Nurse Sattherwhite to enquire if anything were the matter.

"I don't suppose there are any parrots or monkeys in the shrubbery?"

"Ah, no. She could not spare all her treasures." John replied smiling. "But…" He glanced at Nurse who walked to the middle of the porch where the door to the back yard lay hidden behind the linens. With one grand stroke Nurse Sattherwhite parted the curtains.

"…I found another way to bring the animals to you, including the Bengal himself!"

Calla's eyes grew round with amazement. A huge carved door stood before her painted all over with animals. There were parrots and macaws and other tropical birds, monkeys, snakes and boas. She even spied the head and trunk of a large elephant. But all these faded quickly from her sight, for the figure in the middle of the door seized all her attention. It was a crouching, snarling, green-eyed tiger. The girl lay mesmerized for so long that John began to fear that the tiger had frightened her. Then a look of such delight broke out all over her face. She raised her emaciated arms and clapped her hands with all her strength.

"This is a doorway to another world, the world of Kipling." She cried. "When I die, this is where I shall go."

Nurse Sattherwhite encouraged the brave little girl. "Yes, now you know where you will go. You know the door you must pass through. Then all will be well."

***

Calla drifted in and out of consciousness. When she was awake, she knew that someone would be there: Emily and her father or Nettie. Each time the child asked where she would go upon her death, Emily would answer, "Through the Tiger Door to the world of Kipling." Nettie, who often stood next to doors for undetermined periods of time before entering a room, heard this reply as often as the child did. Nettie felt the ominous words held no good for Calla and suspected that Nurse had something fearful in store for her dying patient. The death of the child would set her free of obligation and she could run off with the Master. Nettie felt obligated to contradict Nurse's heathenish reply and when Calla asked her where she was to go after death Nettie's answer was terse, but not unkind: "to be with the angels in Heaven and that's that."

One day at her usual hidden post Nettie watched as Emily had stepped down through the Tiger Door into the yard. "My," the nurse called loudly to Calla, "how lovely the jungle is today! The monsoons are done and the vegetation looks like living emeralds, sparkling and verdant. Shoo! Shoo! It is that rascal Curioso. I believe he has finally escaped the door."

Calla managed a weak smile. She whispered, "Naughty monkey. So disruptive. Box his ears, Nurse." Nurse Sattherwhite passed through

40

the door onto the porch carrying a bouquet of flowers which she deposited in a pitcher. "He has picked these as an apology for his ill behavior." The pair admired them as though they were orchids and other rare tropical flowers.

"I should like to go through the Tiger Door and see all the delights of the jungle."

"You shall," said the nurse gently. "It is the doorway to your new life. All your friends will greet you there – on the other side. You shall romp and play with people and animals. You shall be strong and run about as you used to and never grow tired." Calla drifted to asleep with a smile playing about her lips. Nettie slipped away more fearful than ever.

***

At Belle Magnolia
July, 1906

Eudora wrung her hands over and over, muttering all the while to herself. Finally she summoned her courage and tiptoed into the morning room.

"Victoria, I bear some very, very distressing news. Not about us, here. Lulu is resting quietly. From next door." Her plaintive voice trailed. "So tragic. And at such a time…I have only just learnt of it. If I had known sooner…. Surely I should have come right away."

Victoria stood rigidly but patiently as Eudora muddled through her half sentences which conveyed absolutely nothing of the news she intended to impart.

"A most alarming event. The entire Martin household is in a disheveled state." Eudora whined.

"The little consumptive girl has died, I suppose?" Victoria said. "I am sorry. I shall arrange to have some mourning food sent to the Martin's. I shall see that Mr. Bellingham pays a call on Mr. and Mrs. Martin.

"No! No! Such a visit is not possible. What I mean is that is not advisable. Not under the circumstances. Liliane is ill. At death's door and a mother's concern can be overwhelming…. That is why it happened. I am sure of it. A…"

Cutting off the blather, Victoria interjected propriety into the conversation. "They have experienced an anticipated death in the family, Eudora. Protocol dictates the measures I have outlined. It is extremely advisable."

"Death? Why should you think anyone has died?" Eudora's face looked stupidly at her companion.

Rather than confront the fretful woman's irrationality, Victoria simply commanded firmly, "Please state the event or events which has so discomposed you."

"A startling thing has occurred. A…a condition has overtaken Mrs. Martin."

"A condition?"

"What I mean is that they have sent Mrs. Martin away."

"Away? Mrs. Martin? When? Whatever for?" Victoria had no illusions that the mother cared a whit for her dying child. That Léonie Martin was overcome with grief, so much so that she had to be sent away, was absurd. "Why did Mr. Martin have to send his wife away from home at such a time? Speak clearly, Eudora, if you are able."

"Two days ago. To a fine sanitarium by all accounts. I met Nettie at the greengrocers. Apparently Mrs. Martin suffered a serious nervous reaction as her dear child lay at Death's door. She was overcome with fits of grief and cannot speak…she gibbers and…"

"Enough gossip, Eudora." Victoria was thoroughly irritated with the foolish woman, as often she was. "You have no business fraternizing with the Martin staff. Nettie is a fool. Keep this nonsense to yourself. And for heaven's sake, don't repeat this to Mrs. Bellingham. She suffers enough as it is. We will modify the usual protocol to suit the circumstances. I shall speak to Mr. Bellingham at once to ascertain if there is anything we can do to assist Mr. Martin in the running of the household in his wife's absence. We may be able to lend him some staff."

The efficient Victoria turned abruptly leaving a frazzled Eudora wringing her hands and muttering to herself.

***

Eudora Calls At Lemoyne
August, 1906

Eudora bravely usurped Victoria's position as counsel to Mr. Bellingham and rushed to her father saying she needed to visit their neighbors at Azalea Cottage. Nettie admitted Eudora to the parlor and then departed to inform Mr. Martin of the unexpected arrival of an even more unexpected visitor. The nervous guest tried various uncomfortable chairs before finding the particular uncomfortable one that suited her best. Almost as soon as she sat Emily Sattherwhite, the sick little girl's nurse, entered the room. Of course Eudora had not expected Mrs. Martin, to be sure, but assumed that her husband would greet any guest who came to call upon the sorrowing family. The appearance of the Nurse rattled poor Eudora since she was not sure if it was proper to rise or remain seated in the presence of Nurse Sattherwhite. As it turned out, she half rose and nodded her head vigorously, looking like a court jester engaging in a mock bow to amuse his royal patroness.

"Please." The Nurse gestured for her to sit and Eudora obeyed. Emily rang the bell and a maid appeared – rather too quickly. "Lingering outside the door, no doubt." thought Emily, but addressing the prompt maid she said aloud: "Nettie, ask cook to prepare a plate of ladyfingers. And bring some coffee? Tea?" She looked inquiringly at Eudora.

"Tea, if you please."

"Tea for Miss Bellingham." Nettie gave Eudora a conspiratorial glance (completely lost on the still flustered woman) and left the room.

"Thank you for coming Miss Bellingham. We have appreciated all the kindnesses conveyed by your father and Mrs. Bellingham during these difficult times. How is Mrs. Bellingham?" Nurse Sattherwhite continued to stand throughout the conversation. She knew not to presume above her place.

"Not well. She is slow this time to regain her strength after her, uh, her recent loss. Little Susannah was a darling little thing. We all miss her."

"I can imagine. To lose a child is tragic. Now that my time has become more available, I shall look in on Mrs. Bellingham, unless Mr. Bellingham or Dr. Caldwell objects."

"No, I am certain neither would mind. She herself would love your company. I read to her – quite a bit. She sleeps much, and recently her sleep is disturbed. Being read to is so soothing. Is it not? So, uh, I still, uh, read to Mrs. Bellingham…I…"

As a mercy to the prattling woman, Emily cut her short by remarking: "As I do to little Calla Lily. I believe both my charge and Mrs. Bellingham share a love for Kipling." Eudora nodded vigorously in assent. Nurse paused to consider her next words. "Mr. Martin has asked me to assume housekeeping duties until Mrs. Martin returns from an extended rest. He, of course, realizes that I am trained as a nurse, not a housekeeper, but I am familiar with the routine here and as such can be of use in the interim."

"Oh, yes! Yes! I am sure that is wise. It would be a bother to engage a housekeeper for so short a time. I am sure Mrs. Martin will recuperate quickly and resume her duties." Eudora once again nodded vigorously.

"I imagine so," said the nurse glumly. The room fell silent. An ornate gilded Provence clock chimed loudly as if intent on awakening the two women into conversation.

"Nurse, I had assumed that Mr. Martin would be receiving my call, but I feel…I believe it is fortuitous that it is you instead." Eudora leaned forward in her chair. Although it did not bring her substantially closer to Nurse Sattherwhite, the atmosphere immediately became confidential. "I wonder if I could prevail upon your, your expertise. You see I do not…I cannot…I am not always comfortable speaking with Dr. Caldwell."

The nurse said not a word but inwardly assented. No one as far as she knew could bear the arrogant young doctor. His manner was patronizing and condescending to all he met. Dr. Landry withstood encounters with his younger counterpart by conducting himself with icy professionalism, as did she.

"Lulu, er, Mrs. Bellingham, is of late more distressed in mind. She is not subject to fits, not actual fits, but there are times her speech is disjointed and incomprehensible."

"Feverish?"

"No, she has no fever and that is what disturbs me so greatly. I fear that perhaps she may need to retreat to a quieter place a…"

"…sanitarium, perhaps?"

"Where did Mr. Martin send Mrs. Martin?" Eudora blurted out insensitively. "Everyone knows how dearly Mr. Martin cares for her and so he must have sent her to the finest of institutions."

"St. Dymphna. In New Orleans." Nurse had no doubt that Nettie was the source of the actual events surrounding Léonie's departure. She couldn't help thinking how wrong Eudora was. That John Martin cared a bit for his wife was ludicrous. Emily recalled the relief on his face upon the conclusion of wiring his father in law. Even more so was his look one of joy on the day Léonie left accompanied by her maid and Cephas. No, it was more an expression of exhausted triumph as if he had been engaged in a long, arduous war that had depleted all his resources, but which now had turned, even if temporarily, in his favor.

"Oh!" Eudora was completely taken aback. "So far away. Father would never agree to that."

Nor did Mr. Bellingham need to consider the possibility, not long afterwards Lulu Magnolia Bellingham died in her sleep.

***

What Nettie Saw

Eudora thanked her substitute hostess and tiptoed gingerly down the front stairs. She stopped to admire the ironwork of the porch railing when she heard her name whispered.

"Hello! Who is that?" Eudora found herself speaking to the Bougainvillea that climbed up the latticework.

"Shh! Shh! It's me, Nettie. Meet me at your gazebo in ten minutes."

"Yes, well, what is so urgent?" Eudora asked, but Nettie and her voice were gone.

***

"I thought you weren't coming!" Nettie chided Eudora.

"I had to take tea to Lulu…Mrs. Bellingham, that is. But she was asleep. Then Victoria…"

"Never mind. I needed to tell you something, something horrible. It's a secret. One what only I know."

Eudora conformed to Nettie's conspiratorial tones which perfectly suited the place of their rendezvous. The gazebo was overgrown with wisteria and set back among the dense shrubbery, Eudora leaned in closer.

"It's them that's done it."

"Done what?"

"Driven Madame mad so's she'd be sent off to the lunatic asylum." Nettie grinned showing what few teeth she had, all of them set at haphazard angles. It gave her the appearance of a living jack-o-lantern.

Eudora leaned closer. "Who has driven her mad?"

"Nurse. Nurse and the Master."

The Bellingham daughter stood erect. "I cannot believe you. Why would they? For what purpose?

"Shh! Shh! They stroll about together and may hear us."

Eudora who was quite a bit taller than the maid leaned down again so that their eyes met at the same level. In that posture the pair could be mistaken for lovers.

"Heh! Heh! They're sweet on each other. I seen 'em together. Not that they knows I'm watchin'. I seen the Master go to her room and knock just so light you might not hear. I seen 'im. Alone at night and been received inside, too. Now that the Madame is away they are out in the open."

Eudora almost swooned, clutching her breast and breathing heavily. Nettie grabbed her shoulders and looked her squarely in the eye.

"The two of 'em are up to no good. Not that I likes the Madame. Nobody does, but that the Master and Nurse should carry on while the child lies adyin' and Madame gone lunatic. It ain't Christian. I suffer to guess that the Madame never comes back from her rest." She cackled briefly.

"Sh! Nettie, do not be so insubordinate. Mr. Martin loves his wife. He has sent her to a fine asylum. He wants her to recover. I am sure."

Now Nettie's laughter knew no bounds. Shushing herself with her own finger she whispered, "A crazy house is a crazy house. If he loved 'er, he'd let her be crazy here, not send her away." She stifled another laugh.

The sound of Mrs. Pond calling Nettie's name jolted the pair apart. Nettie ran home leaving a shocked and bewildered Eudora alone in the gazebo.

***

Return Of The Lion
September 18, 1906

The dreaded event had happened. The mistress of the manor returned to LeMoyne: the Lioness to her lair. This time everyone had ample notice of her arrival. Uniforms were starched, the house scrubbed until it shone, delicacies prepared. The verdant grounds were alive and devoid of anything withered; the hearts of John Martin and staff were not so fortunate. These were black and dead, hope having fled the scene, as the carriage bearing the Léonie arrive at LeMoyne.

The imperious lady seemed no worse for the wear. She had spent several weeks at the sanitarium and then completed her recuperation at her father's home in New Orleans, Maison Bienville. Her stay at St. Dymphna's, an event which was never alluded to upon pain of dismissal, seemed to have improved her health. She appeared fuller of face and figure. Despite this, her expression was dour and her posture as stiff as ever. She was assisted from the carriage by Cephas. The servants had lined the sidewalk to greet her. She stepped past them as though they did not exist.

Léonie had business to attend to immediately. She had no time for anyone whether servants, her husband or her dying daughter. During the last week of her stay at Maison Bienville her father had suffered apoplexy. He was quite impaired and it appeared that this would be his final illness. Her brother Langlais, lately wed to Annette, remained in Europe on his honeymoon. This meant that Léonie was for all intents and purposes the head of Bienville Conglomeration.

She went directly to her room and summoned, of all people, Nurse Sattherwhite. The woman tapped at the door and entered when permission was given. She coldly, but politely, welcomed the mistress home. Léonie was seated, her face turned away from Emily. She stared out the window in silence. For some moments there was no conversation on either part and Emily began to wonder if it was incumbent upon her to break the silence.

"How may I help you, Madame?"

Léonie turned to face the nurse. "I have something to relate to you that is for your ears alone. Do you understand?"

"Yes, Madame." Emily was at loss.

"I am aware of the propensity to gossip among the staff, but should any information I am about to impart leave this room, you will find yourself in need of employment, without references and bereft of any means to make a living. No one will offer you a position anywhere insofar as I can arrange it. This matter …" a momentary look of distaste passed over her otherwise expressionless features, "…is between you and myself alone."

Emily was certain that Léonie could arrange whatever she wanted. "I fully take your meaning, Madame and I will say nothing to anyone."

"Very well." The mistress of LeMoyne revealed her message to a sphinxlike Emily Sattherwhite.

***

Emily closed the door behind her. Her world had been turned upside down for the third time in her life: the death of her father, the loss of Jean Langlais and now this. Léonie had left in a deranged state of mind. How could she know anything about them? There was only one answer, but she hardly believed that he would say anything.

***

Repose Of The Lamb
September 22, 1906

Maison LeMoyne was silent. It was one of those Florida nights where the sun's absence is meaningless. The heat refused to abate. No evening breeze dared defy heat's oppression. Calla lay alone on the porch. She had spent a restless day. The doctor was there twice. Nurse's energy was spent so she called Nettie to spend a few hours at Calla's side so she could secure some rest. The housemaid knew the dying girl was deep in a seamless sleep. She didn't meant to abandon the child, but Frank expected her hours ago. If ever there was a time for him to propose, it might be now. She would hate to miss that. She knew if she slipped over to his hut, he would be there.

***

Emily was exhausted. If not the twenty hour days, then it was the oppressive heat which had sapped all her strength. At this stage of Calla's illness Emily questioned the advisability of letting Nettie watch the dying girl, but the stupid maid couldn't do much harm just sitting there. Though Calla was frail and close to the end, she was likely to survive the night. Emily wanted to be with her at the end, along with John. She cursed her own weak condition. Not bothering to wash her face or change, she fell to her bed and was immediately asleep. In her dreams Calla was dancing around the summer porch like a Dervish. One by one the animals broke free from the door and joined her ecstasies. Calla flung the huge door to the side. The creatures followed their leader to the opening. The Tiger grew angrier by the moment knowing that the animals had escaped his protective grasp. At last Shere Khan let out a tremendous roar. Emily jolted awake. It was not a tiger she heard. It was the wind screaming. Not knowing why, she bolted out of her bed and ran to the summer porch.

***

September 23, 1906

Hours after leaving for her rendezvous Nettie snuck onto the porch by way of the larder. She was quite famished. She knew it would soon be light and Nurse would be down. Panic struck her at once. What if Nurse had come down earlier? Shoving a crust of bread into her mouth she rushed to the porch. It was still. Nurse was not there. She lay down on the cot at the opposite end of the dying girl and fell immediately into a deep sleep. She dreamed of a jungle and a prowling tiger. He was gathering coconuts for the poor natives. Then he threw them at the monkeys. Bang! Bang! Bang! They landed at the foot of the palm tree and all the monkeys swarmed down to eat them. The monkeys became birds screeching and shrieking. Nettie woke with a start. Nurse Sattherwhite was shaking her.

"You foolish nitwit," Nurse shouted.

Nettie sat up and saw Calla's bed was empty. She covered her mouth to stifle a scream.

"How could you sleep through all that?"

"Through what?"

A fierce wind blew. The heavy Tiger Door was swinging open and banging shut. "Bang! Bang! Bang!" Nurse stalked over to the door. Nettie leapt from her pallet to join her. Both women peered through the opening in horror.

At the bottom of the porch stairs lay a still, small white figure.

***

Requiem For Calla Lily

Azalea Cottage, as the household thought of itself when Léonie was away, was sorry their mistress had returned in time for the death of little Calla. Had Léonie been gone the inhabitants could have grieved more openly and sought consolation from one another. The stern mistress would not allow it. She demanded that they maintain solemn, but not mournful, countenances especially since callers would be visiting LeMoyne in the wake of the child's death. Servants would show respect, not grief. This left LeMoyne unnaturally quiet. No consolations, even whispered ones, dare occur among the staff members. Lily's death cast a pall over the house, one so thick it was impenetrable by the routine sounds of daily life there. Each grieved privately in his or her own way despite Léonie's orders.

Mrs. Pond, who typically expressed her joviality in song, now quietly and mechanically prepared the meals. Nettie, who normally broke a dish or two, washed each plate with great care, dried it and placed it with the others. Edna, whose dusting skill was mediocre at best, dusted everything meticulously, all the while her tears dripping and making small circular stains on the furniture. Even the high strung and fidgety poodle Très Cher posed like a sphinx for hours at a time.

Léonie's maid Marthe had no great attachment to her mistress, but she loved the child. She wore a glum expression and mused on the loss to the world of this joyous, young girl. Cephas, who had always tended to the grounds, the carriages and horses with the strength of one much younger, suddenly felt his age. He wore the face of a man burdened by the collective troubles of the world.

John, not by nature a man of drink, lay in a whiskey induced stupor on his bed. His grief consumed him. He cared nothing for his life, his home, his future. Had God struck him dead at any moment he would have been grateful. Periodically he eyed the loaded pistol that lay on his desk. He didn't have the energy to rise, much less to walk to the instrument of death and pull the trigger. Even the recent hint of joy he had begun to experience with Emily now receded into the dark corners of his mind. He knew she would leave. There was nothing to keep her at Azalea Cottage now.

Nurse Sattherwhite sat quietly in her room and combed her hair while silent tears ran down her cheeks. She had planned to depart for New Orleans as soon as possible after Calla's death, but now she could not. She sat at her dressing table and looked at the strained face in the mirror. She had not received any answer to her plea. Her recent interview with Léonie explained why that was. The mistress of LeMoyne held the power to alter her intended course. Emily must now subject herself to the Lioness. She brushed her hair mindlessly and set her jaw. There was another way. It horrified her to think of it, but she began the inward journey to the belief that it was not only the preferable way, but the only way out of her current predicament.

While plans for the funeral were made Léonie alone reserved the right to wear publicly the expression she chose. It was not one of grief born of inward sorrow, which is what the household truly felt; rather, it was her usual hard, dispassionate mask. Arrangements were completed; sympathizers came and went. Little Calla was laid to rest. Death drained all meaning from the Martin household. Lily, pure and innocent, took life and joy with her to a tiny plot in the Manawassa cemetery.

***

Conspiracies
September 30, 1906

Nettie, knowing she would not be missed and eager to relate what she suspected, snuck out of the house as soon as it was feasible after the death of Calla Lily. Next door Eudora sat fanning herself on the porch. These days there was little relief for her from the stress of Lulu's death. The end had been so awful and Eudora blamed herself for her stepmother's demise. Her father was consumed with grief and saw no one. Victoria orchestrated all that needed to be done. Eudora stole outside to avoid the efficient and bustling Victoria. There she sat in a typical Eudora reverie without a book or needlework or even a thought in her head. A still, small voice intruded into that emptiness. Eudora began to bob her head about to find its source. Out of the corner of her eye she spotted Nettie in a camellia bush waving frantically and "psst-ting" in her direction. She moved to the furthest side of the porch and engaged the intruder.

"What is it that you want? Has something further happened to your grieving household? We have all learned of Liliane's death. We ourselves have experienced a bitter loss. Poor Lulu! Father is delirious with grief. I am so sorry that we have not come to you to relay our condolences. So very, very sorry. Consumption is such an awful death, especially in one so young…" Eudora would have rattled aimlessly on had not Nettie cut her off.

"Consumption ain't what did it."

Eudora's eyes widened with shock. "She had consumption. We all assumed…"

"O'course she had consumption. But that weren't what killed her. It was Nurse. Nurse and the Master."

"I don't believe it. I dismissed your former propositions about Mr. Martin and Nurse as utter nonsense. Now you are accusing them of killing Liliane Aimée? Nonsense and more nonsense. Nurse Sattherwhite was devoted to the child. She would never…. She couldn't bring harm….

Kill her? You are mistaken, Nettie."

"But I ain't, don't you see? When the Madame left for Newerleens for her brother's wedding, I mean the time before this last one when she was away for the fits, the Master and Nurse moved the child to the summer porch – down from her room."

"I don't see how that could affect Liliane's death. She was frail and weak and bound to die soon. I do not think the venue would much matter."

"Oh, it were part of a clever scheme."

"Nettie, you are being foolish. You…"

"Don't you see? They put the child on the porch and gussied it all with linens. The master had Joe Dorr come paint a wooden door for the porch." Here the maid paused and, completely incongruous to the seriousness of her story, giggled. "Joe Dorr painted the door."

Eudora who was the flighty one in most conversations became the one to check the foolishness of her confidant. "Nettie, do be serious. The accusation you have laid at the door of Mr. Martin and Nurse Sattherwhite is grievous and does not permit such levity. Get on with your story."

"Joe paints this door all over with strange creatures, like those what Mr. Bellingham keeps: monkeys and birds and snakes and all. But right in the middle is this hideous tiger with green eyes and open mouth. Lifelike it is. It stares at you, crouching low towards you like you's to be its next meal. Why would a loving father do that, I asks myself?"

"Why, indeed!" Caution failed Eudora, as it usually did. She was sucked into the center of Nettie's vortex.

"Because he wants the child out of the way. Because he wants to frighten her to death. It frightened the Madame to the lunatic asylum. It were that evil tiger in the door that drove out all her wits. I was there. It's cursed."

Eudora drew a deep breath and closed her eyes. "Nettie, that is blasphemous superstition."

"No it ain't. Besides it were them stories that Mr. Kipple wrote that gave them two the idea. Little Miss Calla loved the stories about India and the Hindoo heathens and the jungle. I never read 'em, but I heard Nurse talk all about this evil tiger what stalks and kills.

"Yes, yes! Kipling. Sheer Khan, but, what had Nurse to do with this? If the girl enjoyed Kipling why should Nurse not read her Kipling?"

"But don't you see? They had a game, the two of them."

"Mr. Martin and Nurse?"

"Yes. The poor sick little girl 'magined she lived in a world of jungles and heathens. Nurse and him egged on her 'maginations, letting her run on about being an officer's wife with children and living in a jungle…"

Eudora's naïveté about servants and their penchant for eavesdropping lent itself to the situation. It never occurred to Eudora to scold the maid or even question how she knew these things. Whatever Eudora heard from anyone, whatever appeared on the surface, whatever presented itself to Eudora was undeniable truth until contradicted by another. Eudora could be so easily persuaded that the reasonableness of whatever she heard dwindled in direct proportion. The fact that sources often conflicted in the information imparted to her was of little consequence. She listened intently to the gossipy maid.

"…living in this magical place. The child's face would light up and go all dreamlike. You could see she wanted to go live there for real. Nurse told her she could. So there. And what with Mr. Martin standing up to Madame and getting her out of the way for a time and him being so forward with Nurse and all. That's how they done it."

As far as Nettie was concerned the explanation was complete. Oblivious to the look of anticipation on Eudora's face the maid crossed her arms and nodded her head vigorously.

Eudora was more confused than usual. She had met her match in the nonsensical Nettie. She prodded the maid for clarity. "What? You are not making sense. Live where? How did that kill the little girl?"

"Because over and over again Nurse would tell the Girl that the way to Kipple's book-world was through the tiger's door. Nurse would step out the door, the big ugly heathen door, and come back to the dyin' child's bedside and tell her of all the charms she seen on t'other side." Once again Nettie assumed a triumphant stance.

"Go on…. For Heaven's sake. I still cannot fathom your meaning. Do you think the child was hastened to her death from consumption because she longed to go through the door? I suppose, if that *is* the case, then Nurse was very wicked to confuse the little girl that Heaven would be like Kipling's jungle, but…"

"Don't you see?" Nettie rolled her eyes and rustled the camellia bush as she waved her arms around. "That's what everyone thinks…that she died of consumption right there in her bed, but she didn't.

"I am so muddled. She had been living on the porch, but she didn't die there. Did she die upstairs?"

"Oh, one would think so. When the doctor came she was laid out all perfect and peaceful-like in her bed, *in her bed upstairs*. But you see, she didn't die there. She was found dead elstwhere.

"Do make sense Nettie. Where? Where was she found dead? If not upstairs or on the porch, then where?" A breathless and shocked Eudora strained every part of herself so that she could fully comprehend what was to come next.

"Downstairs, not on the summer porch, not in her bed there, but on the ground, outside, at the bottom of the steps below that devilish door with the tiger. She fell through, or been tossed through, I say, during her last night here on earth. And who was it pushed her through? It curls my hair to think. If the Master and Nurse would do that to a little girl, what will they do to us servants? Murder us all in our sleep?"

"Shush." Eudora placed her hand over Nettie's mouth. "You are talking like a ninny. Go home." Inwardly, the fretting Bellingham daughter wondered and worried over this new information.

***

CHAPTER III
A NEW ORDER

Death And Life
1907

Death had a short reign. Life returned to its normal misery at LeMoyne. By the beginning of November Léonie had made her condition known to the staff, although they had already surmised that another child was on the way. The staff obliged their mistress and master with mumbled congratulations. The announcement formally acknowledged the reason that Nurse had not been sent away immediately after Calla's funeral. The child's arrival was to be sometime early in the New Year. The only joy that the Christmas season brought to the household was that at the beginning of December Léonie departed for New Orleans to give birth there. Nurse, who had become more and more withdrawn from the household as the weeks wore on, left with her mistress as did Cephas and Marthe. In due course LeMoyne learned that the child, another girl, had entered the world.

***

Léonie returned with her retinue in the new year a month after the birth of little Jacqueline Alexandrine. Her reign reestablished at LeMoyne was not many weeks old when John Martin and Nurse Sattherwhite disappeared simultaneously. The servants were not shocked, but even so, had no time to gossip among themselves. Shortly after the elopement of the pair, Léonie swept LeMoyne clean by dismissing the entire household staff except Marthe who stayed on as nurse. The stunned employees were given good references, except Nettie, and secured positions elsewhere. A new ensemble of servants was summoned from New Orleans. From that time forward the name Martin was severed from Léonie's surname. Léonie Mathilde LeMoyne de Bienville reigned, uncontested, over Maison LeMoyne.

***

Jacqueline Alexandrine Lemoyne De Bienville
Little Girl On A Swing
Summer, 1917

Jacqueline sat so still in the wicker swing which was suspended from a low-lying branch of the giant oak tree that anyone would have thought her to be a very large doll and not a ten year old girl. Her light hair glimmered in the sun giving her a halo, which combined with her white summer dress, completed the angelic effect. The air around her was as still as she. The oppressive Florida humidity caused huge rivulets of sweat to roll down the child's cheeks in hot waterfalls. Her eyes were fixed on some point so far removed from her present venue that she had all the appearance of being in a trance. Her face was expressionless. One hand rested on her lap, the other held the rope and her legs dangled from the basket-chair like whitewashed spindles. A curious expression slowly invaded her countenance. Her brows knit, then lifted. Her mouth formed an 'o' of recognition. She began to nod her head in assent to an invisible petitioner. Slowly she smiled and raising her hand from her lap waved to a departing phantom.

All this was observed by Celestina Crawford as she sat on the verandah mending. She had noticed the child's increasingly peculiar behavior for several weeks now. Celestina was well aware that Jacqueline's mother had suffered a breakdown shortly before the girl was born. The governess had tried in the most oblique ways to determine if the child was suffering the initial stages of some mental condition. Her attempts proved fruitless and the trance-like episodes continued. All children, particularly lonely ones, conjure up imaginary playmates or pets and, had Jacqueline been younger, Mrs. Crawford would have attributed her odd behavior to this infantile practice. But she was newly turned ten and ought to have put away such childish habits.

Still pondering the mystery of Jacqueline's odd behavior, Celestina was startled to find her charge standing next to her, tugging her skirt and calling her name aloud.

"*Puis-je avoir de la citronnade*, Tina."

Mrs. Crawford smiled at the child with great fondness. Tina was Jacqueline's particular name for her governess. Léonie had brought Celestina from New Orleans to Manawassa Springs four years ago when Jacqueline was six. Apparently the child's old nurse Marthe was neither French enough, nor educated enough to suit Léonie. Celestina Dechaine was both. She served in the dual role of governess and French tutor. It was a pleasant living for Celestina for the little girl was quick and pretty.

She was glad that circumstances had not deprived her of this position. A year after her arrival in Manawassa the French girl had incurred the wrath of her employer by marrying the son of the local banker without her mistress's approval. Celestina's dismissal was a fiery one. The marriage was short since the boy was unfortunate enough to have died of typhus not long after the nuptials. Deprived of her husband Celestina approached Léonie and begged to be restored her to her former position. Since Léonie preferred all things of French, particularly of New Orleans, extraction, she received the girl back on the sternest terms. Only in being called "Mrs. Crawford" by the staff did Celestina prevail over her mistress. Léonie basically ignored this child as she had all her other children and depended on Celestina to rear her.

"*Oui, ma petite.*"

Jacqueline seated herself in the shade on the quilt that Celestina had spread under the big oak near the fountain. It was always cooler next to its flowing waters. She lazily waved off a fly that ventured near her. She plucked a small cluster of grapes to eat while awaiting her lemonade.

"*Ici est.*"

"Thank you."

"*En Français.*"

"*Merci. Vous êtes très aimable.* May we speak English now, Tina?"

"The little girl gulped her beverage and then ran her tongue over her upper lip.

No! No! That is not ladylike at all, you little imp!

"Must one always be a lady, Tina?"

"Always."

"Yet I feel at times as though I were two persons. One is a lady and one is decidedly not."

"Then you must exert all your strength to subdue the part of you that will not to follow proper manners, my little one."

Jacqueline sat for some moments nibbling at the grapes and sipping her lemonade. "Yet, the part of me that inclines to being a lady has little fun."

"Fun is for children, not ladies."

Jacqueline turned her little face up to her governess. "But I am a child, am I not?"

"Yes, but a child who is to assume great responsibilities from her mother. Therefore you must cultivate manners as well as the arts of rhetoric and logic in order to hone your skills as woman *formidable* of business."

"Maman is a great woman of business affairs, is she not, Tina?"

"*Oui, c'est vrai.* With Madame's father gone, *Qu'il repose en paix,*" she made a swift sign of the cross, "all things reside in the capable hands of your Maman, as they will one day reside in yours."

The little girl sighed from the depths of her being. "Then I shall not disappoint her."

A prolonged silence followed. The air was so heavy with moisture that even the insects found it difficult to cut through it. They buzzed slowly around the couple who sat on the blanket. In the distance the clock tower chimed ten. There was no wind, no stirring of anything whatsoever.

"*Mon Dieu!*" Celestina cried and pointed to the swing which was arcing back and forth of its own accord.

"Do not fear, Tina. It is only *la petite fille* I call Blanche because she is so pale and white." With that cryptic comment Jacqueline returned her attention to her refreshments leaving a frightened governess to divide her stares between child and swing.

PART II
THE INHERITANCE

CHAPTER I
GENEVIÈVE LEMOYNE DE BIENVILLE

Hall's The Deck
2007

Gena sat staring at the Lake. By now she had a favorite table at her favorite eating establishment. It was there at *Hall's the Deck Café* she sat at the end of the pier which jutted into Lake Manawassa. It afforded a magnificent view of the entire circle of the Lake. How amazing was it that the Lake was perfectly round. She read somewhere that the town's founder Aloysius Bellingham had hired the same men who created the New York subway system to redirect the lake's spring fed waters for his health spa. They had come prepared to meet the challenge of turning a Florida swamp into a deep, cool lake. They discovered upon their arrival a beautiful lake, 100 feet deep with springs in abundance. The engineers from New York had been baffled by the fact that the lake was perfectly circular. "Aliens, maybe." She mused to herself sipping her iced tea.

Directly across the Lake from her, imposing and glorious, stood Belle Magnolia, the icon of Manawassa Springs. A hundred years ago Belle Magnolia had been the domicile of Mr. Bellingham and dominated everything here, both then and now. The house had a persona: The Grand Lady. She was the house that vacationers wanted to tour. Conversations revolved around her lavish grounds, her architectural quirks, her history and especially her founder, although he was long dead and buried in the churchyard. Now a posh bed and breakfast, The Belle drew visitors from all over the United States and even Europe. Gena heard that not long ago Belle Magnolia was all but ready for burial when a new owner revitalized her. The whole town had followed suit. Though Gena herself had been in Manawassa Springs for a while, she had yet to meet the Belle's owner. She preferred to keep it that way. Probably she was some needy little retiree who distinguished herself late in life only by what she had purchased.

Nestled next to the Grand Lady, and far less glorious, sat her own abode – Maison LeMoyne. She leaned on her elbow, cupping her chin in hand and stared at it. She could hardly believe she lived there now. It belonged to Grand-mère and nothing as mundane as her death could alter that fact. She cast her mind back to what her grandmother Jacqueline had told her about de Bienville roots in New Orleans and Manawassa Springs.

They never talked about themselves, except to aggrandize the name of de Bienville. Gena could recite a list of de Bienville family honors and business negotiations, but personal anecdotes about the people that comprised the family were almost nonexistent. It wasn't as though anyone had sat Gena down and narrated a family history. Gena's father said next to nothing about his own father who had died fairly young. Gena relied mostly on Grand-mère for information. From time to time she would spit out comments having to do with her mother Léonie and her father John Martin. She even offered bits about the patriarch of the family and founder of Bienville Enterprises, her grandfather Georges Henri. Gena had pieced these stray facts together to provide herself with some kind of a family story. It wasn't very satisfactory.

Georges Henri, his daughter Léonie and son Jean Langlais lived in an impressive mansion, Maison Bienville, in New Orleans. Grand-mère said that Léonie was a very proud and competent woman. She had reason to be. She was an heiress to a great fortune made from shipping, particularly, cotton and sugar cane. Of equal consequence was her lineage. She was a descendent of the French explorer who founded New Orleans: Jean Baptiste LeMoyne de Bienville. Her branch of the de Bienville family remained in New Orleans (out of necessity, so said Grand-mère) when the famed explorer and ex-governor returned to Paris. Her family was solidly old New Orleans French Creole and held sway there for generations.

By contrast Gena's grandfather John Martin and his family had only recently acquired money from lumber and railroad ventures in Northwest Florida. John's father Robert had small interests in New Orleans, but wanted to induce Georges Henri de Bienville to expand his concerns into the area of timber in the Manawassa Springs area. Robert died before any deal was made and so the task fell to his son John. Since the de Bienville fortune had suffered a little from the vicissitudes of the post-Civil War Reconstruction Georges Henri was eager to diversify into as many profitable avenues as he could find. Martin Lumber and Western Panhandle Railroad were two such.

It was not only profit that de Bienville took under advisement. The French Creole supremacy was waning in the Crescent City and the de Bienville reputation could not suffer indignities. Grand-mère said her mother Léonie was a great beauty, but somewhat wild. Her father wanted her to settle down. It was this particular wish that led to her handshake marriage to John Martin. Any wooing occurred in the Bienville offices and not under moonlit skies. John then brought his French bride from New Orleans to live in Manawassa Springs. Grand-mère, during a particularly maternal moment when Gena was a teenager, warned her against "imprudent marital collaboration." She revealed that that the stately and proud Léonie despised her husband and Manawassa Springs with equal fervor. Nevertheless, John Martin must have been satisfied with his new bride, at least initially, because he had a substantial home built for her, New Orleans style.

Gena looked at LeMoyne and was pleased with what she saw. It was narrowly and deeply built, three stories high. Each story boasted a balcony of elaborate French wrought iron-work. The house's color was the shade of the wild native yellow azaleas. "Aye, there's the rub," Gena mused. Despite the fact that her Grand-mère, her father and herself had always called the dwelling Maison LeMoyne, or LeMoyne for short, the inhabitants of Manawassa Springs dubbed it Azalea Cottage or, occasionally and mockingly, Primrose Manor. "*Les bourgeois.*" Gena said aloud.

"Pardon, mam? More tea?" Gena was startled out of her reverie by the waitress who was poised with a pitcher of tea.

"Thank you, please." She leaned back as her glass was filled by the attentive waitress. "And could I have a slice of the Southern Bourbon Pecan Pie?" Gena had a favorite dessert now, too.

When the pie arrived thoughts of Léonie, John Martin and the roots of LeMoyne receded a hundred years into the past where they belonged. For over ninety of those years Grand-mère had lived at LeMoyne. Well, almost. She considered it her home although she split most of her time between New Orleans and New York with jaunts to Europe. The mystique of LeMoyne persisted. Why was Grand-mère so attached to it? Gena's father, who was raised in New Orleans, saw little of it. Gena, who grew up in New York, had only visited it in a succession of summers as a child. In Grand-mère's absences Maison LeMoyne had been kept up by servants, Tildy and Morris being the most recent. Both survived their mistress and Grand-mère had provided well for them. When Gena asked if they cared to stay on they seemed very uncomfortable. They looked at each other and shook their heads no. Their loyalty was to Grand-mère, Gena supposed, and not to LeMoyne.

She hadn't planned on moving to LeMoyne when her grandmother died. Gena settled on using the house as a retreat from the pressures of the job. Within months of Grand-mère's death, the disturbing dreams started. As time went on the nightmares took their toll. Nothing short of escaping them could have induced her to leave New York, even though the city held older memories from which to escape. Kayton. Dark clouds scuttled overhead momentarily blocking the sun. Her own thoughts darkened in parallel. Had she made the right decision all those years ago? She shoved Kayton down into oblivion.

She once heard her father say that Grand-mère was an odd duck. Jacqueline had married into the lofty Seton-Hayes family of New York, but refused to take her husband's last name. Gena supposed it was a tradition. Her great-grandmother Léonie LeMoyne de Bienville had not kept her husband's name after he ran off, or so Grand-mère had told Gena. The de Bienville name was everything her grandmother said. It would one day be up to her to keep it strong and unstained.

She felt she had let both her father and Grand-mère down. When her father had died unexpectedly she stepped into his shoes at Bienville Enterprises. Initially Grand-mère apprenticed her, but soon gave her full rein, almost. She remained under her grandmother's watchful guidance. At first Gena was exhilarated with the new position. It filled a large void in her life at the time. The shift from her minor executive role in a subsidiary Bienville company to full managing president of the entire conglomeration was not too difficult, at least not for her business life. She had grown up on a steady diet of the spectrum of her father's company interests. Dinner conversations consisted of nothing else. Besides, running a business and turning a profit is basically the same everywhere. Twenty years ago how many women had the experience to do what she had done? But it had ground her down. Her mental health had tottered away from the invincible de Bienville stability. Then there was the recurrent dream. She shoved it down into the depths of her mind to join Kayton.

Before she fell into the trap of maundering over Kayton or panicking over the dream, her mind shouted ferociously: "Relax. You have a new way of life here at LeMoyne." The house may not have the prestige of the Belle, but Henry Ford had "paid an animated and profitable visit" to her great-grandmother Léonie there, or so said Grand-mère. She unsuccessfully tried to cheer herself up. "I am not a failure. I am not going crazy. I am still in control and I could buy and sell a hundred Azalea Cottages or Belle Magnolias with a snap of my fingers." She thought. Her shift of headquarters didn't impact her income at all, though her prestige might be suffering temporarily. She was still Chairman of the Board. She still ran things from her retreat at LeMoyne even if her cousin Langlais had the appearance of it. He was just her mouthpiece.

The pie arrived just in time to distract her any further from dark thoughts. It was heavenly. She glanced down at her waistline. She had put on a full 15 pounds since relocating to Manawassa Springs and was surprised that she didn't mind. She looked suitably fit here in Manawassa. In New York a suitable weight meant addicted to exercise, an anorexic look which meant attractive and that resulted in being socially acceptable. Months ago upon her arrival in Manawassa Springs she had overheard a customer at the Emporium telling the cashier that the new lady from New York had come here to die. "Cancer." She tsk-tsked. "That's why she is so pale and skeletal. Sad, very sad." When Gena went home she took a long, hard look in the mirror. She saw a tall, gaunt, angular woman. Now she was a tall, voluptuous woman. Kayton would have approved. "I won't think about that." She resolved.

Gena decided then and there, in front of that mirror, that it was time to be who she was, not what a city told her to be, not what a parent or lover told her to be, not what a corporation told her to be. She supposed all her life she had been expected to be someone she wasn't. She had been steered clear of food and friends and fun of her own choosing in favor of a grooming process by others. Mother had groomed her for New York society; Father had groomed her for business; boarding schools and universities had groomed her for academia. Grand-mère had groomed her, too, but for what? She wasn't sure. Grand-mère really was an odd duck. One minute she was elegant and proper with a stare that killed any inclination towards impropriety. The next minute she was sparkling with mystery and mischief. Perhaps that was why Grand-mère was her favorite person. In essence (if not in birth date) Grand-mère was a Gemini like Gena herself. Only Grand-mère had let the free spirited side of herself take control on occasion. Gena never had the nerve.

"I will have the nerve now." She thought as she jabbed another ample forkful of pie into her mouth. "I am no skeleton now. I am what my old friends consider fat and what I think of as plump and what Grand-mère had called "womanish." The pie delight was washed down with a gulp of tea, not trendy chai, but just plain old Southern iced tea with sugar. (Chai tea along with all the other fad foods had been left in New York to be replaced by Southern cooking.)

She took in LeMoyne again. Gena was glad to have left it as it was. She kept Grand-mère's furniture. What few things she had added were intentionally integrated to match the eclectic mix of styles that filled the house. Grand-mère had appropriated the definitive fashion from each of her nine decades and placed them in rooms around the house. It wasn't like a museum: the Roaring Twenties Room, the Mid-Century Modern Room, the Seventies Disco Room. No, somehow her grandmother had placed era defined furniture and contrasting accoutrements in each room, blending them to produce a warm and pleasant effect. Gena did her best not to destroy her Grand-mère's achievement.

The first floor had the usual rooms for a home of its vintage: a parlor, a living room, a dining room, a study and a kitchen with a huge butler's pantry. A sun porch ran the length of the back of the house. The second floor had four bedrooms, the largest of which had been renovated to have its own *en suite*. Space for a bathroom had been taken from the back bedroom leaving it to become a small, but pleasant sitting room. The rooms on the other side shared a Jack and Jill bathroom. Katie remembered the third floor best. It was where she had stayed as a child. There were two bedrooms on either side of the landing. These she supposed had originally been for the children's nurse and perhaps a maid. Instead of two more bedrooms at the back of the third floor, which you would have expected, there was long attic room. Its walls were covered with a faded rosebud wallpaper and she believed it had been the nursery when the house was first built by her great-grandfather. As a child, Gena had always stayed in the bedroom to the left of the landing. It was smaller than the one on the right (in which her odious cousin Langlais always stayed), but it was cozy and had the better view. It certainly had nicer décor. She knew Grand-mère had specially chosen that room for her.

The one major alteration she had made to LeMoyne was to enclose the screened in summer porch with energy efficient windows and provide it with independent heating and cooling. Now as a sun porch it was usable year round. It afforded such a wonderful view of the deep back yard that Gena wanted to be able to sit there any time of the year:

sweltering or chilly, rainy or sunny. She had hired Leland Pearse a local contractor to undertake the renovation. She hadn't intended to allow for windows that opened and had screens, but was convinced by Mr. Pearse that there were occasions when she would appreciate the fragrant air that wafted from the outside, especially when the honeysuckle, gardenias or magnolias were in high bloom. Only the horrid old wooden door remained as a source of annoyance. It would soon be replaced.

Suddenly her eye was drawn to the center of the Lake. "Oh, my God! There it is!" She burst aloud without thinking. In the dead center of Lake Manawassa, unaccompanied by any hint of a gust of wind, the waves whipped up into a furious dance. It lasted ten or fifteen seconds and then ceased as suddenly as it began. This most definitely was *"the periodic mysterious action of the surface waters of Lake Manawassa which no one, not even scientists, can explain."* Gena read that in a brochure. She had been living there for months and, until now, had never seen this phenomenon. Her outburst brought the waitress to her side.

"Something else, mam?"

"No. No thank you." Not wanting to appear like the tourists who hung around with cameras waiting to capture the effect on film, she tipped her glass to her mouth and silently reflected: "I am at home. The Lake has officially welcomed me as a resident of Manawassa Springs."

***

CHAPTER II
THE SUN PORCH

Leland Pearse And That Woman

"Mr. Pearse," Laurie shouted as she put the caller on hold. "It's *that* woman again." The receptionist's voice held all the contempt it possibly could.

"That woman. Great." Leland Pearse didn't need a name to go with the gender. He knew it was his client from New York. An unspoken "damn" and a deep breath was all that permitted him to say pleasantly aloud as he picked up the phone: "Yes, Ms. LeMoyne. What can I do for you?" Inwardly he continued his greeting: "Cut my head off and give it to you on a platter? Sure." All this woman had needed for Azalea Cottage was a simple renovation of the back screened porch. You would have thought it was the Empire State Building he was tackling.

"It's Ms. de Bienville, Mr Pearse, not LeMoyne."

"Damn high falootin' hyphenated names." Leland thought maliciously.

Not being privy to his thoughts, Gena had already continued. "The new glass door on the sun porch. It's not quite right yet. It catches when you try to open or close it. I appreciate the hard work your men have done. I did mention to one that I thought it was dragging. It might be best if you came and examined it yourself."

"Yes, mam. I'll swing by this afternoon."

"Well, actually I will be in Pensacola this afternoon. Shall we say tomorrow in the morning, earlier rather than later? I have an appointment at 10." Gena wrapped up with the same tone of voice she used to end all her business calls as CEO.

Lee was counting to ten slowly to give himself time to reply politely. "Morning is fine. I…"

"As early as possible."

That did it. She wasn't Donald Trump. In New York, maybe she was a big-wig, but not in Manawassa Springs. Two can play at this game. "No problem, *Ms. LeMoyne.* See you around 5:30."

"Ms. de Bienville. I said *before* work." Gena replied irritably.

"Right. See you at 5:30 in the morning. I start work at 6 am. Have a nice day." He put the phone down without slamming it, but managed a hearty laugh. "Go back to the Big Apple or the Big Easy or the bottom of the Lake, for all I care." From the room beyond his door he could hear Laurie giggling. "And take my receptionist with you!"

***

An open mouthed Gena stared at her phone as if it had bitten her. How insufferably rude he was. All she wanted was a door to open and shut without dragging on the floor. How hard could that be? He was acting like she wanted him to build a high rise. Well, Leland Pearse was just a fly in the ointment. He was probably a redneck who thought that all women are idiots and only fit to fry chicken. "Actually fried chicken is pretty good." she mused aloud. "What do you want to bet that I wait all day and that he doesn't show up until 5:15 in the afternoon? I have a good mind to sleep in tomorrow."

***

Gena frowned darkly, coffee cup in hand, at Lee Pearse as he inspected the porch door. Her irritation grew with every "Mmm" and "Yeah, right". It may have been 5:30 am in Manawassa Springs, but Gena looked every bit 9:30 pm New York City. To accomplish this she had risen absurdly at 4:30 am and this further angered her.

"You're right." He stated the obvious. "The door is defective. The hinges are wrong. They're too short and slightly angled, and on an extra wide door like this, it caused a droop. So it…"

"…drags on the floor. Yes, I know, Mr. Pearse." Gena interrupted the docile contractor. "Thank you for confirming the obvious." Her barb was not lost on him, but he refused to let irritation get the upper hand especially since his solution was sure to achieve the kind of revenge most contractors were so fond of – a prolonged delay.

"So how long before you can fix it." Gena demanded impatiently.

"I can't."

"Excuse me?"

Cutting her off before she exploded, Lee quickly explained, "The whole door will have to be replaced. It's custom. The hinges were factory set. I imagine it'll take about four to six weeks." Revenge is sweet.

"What do I use for a door in the meantime? Do you have one you can lend me?"

"Like I said, mam, it's custom. We'll just leave this one here…"

"I refuse to have that ruining my newly refinished porch floor for six more weeks!'"

"Well, mam, like I said, the opening is extra wide…"

"Are you sure you can't you find me something?"

Lee had it with her inability to hear what he was saying, but he purposely remained composed. Replying as nonchalantly as he could Lee addressed the strained and irritated Gena, "The only door that'll fit is the original one. I'll have one of my guys here today to take this one off and put the wooden one back on."

"But it's hideous!" Gena shivered slightly at the thought of that door returning to its home. It had always been a source of undefined uneasiness to her. She wondered about the sanity of its originator. She knew it hadn't been her grandmother's idea. "What kind of person puts a huge painted wooden door on a summer porch?"

"This is your family home, Ms. LeMoyne so I can't answer that. Is it still in the shed?"

Deflated she replied, "Yes. It's still there."

"My crew'll be here sometime today."

"Can't *you* do it now? I mean surely you carry adequate tools around in that gas-guzzling monster you drive." It was unusual for Gena to resort to personal attack.

This hit too close to home for Leland Pearse. His patience ran out. "Attack me, but don't mess with my truck!" he thought. He turned to Gena and replied ever so sweetly. "Normally I do, mam, but I need to get to another meeting at 5:45 – a late sleeping client. Not like us." He tipped her a good-bye with the brim of his cap and headed for his beloved Ford F-350. Calling to her from his cab he assured her: "My guys'll be here today."

His guys came two days later. At last the workmen had gathered their tools and departed the premises. Gena stared at the door. A kind of mesmerizing power generated a cold horror throughout her being. She could not look away. The painted figures on it were faded from years of Florida weather, all the figures, that is, except the one that dominated the center: a huge Bengal tiger. She gave an involuntary shudder. He crouched in the middle of the door with his head lowered. The massive jaws gaped and bared glistening fangs. You could feel that he was ready to spring, to devour. His green eyes glowed with anticipation; his wet tongue slathered his ivory fangs with saliva. Gena was not sure what held him captive. She knew that he was fully capable of abandoning the confines of the door to…

What was she thinking? She shook herself mentally and turned away. She would buy a rod and some white linen curtains to hide the menacing figure. Then she wouldn't think about it until the new door was installed. Meanwhile she resigned herself to having the hideous wooden door for four to six more weeks.

***

CHAPTER III
GENA AND KATIE

"Tap, tap, tap." Katie knocked on the front door of Azalea Cottage, an action repeated, who knew how many times, since the new owner had arrived. Each of the other times her efforts were met without success. The owner never seemed to be there or she avoided answering her door. It was aggravating.

Then again, maybe Katie had been pretty busy herself especially after recent events at the Belle. Her brush with death the previous fall caused her to throw herself totally into its management. Its reputation as a destination B&B and the resultant bookings had pretty much overwhelmed her. In fact, once the cleansing of Belle Magnolia had taken place, she almost immediately received a flood of guests that never seemed to recede. The Belle was almost fully booked a year ahead and Katie was turning guests away.

She ceased her knocking temporarily and reflected that a mere four months after the Belle opened Steve sharply observed that both the Belle and Katie herself had become unavailable. He was right, too. To save her sanity and her relationship with Steve she hired a staff which consisted of a youngish retired couple, Addie and Zeph Bagley. It had been her salvation. Addie acted hostess, housekeeper and businesswoman when Katie couldn't and Zeph was all around handyman and gardener.

She resumed her knocking a little louder this time in case the owner was on the third floor. "You might consider investing in a doorbell." Katie observed aloud. As she waited, not too hopefully, her thoughts flew back to the Bagleys and the story Zeph told her the day they met. He and Addie had been a civil servants at NAS in Pensacola for over twenty years when his hermit uncle passed away and left Zeph his house in Manawassa Springs. Though Zeph had grown up in Milton he had on occasion visited his uncle here in Manawassa. Uncle Judd and Aunt Crimmy had a nice little cottage on the corner of the Promenade and a side street. Uncle Judd had worked for the electric coop and Aunt Crimmy was an elementary school teacher. He remembered having fun there the few times he visited. That was before his aunt died from cancer. Judd went off his nut. He shut himself up in his house and built barricades of sticks and other natural rubbish around it. Zeph's dad lost all contact with his brother after that. No one knew how he survived. After a while he became known locally as 'the Hermit of Stick House.' Until the lawyer contacted Zeph, he hadn't thought about Uncle Judd in years.

Addie and Zeph arrived one weekend to take a look at their inheritance. At first glance it hadn't looked too awful. The city of Manawassa must have ordered Uncle Judd to erect a fence that hid the stick fortress on three sides. It was obvious that the old man neatened up the front yard that faced the Lake. The house exterior was somewhat neglected, but in surprisingly good shape for an abode inhabited by a man who had been crazy for over twenty years. They assumed the interior would be the same. They were wrong.

"Uncle Judd was a hoarder." Zeph said. "Bigtime." Zeph described the living room as a nightmarish maze wending its way through seven foot high stacks of twine-bound newspaper, magazines, bills and junk mail. It only got worse the further in you went. China was piled on the surface of every piece of furniture in the dining room. In the kitchen toasters vied for space with old microwaves, blenders, small refrigerators, waffle irons and other dilapidated appliances. Clothing filled every bedroom to the ceiling. Linens lined the hallways. Oddly enough, in the bathroom, row upon row of shelves were lined with Hummel figurines. The sight of all the little figures with their cheery smiles and apple cheeks was in itself enough to frighten the new homeowners. "It was like we had invaded Hummel-Land." Zeph laughed. "The natives looked friendly, but who knew what evil lurked behind those innocent faces."

Undaunted, the couple cleared the yard and hauled the sticks and trash to the dump. Then they rented a gondola to clear out the interior of the house. They had just begun to toss piles of paper into the gondola when the twine around one stack broke. Hundred dollar bills floated around their heads like tufted dandelion seeds wafting on a breeze. "We both looked at each other and jumped into the gondola at the same time. After dumpster diving and going through all the paper in the front room, it hit us that probably all the crap in the house was stashing a fortune. The martial Hummels weren't evil, they were guarding a secret treasure."

It turned out to be true. In addition to the money in all the papers they found teapots full of valuable jewelry in the dining room; Civil War memorabilia inside the appliances in the kitchen; CDs, government bonds and statements of investments in the piles of clothing (some sewn into the linings of jackets). Not everything was valuable, but they knew they had hit the jackpot. When all the cash was counted, the non-cash paper assessed, the jewelry and china (much of which turned out to be quite valuable) auctioned and the Hummels sold to a collector for a small fortune (go figure), the Bagleys were close to two million dollars richer. The only collection they did not sell was the one containing the Civil War paraphernalia. This they donated to the Manawassa Historical Society, much to the boundless joy of that fine institution.

Needless to say they retired. The distressed home and gardens were rehabilitated. The Bagleys did all the work themselves which developed their skills as handypersons and gardeners. The house was christened "Zephyr Cottage" in the hopes of dispelling its shame as "Stick House." It stands now as a delightful bungalow surrounded by a lush yard. At the end of their full time efforts at rehabilitation on the place, the Bagleys wanted an active occupation that wouldn't consume all their time. They had travel plans. Katie found the couple eager to help her around the Belle. They insisted on not being paid; she insisted otherwise. An arrangement was struck to the satisfaction of all.

Even with their valuable assistance Katie still found her schedule blotted out of free time. Aside from inn-keeping, she spent a lot of time with her grand-twins and newborn granddaughter in Pensacola, traveling to visit her other grown children, volunteering here and there for community events and, of course, romancing Steve. So maybe she had miscalculated how many times she had been over to meet her new neighbor. She knocked one more time deciding that this was probably only the third time she had tried to introduce herself to the owner of Azalea Cottage.

***

Gena pulled into the back driveway when she thought she heard knocking on her front door. Abandoning her plunder from the Emporium she walked rapidly around the side of the house to the front door hoping against hope that it was Leland Pearse, or at least his crew, arriving to install the new porch door. Weeks had stretched to over a month and she was pretty impatient.

"Oh, damn." She pulled up abruptly as she saw the retreating figure of a woman and not Leland Pearse or his scraggy crew.

Katie turned and replied cheerfully. "Actually my name is Katie O'Neill, not damn. I'm your neighbor. I own Belle Magnolia Inn. You must be Gena de Bienville." She extended her hand to the figure before her who looked exasperated and not exactly welcoming.

Then Gena's countenance transfigured, in an instant, to one of welcoming grace. As a business woman she had evolved flexibility of facial expression and body language. It was a skill that would always come in useful. Taking the offered hand she mustered a slight blush.

"I am so happy to meet you and a bit ashamed at how long it has taken me to make your acquaintance. I am afraid I have been a rather neglectful neighbor." She intoned the perfect response to put Katie at ease. Gena wanted to appear gracious, but at the same time a little cool. She still felt a bit of superiority over her fellow Manawassans.

"The neglect is all mine. I've been too wrapped up Belle. She sort of runs my life."

"How odd that that she speaks of her inn like a person," Gena thought, but aloud she said, "Perfectly understandable. I hear that the Belle Magnolia Inn is quite famous."

"Well, she is the Grand Lady of Manawassa Springs. And people do come from all over to stay here. It's my first business venture unless you count raising four children. But your house must have quite a history, too. It was built around the same time as Belle I understand."

Gena maintained her distance. "I believe so. My Grand-mère lived here on and off for over ninety years. I visited it on occasion as a child, but lived mostly in New York City. I run Bienville Enterprises."

If Katie was supposed to feel impressed or a little put down, she didn't. She was entirely ignorant of the scope or wealth of Bienville Enterprises and so any attempt at condescension on Gena's part was unsuccessful. Katie did know that she needed to befriend this woman. It was a part of the plan. She couldn't afford to be offended. But it certainly looked as though it was going to take some time to crack Gena's defenses.

"I would love to give you a tour of Belle Magnolia whenever you have time. We're booked solid now, but most of the guests have other things they do during the day. I always check with them to get their permission to show their rooms. So even…"

"That would be lovely sometime, but right now I am expecting workmen."

"Hence the "damn" when you saw me. I was pretty sure you didn't mean it. I understand your situation perfectly. When I was restoring Belle I would periodically consider torture as a way to induce my contractor to show up on time or at all, for that matter.

"Yes. Mr. Pearse can be quite off-putting."

"I actually used Jennings for my major work, but I know that Mr. Pearse is equally dilatory. He's done a few things for me, too."

Gena refrained from scowling at the universal behavior of contractors. "No doubt. You will have to excuse me. I need to unload my car. I am so glad we have finally met."

"Sure. It was great to meet you, too, and any time you want, please call…" Katie rooted around her pocket and pulled out her card and handed it to Gena. "…or just come over. If I'm not there Addie is, and she can show you around. Bye now." Katie stumped down the rest of the walkway and turned at the gate to wave goodbye.

***

CHAPTER IV
REMINISCENCES

Gena woke with a start. At first she thought she had a pillow over her head. No. Sleep apnea. Had she developed sleep apnea? She knew she snored. Kayton had told her. That was a long time ago. What time was it? It was light enough to be after six. She got up feeling less than refreshed. Today she was promised by Mr. Pearse that his crew was coming to install the new door. One could only hope.

As she dressed and went through her morning routine Gena let her mind wander to the door that now hung on the porch. Who in God's name had made the offending door in the first place? It was atrocious. The porch itself was broad and airy and ran the full width of the house. The view of the backyard with its magnolias, crepe myrtles, azaleas, camellias, hydrangeas and other flowering plants was impressive. Their schedules of blooming splendor made for a year round display that was nothing less than spectacular. A row of oleander and yellow anise ran the length of the property on one side and various evergreens along the other. The azaleas bordering the back were enormous. Some of them, she was told, were original to the property. Gena knew very little about gardening in general, much less native flora, but more than one person had remarked on some of the azaleas, that they were the "old fashioned" kind not spoiled by modern hybridization. She had no way of knowing. Some did match the color of LeMoyne. Grand-mère told her the Great Storm of '26 had practically denuded the yard.

In addition to the shrubs, there were plenty of trees in the back yard. Gena particularly liked one huge, luscious old live oak in the right corner. It towered over the back part of the yard. A dilapidated swing with one side drooping almost to the ground hung dangerously by a frayed rope attached to one of its low-lying branches. The swing looked so out of place and lonely. No child had actually lived there since her father was a boy over seventy years ago, and that had only been for a short time. She herself spent only a few weeks each summer there from the time she was seven until she was about fourteen. She remembered whooshing back and forth in that swing during those summers and resolved to have a new swing put up.

The only other noteworthy grand trees were a magnificent

magnolia and another oak, both in the front yard. The flower borders were so wide that there was no real lawn, just a couple of grass medallions on either side of the front walk. The beds, though lush, reflected the abandonment they had experienced since her grandmother's death a few years ago. She brightened at a new idea. She would endeavor to refresh her property and coax it into the lovely state she remembered as a child.

She was not sure where to begin. In New York they had always had a lovely rooftop garden at the penthouse. Her father employed a Japanese gardener who tended it. Gena, who was a lonely child, counted Mr. Hamasaki as one of her best friends. Although he had plenty of duties, he always took time to tell her about the garden. They were never practical conversations that included scientific names or how and when to plant things, they were stories. Japanese spirituality and gardening merged and mingled to produce fascinating legends and reasons why gardens are alive in a unique way. She loved to listen to him and it was there, high above the confusion of New York, that she felt most at peace as a child. There and at Grand-mère's.

Although Gena's visits to LeMoyne were few, they were memorable. While there she thought of the grounds as being her own personal Central Park. The yard was much larger when she was a child, a double-deep lot, a part of which had been sold off. As time wore on many of the people on the Promenade sold their back lots while retaining a right of way to drive to the backs of their houses.

There was a house on the part which Grand-mère sold where the Helpers now lived. Known as "Quarter House" it originally served as housing for servants who were not allowed to use the Promenade and who had to content themselves with access to Circus Avenue. When Gena was a child she had associated Circus Avenue (which ran parallel to the Promenade, behind all the houses facing the Lake) with Mr. P.T. Barnum's domain. She envisioned it as a site of a circus with clowns and elephants and high wire acts. She was very disappointed to find out that 'Circus' meant 'circle' in Latin.

Since most of the interior of LeMoyne was off limits, she spent most of her time outdoors, the opposite of her experience in New York. For a modern woman Grand-mère still clung to the Victorian notion that small children should be seen and not heard. Sometimes they shouldn't even be seen which was why, Gena assumed, she spent so many hours outside.

Grand-mère had let her roam there for hours. She remembered swinging in the now condemned swing. She played hide and seek among the azaleas, usually with an imaginary friend, but sometimes with her horrid cousin Langlais when he was there. When the game was played with him it was more like a game of survival. She crouched in the bushes knowing that if she were discovered Langlais would torture her in some way. To one side of the yard there was a crumbly looking, moss covered fountain surrounded by a wide pavement. For some reason it scared her, so she never ventured near it as a child. Besides, New York and New Orleans had much lovelier fountains.

Grand-mère had servants who tended the needs of LeMoyne. Before Morris and Tildy there were George and Minnie whom she had come to know quite well. She liked them both very much. There were especially kind towards her and they couldn't abide Langlais. Whenever the cousins were at LeMoyne together it was obvious whom they preferred. It was no wonder. Langlais mocked them behind their backs because he thought them beneath himself. He played practical jokes on both of them whenever he got the chance. One time George was gardening in the back. When he broke for lunch Langlais stuck all of George's tools in the shrubbery where he had been working. When George returned to find them gone he was very upset that someone had stolen Miss Jacqueline's things. Langlais and Gena came upon the old man searching frantically. Gena stood helplessly by while Langlais told George that the police were going to put him in jail. When the horrible little boy began to snicker George realized that he had been tricked. He saw the edge of the shovel sticking out of a bush, grabbed it and glared at Langlais. Brandishing the shovel he growled, "Lang-lee, Lang-lee Beenville, you's a bad boy and needs a whuppin'." The child took off like lightening and George, who wouldn't hurt a flea, stood there laughing with Gena joining in.

Gena smiled to herself at the thought of his wife Minnie, who was anything but. She must have weighed well over two hundred pounds, but she could move as quick as a cat. One time Minnie had been out snipping flowers in the yard. Gena was swinging under the oak, higher and higher. She lost her grip on the ropes at the top of her swing and out she flew. From across the yard Minnie saw the girl-missile, and the portly servant flew at an incredible speed towards her. Gena recalled landing quite comfortably on Minnie's ample person. The kindly woman didn't scold. She just laughed. She laughed even harder as she related the episode to George. "Foist I wuz cuttin' daisies, den I wuz toined into a big pillow sos t' catch de girl. She okay. Yeah. She okay."

George and Minnie were the only Negroes in her world. In New York you saw photos in the newspaper of celebrities like Jackie Robinson. She had heard Lena Horne sing on Ed Sullivan once and had met Louis Armstrong at a gathering at her father's penthouse. Somehow they weren't real to her, not like George and Minnie were. George was bent over and had white fuzz all over his dark head. His eyes were rheumy but held a merry sparkle. He was always leaning over at his gardening or handyman work, so much so that Gena deduced that this was why he was unable to straighten up at all. Still he seemed to work as effectively as if he could stand straight. He let her follow him around as he fixed this or that or when he surreptitiously smoked behind the garage so Grand-mère wouldn't find out. "Yeah, yeah. Now you don't go tellin' Miz Beenville I been smoking." He always followed that up with a bribe of peppermints, the same he used unsuccessfully to disguise his tobacco breath. Even as a girl Gena was sure Grand-mère knew all about his trysts with tobacco, but overlooked them.

Gena contrasted the gentle couple with her Grand-mère. Jacqueline LeMoyne de Bienville was reserved, at least most of the time. She cultivated a small circle of family and friends about whom she cared and the rest of the world didn't matter. She was very tall and thin with a gray French twist wound tightly at the back of her head. Gena never saw her dressed any way except extravagantly: sporting the latest fashions, in full makeup and bedecked in jewelry. Her manner was always graciously appropriate in a reserved way, but she could surprise you. Gena found this out the hard way when she was around nine years old. It was her third visit to LeMoyne and the first by herself. Her mother and father were vacationing in Europe. In those days children did not accompany their parents on European vacations or any vacations, now that she thought about it. So she was put on an airplane with Mrs. Lester the housekeeper and flown to Pensacola. From there she was conveyed to LeMoyne in a large Cadillac driven by her grandmother's occasional chauffer Calvin. When they arrived Mrs. Lester set her bag down in the grand foyer and inquired of Grand-mère which room would she be staying in. Grand-mère said: "one at the Holiday Inn. Calvin, take Mrs. Lester back to Pensacola." Then she handed the stunned chaperone plane fare.

Her grandmother had always treated her as kindly as her disposition allowed and, after a few years, Gena was inured to her severity. Still, she was very grateful for the presence of George and Minnie with whom she felt completely at ease. She knew they lived in the house at the very back of the yard, the same inhabited now by the Helpers. The elderly black couple cooked and cleaned and gardened and shopped and ran errands for Grand-mère. It was the early sixties and Gena's young mind had not sorted out the intricacies of the Jim Crow laws especially "separate but equal." In fact, not much of her education had dealt with issues touching the Civil War, much less Civil Rights. So it was only logical that she should innocently ask her grandmother if George and Minnie were her slaves. Gena winced even now, not just at this childish blunder, but at the smack her grandmother gave her. The poor child was momentarily paralyzed by shock. Then she fled in tears from her grandmother and hid.

The old woman took some time finding her, but when she did she apologized and hugged the crying girl. Jacqueline explained to Gena in a very gentle and understandable way all about the horrid institution of slavery, the war that ended it and that ought to have ended every form of racial discrimination, but had not. She said George and Minnie were employees and she paid them handsomely. They stayed in Quarter House, but could leave any time they wished and live wherever they pleased. She said she counted them among her friends and trusted them implicitly which was more than she could say about many whom she knew, especially in the business world. With a touch of anger she related how badly Negroes were still being treated, not just in the South, but all over, and that many people were working together to change all that. Laws were being made and people, both Negroes and White were coming together. She spoke about brave men like Martin Luther King, Jr. who risked their lives to change worn out and prejudicial ideas in America. Gena, though not quite ten years old, took this civics lesson to heart. From that time forward she conceived a detestation for racial injustice in all its forms. It now made her think how remarkable her grandmother was to be so ahead of the times.

That same evening Grand-mère arranged a casual picnic in the yard out back where she (still formally attired), Gena, George and Minnie, Calvin and his wife Darlene (who were both white) sat as equals enjoying a dinner that was brought in from Chilton's Chicken House. Minnie would take a huge bite of chicken then complain about how poorly Mr. Chilton treated "dem chickens" by frying them so badly. Then she would take another bite and complain again with the entire party nodding in agreement. Everyone knew that no one fried chicken like Minnie. She was renowned for it. Grand-mère insisted that she and Gena clear and clean up and let the others chat as the evening shadows grew long. Periodic evening picnics became a tradition for them.

From that summer she loved her grandmother with all her heart. Gena looked beyond the sternness, formality and proper manners and saw a whole other person behind them. As Gena grew older she thought it was as if Jacqueline LeMoyne de Bienville were split into two people, the proper lady and the free spirited girl. Grand-mère contended with both as best she could. Gena learned over the years that this dichotomy of personality was one reason Grand-mère spent as much time away from New York and New Orleans as could be allowed. She still ran Bienville from any locale, but it was always behind the scenes and through some male figurehead. Until Charles her son was ready to take the reins, Jacqueline made sure her corporate president was a perfect male marionette and no threat to her authority whatsoever. It was the way things were done then if you were a powerful woman.

When she thought about it, Gena had truly loved the times at LeMoyne. She never saw much of the rest of Manawassa Springs, not that there was much to see. She could vividly recall her first crush. She was about eleven at the time. Two boys, several years older than she, worked on the yard at Belle Magnolia next door. It was owned then by a very scary and crazy lady, Eudora, the last of the Bellinghams. The boys would take their shirts off when it got really hot, which was most of the time. One was kind of white and pasty and not very attractive, but the other – the dark handsome one – what was his name? It was something unusual. Moss. That was it. She had supposed he was nicknamed for the Spanish moss that adorned all the oaks around Manawassa. She would fantasize that he was the descendent of a Spanish explorer who had survived a shipwreck in which all his companions had died. The truth was much less romantic. In fact, it was his last name. He happened to be Jewish and when Grand-mère caught her pre-teen granddaughter ogling him, she was quite furious with her. At first Gena thought that Negroes were one thing, but apparently Jews did not enjoy Grand-mère's open arm tolerance. Then after a proper dressing down Gena realized that it had nothing to do with his faith or ethnic background; it was Grand-mère's natural disdain of all men. That was an attitude of which Gena became more and more aware the older she got. Perhaps she was hoping to save Gena from an "imprudent marital collaboration." Sadly Gena thought that Grand-mère had succeeded. She lost Kayton.

The ding of the toaster broke into her recollections. She seldom let herself dwell on the past. When she did, it always led to Kayton and that was not acceptable. She plucked the bagel from its cage and winced. Why was it so impossible to obtain a decent bagel in the South? Donuts, yes; sausage biscuits and gravy were to die for, but bagels were nothing more than glorified circular white bread. She would just slather on enough cream cheese to smother her objections to it. Her next trip to New York would be rife with breakfast visits to *Hofstadter's Bagelry*.

Gena carried her tray of cappuccino, tomato juice and the so-called bagel to the sun porch and set it on the wrought iron table. She nestled into the chair and brought up the business section of the *New York Times* on her laptop. There are some forms of civilization that cannot be left behind. The *Manawassa Gazette* just didn't live up to the *Times*. She perused the Wall Street Journal and other periodicals to keep abreast of the world beyond Manawassa Springs. She reviewed her email and dashed off replies as warranted. After thoroughly exhausting this aspect of her morning routine she polished off the so-called bagel.

Glancing up from her computer world to survey her own new surroundings, she felt the momentary assault of doubt about her choice to live in Manawassa. Gena closed her eyes and steeled her mind. Inwardly she would picture the negatives of her former life: the grime of the city, the noise, the crowds, the polluted air, the stress of the job, sparring bouts with Langlais, the nightmares. If Kayton slipped into her thoughts for one nanosecond she would open her eyes and focus on an object around her – any would do – and contemplate it. Right now a fat grey squirrel was running down the side of the oak. It would stop and twitch its tail and chatter, then proceed. It leapt from branch to branch as if to say, "I am free. I have no cares." Her eyes followed the squirrel until it disappeared. Then she caught sight of the dilapidated swing. It had begun to sway limply back and forth though neither hand, nor breeze compelled it. It was a very eerie sight. The swing did that sometimes. Perhaps it was her own personal mysterious phenomenon like the sudden waves in the middle of Lake Manawassa.

***

CHAPTER V
THE DREAM

Katie clicked off her cell phone. Apparently Mr. Pearse's men did not come three days ago as her neighbor Gena had hoped, and it looked as though the delinquent contractor had no intention of showing up today. So Gena was headed over this morning to see Belle Magnolia.

They met at the Belle's front door and Katie began a tour that she had done dozens of times since becoming the owner of the inn. She started with the wrought iron fence and towering lantern at the gate. She elaborated on the landscaping. Katie was an avid gardener and eager to impart her love of this hobby to Gena. She gave common and scientific names to the shrubs, trees and flowers. Gena took it all in and showed polite appreciation. She casually mentioned that Katie might assist her in some points of her own landscaping efforts. Her neighbor said she'd be thrilled to help.

As they walked the yard Katie explained that the house in Mr. Bellingham's heyday had a huge glass solarium where he kept exotic plants and wild animals from South America. Much of it was long gone, only part of it remained. When she gardened she occasionally would find bits of glass here and there from the original structure. She had restored the remaining part for her guests to enjoy.

Over the house and through the rooms they went from the first to the fourth floor where Katie resided. Katie normally kept her personal quarters off guided tours, but she wanted Gena to have full knowledge of the house. There might come a time when it would prove useful. She recounted the process of restoring and furnishing the Grand Lady. Gena politely listened and asked appropriate questions now and again, but otherwise seemed unimpressed. Katie supposed that to someone who had seen palaces and manors and castles of the world, Belle Magnolia probably appeared to be a quaint and provincial dwelling. At the end of the tour Katie asked about Azalea Cottage.

"You said you didn't know much about Azalea Cottage. If you like I can help you find out about her history."

Once again Gena thought it sounded a little eccentric to assign gender to a house the way sailors did to their ships and men did to their sports cars. To Katie, for some reason, Belle Magnolia and LeMoyne were female entities.

"That would be lovely. The background of *LeMoyne* is of interest to me. I know a little of it, but suppose it would be interesting to find out more. I will let you know when I am at the point where I have the time to improve my knowledge of its history."

"Great. Listen… can I treat you to lunch? I know Manawassa Springs is a sleepy town compared to New York, well compared to Crestview for that matter, but we do have a lot of community events. I would love to introduce you to the things of interest here. Of culinary delights we actually have some places to boast about."

Gena felt it would be too rude to decline, and she had to agree that *Hall's* had a boast-worthy menu. There might be other establishments that also had decent cuisine. "I would like that. Where shall we meet?"

"*Blacksmiths*. It has the best sandwiches in town. Their grilled grouper and slaw on a croissant is their signature dish and worth every gram of fat and carbohydrates. It's right on Main Street. You can't miss it. It has old wagon wheels and other blacksmithy things hanging on the wall outside. Meet you there at twelve-thirty tomorrow?"

"I will be there tomorrow."

Tomorrow had other plans because at 11:50 am Mr. Pearse's crew finally arrived. Gena felt like blasting the "Hallelujah Chorus" all over Manawassa Springs. They had the new door. They had tools. They had thermoses of beer or whatever Southern workers put in their thermoses. The hideous jungle door with the tiger on it was returned to its cave. So it was the following day before Gena met her neighbor for lunch, but not before her world was thoroughly shaken.

***

Gena spent several hours admiring the new glass door on the sun porch. She would read a little then get up, open and close it. She did this at least fifty times to make sure nothing was wrong with it. It didn't drag; it didn't squeak; it wasn't too flimsy; it wasn't too heavy. It was perfect.

Her work was done. LeMoyne, at least the interior, was as it should be. That night she ought to have slept soundly, but that did not happen. She settled in at 10:30 and tossed and turned until midnight. A storm had blown up and the flashes of lightning followed so quickly by thunder alerted her to the fact that the storm hovered directly over Manawassa Springs. She had been through others, but not one of this

85

magnitude. She remembered the first bad summer storm she had experienced in Manawassa Springs when she was a child. It must have been the first year she had come. Mother and Father were there with her at that point. The howling wind and booming thunder sent her racing to her parents' room to sleep between them for the rest of the night.

Fully awake, Gena went downstairs and made some Chamomile tea. She was disturbed. For the most part she had slept like a rock from the first day she moved to LeMoyne. Now her old New York pattern of sleep, or rather, lack of it, had retuned. On her way up to her bedroom she grabbed a book from her grandmother's bookcase that stood against the stairway. There seemed to be a predominance of Kipling. She had never read Kipling before. With a shrug she carried it upstairs.

After an hour or so Gena yawned. Kipling was boring which made it choice reading for insomniacs. She set aside the book and again attempted to sleep. There are certain dreams that ought not to be frightening, but, which for some reason unknown to the dreamer's conscious mind, are. When you dream them over and over with variations on a theme, they become terrifying.

There was a little girl all dressed in white. She was beautiful in an old fashioned way. Her hair was lush and shiny, but she was quite pale except for her cheeks that glowed red. She was so frail that even the slightest whisper of a breeze would have carried her off. She sang and danced around the back yard of LeMoyne pulling off azaleas and putting them in her hair. Joining her was a host of animals: leopards and elephants and birds and monkeys and snakes. She looked at them with utter surprise and rushed away stopping suddenly in front of the new glass door to the sun porch. "That will not do! No wonder they have escaped." She looked straight at Gena: the figment of the dream at the dreamer. Gena felt that the figment was more real than she herself.

Then all semblance of rationality fled the dream. A lady dressed in what looked like a medieval gown of rich blue and a pointed hat with a long white scarf appeared atop the back of an enormous Bengal tiger. They had come out of a door in an old live oak in the corner of the back yard. She scooped up the girl who then turned into a tiny baby. Then a man with old fashioned sideburns joined them on the tiger. Another man appeared – tall, dark-skinned and wearing robes. He had a cross in his right earlobe. He opened the new glass door to the sun porch to admit them. When he did, the new door shattered into a million fragments and a massive wooden door replaced it. He beckoned the trio on the tiger to enter. They did, only they didn't go through the door opening; they went into the door or, rather, became a part of the door. Then the dark man looked directly at Gena and nodded. She knew he was inviting her to come. He wasn't evil, but he frightened her nevertheless. Gena knew she was shaking her head no. So the man with the robes followed the ensemble into the door. The oak, the animals, the backyard all vanished. Only the Tiger, huge and menacing, remained.

Gena awoke screaming. She bit her thumb to stop herself. She could not face having nightmares again like in New York. If she did, now where would she go? LeMoyne had been her refuge, her sanctuary. If she went back Langlais would have her committed somewhere. Oh, God! He's here now. He's got hold of me and is dragging me away. Wait. She was still asleep. She knew she had to wake up or she would die.

"I have to wake up now." She shouted. Her eyes flew open and she took in the shadows of the room, her room at LeMoyne. It was a very dark night. Something was wrong. Something had happened. Something horrifying. Could someone have broken in? No, the alarm was not going off. One of the first things she had done, any New Yorker would have done, was to have an alarm system installed. She knew there was no intruder. She lay still breathing deeply in slow silent breaths. She couldn't close her eyes, for when she did she clearly saw the little pale girl, the man, the woman holding a baby and the tiger.

Gena wasn't sure how long she lay there awake. Perhaps she should take some of the sleep aid that she had gotten in New York. She got up, went to the bathroom and retrieved a pill, praying that it would take effect right away. Soon her lids became heavy. The medication was powerful and quick; the image of the people with the tiger faded. She slept.

Her slumber lasted until ten in the morning, but Gena did not wake refreshed. She was worried, but she couldn't say what about. Since it was so close to her luncheon appointment she just had coffee for breakfast. Something was nagging her in the back of her mind, but she couldn't pin it down. She assured herself that it was just a nervous hangover from the wretched nightmare. There weren't enough minor household duties to keep herself busy as she waited to meet Katie at

Blacksmiths. Opting for relaxation and some sun, Gena stepped out onto the porch to enjoy a second cup of coffee and read the New Yorker. An unpleasant surprise met her gaze. She first experienced annoyance, followed by anger. Then consuming all other emotions came terror.

As she settled into her wicker chair she glanced through the window and saw that during the night a huge limb from the oak had crashed into the yard at back. A multitude of smaller limbs and vegetation littered her yard. Several other branches were hanging dangerously from the oak. She realized with irritation that she would need to find an arborist or whatever passed for one here in Manawassa. As if that were not sufficient to ruin her day she noticed that much of the porch floor was wet. Yesterday as she sat contemplating her new life she had opened the windows to enjoy the heavy, sweet scent of honeysuckle in the cool of the evening. "Damn," Gena silently swore. She had forgotten to close them.

She relocated herself at the table which was far enough away from the wet side so that she could sit and read her magazine in whatever peace remained to her. She opened it and started at the beginning. Gena was a cover to cover New Yorker reader. Suddenly a feeling of urgency came over her. Or was it fear? Whatever it was it caused her to turn her attention to the entire porch. She became quite angry now, for the glass in the newly installed porch door was cracked with dozens of lines crisscrossing like a spider's web. It had taken forever to get that door. "Double damn." She was so annoyed now that she could have taken a sledge hammer to the door and to Leland Pearse.

She stared at the mess cursing inwardly, then her entire being stood still for an instant. Her fury was succeeded by a flood of terror. What she knew she had to do, what thoroughly repelled her, what caused the hair on her neck to stand up was that she would have to put the old wooden door back on. No, it was more than that: *she was supposed to put the old hideous door back on because it belonged there. Nothing she did could alter that fact. No other door could reside on the sun porch. The Tiger Door willed itself to return to its home.* She stood as if in a trance and shivered. How did she know that? It was the dream. The dream had told her.

***

The fact that the old door had to go back on scared her very much, but did not abate her caustic attitude as she dialed Leland Pearse. Cutting off the formalities of Laurie's receptionist spiel, Gena exploded,

"Is Mr. Pearse in?"

"Not at the moment. He's in Paradise Springs."

"He'd better stay there until I calm down." Gena thought, but in her most authoritative voice said, "Have him call me at once. It's the door again. For no apparent reason the glass has cracked. It must have been defective." She added a terse "thank you" and hung up without waiting for Laurie's reply.

"Here we go again playing the contractor waiting game," she addressed the door. As she stared at it her eyes were caught by an apparent pattern in the middle of the door. Inexplicably she felt herself being drawn nearer to it. Slowly approaching the door she stared at the shattered glass until her eyes hurt. Gena sprang from it with a scream, covered her face with her hands and fled. What she had seen, what was formed by the crackled lines, what terrified her and sent her fleeing from its presence was a crouching Bengal Tiger clearly visible in the middle of the glass.

***

PART III
FRIENDS, FAMILY, LOVERS, ETC.

CHAPTER I
FRIENDS

At Blacksmiths

"Looks like Gena's fashionably late, per New York social protocol." Katie mused. "In the South we just call it rude." She had secured a table that was nestled in the corner because she hoped that the nature of this lunch would require a private venue. It was necessary to be secluded if she wanted to draw Gena out. Katie had known for some time that Azalea Cottage was in need of a good cleaning of a particular kind. She was sipping the last of her iced tea when Gena gracefully waltzed up to the table and drew the chair back. She smiled, but Katie thought it was rather forced. The former New Yorker's face was strained and visibly tired.

"I hope you haven't been waiting long."

"No, just a few. I love your scarf." Katie ogled Gena's accessory sans the knowledge that it was a designer scarf from Bergdorf's. "I saw one like that at Target and almost bought it. Wouldn't that have been funny? We could have had twin scarves."

Normally Gena would have replied coldly to such an insulting comparison, but her nerves were shot. She managed a sickly smile and ordered sweet tea from the waitress.

"So, you've been here four, five months? I'm very sorry I haven't called on you. I'm afraid I haven't been very neighborly. I should have treated you to lunch long ago."

"I'm sure the Inn has kept you quite busy. I myself have been occupied wrapping up some loose business ends associated with the change of venue. The conveniences of the technological era allowed me to physically move to Manawassa Springs well ahead of my ability to mentally relocate with regard to the network of issues involved at Bienville Enterprises. I've spent a fair amount of time on the computer and iPhone with my corporate officers."

What the heck was an iPhone Katie wondered. No doubt Gena lived on the cutting edge of technology. She nodded as though she understood completely and mentally compared Gena's global wheeling and dealings with her small town inn keeping and babysitting duties. Katie lost.

"There were several mergers and at least one hostile takeover in the works when I moved here. My cousin Langlais," Gena winced fleetingly, "has done his best to smooth things, but I am afraid some of the intricacies are beyond his business competency. Being relatively new to the extent of his duties he is kept under observation, needless to say, by myself, Board members and the other heads of our subsidiaries. I retain the majority interest in the business as well as the consensus of the other large shareholders."

"My God!" Katie thought. "Does this woman know how to speak normal English? She makes cousin Langlais sound like a chimpanzee doing his best at the helm of a nuclear sub. Okay, okay, I must not feel patronized if I am going to bring her out." Aloud she ventured an innocuous statement.

"I noticed that you haven't made any major changes to Azalea Cottage. Are any in the works?"

"No, I plan to keep *LeMoyne* as it is. It was painted two years ago. I may embellish the yard, but I'm afraid I don't have much gardening experience. I was glad of your offer to help. I know you are busy so if am unable to tap your expertise is there anyone else locally to assist me with design and implementation?"

Katie tried very hard not to be irritated with Gena's formality of poise and language, but it was a challenge. "Sure. The folks at Sanders landscaping are pretty good. Morrison's nursery, ditto. Then there's Mr. Crippett. He lives here on the Promenade at Stokely. He's very old and you wouldn't think he could keep up with the work, but he has the most amazing garden in Manawassa. He has a handyman appropriately named Clipper who helps him. There's pretty much nothing Mr. Crippett doesn't know. I will warn you that, aged or not, he likes the ladies. But he's harmless. I mean he isn't a dirty old man or anything. He's just Old South Gentleman when it comes to women. To him we are the weaker sex – in a nice way. He considers us all genteel and in need of continual accommodating. It's actually kind of quaint. But if you can get over that, he'll spill everything you want to know and, if he likes you, give you a cutting or rooting of just about anything in his garden."

"Thank you for the leads. I will investigate them." The tea and a straw were placed before Gena. Eschewing the latter she lifted the glass and took a polite sip.

"We were all sad to see your grandmother pass away. I know she only lived here full time the last few years, but she always made her presence felt. I liked her. She was a character. We were afraid that the house would be put on the market and sold to some Snowbirds."

"Snowbirds?"

"Yankees who flit down here when it gets cold up North, then flit back home. They used to own a lot of the houses on the Promenade and most were either neglected to varying degrees or modified out of recognition. It didn't make for a community feeling. Fifteen or twenty years ago they found other places to nest in the winter. Most of them fly to Sugar Beach or Destin now days. Thank God! Oh, I didn't mean you. You're considered local by association…your grandmother and all…" She trailed off lamely.

"I see." Gena's response was as cold as her tea.

Katie blundered on in further attempts at friendliness. Internally she likened this New Yorker to Mt. Everest: beautiful, tall, icy and a challenge to conquer. "It was back in the eighties, may have been the seventies – I'm not sure, that the town council began to realize what a special place this is. They imposed zoning and building laws on the Promenade and Circus areas and the little downtown. They wanted to recapture the feel of Manawassa Springs in its heyday at the turn of the 20th Century."

"Then I'm glad I don't plan to do anything to LeMoyne. I won't have to deal with the local authorities."

Katie glanced down at the menu to hide her rolling eyes. She was almost ready to give up on her patronizing neighbor. Maybe it wasn't intentional. The waitress returned and took their orders. Katie heartily praised the grouper croissant and Gena acquiesced to her recommendation. Katie splurged on Blacksmiths Gumbo Filé, a spicy dish that required ongoing refills of water.

"Do the codes dictate what color one can paint her house?"

"Good question. They do and don't. That is, unless you plan to paint it in psychedelic colors, you can paint it whatever. Many of the homes have been restored to the original color – white – which I find boring. I know Belle Magnolia is white, but the aqua shutters make all the difference in the world. They were quite a shock to proper society when Mr. Bellingham painted them that color back in the day. Anyway, you can see that other houses are pastel colors… except for LeMoyne. I am assuming that primrose was its original color. It's pretty bright for the Promenade, but as far as I'm concerned, quite a welcome relief from color boredom."

"Yes. Grand-mère told me her father had selected LeMoyne's color after a grand house in New Orleans. It was intended to please my great-grandmother. He felt it matched the wild azaleas and complemented the pinks and purples of many of the other azaleas. The yard held more azaleas than now, the azalea being my great-grandfather's favorite shrub."

"If you are considering any alterations or want to paint Azalea Cottage luminescent green you can get the codes from the city hall."

"Thank you."

The meal was brought and conversation ran along the lines of the historical character of Manawassa Springs. Katie filled Gena in on all she knew, but being a fairly new resident herself, Katie often had to refer LeMoyne's mistress to the more informed natives of the town. In addition to Mr. Crippett, Gena made mental notes of Carrie and Shelby Easley, octogenarians, who might have known her Grand-mère, Polly Price who was the local genealogical enthusiast, Hefty Porter who could do whatever odd jobs she needed to get done and a half dozen more locals whose acquaintance would prove beneficial to her residence in Manawassa.

The meal was drawing to a close and Katie was feeling quite frustrated. She knew that Azalea Cottage was in need of a kind of restoration that would be foreign to Gena, and she sensed that Gena had experienced something while living there, but was withholding information. Discovering that Gena had walked to *Blacksmiths,* as had she, Katie suggested they walk home together.

It was a hot and listless sort of day. The air was stifling. The leaves on the trees hung limply awaiting some welcome change: wind, rain, coolness. They were halfway around the Promenade when an agitation of water became clearly visible in the middle of the Lake. Little whitecaps peaked and fell.

"Oh!" An involuntary exclamation escaped from Gena.

They stood together and watched as it came to a crescendo and abruptly ceased. The appearances of the mysterious white caps in the middle of Lake Manawassa had been increasing since Katie moved to Manawassa Springs. Everyone had noticed it, but no one knew why it was happening. Katie was sure she did. She simply said:

"It does that sometimes."

***

Amaryllis In The Hedge

"You don't do much gardening, do you," floated a disembodied voice over the hedge behind LeMoyne.

"Gena looked up swiveling her head in all directions and replying to the air. "Yes I do…well, not really. I'm learning. I suppose it shows."

A head poked itself through the azalea hedge, a mop of thick, unruly curls enveloping a tiny face. Gradually the entire form of a young girl slipped through the thick bushes. Unaccustomed to children as she was, Gena could only estimate her age as pre-pubescent. The child's loose white shorts and faded top that hung off one shoulder, together with the stray leaves and flower petals caught in her long curls gave her the appearance of a Greek maenad awaking after a bacchanal rite. A pair of wide set green eyes met Gena's. "I'm Reese. I just moved here from Mobile. I live in that house." She indicated the house behind the back shrubbery of LeMoyne. "It has a name. It's called Quarter House. I don't know why. At first I thought it was Quarter Horse. I know what a Quarter Horse is. What's your name?"

"My name is Ms. De…my name is Gena. I recently moved here from New York City."

"New York City! That's far away. I used to live in Biloxi and then Mobile. That's just a hop, skip and a jump away my mom says. I went to Atlanta once. It was far away. There's a zoo there. We drove for a long time. Aren't there any gardens in New York City? I've seen pictures of Central Park. It has lots of trees. Does it have gardens, too? If they do, I bet New York gardens probably don't grow vegetables, just flowers. I was named after my grandmother. My mom insisted. That means she got her way. Her name was Amaryllis – my grandmother's, not my mother's. Mama's name is Rose. I like the name Rose, but not so much Amaryllis. But I loved Grandma. She went to Heaven last year. I miss her lots. Since Daddy didn't like the name Amaryllis very much he called me Reese. So after a while Mama did, too. Daddy loved Grandma, just not her name. Everybody calls me Reese except Grandma. She used to call me 'Pigeon.' She said when I was born I looked just like a little pigeon. She used to live here in my house when she was a little girl, only it was her house then.

95

That was a long time ago. She moved a lot, but after Grampy Frank died she moved back here, only not right here. She lived in Destin by the beach. She got sick and then had to live with lots of sick people, but she said she wasn't like them. She was young at heart. She said we were like-spirited. She said I was a throwback. What's a throwback?" Here she drew a deep breath obviously deflated from her discourse.

Gena barely knew where to begin her response. Corporate life had prepared her to deal with negotiations with the toughest talking businessmen, but not with the stream of conscious monologue of a voluble ten year old.

"Nice to meet you, Reese." Gena stabbed her spade into the ground, removed her gloves and dusted off her hands as she walked over to the little girl. She extended her hand to Reese. For someone who had been so talkative just a moment before the girl sucked in her lips and made the pretense of being cautiously shy. Slowly she reached out to Gena and wagged the proffered hand.

"Are you a stranger? I'm not supposed to talk to strangers."

"Well, my grandmother lived here before me and probably knew your grandmother, or maybe your parents. Also we've introduced ourselves, but if you are uncomfortable I suppose we can go talk to your mother."

"She's at work now. Casey watches me when Mama works. She's a nurse, Mama, not Casey. Mama only works sometimes, not all the time like Dad. Do you want to meet Casey?"

"Sure, but can we walk around to the gap over there? I'm not quite as small as you are. I don't think I would fit through the bushes here."

The pair walked to the other side where there was an opening between the two yards next to Gena's driveway. Reese, her curls whipped into a frenzy, ran to the back door with Gena following more sedately. The little girl had barely entered the screened porch when she yelled.

"Casey, can you come meet Gena so she's not a stranger anymore?"

A young woman in her late teens or early twenties emerged from door at the same time stowing her cell phone in her pocket. She looked both guilty and surprised.

"Reese, where have you been?" She scolded, though the guilty look did not leave her face. "I, uh, just went to the bathroom and you disappeared. You're supposed to tell me when you want to go outside."

"I'm sorry. I met the lady who lives in the yellow house. Her name is Gena and she's from New York City. I don't want her to be a stranger so I brought her here to meet you."

Gena stepped forward and introduced herself to Casey. She immediately recognized her as the server who frequently waited on her at *Hall's the Deck*. Gena mentioned this fact and the young woman relaxed visibly.

"Southern Bourbon Pecan Pie. It's my favorite, too. My name's Casey Halloway.

"So you work at *Hall's* and babysit…"

"I'm not a baby," protested Reese.

"Duly noted," Gena nodded to the little girl. "You work at the café and also play with Reese when her mother's away."

"Mmm-uh. It helps with college. Right now I'm at Panhandle Junior College, but next year I'll be going to West Florida."

"Wonderful. What are you studying?"

"My core courses are just about out of the way. I'm going into business administration. Eventually I plan to get my masters. I'm thinking of specializing in restaurant management. I like to cook, too." She grinned. "And eat."

"That's a wide open field. I've been in business more years than I like to count. I would be glad to talk to you some time at greater length, when you're not busy. I also have plenty of restaurant contacts on East Coast and, when you are ready, maybe I can be of help." Gena was amazed at herself for how glibly these words flowed from her. She had been used to dispensing them to graduates of Harvard and Yale, not Panhandle College, but it gave her an incipient sense of belonging to offer a helping hand to a local.

"Thanks."

Reese had been patiently waiting for the grown-ups to end their boring conversation, but since there seemed to be no end she blurted, "Can I have something to drink? Gena, too."

Casey escorted them to the kitchen where she prepared tea all around. After a little more small talk Gena took her leave and returned to gardening. Somehow the small episode lifted her spirits. It made her feel like a neighbor. There were no such things as neighbors in her New York City world. She knew that they existed for some people there, but not for her. Lofty penthouses preclude neighborliness as a rule. She smiled to herself and, drawing on her gloves, resumed digging up weeds.

***

Over the next few weeks Gena became accustomed to and actually welcomed the frequent intrusions of the next door nymph into her backyard. She always asked if Reese had first let Casey know she was going over for a visit. It was true that the child babbled incessantly, but Gena enjoyed the imaginative stream that flowed from the child. Reese covered every topic from worms to an upcoming trip Disneyworld. She could barely restrain her excited anticipation of seeing Mickey Mouse and Cinderella, not to mention riding in the teacups. Apparently a visit to this children's paradise was to be a present for her 10th birthday which was in a few weeks. It was an event that Reese had anticipated since she was five. "Lots of kids go when they are like seven or eight, but I'm 'putty' for my age. That's French. It means I'm very small, like Mama." Gena hid a smile at the child's butchering of the word 'petite', but restrained the urge to correct her. "Mama and Daddy had to wait until I was big enough to go on all the rides. They measured me every month and last Christmas I was big enough. So for my tenth birthday they said we could all go to Disneyworld."

One morning right after Reese had been called home by Casey, Gena took a break from gardening in order to stretch her legs. She strolled around the yard to assess her progress. She did not have enough knowledge to plant anything quite yet, but was quite learned in what to pull up. Her first skill after studying a book on gardening was the ability to identify weeds. And in Florida there were a plethora of these insidious invaders in all shapes and sizes. She discovered how much she hated vines. She came to the front yard and stopped. The gate was unlocked and swinging.

"Why does it keep doing that?" She asked herself as she walked to secure the latch for the umpteenth time. "There's not a bit of wind and it's too early for the mail." She locked the gate then jiggled the latch to see if it was defective and could be loosened inadvertently. That was not the case. To open it took a great deal of effort. No casual action she tried would unlock the gate. She knelt and examined the hinges. She unlocked and swung the gate. Her personality was such that she was determined to find the answer. This had served her well in transactions in New York, but did little to resolve the problem of the self-opening gate. "Maybe I will ask Mr. Pearse to take a look when he comes."

That touched a sore point as always happened when the words "Mr. Pearse" came up. Surprisingly he had come the same day she called and took a look at the shattered glass door. Gena had accompanied him to the porch but could not make herself look at the door itself. At first she hoped he would notice the tiger and justify her observation. This was succeeded by chills shooting throughout her body. So she altered her hope that he would see nothing unusual. This left her feeling fragile of mind as if she were slowly going mad. In the end, she just pushed the thought of the tiger-in-the-door entirely from her mind and stood blankly behind Mr. Pearse with a cup of coffee in her hand.

"It doesn't show any signs of having been hit by anything. There's no central spot for the shatter. So I reckon you're right. It was defective, the glass that is. We did have a swing in temperature from the daytime highs in the last few nights and there was that storm. The drop in pressure and all. I'll just get my boys to take the door off and we'll send it back. 'Til then…"

The rest of his words became inaudible. Again, a horror swept over her at the thought of the old wooden door being put back on. Nevertheless, she knew that if it were not something, something very awful, would happen. Robotically she assented. She was powerless to contradict his conclusion.

"…Ms. LeMoyne?" The contractor was facing her and for some moments had obviously been waiting for her reply.

"Fine." Gena left the porch swiftly.

While waiting for Pearse's boys to come and restore the Tiger Door to its rightful place, Gena pushed all thoughts of the porch, especially the door, out of her mind and pretended they did not exist. Now she had a little miscreant gate to annoy her.

***

Mr. Crippett

When Gena was able to push her cares aside, she began to feel acclimated to her new surroundings so that the words "relaxation" and "friends" partially replaced the words "stress" and "business associates."

She counted Reese, her parents Rose and Sam (whom finally met), Casey and Katie among her friends, although the latter was most uncomfortable to be around at times. Other than thoughts of the Tiger Door which nipped at her consciousness occasionally, she began to suspect that serenity was obtainable, if she worked hard at it. She chatted frequently with Casey who sat for Reese Mondays, Wednesdays and Fridays. As was typical for those of her youth Casey held forth frankly on every subject under the sun. Gena learned a lot about Manawassa, at least from the perspective of a twenty year old. Reese's mother Rose was a diminutive woman who was very calm, quiet and soft spoken, the antithesis of her young daughter in personality. Rose grew up in Mississippi, but had lived all over the world. Her career as a nurse in the army had seen to that. It was in Germany she had met her husband Sam Helper who was an engineer and contracted private security for the military. When Rose retired Sam moved his family to Manawassa Springs where he and his wife had family roots. Sam Helper was a big cheerful man after whom Reese seems to have taken, in all but appearance. Gena now knew many of the shopkeepers well enough to chat with them about their families. It was an odd, but liberating feeling to undergo the process of becoming a small town resident. She lunched on occasion with Katie, though there was always something strained there. It was as if Katie wanted something from her, something Gena was clueless to provide.

Early one morning Gena strolled out to the fountain which had become her substitute venue for the disconcerting sun porch. It was far less threatening to her as an adult than when she was a child. There was a certain charm about the moss and dilapidated condition. It was one of those rare milder mornings of late July. She sat on her lounger under the canopy of a large umbrella. Light filtered pleasantly through the branches of the tall live oaks not far away. This provided additional protection from the brunt of the sun's rays. She sipped her tea and read the local *Manawassa Gazette*.

She had risen early and had lazily accomplished a few small projects in the yard. She opted to relax a bit before she met Katie for the tour of Mr. Crippett's gardens at Stokely Plantation. The anticipation of learning about plants and design now excited her interest just as the thoughts of acquiring new companies once had. How strange her old way of life had begun to seem. Gone were the mornings of black coffee

breakfasts and board meetings. She smiled and took a large bite of
Southern Bourbon Pecan Pie that Casey had brought her from *Hall's* the
day before. She switched her attention to Panhandle Gardening Magazine.
Gardening was becoming her passion and lent thorough enjoyment to her
life in Manawassa.

She was looking forward to the upcoming tour. Mr. Crippett's
plantation manor, as it were, lay only a few houses away from LeMoyne. It
was one of the grander houses on the Promenade along with Bell
Magnolia, LeMoyne and Lady Anne. Gena had thought it rather
pretentious the first time she saw it and mentally referred to it as "Tara,"
but admitted that it was a lovely white Southern style home with thick
columns, enormous green shutters and a broad front verandah. She
wondered if it were once a plantation before the town had sprung up so
she had asked Katie, who seemed to know the stories of all the houses on
the Promenade.

Katie held forth on the topic with ease. She had come to know
Mr. Crippett quite well and, aside from his garden, nothing pleased him
more than to expound on his family history. The Crippetts were an old
New England family who had derived their fortune from the aircraft
industry and, before that, from worldwide shipping. It was the shipping of
lumber that introduced Mr. Crippett's grandfather Ethan to Manawassa
Springs in general, and to timber baron John Martin, Gena's great-
grandfather, in particular. The mundane affairs of business that brought
Ethan to Manawassa also introduced him to the raptures of Aloysius
Bellingham's intellectual society, the Stoa. Even after Ethan employed
locals to manage his affairs in Manawassa Springs, it was Aloysius's Stoa
that drew him and his wife Sarah there year after year.

While staying in the town to broaden their intellectual horizons
they resided, as did most prominent visitors, in the Majestic Oaks Hotel.
Ethan had a predilection for ancient history and it was to this that his son
owed his name. The Vermont couple's son was born shortly after a
lecture on the poet Vergil's *Aeneid*. The child barely escaped being named
after the poem's hero. His mother strongly pressed for the poem's
author's name instead. Young Vergil spent occasional summers in
Manawassa and vowed one day to live there.

His oath was fulfilled by the way of marriage to a young woman
whom he met in Boston. Lucinda McCall, a Manawassa Springs native,

was visiting Nancy Endicott her dearest friend from Sweet Briar College. Nancy was from a Boston Brahmin family. The family hosted a gala for Nancy's twenty first birthday. Vergil was invited and upon laying eyes on Lucida was besotted by the lovely Southern belle. They found that they had Manawassa Springs in common. He wooed, wed and returned with her to the South.

After the market crash in 1929 when the Bellingham fortunes were waning, Manawassa, like many small towns, slid into the murky waters of the depression. Vergil, intending to escape the harsh winters of Vermont, purchased an abandoned lot on the Promenade. It was doubled both in depth and width, the largest available property at that time. An older structure stood precariously on the property. It had been built decades before as a summer home for a family from Pennsylvania. The fortune of the house seemed to have matched the fortunes of the Philadelphia family which was destroyed by betrayal, bankruptcy and suicide. Vergil demolished it.

Whether it was Vergil's aim to outdo Aloysius Bellingham is debatable, but he did erect a venerable Southern manor to rival Belle Magnolia's magnificence. Ironically, he christened it with a very New England name, Stokely, which was his mother's maiden name. The Yankee appellation agitated Manawassans, but stuck nevertheless. It was amended by the locals with the addition of the word "Plantation," which to every Southern mind covers a multitude of sins. Except for a few who mysteriously referred to it as Cripp's Crypt, the townsfolk eventually adopted Stokely Plantation as one of their pride and joys.

Mr. Crippett, whose Christian name was non-existent as far as Katie could tell, was born at Stokely and grew up in Manawassa. He lived well after inheriting his father Vergil's fortune. Mr. Crippett, the younger, had worked on the Manhattan Project or so it was rumored among Manawassans. His age belied this rumor, unless he had been a nine year old genius recruited by the government. At any rate, Crippett was an engineer of some sort who, in addition to working for his own company, had been engaged in nebulous undertakings for the government during his younger days. He never said more than that, and Katie never pried further. She estimated him to be in his late seventies, but he was incredibly hearty in spite of his years.

As she mentally reviewed her soon-to-be host's history Gena's peace was broken by the harsh buzz of her cell phone.

"Gena de Bienville. Katie...not today? That's disappointing. Perhaps we can reschedule another time... All right. Good-bye."

Gena leaned back to absorb more of the oblique rays of the sun. She would meet Mr. Crippett some other day.

***

CHAPTER II
FAMILY

Langlais Bourgogne Lemoyne de Bienville
Necessity

Putting his phone down Langlais blew slowly out of the side of his mouth, an action which served as an oath. The merger had to go forward and that meant securing Gena's approval. The acting chief executive of Bienville Enterprises chewed the inside of his cheek while spinning a pen on his desk, two actions he had performed so often that he did not realize he was doing them. A year and a half ago Gena had been so adamantly opposed to the merger that the matter had been sidelined, permanently she supposed, but Langlais thought otherwise.

It had been, what, six or so months since her self-imposed exile? He couldn't remember. The fact that she was still there lingering in the background gnawed at him. He maintained as little contact with her as possible. So except for an occasional memo when she felt things were not being conducted according to her methodology, Langlais did as he pleased. He spent that time behind the scenes schmoozing the other shareholders of Bienville, wooing them to his way of thinking. Gena's frame of mind when she left had not inspired confidence in her abilities to run the company remotely or otherwise, and he had taken advantage of that. He was certain that whatever course he pursued at this point would be backed up by most of the others. As the controlling shareholder Gena was the problem. He didn't want her to come to New York. An invitation to come to the headquarters would probably pique her interest in a bad way for him and allow her to prepare an arsenal against his course of action. That meant he would need to head for Manawassa Springs.

Manawassa Springs. The name had the taste of bile to him. As a child he called it "Man-a-wussy," except in his Great Aunt Jacqueline's hearing. He hated every minute he spent at her house there, and that feeling was doubled when his visits coincided with his cousin Gena's. They never saw each other much as youths: she lived in New York and he, in New Orleans. So usually when their paths crossed it was at LeMoyne. He had loved to torment her whenever possible. Gena had been a shy and sensitive girl. She preferred reading to running, propriety to misbehavior and solitude to crowds. Her voice never rose above a whisper. Langlais had despised her inability to make even the simplest decision. When Great Aunt Jacqueline offered the two of them choices of ice cream or snow cones, cookies or cake, she would wrinkle her brow and turn red as if the old lady had called upon her to decide which form of torture she would prefer. Langlais made decisions for both of them. No matter how miserable Gena felt, she never objected. Then things changed.

Langlais rubbed the scar that peeped from under the hair over his right eye. If she had been a boy Langlais would have engaged in physical bullying, but it was words that tormented Gena. One day when they were about ten years old he was amusing himself at her expense. Vividly he remembered Gena sitting in the old rope swing that hung from one of the big oak trees. She seemed far away and wasn't responding in her usual manner to his insults. She wasn't turning red or crying or running away. She just sat there and stared off into the distance. He drew closer to her inanimate form wondering if his sheer meanness had killed her. When he was about ten feet away she turned her blank eyes on him and spoke.

"*Sic semper tyrranis.*"

The next thing he knew she had hurled an empty coke bottle at his face. The skin of his forehead burst and blood spewed like a fountain all over him. She just sat immobile, but with such a look of satisfaction that Langlais, in the depths of his being, was terrified. He had run like a rabbit to his great aunt fabricating a story about falling out of a tree. Langlais always saved face, no matter what. Since that time Gena had no problem dominating him, and everyone else for that matter.

Shaking himself out of his reverie he tapped out an email to his PA.

Stephana – Call Cody to get jet ready for Friday, 10 am. Flying to airport nearest Manawassa Springs, Florida. Reserve suitable car. Make reservations at best accommodations in or as near possible to MS. Prefer a B and B.

***

It had been an hour ride from De Luna Regional Airport to Manawassa Springs. Cody drove in silence as usual while Langlais conducted business on his laptop and phone. Occasional four letter words filtered from the back of the car as phone reception dropped out.

"Who the hell would intentionally move back to this rotten place?" Langlais fumed.

"A nut job or a masochist, maybe?" Cody guffawed. Anthony Franconelli knew exactly to whom Langlais referred and took every opportunity to belittle Gena. It wasn't that he needed to ingratiate himself to his boss. Franconelli was about as close to a best friend that Langlais had. Unlike his employer, he had grown up on the wrong side of New Orleans. The two met during Langlais's wild and rebellious days before he was forced to assume responsibility in the family business. Langlais had dubbed him "Cody" after William "Buffalo Bill" Cody. Cody had taken a real liking to the Rich Jackass as he called him. When Cody and R. J. (Langlais let Cody alone call him this and no one knew why) had gotten into any kind of trouble, the loyal sidekick always took the fall, even if it meant jail. Langlais was blessed with the type of personality typically born of privilege which never questions why someone would take a bullet for him. It was assumed. After all he was a LeMoyne de Bienville. When Cody had gotten out of prison Langlais saw to it that he got his pilot's and chauffeur's licenses. Cody had been great with anything mechanical, the logical result of stealing and chopping cars, so it seemed a natural progression for him to ascend to the position of Langlais's chauffeur and pilot.

He adored Langlais and despised his boss's cousin Gena. Cody was a looker and all his life no woman had been able to resist his charm. It didn't matter whether the woman was a bar-fly or a professional. He had his pick. He knew how to play women, and, at one point long before prison, was poised to marry a prestigious doctor whom he had wrapped around his finger. He figured he'd be set for life. Meeting Langlais disrupted that dream. He had a choice to make and he made the right one. No one woman could be more satisfying, no crime could be more lucrative, no pastime provide more excitement, no job carry more fringe benefits than what Langlais had offered him. Fortunately for Cody, Langlais had pulled strings so that prison was short lived. Anthony Franconelli had a great boss, a great life and all the women he wanted in whatever city his job took him. There was one exception.

He had been attracted to Gena from the start. When Langlais flew into New York for meetings or, on the rare occasions Gena flew to

New Orleans, Cody had always taken the opportunities that presented themselves to hit on Gena. She wasn't having any, and that pissed Cody off. From that point forward Gena morphed from warm meat to cold bitch in his opinion. "The icicle" was what Langlais called her because she was long, thin and sharp, like a deadly weapon. After that Cody added spying to the list of duties for his boss. It was he that uncovered how loony Gena had become. He fed Langlais exaggerated accounts of her unstable behavior in order to avenge his wounded ego. Langlais's gratitude was overwhelming.

Langlais slammed his laptop shut. "Gena's breakdown is inevitable. Between the old lady's death and her eternal obsession with Kayton, I knew one day she'd crack under the pressure of the job." Langlais snorted a laugh through his nose and Cody joined in.

"All the better for you, R.J."

"Oh, yeah. The crappiest thing is that she retained the controlling interest. My job is to divest her of her shares as soon as possible."

"Won't be easy."

"It'll be marginally easy. The other shareholders know she's had a mini-breakdown already. Moving to Man-a-wussy Springs proves it as far as I'm concerned."

"So what's your tack?"

"Like always. Show up and make it happen."

***

CHAPTER III
LOVERS

Kayton Bidwell Landry

"I met a girl."

Dr. Kayton Landry had been eating his breakfast in silence wondering what had tied the tongue of his 22 year old son. Joe was usually pretty talkative, but for the last few days since his return from Tulane seemed almost zombie-like.

"That explains it."

"Explains what?"

Like all youth, an awareness of temperament and mood changes was hidden to his conscious mind. His father kept silent seeing that Joe was about to return to his normal mode of fervent conversation.

"I only met her a few months before graduation. She's a junior — well she'll be a senior next year. I wasn't sure how to break it to you."

"You never needed to break any of your other girlfriends to me."

"This one's…"

"Different?"

"Yes. Maybe. I don't know. Anyway, I think so…."

"There's nothing like the decisiveness of youth." The good doctor imbued enough affection in his remark that his son took no offense.

"Dad, I'm serious," he smiled at his father, then a serious look overtook his face. "We hit it off right away. She's an art major. Like Mom was. She told me I was too serious, studying all the time. She said I needed to lighten up. I tried to explain to her that I was pre-med, but she won. We got to know each other and well, um, her dad offered me a job for the summer."

Kayton's eyebrows went up and he tilted his head to one side. "And that would be doing what?"

"Construction type things."

"You're going to risk those surgeon hands even before your career begins," he teased.

"Dad, you know I want to be an ophthalmologist. I think I can risk it."

"Okay, I give up. When do you start?"

"Next week. There is one thing though. It isn't in New Orleans."

"Where is it then?"

"Manawassa Springs. That's in Florida, not south, but up north in the Panhandle. It's not far, only a few hours away."

Something inside Kayton stood still at hearing "Manawassa Springs." His mind flashed back to the times he was there at the same time as Gena was staying at her grandmother's. That was a long time ago.

"You used to go there when you were a kid, didn't you?"

"A few times." Snapping back to the present the doctor began his inquisition. "Will you be living with the young lady?"

"Only if I have a death wish. Her dad's an elder or something in the Baptist church. She's pretty religious, too."

"Ah! No wedding, no bedding. So will your earnings cover rent for a place there?"

"That's the great thing. Talia – that's her name Talia Pearse – has a couple of cousins, male cousins, who have a house and I can crash there practically rent free."

"Practically. Sounds affordable. But there'll be gas and car maintenance and your girlfriend. Cars and women don't come cheap."

"Dad." The rise and fall of Joe's voice expressed sufficient annoyance that Kayton temporarily suspended his line of questioning. "Anyway, I can start next week and be back in August in time for orientation."

"Is there anything you need: steel toed boots, coveralls, fried chicken and a corn-cob pipe?"

Father and son laughed. Dr. Landry had spent most of his career as a medical missionary. Kayton, Marla and Joe had lived for short spurts in every third world country imaginable. The family had gotten used to adapting their lifestyle, wardrobe and diet to whatever locale they called home.

"I don't think it's that backwards, Dad."

"It isn't, from what I can remember. You don't think your time would be better spent interning or volunteering at a hospital?" Kayton couldn't resist one last serious question.

"I've already gotten accepted to med school. I worked my ass off for the last five years, winter and summer. I need a break before the real grind starts."

Kayton looked across the table at his son sitting there with that determined look on his face. Most of the time the Landry genes dictated a laid back and mellow personality, but once in a while the long buried de Bienville genes took precedence, and neither Heaven nor Hell could conquer them.

"It sounds like you have a plan and I won't stand in your way."

"Dad, I hate to leave you alone."

"Alone is my middle name since your mom died and you went off to school. I'll survive."

With that Joe shot up from the table, whipped out his cell and bolted from the room in one swift movement. "Talia, guess what?"

Kayton stared at the doorway his son had exited and tried hard not to think about his life at that age, about the true love of his own youth.

***

It Can't Be

When the contractor pronounced the glass door irreparably damaged, Gena hoped it could remain in place until the new one arrived. Pearse nixed that and promised to send his crew to switch out the doors. He said he needed the door for the warranty. Gena resigned herself to having the wooden door put back on temporarily. Pearse had sealed the glass door with some tarps from his truck, then left Gena to play the contractor waiting game. "At least," she thought, "the image of the tiger is covered out of sight."

Days later she heard heavy knocking on the front door. Certain that it was the crew Gena responded quickly. She opened the door and found herself staring into an intense pair of hazel eyes which peeped out from under a shock of sandy colored hair. The young man tilted his head slightly forward and to the side. He raised his eyebrows and looked at Gena. For some reason she experienced a mild feeling of recognition.

"Ms. LeMoyne?"

"It's Ms. *de Bienville*."

The young man looked at his work order.

"Sorry, Ms. de Bienville. We came to replace your door, Mam."

His voice was oddly familiar, too. She stood silently and stared at him.

"Mam? We're from Pearse's Construction…," he said indicating

110

an older scruffy looking man that Gena recognized. "…about the door?"

"Oh, yes. It's in the back."

She stepped outside onto the front porch and ushered the pair to the shed at the very back of the property. Flinging open the doors she indicated the wooden monstrosity.

"Here it is."

"Wow, that's pretty interesting." The young man tilted his head this way and that in order to take in the full complement of its jungle inhabitants.

"It's hideous. I will leave the two of you to your task. It goes on over there where the tarp is."

Gena walked away without another word. Like all the other appointments she had scheduled with Mr. Pearse, this one was inconvenient by homeowner standards, if not by contractor standards. She had made plans for the morning and was thoroughly annoyed when she got a call, ten minutes before she left the house, that they would be coming. To calm herself down she donned her gardening habit, walked to the side border not far from the workmen and began tugging centipede grass which had encroached into her flower border.

As she tugged and dug at the offending tendrils, snatches of typical working class conversation floated past her hearing: beer, trucks, sports and women. Nothing much registered in her consciousness until she heard something that made her temporarily pause the activity of her trowel. The older man, Snuffy, was calling to the younger boy who had headed for the truck to get some more tools.

"Joe." The boy didn't respond. "Joe!" The boy still did not turn or acknowledge him. "Hey, LANDRY. Get me a coke from the cooler." The boy signaled his response with the wave of a hand.

Gena's heart began to pound for all its worth. The head tilt, the thick sandy hair, the hazel eyes, the voice were summed up in the last name: Landry. "It can't be." She thought as she watched the boy round the corner of the house. He walked liked Kayton – a gentle laid back lope that she had found so irresistible. Had this young man been a little taller with a little more heft, had his nose been slightly different, and had he started whistling "When the Saints Go Marching In" Gena swore she would have been seeing Kayton Landry as a twenty-two year old. "It can't be," she thought for the second time. "It must be my imagination which has been rampantly insane of late." She sat for some minutes, trowel in hand.

"No more cokes, Snuffy, just water. You'll just have to suffer. Or "snuffer."'" A huge grin split his boyish face and Gena was almost a hundred percent sure he was the son of Kayton Landry.

Her instincts next said, "If it is Kayton's son, verify it." She dropped her trowel and strode back to the house using the side door nearest the kitchen. With the swiftness of a trained Southern hostess she placed two glasses on a silver tray along with a crystal pitcher of iced tea, a sugar bowl, silverware and linen napkins. She set the remainder of the pecan pie on it with two plates. Deftly she carried the beverages and pie to the sun porch. Gena arranged her face and put on her friendliest smile.

"I am sorry you don't have any cokes. Will iced tea do?" Looking the epitome of a genteel Southern lady, she set the tray on the white wrought iron table and poured out the tea. "I thought some Southern Bourbon Pecan Pie from *Hall*'s might be nice, too."

"Thanks, Mam." Snuffy quickly repaired to the table and snatched a glass of tea, downing it even before she indicated that there was sugar available. Realizing there was no sugar in it he made a face and set his glass down.

"Some more?" Gena raised the pitcher. "There's sugar here if you like."

She refilled his glass. He grabbed the spoon and put half the bowl of sugar in his glass. Then he scooped up the pie Gena had sliced and started in on it.

"Thank you." The lanky assistant took his glass, waited for his buddy and stirred in a couple of teaspoons of sugar.

Gena turned to the older man.

"So you're a native of Manawassa Springs?"

Snuffy looked a little puzzled. Gulping a bite of pie he politely answered her question as best he could.

"No, Mam. No native Indian blood in me, though I had a cousin that married a girl with Indian blood. She claimed her great-great-great grandmother was Takawhatchee the Indian princess famous 'round these here parts." At this Joe smiled appreciating his companion's honest naiveté and wondering how their hostess would treat humble Snuffy's misunderstanding.

"How interesting. What I meant by being a native is have you lived here in Manawassa all your life?" Gena restated her question in terms she felt were more compatible to Snuffy's understanding. Gena never thought of herself as condescending, only practical, especially when she needed something.

"No Mam. Grew up at Blount Springs, Blount Swamp as it was when I was a kid. Somebody got elected and gave it a fancier name, but it's still a swamp. I liked growin' up there. Plenty to do. Swamps are interstin'. Now the National Graffic has TV shows about 'em.

"I didn't know that," came her disinterested response. "Have you worked for Mr. Pearse long?"

"Ten years. He's a good man and a good boss. I had my own construction binness fer 'bout twenty years, but it didn't work out. Lee come by, bought out my stuff and hired me right on the spot. Pays me good. Never lost a cent. He's a pretty smart binnessman."

"I'm sure he is, and I imagine you were, too. The economy is so unpredictable. It is difficult to maintain an enterprise for a substantial number of years when you consider the market's vagaries."

Another look of bewilderment crossed the old man's face. "I reckon the 'conomy didn't work out for some market bakeries either, Mam." Snuffy rubbed tea and pie crumbs from his beard. "But fer me it was my bookkeeper – my ex-wife – that done me in. She cleaned out my bank account and ran off with my foreman."

"I see. What a terribly emotional event." She spoke with little sympathy in her voice. Whatever was expressed did not seem particularly genuine. Gena's face reflected a certain amount of frustration with Snuffy.

All the while Joe was eating his pie and drinking tea using these actions to hide his frowns. The frowns weren't for Snuffy for whom he had a ton of respect. Snuffy was an unpretentious man who liked most everyone and had an aptitude for anything mechanical. His problem solving skills in construction were off the chart. But none of this inflated his ego. Snuffy was content being Snuffy

Ms. de Bienville was another matter. Since Joe had lived in poor countries all over the world, one thing he hated was prejudice against the poor or undereducated. When so many people automatically assumed that poverty and lack of a broad education meant stupidity or immorality, Kayton and Marla taught their son that each person was imbued with dignity no matter what their circumstances. Each person had value and everyone was to be met as an equal. Joe was taught that you could learn something from everyone no matter what their station in life. Between his parent's teaching and their selfless actions in the underprivileged countries, Joe Landry learned to have regard for each individual. It was unnatural for him to divide people into this class which you treated one way and that class which you treated another. If Joe had a judgmental streak that caused him to struggle with this philosophy, it was against those who lived in their own little world, a Cloud Cuckoo Land of wealth and privilege.

Ms. De Bienville apparently lived there and held to different school of thought. Throughout the dialogue Joe kept thinking how silly she appeared trying to be nice to a man who could be thrown into a swamp and not only survive, but prosper. For a guy like Snuffy that swamp could be in Blount Springs or New York City. Joe wasn't so sure about this Southern lady with her silver tray and linen napkins. He felt a little sorry for her but gave no indication of this, or any of his thoughts, when she turned her stilted conversation towards him.

"And are you from Manawassa Springs?" Gena held her breath.

Despite his misgivings about her sincerity, Joe's behavior towards her was true to his upbringing.

"No Mam. New Orleans. At least for the last five years or so." He set his glass on the table and gazed at her steadily. Eye contact was another thing that his parents taught him. If you have no guilt, no shame, no fear you can look directly into the eyes of anyone on the face of the earth. "Most of my childhood was spent living among people in third world countries until I was in high school. It was our way of life, so until I moved to New Orleans I had no permanent home. It was a great way to grow up. I learned a lot about other cultures, met a lot of great folks." This last comment was not meant to call Gena to task, but to let her know how he felt about people.

It relayed to her a completely different set of facts that were meaningful to her past. If Gena's heart was pounding she gave no evidence of it.

"I've traveled extensively. Where have you been abroad exactly?"

"Mostly Africa, South and Central America, the Caribbean. I doubt you've been to the areas I grew up in. My dad's a doctor and did medical missionary work. My mom was an artist, but wherever we went she worked to improve the lives of the women in the villages." The young man seemed very proud, but a little choked up at the mention of his mother. "She'd look at what their culture's art forms were. Sometimes it was clothing; sometimes, stuff we call crafts. She had a good eye for what could be sold in prosperous countries. I think they call it "fair trade" now. Mom just called it helping others. Once she produced a cookbook of local food from a tribe in Uganda. It was a best seller. All the income goes to the village. They're still profiting from it. Like my dad, she always made a difference."

Ignoring all the noble things done by husband and wife, Gena heard only one phrase: "My mom *was* an artist." In fact, everything he said about her was cast in the past tense. Gena made a mental note. It didn't necessarily mean that she was dead. It could mean that now in the States she pursued something else. It didn't follow that Kayton was unmarried now. She pressed for more information.

"I used to visit New Orleans as a child. Is your father practicing there or has he returned abroad?"

"He's still in New Orleans."

"And your mother? Has she been able to concentrate on art for herself now that she is back in the States?"

The pause that ensued exposed a wave of sorrow passing over the boy's handsome face. He lowered his eyes for a moment. "She died about six years ago before we came back to the States." His eyes lifted and returned to their piercing gaze.

The hard shell that had enveloped the real Gena for most of her adult life cracked, even if a little. The boy knew her next words were genuinely from her heart. "I am sorry. My mother died when I was not too many years older than you. Both my parents are gone now. My Grand-mère outlived them both and was very important to me. I inherited this house from her." Gena swept her arm around and avoided the hazel eyes. She experienced a phenomenon for her: she wanted to cry for someone else. The silence lasted for a number of seconds, but seemed an eternity while she fought back her tears.

Joe sipped his tea and took the last bite of his pie during the silence. Then he finished his story.

"When she died, Dad wanted me to return for my last year at

high school. That's when we moved to New Orleans where he grew up. By then I was pretty sure I wanted to be a doctor. We felt like I needed to be here, in the States, to prepare for college. I just graduated from Tulane."

The old Gena returned. "So what brought you to Manawassa Springs?"

A downward glance as he set his plate on the table concealed a blush. "Well, uh…"

"…a job." The scruffy old man rescued his younger counterpart. "You need to finish that tea off so we can get to it if we want to beat the rain."

Joe and Snuffy thanked their hostess again and set about to finish restoring the Tiger Door to its rightful place.

***

The workers from Pearse's crew were gone and a preoccupied Gena returned to her gardening. She knew she had just met Kayton's son. She forced herself to think back to that awful time in New York well over twenty years ago. Gena was resolved to be the incontrovertible head of Bienville Enterprises; Kayton believed she had chosen business over him. And so they parted. The anger and sorrow of their parting returned to overwhelm her. For a number of years after that she lost track of Kayton. Then twelve years ago she encountered him by sheer coincidence in New Orleans. It was a brief, cold and awkward meeting. During that strained reunion Gena had conducted herself in a particularly business-like manner as she inquired about the intervening years. She expressed each of her responses with the appropriate pleasure while inwardly she felt her heart sink lower with each of his replies. How nice that he had married and had a son. How interesting that his family lived with him on his medical missions. How rewarding to have brought his skills to Kenya, Haiti, Guatemala and the like. How fortunate his wife was so helpful. How the natives much appreciate them both. How lucky they all survived that coup. She replied that for her part, she was now in total control of Bienville. Yes, it was rewarding. There had been tremendous expansion. Profits were higher than ever. She had a full social life. Her horizons were endless. So they played the game out: neither impressed with the other's life, neither admitting to that opinion. It was all frigidly amicable and polite.

116

***

Can It Be?

"Dad."

"Joe, my son, right? It's been so long I've forgotten how you sound."

"Sorry I haven't been in touch," came the sheepish reply. "I've been working pretty hard. I didn't realize how tired you get after a day of construction. I come home, eat and drop like a dog. I haven't even seen much of Talia either. She's working, too. We finally had dinner together last night."

"That's some consolation. So you haven't seen much of Manawassa Springs, I take it. Not that there's much to see."

"Actually it's kinda weird, but in a good way. I feel like I stepped into the 50's. People are nice and friendly. Living is cheap. The town is clean and neat."

"Do you thinks it's backwards?"

"No. It's not like people don't know about computers or anything." Joe laughed. "It's different than living in a city like New Orleans. Everybody you run into is, well personal. They're friendly, well-mannered and religious and all."

"There are worse things, you know. Besides, it's closer to the world you grew up in. After all, it's not like you spent your childhood mingling with the jet set. I think you probably find a more sociable class of people where you are than among the careless billionaires." Kayton tried to keep the bitterness he felt out of his comment.

"Probably. So far even the upper crust folks of Manawassa Springs are pretty nice. We've worked on some of the old Victorians on the Promenade, including the famous one, Belle Magnolia. The lady that runs it is pretty funny. She hung around while we were doing some small stuff for her and kept us laughing. I guess I've only met one person you might call snobby. The other day Snuffy and I were at her house to put a door on. The house looked a lot like some of the old houses in New Orleans. It was bright yellow and had iron railings. It's pretty different from most of the places here. The owner was a little different, too. She seemed out of place. She brought us iced tea on a silver platter. No joke. Silver with cloth napkins. She said she inherited the house from her grandmother. Talia said her dad told her the lady was a little high and

117

mighty for Manawassa Springs. She's some big CEO from New York. Her name's Bonneville or something like that. She tried to be friendly, but came off a little patronizing – at least to Snuffy. She tried to make small talk, but it wasn't very casual. It was more like an interrogation. She asked us all about who we were and if we grew up here..."

Kayton didn't hear the rest of his son's discourse. A New Orleans-type house, inherited. A CEO from New York. Ms. Bonneville. Bienville? Could it be Gena?

***

CHAPTER IV
A FOUNTAIN

The blush of early summer had long faded and the muggy, hot days of mid-summer succeeded them. Gena found that she coped with the heat very well. In fact, she seemed to be born to it. She assumed it was in her genes. The de Bienville's were originally from the South of France and the Mediterranean climate had already adapted them to the sweltering atmosphere of New Orleans. Gena remembered how much she had hated New York winters and how her brief stints in New Orleans on business, in Manawassa as a child and in the Caribbean with Kayton had provided the necessary antidote.

She had quite forgotten about the porch, the door and all the frightening incongruities associated with them. The hideous door was returned to its place while the glass door was repaired. Instead she spent time of late trying to process her encounter with Kayton's son Joe. For that she needed a place of relaxation, at least her version of it. It definitely was not the sun porch. She never went to there anymore, but instead retreated to the back yard. She replaced the old swing with a new one. She was grateful to Katie for telling her about Hefty Porter. Unlike Pearse, he was prompt. He came the day he said he would. He put up a new rope swing with a beautiful oak seat. Reese had been delighted as she undertook the honor of inaugurating the new equipment. It frightened Gena a little at how high the little girl went, but she refrained from chastising her.

Gena chose the fountain as her place for leisure. It was situated toward the back of the yard in an open space amid the towering trees. It was a granite structure, built God knows when, chipped in places and covered with moss and lichen. Holes had been drilled purposely in the floor of the surrounding mote to drain any rainwater, but small pools of algae green water mottled much of its surface. Gena recalled the fountain had been deteriorating even then. She wondered why Grand-mère, who in every other respect kept up LeMoyne immaculately, had let it deteriorate. She once asked her grandmother why it didn't have any water and the old woman said, "It's like the inside of a rotten pecan. It's better not to open it. Gena dropped the subject and never broached it again.

When Gena inherited LeMoyne she had gone back and forth as

to whether she would even keep the fountain. Even though it was in a beautiful location and must have once been grand, it was an eyesore now. It was obvious that a full restoration would be expensive. She called some friends of hers from Connecticut who had a magnificent fountain in the middle of an ornate stone pool and, being given the name of the company who had built it, Gena summarily called them. Her friend had warned her that with her own fountain it had taken eighteen months for the stonemasons to begin the project. Gena reverted to her New York methodology and flew the head of the company to Manawassa at her expense in her private jet. He was familiar with both the material and era of the fountain. It was much older than she had thought. The architect said it dated to the turn of the twentieth century. He gave her an exorbitant estimate, which she agreed to only on the condition that he schedule the restoration for no later than this fall. He vehemently protested saying that his work was scheduled at least a year ahead. He had deadlines to meet in such far flung places as Italy and Brazil. The negotiations volleyed back and forth until Gena enticed him with additional money to complete the fountain by September's end. While awaiting the restoration she had Hefty Porter power wash it to remove the most objectionable green splotches. Then she moved her morning routine to one of the lesser decayed areas of the fountain pavement. It was there that she relaxed in exquisite furniture and imagined the cool waters that would soon flow from the fountain. Her porch woes receded into the background temporarily.

***

CHAPTER V
A SWING

Amaryllis On A Swing

"There it goes again." She walked to the front gate for the fourth time that day. It had mysteriously unlatched itself yet again and was banging. This annoyance was ongoing. If Pearse's crew had worked anywhere near the gate, she would have irrationally attributed it to something they did. "Pearse's fault" was a standard thought when something at LeMoyne went awry. Though she mentioned it to the crew when they came to replace the porch door, no action had been taken on the gate. "Another time we'll stop by." Snuffy had said. "Just let the boss know."

She closed and latched the gate with a shiver. Once again she thought how odd it was that each time she had walked to secure it, she noticed that there was no wind to blow it open, no scurrying animal to trip the latch, no person passing by. It was just one more thing to fray her nerves.

Every day Gena seemed to grow increasingly jittery. Her nerves had begun to give out in New York. She came to meetings tired and unfocused. She had to correct herself at meetings. When friends and business associates asked she told them it was the result of stress. She would rather have died than admit she was having nightmares. More than anything else, it was connected with Grand-mère's passing. Everything began to go wrong then. Langlais knew something strange was going on with Gena and that it was impacting her abilities to direct Bienville. He was crouched to spring upon her like a predator, like the tiger in the horrible door. The cousins outwardly displayed mutual ignorance during the months preceding her retreat to Manawassa: she not admitting that she was having mental issues; he knowing that she was losing it, but not acknowledging the fact. She resolved to control her future rather than let Langlais dictate it for her. She still held the upper hand and he knew it.

She returned to the back yard and gave a cry of surprise. There on the restored rope swing suspended from the huge oak someone was sitting and staring her way. Gena relaxed when she realized it was just Reese, newly returned from Disneyworld. Her relief was short lived. She hailed the little girl, but Reese just sat and stared straight ahead at her.

"Surely she heard me." Gena approached the child. The swing with Reese in it began swaying slowly back and forth. Reese hummed a tune. There was something strange about the melody. It was not a modern song or a child's ditty. Gena searched her memory. That was it. She was humming *I Dream of Jeannie With The Light Brown Hair.* Grand-mère used to rock in the evenings on the porch at LeMoyne doing crosswords and idly singing snatches of songs from bygone eras. Gena was particularly captivated by this one and had asked her to sing it over and over. Her grandmother would lean back with her eyes closed and sing her the song as if it held some mystic significance. Gena had never forgotten the words.

I dream of Jeannie with the light brown hair
Borne, like a vapor, on the summer air
I see her tripping where the bright streams play
Happy as the daisies that dance on her way

Many were the wild notes her merry voice would pour
Many were the blithe birds that warbled them o'er
Oh! I dream of Jeannie with the light brown hair
Floating, like a vapor, on the soft, summer air

I long for Jeannie with the day dawn smile
Radiant in gladness, warm with winning guile
I hear her melodies, like joys gone by
Sighing round my heart o'er the fond hopes that die

Sighing like the night wind and sobbing like the rain
Wailing for the lost one that comes not again
Oh! I long for Jeannie, and my heart bows low
Never more to find her where the bright waters flow

I sigh for Jeannie, but her light form strayed
Far from the fond hearts round her native glade
Her smiles have vanished and her sweet songs flown
Flitting like the dreams that have cheered us and gone

Now the nodding wild flow'rs may wither on the shore
While her gentle fingers will cull them no more
Oh! I sigh for Jeannie with the light brown hair
Floating like a vapor, on the soft summer air[3]

Her heart thumped wildly at those words. Gena had always thought it a frighteningly eerie song. She didn't understand why Grandmère liked it so much. It was a cruel, heartless song. Poor Jeannie who had been so lovely, now gone. Dead. Her fingers white and stiff, never picking wild flowers again. Her smiled faded away. Her songs stilled by the grave. She was only a ghost now floating on the summer breeze.

Gena stopped in front of the child. It took all her courage to examine her more closely. The girl was dressed very oddly. A long, flowing, white gauzy dress was cinched below the waist with a wide blue satin ribbon. Another blue ribbon was tied in a bow and nestled among her curls. She wore white stockings and brown leather shoes. Gena stared. Her whole appearance brought back memories of the movie *Pollyanna* that she had seen when she was a girl. Then Reese spoke in a strange voice.

"It won't do, you know. You don't live in New York anymore. Your life is here. Your mission is here. You cannot ignore me forever. Shere Khan will not let you." She hummed a little more and stared straight ahead.

Gena had no idea what to say. She stood stock still, arms at her side, her mouth parted in shock. The child's sweet voice continued.

"I don't mean to frighten you. I have been calling you for so long, so many years. You heard me, didn't you? In New York. Especially when you were in here in Manawassa Springs." The child stared directly into Gena's eyes. Green eyes sparkling like the finest emeralds bored into hers. Somehow she knew the child, but it wasn't Reese. It was *the Child*, the one from her dream. "Help me."

Despite the heat and humidity a cold chill swept over Gena's body. She began stepping backward and tripped over her garden tools. Her head hit the ground with a loud thud and everything went black.

When Gena opened her eyes she was in a jungle. It was lush and green. It was noisy. She began to parse the sounds: monkeys, birds,

---

[3] Words and lyrics by Stephen Foster. First published in 1854 as *I Dream of Jeanie with the Light Brown Hair*. Subsequently another "n" crept into the name most used today.

snakes, insects, elephants and, above all the din, a tiger. She swiveled her head around to look for the tiger. The animal sounds grew to a deafening crescendo, then ceased. There was utter silence. Gena knew what was about to happen, but could not make herself move. It would be useless to run. She could not escape. The tiger would get her no matter what she did. There was no child, no woman and baby, no man to protect her this time.

She stared at the edge of the silent jungle. The verdant brush rustled. It was a sickening sound, a sound of inevitability. Then He emerged from the jungle: an enormous Bengal Tiger. He slinked towards her, every sinew in his body outlined from his tenseness. He lowered his head and shot out a long pink tongue over his ivory fangs. Teethed bared, he sprang at Gena.

***

"Is she going to be okay?"

"I think so. I called the ambulance."

Reese was sobbing. Katie O'Neill was trying to get information from the little girl while she knelt down to make sure Gena was breathing.

"I don't know what happened. She saw me and I said "hi" but she looked all scared and fell backwards and hit her head and wouldn't move. That's when I screamed."

"It's okay, Reese." Katie stood and gave the girl a hug. "As soon as the emergency team gets here I'll walk you home. Where's Casey? Did she know you'd come over?"

At the same time the sirens became audible, Casey rushed over from Quarter House behind LeMoyne. Relief flooded her face when she saw that Reese was all right. "What happened?"

"I don't know exactly. Reese said she came over to visit Gena, but didn't see her so she decided to swing and wait for her. Then Gena came around from the front. After that I'm not sure what happened or why, that is. Apparently Gena tripped over her tools and was knocked unconscious. I just happened to be coming over to see her when I heard Reese screaming back here." Katie wondered how it was that Casey hadn't heard, but let it pass.

"Oh, my God!" The distraught sitter began to cry both from the horror at her neglect of the little girl and the sight of Gena lying there unconscious. Now Katie had a pair of hysterical girls to keep under control.

She did her best alternating comfort between the two when the emergency team arrived. Katie explained what she knew. She passed Reese into the hands of a calmer Casey and followed the stretcher until it was stowed inside the ambulance. The vehicle sped away with its sirens blaring. She sent up a silent prayer. She went into LeMoyne, located Gena's purse and ran to her SUV. Memories of her own journey to the hospital under strange circumstances returned to her as she hopped into her car to follow the ambulance. That trip for Katie, similar to the one Gena was now taking, had revealed the mystery of Belle Magnolia to Katie. What was it that Gena would discover as she wandered in that murky world of unconsciousness?

***

CHAPTER VI
A HOSPITAL VISIT, A CONFERENCE AND LUNCH

"Knock, knock," Katie stuck her head inside the door of Gena's room. The unfortunate woman had been kept overnight for observation and Katie came, unsolicited, to see about getting her back home. Gena was very pale and all traces of her usual formidable appearance had vanished.

"They told me you'd be released today, so I thought I'd stop by and offer my services as an escort home." The visitor swept a low bow to the patient.

"That is very kind of you, Katie. Yes, I would like that." She spoke softly. It was a vulnerable Gena that lay on the bed in front of Katie.

"Do you want me to bring you a change of clothes? I brought your purse along yesterday to get your insurance information for the hospital. I hope that was okay. You were out cold."

"Oh, of course."

"Don't worry. I locked up Azalea Cottage. Since I have the key I can bring you whatever you need."

Gena instructed her neighbor where to find the things she wanted. As the conversation wrapped up, the doctor stepped in to confirm the patient's condition and authorize the discharge. As soon as he came into the room the old Gena returned. She sat upright, put her authoritative look on and resumed her normal hard voice. Katie excused herself and quietly left the room.

***

"She's seen something, I know." Katie poured a mug of coffee for Steve. She had deposited the old Gena on her door step several hours before. Gena had given her a curt "thank you" and disappeared into her house.

"Well, you've known for some time that Azalea Cottage needed fixing."

"That's one way to put it."

"Are you sure you weren't imagining things. Maybe she just had an accident. They do happen, you know. I mean, after all, just because you had to have a traumatic experience to get your message, it doesn't follow that Gena does."

"No, I'm sure it had to do with Azalea Cottage. Gena probably thinks she's going nuts and, knowing how that feels, I want to help her as soon as possible."

"Aye, aye, Captain." Steve saluted her with his mug.

"Seriously, do you think I should just ask outright or should I be low-key? I could check in on her and subtly approach the subject."

"Yeah, like subtly and deviousness are your strong suits. I can see it now. "Gena, when you were knocked out did you see anything unusual? Dead people, as in ghosts, or house-spirits? Elvis, maybe?""

Katie gave her handsome retired naval officer a playful mock swat on the arm.

"Hey, watch the coffee."

"I may not be the most subtle person, but I will give it a try. Now about our trip to New Orleans...."

The lovebirds put their heads together making plans for the upcoming trip and forgot all about Azalea Cottage, Gena LeMoyne de Bienville and ghosts.

***

"Well, that's the long and short of it." Katie was sipping tea with Gena at *Hall's*. It was a week after the hospital incident and Katie had not found an opportunity to see Gena, much less talk to her about what had happened. Gena had become more reclusive than usual. Her frame had begun to melt away the last few weeks, headed straight for the anorexic form it had upon her arrival in Manawassa Springs. Katie was pretending to be in need of information about New Orleans, ostensibly for the purpose of her upcoming trip with Steve. She was hoping to segue into Gena's recent experience. Unfortunately for Katie it wasn't working out the way she had planned. Her neighbor was fully recovered from her hospital vulnerability and was once again stiff and formal.

"I do, in some sense, consider New Orleans a second home, but it sounds as if you are familiar with it from your previous trips there with Steve. I don't know if I can add anything. My familiarity with the city as an adult, although family roots go deep there, is strictly based on business. I never had much time to enjoy the New Orleans is what I am trying to say."

"Well it was worth a shot. We'll manage. Speaking of

managing… how's your head?" Internally Katie winced at her blunt transition. So much for subtlety. "I mean, are you fully recovered from the accident?" Katie couldn't help noticing a slight shudder come over her lunch companion.

"I am perfectly recovered, thank you." Gena's response was frosty. Up until then she had warmed infinitesimally over the course of lunch. Other than New Orleans they had talked about topics of mutual interest, which were few: antiques, gardening and their houses.

"Have you visited Mr. Crippett yet?" Katie inquired.

"No, not yet."

"Would you like to try again to go together? I never get tired of seeing his place."

"Well, yes, that sounds fine."

Let's plan on Thursday, 9 am?

Although she knew of nothing on her schedule for that day, Gena dutifully consulted her iPhone before she replied. "Thursday will be fine."

***

CHAPTER VII
THE SHARK PAYS A VISIT

With Zeph and Addie on a brief vacation, Katie had taken on a lot of their work. So much for spending more time with Steve. She established herself as the temporary gardener and hired a retired friend, Nancy Fuller, to watch the desk when she was busy. Nancy was a wonderful friend, but a little deficient in inn-keeping. Thank the Lord Addie and Zeph said they'd return before she left for New Orleans.

It was a beautiful and not too hot day, when she decked herself out in her junkiest clothes, donned a wide brimmed straw hat and grabbed her tools to spend the day in the garden. After some intense wrangling with dead branches and engaging in some on-her-knees heavy vine pulling, Katie turned to something less strenuous. She went to the front of the Belle with her clippers and began deadheading flowers. While snipping the spent marigolds she saw a large impressive car draw up in front of Belle Magnolia. She stood up and cocked her broad brimmed hat a little backwards to take in the arrival. Katie didn't know much about cars, but this one looked like it cost about as much as she had paid for the Belle. She mentally reviewed the Belle's reservations and tried to recall who was to be arriving that day: no one as far as she knew. The family which had planned to be there and use two of the nicer second floor rooms cancelled because of an unexpected death in the family. So who was this?

The driver who stepped out of the front was casually dressed: casually for a big city, not Manawassa Springs. That is to say, he was wearing immaculate designer slacks and an open collar shirt instead of worn out jeans and a tee-shirt from Wal-Mart. He drew his fashionable sunglasses off and looked quickly around before donning them again. He was quite a good looking man Katie noted without any guilt. He was not her type. He looked younger than Steve, had jet black hair and a dark complexion. He was of medium height and a muscular, compact build. That was not bad in and of itself, but there was something unsettling about him. He moved like a snake. He planted his feet and started swaying from side to side. Then he stretched his arms in a sinuous manner, twisted his torso and writhed his head around. He had all the appearance of a Cobra perpetually ready to strike. Some woman might be held mesmerized by him, but Katie had better judgment. If her own unfortunate marital experience had taught her anything it had taught her how to spot a snake.

He wasn't alone, but his companion sat in the back seat instead of the front. Apparently he was disabled since he sat there without attempting to open the car door and get out. Snake-Man (as Katie now dubbed the driver) walked around and opened the door for the passenger. Backseat-Man emerged from the door looking perfectly healthy and sound. That, together with the front seat/back seat arrangement as well as the expensive model of the car, led Katie to the conclusion that the Snake-Man must be the chauffeur and the man in the back, an incredibly wealthy somebody.

The man who emerged from the backseat was the complete opposite of the driver. He was tall and lean. He had a wide forehead, high cheekbones and what they used to call "an aristocratic nose." His light brown hair was slicked back except for a shock that fell over his right eye; a very intense green eye it was. Both of them were. He was dressed less casually than Snake-Man and probably more expensively. All assembled it gave him a boyish, disarming look, though he had to be closer to fifty than forty. He was not exactly pasty, but Katie figured he got most of his exercise in a gym and not outdoors like Snake-man probably did. As he stood upright Katie noticed that his face was expressionless. As soon as he saw her he turned on a mechanical smile as if to accompany the role he was about to play. She expected him to blurt out "aw, shucks" as a greeting. Katie didn't like either of them and wished very much that Steve were there.

"Good Morning." He intoned in a sing-song, heavy New Orleans accent. "It's quite a beautiful day for bein' outdoors. And here I've been cooped up in this ol' car all morning. It feels good to get out and stretch a bit." He came through the gate toward her; Snake-Man remained by the limousine. Her unwelcome guest had a lot of teeth for his mouth making him look like a shark. His shark-grin widened as he extended his hand towards Katie. At that point she silently dubbed him the Shark. "My name is Langlais LeMoyne de Bienville." He drawled. "My friend and I are in need of a couple o' rooms. I understand that this is an inn."

"Duh," thought Katie. "Maybe it was the sign that said *Belle Magnolia Inn* that gave it away." But she said nothing. She just stood there with gloves still on, her garden clippers clutched tightly and ignored his invitation to shake hands. The Shark dropped his hand and continued.

"Is your employer here, Miss? The innkeeper that is?"

His whole attitude was so patronizing that Katie wanted to eliminate some of his teeth with her clippers. "Patronizing S.O.B." She thought. It dawned on her that, dressed as she was, standing still and staring, she must look like the village idiot. Then his last name hit her: de Bienville. This slime ball must be a relative of Gena's. How was she going to play this?

"Yes, sir… but she's busy."

"My chauffeur and I are here for a day or two. We were booked at a B&B yonder in Wisteria, but now that I'm here I find that this place is much more charmin'." Taking advantage of his boyish looks he paused and cocked his head to the side. "Do you, by chance, know if there are any rooms available?"

Katie mentally summed up Langlais to her satisfaction. "There is some family resemblance to Gena. His little lost boy act doesn't disguise the fact that he's a carnivore, and he doesn't have that vulnerability I see in Gena, buried though it may be. In short, he's a nasty piece of work. No wonder Gena never said anything about him." Aloud she said in a syrupy Southern accent, "As a matter of fact there are. Miss Nancy is inside. Just go in and ring the bell. She'll tend to you." Without so much as a "good day," Katie turned away and resumed her deadheading.

***

Reese And The Shark

After a lunch at *Blacksmiths* (recommended by Miss Nancy) Langlais sauntered next door to LeMoyne. Cody was left on his own to prowl. Langlais practiced his spiel in his head and anticipated Gena's replies. He made sure that he had every possible angle of their conversation covered so his reasoning would be logical, his arguments, persuasive and his repartees, invincible. He had just put his hand to the wrought iron gate when a little girl appeared from nowhere.

"Hi, I'm Reese. Are you a friend of Gena's? She's from New York. Are you from New York? She's learning how to garden, but she's not very good at it yet. I come over sometimes to help her. Gena's my friend. She says I can call her just plain Gena even though she's a grownup. I don't have to call her Miss or Mrs. or Ms. Just Gena. She's nice. Sometimes she gets a little weird, but usually she's normal just like me."

At the word "weird' Langlais saw an opportunity to take advantage of what the child might know of Gena's mental state. He put on his most condescending manner and stooped down to the little girl's level.

"I'm Langlais, Gena's cousin." He held out his hand which caused Reese to retreat a step. Langlais gave her some space. Convinced that a cousin of Gena's must be okay, she took his hand and shook it.

"I do live in New York most o' the time. I'm glad Gena has you for a friend. She was a very busy lady in New York and didn't' have a lot of time to make friends there. Does she have a lot of friends her in Manawassa Springs?"

"She knows my mom and dad and Casey."

"Your sister?"

"No. Casey is my baby…Casey plays with me when mom and dad are at work. I don't have any brothers or sisters."

"She doesn't have any brothers or sisters either. So, then, I guess Gena can be like a big sister to you, Whadd'ya think?"

Reese screwed up her face as she pondered this. "No, I don't think so. She's too old. She's just my friend. She's Ms. Katie's friend, too.

"Who is Ms. Katie?"

"She lives there." The child pointed to Belle Magnolia. "She's the innkeeper lady. I think Ms. Katie must be Gena's best friend because she visits a lot. I'm glad she comes over a lot because the other day when Gena had a fit and fell down, Ms. Katie was already on her way over and made sure she got to the hospital."

Langlais could not have been more gratified. So Gena had had a fit.

"I'm so sorry that my cousin isn't well. That's why she came here. She had fits in New York, too. We all hoped that coming here to Manawassa Springs would make her better. What happened exactly?" A cruel smile, completely lost on the innocent little girl, darted across Langlais's face.

"I came over to help Gena in the garden, but I didn't see her. She said it was all right if I came over and used her tree swing even if she wasn't here as long as I told Mom or Dad or Casey. So I came over to swing. I like to swing high, but it makes Gena nervous so I try not to swing too high when she's watching. I just got into the swing and she came around from the front, but when she saw me she looked all scared. I wasn't even swinging. I was just sitting there. I said "hi," but she didn't say anything. She just had a fit and fell on the ground and hit her head."

Langlais had suppressed a shiver when the child began chattering about the swing. His thoughts flew back to the day of the coke bottle incident. That day it was he that wore a terrified look on his face when he saw his cousin in the swing sitting there like a zombie. He inadvertently rubbed his scar. In his entire life he'd never told anyone how he'd gotten it. He stuck to the story about falling out of the old oak. He always embellished it to his own glory by saying he was putting a baby bird back in its nest.

"It didn't bleed or anything," the child continued, "but I screamed and Ms. Katie came running. Casey did too. Then Gena went to the hospital and got better. Most of the time she's better, but sometimes she gets jumpy, especially about the jungle animal door. She doesn't like it. I like it, but she keeps sticking it in the shed. I snuck in there one day to see it. It has monkeys and birds and snakes and a big tiger in the middle. I thinks it's cool, but I think she's afraid of it."

"Better and better." Langlais thought. "She's afraid of that old battered door Grandmother had on the screened porch. I loved spitting at the stupid tiger, but come to think of it, Gena always avoided it." Langlais was inwardly laughing with joy while maintaining a concerned look.

"Gena tried to put a glass door on the porch, but it kept breaking so she had to put the jungle door back. One day she got into one of her weird moods and said that the Tiger Door, she calls it the Tiger Door, had to be on the porch because it was inedible or something like that. I asked Casey what inedible meant and she said it meant something you can't eat. Why would anyone want to eat a door anyway?" The little girl stopped the flow of chatter to let Langlais answer.

"She meant inevitable. That means that the Tiger Door must be on the screened porch or something bad will happen. That is part of her illness, Reese. Sometimes she has strange thoughts and fears. We played at this house when we were little. She was always afraid of that door. She's afraid of common things that people like you and I aren't afraid of.

"Did she see things, too?"

"Why'dya ask that?"

"Because one day she was gardening and I was coming through the hedge. I usually come through the azaleas. There's a little place I call a door. It's big enough for me to get through, but grownups have to walk around to the other side."

Langlais was thoroughly sick of the child's tangents. Having to wade through her babbling was driving him crazy. He summoned all his patience and waited.

"Right when I got through I saw Gena pulling up some *liriope*. That's the science name for monkey grass." Reese beamed proudly. "Gena is learning all the science names. Most of them are in Latin which is a dead language. How can a language be dead? It's not a person or an animal." Once again Reese stopped and stared at her companion awaiting an answer.

"That's what they say when no one speaks a language anymore. We use Latin for scientific names in medicine and for gardening." If he could have shaken her into finishing her story he would have.

"Oh. Anyway, when she saw me come through the azaleas she stood up and stopped, all frozen like. She got all white and she said something like, "what happened to your tiger?" But I don't have a tiger. I have a cat named Smokey, but she's all gray and doesn't look anything like a tiger."

Reese continued to prattle but it was lost on Langlais. He could not have asked for a better source for ascertaining Gena's mental state. Apparently she had gotten worse. She was afraid of a door, saw things and had fits. He had a witness. True it was a child, but he needn't divulge that. There would be a record of her hospital visit. He silently thanked a God he didn't believe in for this encounter with the little girl. Great Aunt Jacqueline, before she died, had parsed the deputations of power for Bienville Enterprises very carefully. Gena had the reins, but they could be taken away, and he knew how to do it. It was in the works. His lack of scruples had never done him more good than now.

When the child paused to take a breath, Langlais stood up. "It was nice to meet you, Lisa. Thank you for watchin' over my cousin. I think I'll go in and see how Gena's doing."

Reese watched him knock on the door. Whether it was the fact that he hadn't gotten her name right or the mean look he had on his face as he walked away, she did not like Gena's cousin from New York. Not one bit.

***

Hissing Cousins

Gena mustered every effort not to look horrified at finding her cousin Langlais at the door. At least that vermin of a friend wasn't with him. She smiled and greeted him calmly.

Langlais did a quick assessment. Her frame was somewhat more filled out that when he had last seen her, but that was not what gratified his hope that her condition had deteriorated. His cousin had dark circles under her eyes. The lines that had creased her face when she smiled remained long after the smile had vanished and were joined by numerous other worry lines. She looked like hell.

"Cousin Gena. Where y'at?" Langlais greeted his cousin New Orleans style. He rested his clammy hands on her shoulders and pecked her cheek while she stood like a statue. "You seem fit. Manawassa Springs seems to have agreed with you."

She recoiled as quickly as possible and stepped back into the hall. She showed her unwanted guest into the grand salon of LeMoyne.

"Welcome to Manawassa Springs. Perhaps I should say welcome back to Manawassa Springs. How long has it been since you were last here?"

She made no attempt to keep the bitterness out of her voice. When word had come that Grand-mère lay close to death here in this house, in this little town, Gena had dropped her affairs in New York and flown down. Langlais couldn't be bothered to make the much shorter trip from New Orleans to see her. Even after she had emailed Langlais of Grand-mère's death, he had neither helped arrange for the removal of her body to New Orleans, nor attended the funeral. By that time he had been caught up in negotiations on the West Coast. He apologized profusely (and insincerely) for his absence and publicly atoned for his sin by throwing a grand memorial soirée for Grand-mère in New Orleans.

"Oh, I imagine it has been some time now. Twenty-five years, thirty perhaps? It don' madda. I'd forgotten how charmin' this little town was," he lied. Langlais had completely lapsed into his most endearing Southern accent and colloquialisms. "I was fixin' to go to Atlanta from N'awlins and was inclined to pass by my cousin's place. I wanted to see how you're getting' along down here amongst the natives. I've, that is all of us, have been concerned for your state of health."

Ignoring his implication Gena offered him hospitality. "Can I get you some refreshments?"

While Gena went to prepare some coffee Langlais seated himself in the salon on the sofa and stretched his arms along the back. He surveyed the contents. It looked about the same as when he had visited as a child. It still reeked of his late great aunt. How could Gena endure this crap? The musty old town, the musty house, provincial idiots like the garden lady next door. That was her world now and it didn't seem to be doing her any good. She looked wretched, pale and exhausted. Even heavy makeup couldn't disguise that. For sure Manawassa hadn't cured her. She was loonier than ever. Maybe she would crack and he wouldn't need to procure her approval for this deal. Who had her power of attorney he wondered. Did it really matter? How long before she could be severed from power or even committed?

While these pleasant thoughts darted around inside his head, coffee arrived on an ornate silver tray dotted with pastries. Langlais stirred his coffee, took one of the delicacies and pursued his strategy. First, he expressed belated grief at Grand-mère's passing and praised the fact Gena had kept LeMoyne as it had been. (Gena was not taken in by any of it.) Next, he inquired of her and made suitable approbations to her declarations about enjoying her new life in Manawassa. (Gena knew he despised her situation.) Third, he dabbled in the general state of Bienville Enterprises: its worth, its policies, a few IRS issues, its direction. (Gena sat and waited for the punchline to this comedic discourse.) Finally it came.

"You remember Chip Creighton of Creighton-Howard. We were playing golf the other day and he asked how you were. I told him fine. He'd heard of your, uh, retirement, but I assured him it was just a Sabbatical from the New York office and that you were still in charge o' runnin' things from down this way. He said he couldn't imagine Bienville letting you while away your time sipping mint juleps when we were facing some crucial negotiations. I let him know that even from this foreign abode you were still on top o' things like a hound dog on a 'coon." Langlais raised his cup to his mouth to disguise the expression on his face.

"I remember Chip. He was pressing for a big merger before I left. I think we nipped that in the bud." Gena stared coldly at her cousin.

136

"Oh. Of course you were well in your rights *at that time*."

"And at this time as well. I still have the same "rights" as you call them." She referred to her controlling interest.

"Now, Cousin, don't get all riled. What I meant was…" Langlais damned Gena for unnerving him. She had a knack for it. "…things have changed. That is to say, you were right back then, f'sho. The timin' was off. Thing is, we now have the upper hand. I have to hand it to your superb intuition. That year made all the difference in the world. Creighton-Howard stocks have fallen off. Their Asian market is on the verge of collapse. Why, I bet if we were to stir up talk of a merger now, old Chip would be on his knees just beggin' us to deal on our terms – a full buyout at a ridiculously low figure. It would be a relief to ol' Chip to have creditors and the IRS off his back. I s'pose I could bring it up to the Board, with your approval, naturally. I estimate we could expand our Asian market by almost a third and, say, in two years be the top grossing company…"

"No." Gena was looking down at her lap and spoke barely above a whisper.

"Pardon?"

"I said no." Gena looked up into Langlais eyes with the ferocity of the old coke bottle-wielding Gena. "You won't secure my vote or the votes of the other big shareholders. The board would agree with me. Creighton-Howard is riddled with malfeasance, shady practices, serious IRS woes and a multitude of other scandals. Of course they want the merger or a buyout. Chip floats away on a golden parachute and the company walks away with billions leaving us to clean up a mess that's beyond an affordable solution. Bienville may have a few unsavory issues, but they are not intentional. All Creighton-Howard's troubles are self-manufactured."

"Granted, granted. Their name is a little under a cloud, but what we can offer…"

"No."

"Now, Gena, be reasonable, if you're able." His ire was fully up and his boyish charm fled.

"An idiot understands the meaning of "no". What is it that eludes you, Langlais?"

Langlais lost it. "I see. Somewhere inside that disheveled body and mind of yours, the old Gena is alive and well. As long as we are being perfectly honest. You look like shit. However mentally incompetent you were in New York, you're worse now. Anyone can see it. And if they can't, I have, shall we say, proof. But I don't need your support, cousin. I reckon inside a month, maybe two… you'll be shut up in some cushy mental facility. At least I'll see to it that it's nice and comfy like any good cousin would." The scar over his eye was swollen red with blood.

"Get out. Now." Gena's voice never stirred above a whisper, but that whisper, those flashing green eyes, that threatening face so deadly pale, all terrorized Langlais. He had seen it years ago as she sat on the swing. His scar throbbed mercilessly as he raced to the door fearing that a huge silver coffee pot would be hurled his way.

***

The Angry Departure

"Boss man, I barely had time to scope out the local sights."

"There aren't any local sights in Manawassa." Langlais clearly understood the meaning of Cody's sights. "You want women? You're a few miles north of the bikini crowd." He threw a shirt into his suitcase. Langlais had completely forsaken his charming Southern self. "Try Sugar Beach."

"I would if you weren't skipping out. Where you go I go. I guess Ms. Sour Face didn't give you what you wanted."

"Doesn't matter what she wants. In a few weeks it'll be settled my way. She won't know what hit her."

"Are you referring to my Uncle Roscoe?" Cody snickered.

"Just get the damn limousine."

***

As the limo sped off Katie felt relief flood her body. Her last encounter with Langlais had left her both angry and afraid for Gena's sake. She knew that there was no more time to waste. As he stood there checking out, Gena's cousin had abandoned all pretense of winsome boyhood. It was a flushed and loud Langlais that checked out of the Belle. He had seen Katie behind the desk and realized that she was the proprietress, not a garden slave. Recalling his previous patronizing towards her only produced unacknowledged embarrassment which translated into anger. That did not sweeten his mood.

"I am sorry you need to leave so soon, Mr. de Bienville. Gena is a friend of mine and I was so glad to see that she had family visiting. It must have been so nice for you both even if it was brief." She sang the words oh-so-sweetly and batted her lashes while inwardly thinking, "Who's doing the patronizing now, you S.O.B."

"Friends? Gena doesn't have friends. She has slaves, minions to do her bidding. Someone needs to inform her that the Union won the War. She'll be coming off her high horse. She's mentally unstable. I'm sure you noticed, if you're a friend." He spit the last word out. "I expect any time now I, that is, the family will have to have her committed. She began losing a grip on reality after her sainted grandmother died. We haven't heard much from her and it worried us. So I was sent to check on her. It looks bad, I'm sorry to say. I plan to send down a specialist soon." He pulled out his wallet and handed his business card to Katie. "If she gets worse, you call me right away. I'm sure you wouldn't want her to do harm to herself, now would you?" He slapped down cash for the room. "For the whole weekend." Then Langlais Bourgogne LeMoyne de Bienville stormed out of Belle Magnolia.

***

Langlais got down to business as soon as he was in the limo. He was in his clamshell mood. Cody swung the luggage into the back and slid into the driver's seat. The chauffeur was used to his boss's silences. In situations like this the two of them shared a unity of mental processes. Cody knew not to bother the boss, but to go into automatic. He headed for the airport.

Langlais concocted his plan and quickly began making calls. The first, and most important, was to a shady medical friend of his. Without mincing words he laid out the course of action to the doctor. Cody glanced in the rearview mirror. The smile on his boss's face told him everything he needed to know: Gena was in big trouble.

***

CHAPTER VIII
STEVE TELLS THE STORY OF BELLE MAGNOLIA

Strength and Love

Gena was thoroughly rattled. It wasn't just Langlais's visit. It was Kayton, his son Joe, her visions. She herself had begun to doubt her sanity. All her life she had relied on others' approval to give her life stability. Most people had some deep seated love or passion to sustain them. They relied on religion or family or noble causes. Gena had none of those. She had abandoned religion when she lost Kayton. The only family members she cared about were dead. Bienville crowded out any time for noble causes. She always believed that all she needed for happiness, strength and stability, was held in a reservoir inside her. The reservoir was continually replenished by a succession of approvals. This cycle had proved trustworthy up until now. Could it be that collecting approval lacked sustaining power to deliver happiness and inner strength? Could it be that eventually that system failed you?

She thought honestly about her childhood. She had wanted to be close to her parents, but they never seemed to have time for her. Gena was sure they loved her. It wasn't a lack of love. It was a barrenness of love's expression. When their attention was present it ought to have included affection. When had she ever been hugged? When did she ever sit on her father's lap or receive comfort from her mother when she was in distress? Why had they never lovingly corrected her or playfully teased her? The substance of a good upbringing had been given her, but without the necessary attendant expression of parental affection.

She simply assumed they loved her because that is what parents did. It was incomprehensible that they wouldn't love her. They provided all the physical necessities. They gave her a wonderful place to live, nannies and a good education. Gena conformed to all their rules and a proper way of life because she saw that this brought success. She equated success with approval and approval with love. That was where all her strength had come from. This is why it had been so perplexing when Kayton left. How could he not approve of her success? He said he loved her. Did that mean something different than what her parents had demonstrated? She had thrown herself into her work and was successful. Wasn't Kayton proud of her? Didn't he approve? If no, then what did he mean by his love?"

Her parents died, Kayton left and even Grand-mère passed away. There was no parent, no lover, no mentor to tell her she was approved, to make her feel loved. She felt weak and alone. She ought to have been able to tap strength and love from the reservoir inside her, but it was empty. A self-satisfied feeling which she associated with approval, thus love, had followed each successful business venture, but it didn't last. It evaporated quickly like the dew from the grass when the midmorning sun hits it. She never noticed its departure because she was already on her way to the next undertaking for acquiring success. And so she went on to the next dealing and the next. She was being filled up and emptied, then refilled in a merciless cycle.

Love couldn't be like that. It was supposed to be something that filled you up and stayed, no matter how you were tossed around, no matter how circumstances tried to drain you. It might be taken for granted, but it wasn't continually depleted. Real love was strength. She didn't have any. She sat and cried for what seemed like hours. A knock came at the front door and she rose to answer it. In her emptiness Gena didn't bother to disguise the fact she had been crying. She answered Katie's knock with red swollen eyes and fell upon her neighbor sobbing uncontrollably.

***

As best she was able Gena related her experiences of late. Due to pride or embarrassment she left out many details. Basically she focused on the girl and the tiger. She began with the incident of Reese, or rather the girl who appeared to be on the swing. She spoke quietly and almost childlike.

"You're not crazy, Gena. These things, these visions are happening to you for a reason."

Katie had taken advantage of the fact that Gena's defenses were down. She summoned a meeting. Katie, who never ordered anything, except goods online, ordered Steve to drop whatever he was doing and come to LeMoyne immediately. While she waited for him Gena poured out her story of the dreams and other odd incidences. She left Langlais out of the picture, at least the seriousness of his threat to her. At first Katie had wanted Steve to hear, but perhaps this was the better way. Gena was comfortable relating her frailties to another woman. Steve at this point might have been an impediment.

"Langlais was right. These are happening to me to drive me crazy so he can push me out of Bienville completely. He wants all my shares, all my control."

"It has nothing to do with Langlais, at least not the way you think. It has everything to do with Azalea… LeMoyne. She needs help."

"You're crazy, too, always talking about your inn like it's a person." Gena spoke angrily, but deep inside knew she was ready to hear whatever Katie had to say. "I'm sorry. Please go on."

"She…Belle Magnolia is not a person, but she is a Presence. You need to hear the story. You may think I'm nuts, but do you trust Steve?"

"Well, yes. I think so." Gena trusted Steve very much. He may have seemed a little devil-may-care in his comments at times, but there was solidness, like granite, underlying everything about him.

"Then would you hear the story from him? He is the biggest skeptic in the world, believe me. He's also the person who has kept me grounded when I thought I was losing my mind. In fact, he saved my life. Please."

Gena's nerves were so frazzled that all resolve was burnt out of her. "Certainly. I will listen, but I can't promise you that I will believe it, even if it comes from someone like Steve." Nevertheless, Gena wanted desperately to believe every word he said.

"Fair enough." Katie wrapped a consoling arm around her neighbor and prayed that Gena would embrace what she was about to hear.

***

Katie felt that the Belle would be a more appropriate venue to hear Steve's narration. After Steve arrived the trio walked next door from LeMoyne to settle themselves on the back patio. Steve and Gena sat in two of the wicker chairs around the table while Katie went to get refreshments. With the vacancy left by Langlais and friend, it was one of those rare down days where her current guests were not returning until late that evening and her new guests weren't arriving until the next morning. She had given Miss Nancy the day off. They were assured of complete privacy.

Katie came out bearing a large tray with the beverages of their choice: iced tea for Gena, beer for Steve and a diet coke for herself. She had compiled an assortment of goodies in case anyone wanted something to eat. She set the things down and settled into her chair.

"It's now or never." She glanced over at Steve's serene face and smiled. "Mr. Practical-Skeptic, you may begin."

Steve was a good story teller. If Katie had attempted the task she would have started at one point and retreated to another, then gotten sidetracked by this or that. Steve's presentation was straightforward, clear and logical. It was so much so that Katie was a little miffed that it made their whole romance sound pretty sterile, which it wasn't at all. Steve didn't hold back anything, including his own involvement: seeing a ghost at the Belle when he was a child. Gena, who had been silent up to that point, broke in.

"I remember two boys working in this yard. I guess you were one of them. I especially remember your friend, the tanned one, the one you called Moss. Does he still live here?"

"You remember him and not me? It's wounded ego time. Moss, David Moss, moved to Pensacola. His family owned a brewery there. His dad and uncle were partners in the business, but his uncle, who lived in Pensacola, did most of the day to day factory management. Moss didn't go to college. He went into the family business and moved in with his uncle. He just stayed there after his uncle died. I think he now owns several other businesses."

"Pensacola. A more culturally diverse venue in which to raise his children, I suppose?" Gena remarked hoping to appear nonchalant, but she actually wondered if the young man that she remembered as handsome and sexy was married.

"I guess. He's settled, all right, with kids in abundance, four or five, I think. All grown." Steve resumed his narrative. Gena and Katie sipped their tea and soda respectively, munched on appetizers and listened quietly. Katie periodically let her eyes drift over to observe Gena's facial expression, especially during the more bizarre events of the story. It never varied. Inscrutable. At least she didn't leap up and run away screaming.

When Steve finished they all sat in silence for a minute or two. The natural inclination of both Steve and Katie was to break the silence with some humorous remark, but they refrained.

"There are more things in Heaven and earth, Horatio, than are dreamt of in your philosophy." Gena stared at her empty glass of tea. "Even Shakespeare dealt with ghosts. Do you suppose it is possible that the Bard was speaking from an experience in his life? I wonder. There are things seen and unseen, after all. That is what the Creed says." Gena had not been to Mass in over twenty years except for funerals and weddings.

Katie and Steve sat quietly in order to allow their guest to ponder her last observation.

"Thank you. I thank both of you. Let me go now. I want to... I need time to think some more. If anything unusual or frightening should happen to me, I will need both of you."

"Don't hesitate. Call me or Steve." Katie looked at him for confirmation. He nodded. "You have my number, but Steve's is..." He had already pulled a pen from his pocket and was scribbling his number on a napkin. He passed it to Gena.

"Thank you again." She rose, turned and left.

Steve reached for Katie's hand and gave it a squeeze. He leaned over and kissed her tenderly. She smiled back at him, grateful that he was the man he was. She never would have made it through her trial with Belle Magnolia if he hadn't been.

***

Two days later Gena was once more sitting on the terrace behind Belle Magnolia. She and her hostess sipped coffee and chatted in a manner friendlier than any which had passed between them. Gena seemed relieved, if not relaxed, and worked up the nerve to what would have been seven months ago an irrational admission.

"I've thought it over and, as crazy as it sounds, I believe Steve. I mean I believe Steve and you, Katie. I believe both of you. What I am trying to say is that I am ready for... I don't know what I am ready for." A smile like Katie had never seen erupted on Gena's face. She actually laughed. "What am I supposed to be doing?"

"It's a gorgeous day. Let's take a walk." Katie set down her cup and grabbed her straw hat. "I have another if you need?"

Soon Gena and Katie were strolling around the Lake Grove for the second time. It was just past nine in the morning and already hot and humid. Katie indicated one of the quaint benches and both sat down.

"I've thought a lot about a course of action, too. I'm slowly getting familiar with local history. It's taken me a while. Sometimes the investigation has interesting." Katie thought about her first encounter with the Owl. "I think finding out as much about the house itself is crucial."

"I've told you everything I know, everything that Grand-mère told me. There isn't anyone else in the family who would know more than that. There is something that happened here when I was a child about ten years old, here, at LeMoyne." She stopped. The openness in her face was replaced by fear. She tried to sound blasé. "Oh, it wasn't anything. I'm beginning to be paranoid."

"No, you're not. You can tell me. It may or may not mean something. What happened when you were a child?"

"I throttled my cousin Langlais in the head with a coke bottle." She laughed. "I don't know what possessed me to do it. It scarred him for life. Maybe that is what the house is angry about."

"Having met your cousin, I'd say you were thoroughly justified." Katie knew that there was more to the story than that, but didn't want to press Gena further. "Back to local history. When I first came I started at the Library and found that to be useful. Have you been yet? It's an historical landmark, you know."

"No, I haven't been. Not yet. I planned to…" Gena sounded embarrassed as if she had lived in Paris all her life, but had never been to the Louvre.

"I'm sure you're used to grander things, but it is charming. It's the oldest library in Florida, as the Owl will let you know right off."

"The Owl?"

"You'll see."

***

CHAPTER IX
STOKELY PLANTATION

Before Gena could pay a visit to the Owl, the day arrived for the pair of friends to see Mr. Crippett. They met at eight in the morning and strolled down the Promenade to Stokely Plantation. One of the most notable features of Stokely was that it was set further back from the road than all the other houses on the Promenade making it seem as though it was all front yard and had no back yard whatsoever. This was deceiving since it sat on a double deep lot, one which it still retained long after other houses on the Promenade had sold their hinder portions. Looking at the dramatic sweep of the front yard Gena could imagine it being a grand Southern plantation set in Mississippi or Georgia instead of fronting a small circular lake in Florida. The depth of lawn gave it a grandeur that even Belle Magnolia lacked, though she would never have said that to Katie. The fact that it had been built in the 1920s meant that all the trees had close to a century to grow and spread their branches. There were two magnificent Southern Magnolias that flanked either side of the "avenue" to the front door. An avenue it was; the broad pathway to the front door could hardly be called a sidewalk. It was at least ten feet wide and was made of old fashioned cobbled brick. No shrubs or flowers lined it. This utter lack of flanking vegetation served the purpose of drawing the eye immediately to the front of the house. Although the entire front yard was landscaped with beautiful shrubbery and ornamental trees, when one looked at Stokely one saw first the giant magnolias and then the sweep of the avenue leading to the wide front porch with its magnificent fluted Doric columns.

As Gena approached the house she marveled at the Greek revival architecture. She had not realized how immense the structure was. The columns might rival those of the Parthenon in proportion to their setting. Other than these pillars the porch had no adornment to catch the eye. The windows were large and shuttered. The massive double door was plain but of beautifully finished mahogany. When she reflected on what she saw Gena realized she had attributed to Stokely what it did not deserve: pretention. The structure was quite simple in its lines. She supposed it was the scale of the thing and the plantation style which had prejudiced her. Perhaps for Gena all first impressions were invariably biased. People or things which inspired initial prejudices were seldom allowed to overcome these judgments even when Gena misapplied them.

She began to feel a little abashed that she had written off Stokely as a pompous edifice. She no longer thought of it as "Tara," built to proclaim itself master over the Promenade. She would simply let Stokely be Stokely and enjoy the tour of both house and garden.

***

Their knock at the door was answered promptly by a man in full butler regalia. Katie took the lead and explained that she and Gena had an appointment with Mr. Crippett to view the house and gardens. They were ushered into the small parlor, quite undeserving of its name since each of the walls was at least twenty feet long. Instead of sitting, the two wandered about the room, Katie pointing out the artwork. It was all very fine. There were some masterful individual portraits of Ethan and Sarah Crippett over the fireplace. There was one of their son Vergil as a boy, posed in a separate picture, with a pair of Welsh Corgis at his feet. There were oils of New England scenes, of other Crippett family members and of various subjects scattered around the room. The picture that dominated the room and put all others to shame was the enormous portrait that filled the space between the windows that faced the Promenade. It was definitely of Sarah Crippett and the artist couldn't be mistaken. Gena gasped with recognition. She stood speechless as she faced a John Singer Sargent with its surprising bursts of white in the foreground against the deep shadows.

"It's magnificent. I'm sure it's a Sargent." She said as she scrutinized the lower corner of the canvas. "Unbelievable to find one here in the middle of nowhere."

Katie overlooked her slight to Manawassa and answered her unspoken question.

"The story goes like this. Ethan Crippett was a very wealthy man and traveled abroad extensively with his wife Sarah. This would have been in the late 1800s. During their travels on the continent they met Sargent. He was captivated by Sarah's beauty and wanted to do her portrait. Ethan agreed, but on the condition that the portrait never be publicly displayed. An agreement was struck, but before the portrait was completed Sargent, who was a rising portraitist at the time, received a hefty commission to do another portrait for a prominent European family. He left it unfinished and unsigned."

"Very unusual for an artist to…"

"As the charming Katie said, it is just a story. I have had it scrutinized in an attempt to have it authenticated. There have been conflicting opinions." A very handsome elderly man entered from the hallway.

"Nevertheless, if it isn't a Sargent, it is still magnificent." Gena didn't realize it but she had just made a lifelong friend of Mr. Crippett.

"I believe it is. The only experts who shied away from verifying it were just young cowards still looking to make a place for themselves in the art world, afraid to take a risk."

He showed the way out of the parlor. The tour of the house and yard proceeded. The house, by Manawassa standards, was grand and impressive. For Gena, who had travelled in social circles with billionaires, it seemed lovely, rather than imposing, a home with great Southern charm. The grounds were another matter. They were spectacular. There were five areas of theme gardens, each flowing seamlessly into the other: a tropical garden, a garden of plants native to the Panhandle, an English garden, an herb and cutting garden and, much to Gena's delight, a Japanese garden.

Following the tour they took tea and coffee on the expansive verandah in the back. Gena surveyed the lush surroundings with envy. She would never make LeMoyne look like this. Mr. Crippett engaged them in diverse conversation. He was at ease with any topic that was brought up, ready to offer unusual information. He listened well and commented only when he had something complementary to the conversation. His manner was neither officious nor ingratiating.

As they were walking home Gena reflected aloud to Katie on their visit.

"I liked Mr. Crippett a lot. I don't see how one could not enjoy his company. It's strange, though. I know that we all contributed a great deal to our conversation, but I think Mr. Crippett learned more about us than we about him. Don't you think so?"

"Yes. The times that I've been to Stokely I felt like I drained him of information about his family, the house, the garden. Today I felt he returned the favor without me even realizing it."

"That's what I mean. I heard all about his grandfather,

grandmother, father and mother. I know he is distantly related to the Roosevelts, but I can't tell you what he has done all his life or even if he was married and has children." Gena shivered. "He knows all about me. I seemed to have unconsciously poured out my life to him. At one point I was remarking on his Japanese garden and ended up telling him all about Mr. Hamasaki and the rooftop Japanese garden where I grew up. Then for some reason I mentioned Grand-mère. I could tell he knew all about her. There was a look in his eye. She would have been older than he, but still, I think that there was something between them. I don't think it was romantic."

"All that from a look in his eye? My goodness! We have gone from ghosts to intrigue."

Gena clammed up and put on her coldest look. Katie bit her tongue and apologized.

"I'm sorry, Gena. You're probably right. I think Mr. Crippett knows a lot more about your family, and about Manawassa Springs in general, than he lets on.

***

CHAPTER X
THE OWL AND MARGIDDY

The Owl

"Thank you, Ms. Bradley. These have been somewhat helpful. I..."

"Well I indicated that they were not complete. The Great Storm of 1926 and the town fire..."

"...destroyed a lot of records." She cut the librarian off as politely as possible. Katie had warned her about the Owl's loquaciousness. Drawing on her experience in business Gena plied the technique of anticipating the substance of her opponent's comments and softening any abruptness of her rely by the use of flattery. "That is so tragic. These were superior in what they did contain." She placed the material on the counter. "Thank you. You have been extraordinarily helpful. This is a wonderful library and I am so ashamed not to have stopped by earlier."

"Yes, we are very proud of our Library. Our founder..."

"Aloysius Bellingham would have smiled on all you have accomplished here. Any other information you can discover about LeMoyne, Azalea Cottage that is, would be immensely gratifying to me. Good day, now, Ms. Bradley." Gena turned to leave, but the Owl (a nick name that certainly suited the wide eyed, bobble-headed librarian) continued her stream of consciousness aloud. Gena remained on course to the door as if not hearing until the Owl cried out.

"There is Margiddy." The name struck a chord in Gena. She wasn't sure why.

"Who?"

"Margiddy. He is an eccentric retired... I hate to sound prejudicial... old seaman. I don't mean that I am prejudiced against seafarers or old people. I mean that he is a little off center. He is certainly in his eighties by now or even nineties. Perhaps he has dementia. I believe his family was slightly connected with yours, the de Bienville-Martins. It was John Martin who built your house you know. He..."

"I do know that, Ms. Bradley. About this Mr. Margiddy?"

"I haven't seen him in a while, but I know he is alive. Of course, he was always an odd fellow. I remember..."

"Where is his house?"

The Owl began a low chirruping that mutated into a louder twitter while her head almost bobbled off her neck. Gena stared at the old bird and waited patiently. The librarian reminded her of a personal assistant she use to employ. Ms. Brenner lasted three weeks. She flitted rather than walked. She chirped rather than talked and she simply could not look at anyone straight on. Her head was always dramatically turned to one side staring at you with one eyeball. Gena wondered if the other eye was glass. Even more annoying, she blinked her eyes continuously. Gena had let her go. Since, other than the personal foibles which grated on her employer, she had much to recommend her, Gena found Ms. Brenner a more suitable position elsewhere in Bienville Enterprises.

"He doesn't live in a house exactly." The Owl continued amusing herself with her cackling. She put her hand to her mouth so as not to further disturb the nearby library patrons who were already glancing in her direction.

"Then where does he live?"

The Owl now flew completely out of control. Her arms began to flap at her sides. Despite her attempts at maintaining decorum, she continued twittering. Library patrons were now more than a little irritated. Gena wanted to slap her into sensibility when all the sudden she ceased all noise and movement. She adjusted her thick glasses and stared into Gena's eyes, "In the middle of nowhere." Then she turned and left a bewildered Gena.

***

Margiddy

"Where on earth are we going?" Gena and Katie had just finished breakfast at LeMoyne.

"To see Margiddy." Katie replied. "If the Owl says we have to go see an old timer named Margiddy, then we do. I asked Steve about him. He checks on him occasionally but doesn't know much about him personally. He says he's quite a character. I'm assuming that he will probably be able to tell you something about the house and your family's past."

They climbed into Katie's Suburban (more practical for their destination than Gena's Beamer) and pulled onto the Promenade. Soon they were flying down a country road, unusually curvy for northwest Florida. They drove and drove until Civilization had receded far into their rear view mirror. As the sun hit its zenith they pulled off the main road, or what by that time passed for a road, and bumped along an oyster paved lane.

"Where is this place?" Gena asked Katie for the third time. She was trying not to be impatient, but they had been driving for what seemed like hours on narrow roads amid scrubby brush and tall pines.

"I've never been there. Steve gave me directions, such as they are. At this point I'm thinking he should have given me Takawhatchee."

"Who?"

"Local lore. She was an Indian princess guide who the Spanish thought would lead them to stashes of gold."

Not long after that they came to an abrupt stop. In front of them at a distance in the middle of a broad field sat an old rusty tugboat. It listed slightly starboard. The wind ruffling the tall grass gave the illusion that the boat was being tossed upon a roiling ocean. The overall effect it gave was that the tugboat and its inhabitants were soon to be acquainted with Davy Jones Locker. Gena swiveled her head and, seeing no house in sight, said nervously, "Where are we?"

"Margiddy's."

"Where's his house?" She continued straining her neck and eye muscles.

"There." Katie pointed to the boat.

"He lives on a boat...in a field...in the middle of nowhere." Gena said flatly.

"Think of it as a sea of weeds."

"I can deal with that. After all, it isn't the strangest thing that I have experienced lately. Let's go see Mr. Margiddy." Gena started to open the door but ceased immediately when Katie shouted in a cautionary tone, "Stop!"

"What's wrong?"

"We've to get his attention and see if he can have visitors."

"You think he wouldn't be so picky about guests. Is he armed?"

"Well, it's weirdly complicated, Steve told me." Katie honked several blasts on the horn as instructed her by Steve. "Morse code for "ahoy there,"" she explained.

They seemed to wait forever. Gena began to wonder if this trek was worth it when ambling around the bow of the boat came a stooped over figure. A battered captain's hat sat askew on his head. White fringe burst out all over his head. He was so brown that Gena wasn't sure of his ethnicity, but as he drew closer she was certain it was mixed. He wore a tattered blue, sleeveless work shirt and stained khaki cut-offs that straggled between knee and shin.

Margiddy eventually reached the car and leaned over at the driver's side.

Katie rolled her window down. Steve had not told her exactly what to say, but just to turn on her feminine charm. She did her best.

"Up for some visitors today, Captain?" She said cheerfully.

Margiddy pursed his lips and screwed up his face as if he had just been asked to expound on the meaning of the universe.

"Aye." He turned and began to hobble back to the tug.

"What about Tootsie?" Katie yelled after him. This was something Steve had warned her about, something that she kept from Gena.

"Out somewhere hunting in the swamp. She won't bother us. C'mon in."

Only then did Katie beckon her passenger to venture outside the SUV. As Gena threaded her way along a sort of path she caught sight of the name on the side of the tug. In crudely painted letters it read: *The High and Dry*. Gena's thoughts wavered between curiosity and vexation. Apparently someone named Tootsie was armed, but at least she was out hunting and not on the boat.

"I assume that this Tootsie is his wife?" Gena tried to conjure up a picture of a woman to match Margiddy and failed.

"Not exactly." Katie was glad Gena could not see her face.

"Oh. A girlfriend, I suppose. I take it that whoever she is, Tootsie doesn't care for visitors. She must not be nearly as sociable as her companion."

"You might say that." Katie couldn't bring herself to offer more, at least not until they were closer to the boat.

"I assume she freely indulges in her Second Amendment right and brandishes firearms whenever she can."

"No, I doubt it."

"I suppose she's suspicious when it comes to people invading her territory. She isn't a predatory sharpshooter is she?"

"Not a sharpshooter." They were almost at the bow, so Katie gave way. "Tootsie's an alligator."

***

Unwelcome words if there were ever any, especially as the car was lost in high weeds some fifteen or twenty yards behind them. It was *The High and Dry* or nothing. Recovering from the shock that an alligator was loose somewhere nearby Gena quickened her pace. As she rounded the bow, she saw the entrance to *The High and Dry*. It was a long upward sloping gangway bordered on either side by rope railings. She barely restrained herself from sprinting up and rushing into Margiddy's domicile.

Both women gave sighs of relief as they entered the belly of the boat. It was dark and a little musty. Gena had expected half-kegs for tables and stools for chairs, but the furniture would have been appropriate for any mobile home. It was not new, but appeared to be clean and comfortable. Other than the fact they were in a boat, there were not many indications of a seafaring life. There was no parrot on a perch, no nets draped around, no smell of fish, no shells, only a few nautical instruments hanging on one wall.

By the time Katie and Gena were settled Margiddy offered them something to drink. Gena was about to decline, but a look from Katie warned her against that, so she chose a coke. Southern hospitality was never to be rebuffed no matter where it was offered.

They had a little more time to survey their host. Despite his mass of unruly white hair, his age was indeterminate. He could have been a very old seventy-five or a very young ninety-five. He definitely had strong African-American genes, but there was some other ethnicity that neither Katie nor Gena could pin down. His eyes, which looked to have to have been hazel in younger days, were clouded by the milkiness of cataracts. Katie saw in Margiddy the perfect description of "sinewy". Everything about him was stringy. He moved as though *The High and Dry* were riding the waves at sea, shifting now to one leg and now to another as he returned to his guests from the galley.

They had their drinks in hand and Katie turned to Gena and said, "Margiddy here may have a lot of information for you." Looking at Margiddy she said, "Gena wants to know a little more about her house and her family. Her roots are here, but she has only visited a few times when she was young. Now she lives here. Ms. Bradley our librarian told us

154

your family was from here and connected in some way with Gena's." She nodded to her friend to begin.

Gena cleared her throat and spoke. "My name is Gena LeMoyne de Bienville, I just moved into Maison LeMoyne."

Here Margiddy broke into a big smile then roared with laughter. "Mason Leemin. It's yeller, all right. But you mean 'Zalea Cottage."

"Yes, Azalea Cottage. It's the house left to me by Grand-mère."

Margiddy broke into another series of hee-haws. "Grammar!" He choked. "Grammar is whut makes you talk good. Grammar ain't no person."

Gena began to doubt the old man's sanity and questioned her being there at all. He did not seem to be of much use. She attempted to justify the use of the French appellation for her grandmother.

"I always called Grandmother Bienville "Grand-mère." I think she preferred it because she cherished her French roots. I know a little about the family. My great-grandfather John Martin was from Manawassa Springs. He was in lumber and met my great-grandmother Léonie in New Orleans. They courted and wed in New Orleans. He built LeMoyne, Azalea Cottage, for her. Jacqueline, my grandmother, was their daughter."

"Don't know there wuz courtin' or love. Mammy tol' me Leenie didn't love nobody, 'cept herself. Liked money though." The old captain seemed oblivious to the insult to Gena's kin.

Ignoring his rudeness Gena pursued her line of inquiry setting aside anything her grandmother had told her. She did not want to influence what the old salt had to say.

"I know Grand-mère said she had siblings, but never knew any of them. I supposed they were all dead before she was born. She didn't really say. I don't even know if any of them have descendants. Perhaps you can enlighten me."

"Cawlege teachers 'lightens folks. I kin jes' tell you whut I know." He paused and leaned back in his rocker and laughed. "Yepp, yepp, yepp. There wuz four of 'em. Mammy tol' me about 'em. "Now there wuz de boy. He wuz de oldest. Ahn-ree was what Mammy called him 'cause Leenie called him that. His pappy called him Herry. Weak like his papa. No gumption. Leenie sent him to make his fortune in Sou' Merica. Got et by cannonballs. They still had cannonballs there."

"Oh my! Poor…"

"Miss Aureelee wuz the purty one. Lot's o' men sweet on her, but most wuzn't fancy or rich enough for her. Married Caleb Peyton, owned lots o' de prop'ty in Manawassy. Probably best. He wuz no good and she was a Jonah.

"A Jonah?" Gena recognized the biblical reference but had no idea what being swallowed by a whale had to do with anything.

"Bad luck. Lost her babies afore they wuz a year. Two of 'em. She wuz drove crazy…pizened herself wi' medicine."

"How sad. I…"

"Then there wuz Lily. Calla Lily she wuz called most. Leenie called her t'other name, Lilyanne A-mee. She wuz born afore her time. Fit in a hatbox Mammy said. Never wuz strong. She wuz like a fairy. Didn't belong in dis world. Died o' consumption when she wuz a girl. Somethin' not right about her death, but nobody noticed. Shadowed over by the rich lady next door dyin' the same day.

"All her chil'uns were sickly things. Leenie couldn't abide weakuns'. She wuz glad to be rid of 'em, I 'spect. Yer Grmmar wuz different, strong like Leenie."

The old man closed his eyes and fell silent for a minute or so. Katie and Gena exchanged glances wondering if he was all right. Katie was just about to poke him when he erupted in laughter.

"Leenie had her poor moments. Got drove over the edge by sumpin'. Her husband packed her off to Chattahoochee or someplace like dat. She cum back, but wuzn't long after, Lily died and her man John up and run away with the nurse." He shook his head.

"So Grand…my grandmother was alone except for her mother Léonie."

"Bein' with Leenie wuz same as bein' alone. Mammy said a colder woman never walked d'earth.

"So your mother worked for the Martins?"

"Fer a long while, but dat wuz afore I wuz born. Mammy's fambly was from right here – Blount Swamp as it wuz then. Blount Springs now." Here the old man gave a low chuckle. "A swamp it wuz, a swamp it is no matter whut they call it. This here is my 'cestral land. Mammy wuz from here, but Pappy weren't. He'd a been from N'wlins. Pappy wuz a big man. Was awled." Picking up his pipe he tapped it on his ear. "Lot o' slaves wuz awled like in the Bible. Pappy wuzn't born a slave.

His pappy wuz one. Killed in the War between the States.

"Mammy left here and moved to N'awlins where I wuz born. Pappy wuz a sailor. One day when I wuz a boy, he went and never cum back. Died in a big storm, a hurry-cane. Left Mammy wid nuthin' 'cept his record." He jerked the pipe over his shoulder indicating the wall behind him. Gena and Katie looked at the old mariner instruments hanging there. "Pappy weren't one fer cummulatin' things, not like me. No, sir, not like me."

Beaming proudly he waved his unlit pipe around, slapped it on his knee, stuck it in his mouth and worked his jaw on the stem. Gena's eyes swept the interior again and marveled that this man felt he had amassed some sort of treasure.

"Not long after he died I heered him callin' me from Davy Jones and I went to sea. I wuz thirteen. Mammy moved back to Blount Swamp to be wid her folks who still lived on old fambly land. I sailed in an' outta N'awlins fer over sixty years." Much to Gena's displeasure he lit the pipe and began to smoke.

"So you never knew my grandmother."

He burst into laughter again. "I tol' you, I knowed a little from whut Mammy tol' me, but never laid eyes on Leenie. After I's too old for de sea I came here to fambly land, too. Mammy was long gone, too."

Gena was utterly frustrated by now. Margiddy had told her nothing of what she had hoped to hear. "I was hoping you knew more about my family and LeMoyne, I mean Azalea cottage. I am sorry to have troubled you, Mr. Margiddy…" Gena rose abruptly.

"Mister!" he laughed and puffed on his pipe. "Jus' Margiddy." He stuck the pipe to his lip and puffed.

Katie got up and could tell by Gena's tightly pursed lips that she was not a happy camper. Her time had been wasted. They hadn't discovered a thing. Since it was obvious that Gena had nothing else to say, Katie took leave for the pair.

"Well, thank you so much Margiddy. We appreciate letting us visit. Thanks for the drinks and helping us to know more about Gena's family. I guess we better go before Tootsie comes home. We wouldn't want to be her supper!"

The old man laughed and shook his head. "She don't eat people, jus' fish."

On the drive home Gena did not spare Katie. It had been a thorough waste of time and she let Katie know it.

***

CHAPTER XI
FAMILY MATTERS

Gena's anger at Margiddy and, by association, Katie, only lasted a few days during which time she had another disturbing dream and an even more disturbing phone call from one of her board members. It seemed Langlais was full tilt into the process of undermining her authority. She sat down and cried after the call and thought how unlike Grand-mère she was. Grand-mère could have kept the entire world spinning while based in Manawassa if God had asked her to do so. Gena couldn't even manage the oversight of Langlais. She put that out of her mind for the present and returned to the problem of LeMoyne. Eventually she would get back to Katie, perhaps after she and Steve returned from New Orleans. Waiting would give her time to dig into her family history. She poured some morning coffee and began her task.

The library gave her plenty of information on the Martin side of her family. None of it seemed relevant to her quest so she began investigating her family tree on the de Bienville side. She had an acquaintance in the genealogical world of New Orleans who kept track of all the prominent families which included the LeMoyne de Bienvilles. He faxed her a genealogy that went back to Jean Baptiste LeMoyne de Bienville who was governor of New Orleans in the 1700s. It wasn't necessary to go back that far for her purposes. She made a list of everything culled from her sources: the genealogy report, her grandmother, the Manawassa Library and even Margiddy. She began in the mid-1800s. That meant starting with the man whom the family considered the Grand Patriarch and founder of their current fortune, Georges Henri LeMoyne de Bienville. She focused on this branch.

Georges Henri m Seraphine Bernadette Balestrieu in 1853

Leonie Mathilde (m John Martin)	Jean Langlais (m Antoinette Pariseault)
Jacqueline (m Alfred Seton-Hayes)	Charles Chretienne (m Marie Fouche)
Charles Alexander (m Claire Ford)	Jean Henri (m Grace Thoreau)
Genevieve (Gena)	Langlais Bourgogne

As she glanced over this part of the family tree, she was struck by two things. The first was that neither she nor Langlais had children. This line of the de Bienvilles was destined to die out. She ought to have been horrified, but she was not. She felt a calm that she couldn't explain. She mused that it was time for new blood. The other thought that came to her concerned certain persistent de Bienville traits that appeared in every generation. She had seen enough old family portraits to recognize them. There was always some play upon the long, straight French aristocratic nose. Luckily Langlais got that. The tall, lean frame was something they both shared. The thick de Bienville hair of the darkest brown, so that it almost appeared black, was her crowning glory. She smiled as she thought how Langlais was cursed with dirty brown hair that was thinning at an alarming rate. Of all of these, the most prominent trait was the piercing green eye color. It was deep and rich and almost imperceptibly flecked with gold. Langlais had gotten only the gold flecks that darted around his dark eyes, but she had gotten the whole of that trait. She now began a very short list of other facts.

1. John Martin m. Léonie LeMoyne de Bienville.
2. Léonie runs Bienville and Martin businesses de facto.
3. They have four children.
4. Non-Surviving Issue of John and Léonie Martin
   a. Henri Martin (1883-1904) - Was sent to South America; caught fever and died. No issue.
   b. Aurélie Martin (1884-1905) - Married; all issue died as infants.
   c. Liliane Aimée Martin (1896-1906) - Died of consumption, age ten.

Gena stopped and looked at her last entry. Something struck her about the year, but she wasn't sure what that was. The age at which the child died, however, made her catch her breath: a ten year old girl. Why did that seem important? She recalled what Margiddy had said about something not right about the girl's death. The child was ten when she died in 1906. Gena grabbed her laptop and searched for children's fashion circa that date. That was it: white dresses with sashes, ringlets. Just like Pollyanna in the movie. The child on the swing must have been the dead child Liliane Aimée or Calla Lily as Margiddy called her. Now she was excited. She called Katie to meet her right away. Although she had told Katie about the current visions, she withheld from her the whole truth. Now it was time to divulge all.

***

An Old Family Friend

She couldn't reach Katie, but left a message on her voicemail. As she was waiting for a callback Gena received an unexpected visitor. John Franklin was an old friend of her parents. Gena could not remember him *per se*, although she did recall that her mother and father had some close acquaintances by the name of Franklin who lived in Massachusetts. She invited her guest in and asked if he wanted any refreshments.

Ten minutes later they were seated and he was sheepishly apologizing for this unexpected intrusion. He was recently retired and had come down to look for a house to buy at Sugar Beach. He vaguely remembered that the de Bienvilles had a home nearby. After some investigation Mr. Franklin had found that one of the de Bienvilles, Gena, still lived in the old family house in Manawassa Springs. He took a chance on paying a visit.

Gena commented that Mr. Franklin looked to be a great deal younger than her father. She told him her father had been deceased for some years. He said he recalled reading that. She asked how well he knew him. Mr. Franklin went on to explain that it was actually his parents who had been good friends of the de Bienvilles. The Franklins had a large place outside of Boston where Gena's father and mother visited from time to time. He remembered them well as a child and as a teen when he was home from boarding school.

"Wait a minute. I remember the Franklins. They visited us in New York sometimes. I do recall going up to Massachusetts once, I think. I was seven or so at the time, so I don't remember much about it, I'm afraid. I suppose you would have been away at boarding school or college."

"Probably. I went to Phillips when I was in high school, then Harvard."

"You say you've retired. What business were you in?"

"You never quite retire from your lifelong business, but I guess something happens to a person as they get older. They start a journey

161

back to their childhood, revisiting old times along the way. I have one particular memory of your dad when I was about seven years old. I'm afraid I had done something not very nice to a friend of mine. I was pretty sure my father was going to kill me. Your dad got to me first. He ruffled my hair and said, "Son, never take advantage of anyone especially when they are weak. That isn't honorable."

Gena's eyes watered upon hearing these familiar words. It had been her father's philosophy of life. In a world of business where practices had been cutthroat, her father had always acted the gentleman. They spent a pleasant afternoon chatting. His memories were few, but solid in their depiction of her mother and father. It warmed Gena's heart to connect to her parents so long after they had been dead. Finally her cell phone rang. She ignored it, but her guest said he needed to be on his way. After a gracious parting she called Katie back and made arrangements to meet her as soon as possible.

Gena was grateful for Mr. Franklin's visit. It was a welcome healing balm in contrast to her confrontation with Langlais.

***

Tell All

"There's something I haven't told you." Gena and Katie were seated in the small tea room parlor at Belle Magnolia for their tête-à-tête. Katie noticed that Gena seemed even more nervous than the last few weeks. Her descent into fear and paranoia had revived with the arrival of Langlais. Katie pried some information out of Gena about that visit, but not much. So she braced herself for Gena's forthcoming confession. Hoping that her friend would be completely open, Katie sat still and quietly waited for Gena to continue. She put on her most understanding look to convey her willingness to listen without judging.

"It isn't that I didn't want to tell you. I had forgotten it all for years until recently. It began to surface again after Grand-mère died while I was still in New York. No, it started long before that." Here Gena closed her eyes and took a deep breath. "I told you only a part of my recent dream. I left things out. I did tell you everything about seeing the girl on the swing – the girl that ought to have been Reese, but wasn't. What I didn't tell you is that there are other characters in my dreams and...I have seen the little girl before. Even after Steve told me about his ghost and yours, and you told me about Anna's "Lady with the Lantern,"

I couldn't bring myself to tell you everything. Pride, I suppose. Now I am prepared to lay it all before you.

"When I was about to turn ten years old, my mother and father wanted to give me a special birthday. Grand-mère persuaded them to have the celebration at LeMoyne. I don't know why. What friends I had, and I didn't have many, were in New York. At any rate, Mother and Father agreed. I was allowed to bring one friend from New York. Her name was Connie, Connie Hodges. We all flew to Manawassa Springs in my father's plane about a week before my birthday. The only other people invited were my Uncle Henri and Aunt Grace from New Orleans and their son, Langlais, whom you have met."

Gena's face reflected the disgust she felt at having to mention her cousin's name, but her voice remained calm and unemotional.

"Langlais and I have always hated each other, but I suppose family is family so I had to endure his presence. The party was dull from a child's point of view. I don't think Grand-mère had any idea how to arrange a child's party. The adults ate and drank and chatted. We three children were supposed to eat cake and ice cream and play with each other. I vividly remember Langlais flicking the half melted cake candles at Connie and me and sneering at us. Connie and I tried to stay as far from him as possible, but to no avail. No matter what we did or where we went he followed, taunting and throwing things at us.

"I know this seems irrelevant, but it sets the scene for what was to come. That night, the night of my birthday, was the first time I had the dream; no, it was a nightmare. It was almost the same every time I dreamt it after that, with only minor differences. The feeling was always the same. I had the dream over and over for a year or so and then it faded away. Since Grand-mère died the dream has returned, first in New York and now here. There are variations on the one I had as a child, but in essence it is the same. It gives me the same feeling, the same understanding. After I moved here it became a waking dream. I cannot *not* dream it, if you know what I mean. That is, it's like trying to escape Langlais at my birthday party. It's impossible. I am sure it won't sound nearly as frightening as it was to me when I was ten years old, but here it is.

"In the dream I am always in the dark, and I mean seamless darkness. I literally cannot see my hand in front of my face. I am in a very small room. The air is close and I feel claustrophobic. I know that I am going to have a panic attack. I am lying on the floor. For some reason I sit up and look to my right. I don't hear anything in that direction; I just know that I am supposed to do that. I wait in the darkness for a long time and then she comes. She's a little girl all dressed in white. Her clothes are very old fashioned and her hair is too – all in ringlets. She is very pale, as pale as her clothing, except for her cheeks which are tight little red spots. It makes her face look like a doll's face, one of those old fashioned dolls that has a cloth body and a ceramic head and hands. She has no expression at all, which is amazing since she's riding a huge tiger. You would expect her to look terrified or superior riding on this magnificent savage, creature, but she doesn't. At first they seem far away, floating in space. Then slowly they come towards me. They stop and face me, no more than a foot away. I can feel the tiger's breath, hot and heavy. It smells wild, if you know what I mean. Both of them are staring at me. Both of them have eyes that are so green that they don't look real. Then the little girl says, "Come with us. You will find the truth." I always shake my head no because I'm afraid to get on the tiger. Next, I start hearing loud noises, jungle animals all cackling and chattering until the din is unbearable. Then I wake up."

"You said that sometimes the dream is different, that there are other people in it."

"Yes. When I was ten years old the dream I described was almost always the same. I vaguely remember other people in it, but I think the girl and the tiger were so larger than life that they crowded the others out. Now it's different. There are times that other people are in the dream and I clearly remember them. Sometimes they are riding the tiger with the girl and sometimes they are standing behind the girl and the tiger. A man and a woman are always present. She's usually wearing a long old fashioned blue dress, but he has a modern suit on. Sometimes there's a small child, no, an infant and a foreign looking man dressed in robes. They dress a little differently each time, but they are the same people. I know they're very important. I don't know why."

"And the most recent was the one before you found the shattered door?"

"Yes." Gena related the one now in full detail along with a couple of more recent ones. "This time they were all there. This time the tiger was angry I wouldn't go with him. He wanted to eat me. It was horrible.

Now it seems that my nightmare is coming to life, like when I saw the child on the swing, only it turned out to be Reese. I've had other frightening moments. I'll be gardening and look up and see the little girl beckoning me. She doesn't look threatening, but I am afraid of her. I know she is a ghost – a ghost of someone who lived in this house. In fact, I am sure she must be the ghost of the little girl who died of consumption – the one that Margiddy mentioned, Calla Lily.

"Speaking of Margiddy. I'm sorry I gave you such a hard time about the visit. I now believe it was for this purpose: to identify the little girl of my dream. It all fits together. She died when she was ten. She wears the clothes and hairstyle of the early twentieth century. Lily is a white flower and this girl is always in white. She was my great aunt, Grand-mère's sister, and I might have known her if she had lived. Margiddy said that there was something unnatural about her death. I am convinced that she has come back to tell me this: she did not die of consumption. She was murdered.

***

Although Katie was gratified that Gena was now quite serious about her quest, she had misgivings about her direction. How could Katie explain to her neighbor that she was making the same mistake Katie herself had made by thinking that a dead person returned as a ghost? After Steve had so carefully explained all about her adventures with Belle Magnolia, Katie hoped that Gena understood about the nature of these particular spirits, but apparently she did not. She let Gena continue without interruption.

"I've thought a lot about the current dreams. I believe that Calla was murdered. The suspects have to be my grandfather John, the nurse or my grandmother Léonie. If my grandfather John and the nurse were planning to run off, then either or both of them might have hurried the child' death. Maybe they didn't want her to linger in suffering. They could have given her an overdose of morphine or smothered her. Then they slipped away."

"I don't think that makes sense, Gena. She was going to die. Why would they be in a hurry?"

"I don't know. Maybe they couldn't stand being around Léonie any longer. Anyway that's not the real theory I have. The other possibility is that Léonie murdered the girl. Through Grand-mère I know enough of

Léonie's character to say that she despised weakness in people. In fact, Margiddy said the same thing and he added that all Léonie's children were weak. He meant the first three, not Grand-mère. Then he said that Léonie went crazy and was sent to an institution. I understand now a few things Grand-mère referred to, some oblique references to Léonie's rest in a sanitarium. I assumed she was having difficulties during her pregnancy with my grandmother. This would have been before Calla died. I think Léonie was a little crazy even after she returned from her so-called rest. She murdered Calla Lily hoping the new baby would be strong. John and the nurse may have suspected and that's why they left. The dream makes sense. Calla has come back to show me that the man is John, the woman is the nurse and the baby is Grand-mère."

"Why would your grandmother be the baby? In the dream doesn't the baby go away with John and the nurse?"

"True. I think her presence there is symbolic. The baby, my grandmother, is there, alive. Poor Calla Lily was dead, murdered. She is showing me her sister, Jacqueline – Grand-mère. That's the important thing. Léonie had what she wanted: a strong heir."

"I don't know." Katie made a skeptical face. You still haven't explained the man in the robes."

"He never does anything except stand there and look solemn. He opens the tiger Door. He's the doorman for I know. He looks so foreign that I assume he's a part of the whole jungle imagery. I don't think he's important."

Katie knew that all the parts were probably important but she said nothing."

"Katie, I truly believe Little Calla Lily is haunting me, telling me my great-grandmother killed her."

Katie couldn't hold back her reservations any longer. "It could very well be that the child was murdered and that is why you've been called. I don't think that Calla Lily has been hanging around for a hundred years in limbo putting off heaven to wait for your discovery."

"What does heaven have to do with anything?" Gena snapped.

"I mean there aren't people ghosts. You die and you're gone from this earth. These are house spirits. They're like spiritual house protectors. I guess you could call them guardian angels for houses...like real-life gargoyles or garden gnomes..." her voice trailed off. Gena's look told Katie everything she needed to know.

Gena was angry. She felt that all her efforts to conform to the supernatural world which Katie and Steve shared with her was now being mocked. She remain composed, but rose and spoke curtly.

"You have more important things to do. I am sure you need to prepare for your trip to New Orleans. I will just continue my pursuit." She walked to the front door of Belle Magnolia with Katie in pursuit. As she was opening the door she paused and turned to Katie for a parting shot.

"I recognize that your experience with the ghosts of Belle Magnolia is perfectly valid. Perhaps it hasn't occurred to you that their nature was peculiar to Belle Magnolia. *She*, that grand house of yours, seems to have a place of undisputed supremacy here in Manawassa Springs. Perhaps for other residences of lesser importance there are different methods for finding out the truth. Have a good trip."

With that Gena closed the door.

***

CHAPTER XII
LOVERS AND FRIENDS

An Angry Interlude from Mystery

"My trip to New Orleans couldn't have come at a worse time," Katie commented to Steve as she packed for their upcoming trip.

Steve had stopped by to tweak some of their plans. Katie insisted he follow her up to the tower room so she could discuss and pack at the same time. He settled comfortably and quietly in his favorite chair and put his feet up on a Victorian ottoman. Katie held up a shirt, scrutinized it and then tossed it on the floor.

"Gena and I haven't had any time to talk about what direction to take, I mean about Azalea Cottage. I think she's avoiding me."

Katie had returned in a huff after the visit to the Margiddy. Then she met with Gena afterward and that had not gone well Steve surmised. Now she was taking her frustration out on him. Ever the gentleman, he abandoned his plan to discuss trip details and was helping her pack by listening to her complaints.

"She was so angry about our trip to Margiddy's. Then he calmed down and spilled the proverbial beans about the fact that she was having visions long before the conk on her head, long before she even moved here. Apparently she's had these glimpses since childhood. Why not tell me sooner?" She slammed a piece of her wardrobe into her suitcase.

"I don't think that dress deserved punishment." Steve was hoping to diffuse some of her frustration with his particular brand of humor.

"Ha. Ha." She retorted sarcastically. "Besides it's a negligee." She held up the little-something.

"In that case I am looking forward to seeing you in what there is of it."

Katie stuffed it in her suitcase. "I feel like Gena isn't handling this properly. She thinks that the little girl, Lily, has come back from the dead to haunt Azalea cottage. I tried explaining to her that when people die, they're dead. They don't come back. Their spirits go up or down, not stuck in the middle. This bit of logic seems to have made her angry at me."

She picked up a pair of bedroom slippers and looked around her suitcase for an appropriate place for them. In they went with undeserved violence.

"It makes much more sense that houses have their own ghosts." Steve teased.

"Exactly. Spirits to protect them." Katie looked over at her smiling lover and, realizing that he was being sarcastic, withdrew a slipper and threw it at him. He caught it and tossed it back.

"Besides, she doesn't seem to have the drive for it." A tiny voice nagged at Katie and again tried to tell her that this was not her mystery to solve; it was Gena's. This only made her toss her clothes into the suitcase a little more hastily and disorderly.

As if reading her thoughts Steve reminded her that whatever was going on with Azalea Cottage, it was up to Gena to discover the solution, not her.

"Katie, let's leave Gena alone. This is supposed to be a relaxing trip to New Orleans for the two of us. We don't need any third parties, or fourth if you count Azalea Cottage's house-spirit." Steve got up and walked over to Katie and took her in his arms. "I'm the guy who is supposed to be teaching you the meaning of the word relax." That seemed to have the reverse effect on Katie. She pushed him away and pulled several garments out of her suitcase. These she flung on the bed. "These aren't right." She walked to her closet and yanked out some other outfits.

Steve changed tactics to distract her. If humor didn't work or romance, then aggravation might.

"So what'll you be doing when I am conducting my important business?" Steve stressed the word "important" knowing full well how to get a rise out of Katie. His slate eyes twinkled. She bristled at the implication that she wasn't in New Orleans doing anything important. She had told him a million times that she had wanted to hit some of the antique stores to flesh out a few empty corners at Belle Magnolia.

"First I'm going to *Bon Temps Vintage Furniture*, then *Fairweather's Antiques* and then..."

"An excursion to the exalted flea markets. Very essential to the state of the world."

Sometimes she hated it when he teased her because it made her fall back into her defensive mode, an automatic response lingering from her marriage to Dave. Under typical circumstances she quickly recognized this self-protection was unnecessary with Steve. She had trained herself not to take little jests seriously. Dave had always treated her like a mindless pet. Her ex-husband hadn't teased her; he had patronized her. Katie knew she had to learn that teasing from Steve, a man who not only loved her, but respected her, was just fine. On the other hand, when she felt a little snippy, she could dish it right back.

"They are authentic antique stores…and very expensive. Anyway, after that, since you'll be busy, I'm meeting Hugh Carlisle for a little afternoon delight. Hope that's okay." She shrugged her shoulders and toyed with the negligee.

Steve had retreated to his chair, slouched down and was about to put his legs up on the ottoman. At the mention of Hugh Carlisle he sat up straight and glared at her. Hugh was an old high school flame of Katie's who had recently reconnected with her. It happened two trips ago to New Orleans. They were having a great dinner when a tall, nice looking middle aged man approached their table. After apologizing for the interruption, he had looked right at Katie and asked if she were Katie O'Neill who grew up in Pensacola. It was all downhill from there as far as Steve was concerned. Hugh was the owner of that restaurant and the man that he would be negotiating with to buy from *Triple-S Farms*.

"Very funny." He hoped she had no intention of seeing Hugh and was pretty sure she didn't, but insecurity prickled him. "I'm grateful that your old friendship helped get me the deal with his restaurant, but I don't think you need to go to any more extraordinary lengths."

Steve's ploy had not gone exactly the way he planned, but all thoughts of Gena and Azalea Cottage had been driven from the room. Katie looked at the man sitting across the room from her and thought for the millionth time how much she loved him. Her eyes began to tear up.

"You know damn well I didn't help your cause a bit. He's happily married and I'm, well I'm happy. You're a terrific salesman and *Triple-S* has gained such a great reputation that it sells itself. And I love you." Abandoning her packing she walked over and sat on his lap. It was obvious to anyone looking at the pair that they were in love.

"I love you, too." He said giving her a big kiss. "Good luck on your antiquing. It'll be fun. Hey, are you going to *Buster's?*"

"I hadn't planned to." *Buster's* was a true flea market with no pretensions to being an antique store. It held some good finds, but getting at them was another thing. The whole place looked like a champion hoarder had decorated it. Katie had been there once. She found herself continually on the lookout for spiders and other creepy things, so much so that she never found anything to buy. "Why? Are you in the market for fine furniture?"

"I thought they might have a spittoon."

"Here we go again. I am not putting a spittoon in Belle Magnolia. No one uses a spittoon anymore." The acquisition of a spittoon was an ongoing conversation. At first Katie had thought he was joking, but when it turned out he was serious her sense of décor rebelled.

"Just hide it somewhere, in a corner or behind a plant. You have a chamber pot in one of the guestrooms."

"It's not a chamber pot. It's a standing commode cabinet and a valuable antique. It's made of wormy chestnut and has the original enamel basin…"

"And takes up a huge amount of space. A spittoon on the other hand…"

"The whole point is that the commode doesn't look like what it is used for. The same can't be said for a spittoon. The commode is an authentic piece and still functional."

"But no one actually uses it, I hope."

"That's because I made sure that Belle Magnolia has all the modern conveniences like bathrooms with indoor plumbing. Like I said, it's primarily a piece of furniture…"

"All right, all right."

"But if I do see a pretty spittoon, I'll get it." With that Katie leaned over and kissed him.

***

Face To Face With The Past

Dr. Kayton Landry tossed his suitcase onto one of the mahogany beds at the Belle Magnolia Inn. He couldn't help wondering what the hell he was doing there. He had told himself the trip was to visit his son and meet his girlfriend, but the truthful part of him knew that was a lie. He had come to see Gena again.

There had been plenty of restless nights and distracted days for Kayton since he first found out that his son was taking summer employment in Manawassa Springs. Of all the small, insignificant rural

Florida towns, this had to be the residence of his son's college infatuation. He had seldom mentioned his own connection to Manawassa to his son, or to his late wife, for that matter. It was a place he visited in his younger days is all they knew. Marla knew about his past flame Gena, but only as a high powered CEO who grew up and now lived in New York. Kayton yawned. He felt weary, but too reflective to take a nap.

Looking around the room for a comfortable chair to plop into, he realized that "comfortable Victorian furniture" was an oxymoron. He settled into a straight back tapestry upholstered chair and pulled the fringed round ottoman up for his feet. Maybe this tortuous seating arrangement was the perfect place to reflect on his and Gena's past. The Landry's and de Bienville's were distant relations and the families had a certain amount of social intercourse. Jacqueline de Bienville acted as patroness to both families and her house in Manawassa Springs was at the disposal of the Landry family at certain times. Kayton had spent time there as a young child. Most of those times were generically fun, but pretty forgettable, until he was twelve. That was the first time he was at LeMoyne when Gena was. Up until then they had seen each other off and on at extended family gatherings in New Orleans, but it was in Manawassa Springs that they became friends.

He and Gena had liked each other at once and, despite the fact that they both were shy children, got along happily together. It was their quiet dispositions that actually cemented their bond since, as is often the case, their exploration and adventures were derived from reading, rather than activity. They spent hours in conversation. They talked to each other about seeing the world and all the exotic charms it held. They shared a love for *National Geographic*. In the innocence of childhood they made a pact to travel to darkest Africa as missionaries to help the poor and suffering there.

Kayton looked out the window. He hadn't realized that his room afforded him a view of Le Moyne. The childhood pact was destined never to be fulfilled. Yet, in a way it had been, just not by him and Gena. It was Marla and he who saw deepest Africa and the wilds of South and Central America. His medical missions had taken him all over the world. Meanwhile Gena had taken up the reins to drive a billion dollar corporation. How it all had fallen apart he could barely remember. Their love degenerated slowly, just as their friendship had evolved slowly.

As teens they remained fast friends even when they lived in different cities. At some point he and Gena became more than childhood friends. They became lovers. He remembered the first realization that they loved each other. They were both in college and, like many coeds, were eager to escape their families. It was the summer after their freshman year and, however it came about, they both ended up in Manawassa Springs at LeMoyne. Since they attended different institutions they had lost contact that year, that watershed year where most children away from home revel in the liberation from parents. This particular insanity had affected neither of them and when they met at Le Moyne they met as sound-minded adults. The two of them soon became lovers. They navigated the disparate waters of their educational streams: he on the course of becoming a doctor and she, a business woman. After graduation they made New York City their home and postponed marriage until they both had stable careers under their belts.

Kayton ran his hand through his hair and sighed bitterly. It had fallen apart because Gena changed. It was ridiculous to think that he could just stroll over to Le Moyne after twenty plus years and renew an old relationship, even on a Platonic level. The doctor got up from his chair. Enough of fruitless reflections. He glanced at his watch to check the time. He wasn't to meet his son and the girl for another few hours. Since he didn't stop to eat along the drive from New Orleans he thought he might venture out to find a restaurant.

He picked up some brochures at the welcome desk and looked over several recommended places to eat. Settling on *Hall's the Deck* because it was the closest, he took to the sidewalk on the Promenade and walked. The restaurant was a small affair with local charm. Since it was the off time of day he found out that a table could be secured on the pier that jutted out into Lake Manawassa. Kayton sat down and ordered grilled shrimp. He glanced around the rest of the circumference of the Lake. It appeared to be unaltered from his youth as far as he could tell. He marveled that on this part of the Lake bank, which had been a grove of pines and oaks when he was a child, there was now a restaurant. For a city whose council had not been very forward thinking, this apparent intrusion on Lake Manawassa was nothing short of a miracle. When his waitress returned he inquired about it.

"Casey," he spotted her name tag, "I visited here in my younger days off and on and don't remember this restaurant. Everything else around the Lake looks the same, except in much better condition than when I was a child. When was this built and how in the world did they persuade the city to let them do it?"

"I don't know exactly when it was built." She topped off his coffee with an expert hand. "It's always been here since before I was born. I know some people are still mad about it. I think my mom said that there was a bad hurricane and it destroyed a lot of the trees so they built *Hall's* here because the trees were already knocked down. But I'm not sure exactly when that was. Is there anything else I can get you?"

"How about your signature dessert, Southern Bourbon Pecan Pie." Kayton settled back to enjoy his coffee when there came a voice from behind him, a familiar voice.

"Kayton?"

He didn't need to turn around to know that it was Gena LeMoyne de Bienville standing there calling his name.

***

Dr. Kayton Landry rose rather clumsily from his chair. He was certain that he looked like an idiot standing there speechless and staring at the woman he had loved so long ago. To his eyes she looked the same – beautiful, though somewhat haunted. Perhaps she was as haunted as he was about their past. It seemed as if minutes went by before he spoke, though it was only a few seconds.

"My, God. Gena de Bienville. I can't believe it's you. Pardon my manners. Please have a seat." He indicated the chair across from him and she sank gracefully into it. "It's been years. How are you? You look very fit and unchanged since…"

"I live here now." She cut him off intentionally. "Grand-mère passed away a couple of years ago and left me LeMoyne." She directed her glance across the waters of Lake Manawassa and Kayton's followed suit.

"You're retired, then?" Try as he would he could not keep the note of hopefulness out of his voice. Thoughts of a Gena free from business cares, a Gena like the one he knew long ago danced in his mind like sparks in a fire.

Her next words quenched the flame. "No. I run things from here temporarily. I only came to settle Grand-mère's affairs thoroughly." It was only a partial lie; Gena had to maintain a cold superiority if for no other reason than to steel herself against the memory of their former life together.

"Ah."

"What brings you to Manawassa?"

"My son Joe. He just graduated from Tulane. He's got a job here. He needed a break from academia this summer since he'll start med school next year."

"Following in his father's footsteps. You must be proud."

"Very." Kayton was feeling uncomfortable. This was the Gena he had fled from. She was cold and impervious.

"Why did your son choose Manawassa Springs for employment? Why not New Orleans or even Sugar Beach? Let's face it there's a lot more for a young man at both those venues than here."

"That's true, but his girlfriend is here and he's working for her father. He's in construction. Pearse, I think's the name."

"Mr. Pearse and I are acquaintances." Her tone was decidedly frosty now.

"Actually I'm to meet the two of them for Dinner at, uh, *Le Monde*. I understand it's the haute cuisine of Manawassa."

"It is quite a good place. A refugee chef from New York City owns it. You'll find it up to your standards, I'm sure."

Conversation languished. The awkwardness was temporarily set aside when Casey came to bring the pie and take Gena's order.

"Hi, Ms. de Bienville. What can I get for you today? The usual?"

Whether from a desire to hide her recently acquired taste for Southern fare or a self-consciousness of her fuller, less emaciated frame, Gena ordered a salad and water.

"You know the waitress. I guess in a small town you get to know pretty much everyone."

"Other than her work here she sits for the child of a neighbor of mine. I see her occasionally. That's all. It would be rude not to introduce oneself in a small town." Her apathy was pronounced.

Kayton wondered what it would take to defrost Gena. Her body language spoke tension and rigidity; her voice, icy reluctance. He looked her full in the face, something he had been avoiding, and was caught unawares by her eyes. They conveyed nothing of her manner or speech. They were the terrified eyes of a defenseless child. They were pleading for help. She was haunted, but by what? Gena quickly broke eye contact and shifted in her chair. The connection had lasted but a moment, but he knew she needed help. Gena deftly turned their conversation to generic observances. She mentioned the changes in Manawassa from their childhood days, yet without alluding to any intimacy that had existed between them then or afterwards.

The salad came and was consumed. Kayton sipped his cold coffee and picked at his pie. He described his marriage and career in the most objective way possible picking up from their accidental meeting twelve years ago. Gena unemotionally expressed admiration for the self-sacrifice that he and his wife had made in bettering mankind. He dully accepted her praises and prayed for an end to their luncheon. It came in due course and they politely escaped each other's company.

Kayton headed for Belle Magnolia. Being a little agitated he chose the longer route which meandered around the Lake through the Grove. As he strolled among the oaks, pines and magnolias the suffocation of his luncheon interview was dissipated. He breathed in the sweet scent of wild honeysuckle. It cleansed his soul. The bird song that wafted above in the warm air, each individual voice merging into a unified melody of wholesomeness, banished the cold words which he and Gena had exchanged. Even the squirrels who chattered at him for driving them away from their acorn feast on the ground, offered him friendly fellowship. By the time he reached Belle Magnolia he felt an unexpected hope. He still loved her. He was in Manawassa to rescue Gena from a dragon of some sort. He was to be her knight in shining armor.

***

Past Acquaintances

Gena refused to let Kayton pay for her salad. This gesture did not sweeten their farewell. Uncharacteristically of the Kayton she knew, he stalked rather than walked away from the table leaving a very angry and confused Gena. For the life of her she did not know why she had been so unfriendly to him. She left *Hall's* feeling so confused that her afternoon plans fled her mind. Feeling there was nothing else to do she began strolling aimlessly around the Promenade until she found herself in front of Stokely Plantation staring at the Southern mansion. The massiveness of the building, the huge white columns, the enormous green shutters mesmerized her. She sauntered up to the long sidewalk to the front door as if a magnet had drawn her. Without any reason for the visit forming itself in her mind, she summoned her courage to knock at the door.

After a brief interim during which Gena formulated various excuses for intruding on Mr. Crippett unannounced, his butler Carroll opened the door.

"Is Mr. Crippett in?" She inquired

"Are you expected?" His stone face looked at her steadily.

"No, but could you give him my card, please."

The butler took her card and asked her into the grand foyer. While he sought his master she looked around at the pictures on the walls of the cavernous hallway. She had not noticed them before. As with the works of art she had seen in the drawing rooms, they were masterpieces in their own right. While she was inspecting a landscape that looked remarkably like a Constable, Carroll returned.

"Come this way, please."

He escorted her into a room that she didn't remember seeing on her original tour with Katie. It appeared to be a small, snug private office. Her host was not there so she began to look around. First she searched the walls for the fine art that she had seen in the other rooms of the house, but failing to find anything significant, she turned to the photographs that dotted the tables and shelves. Most of the photos were inhabited by people who were strangers to her, that is, until she picked up one that rested on a lady's desk in the corner. There she recognized her grandmother in her younger days. Judging by her age and the style of clothing it must have been taken in the early nineteen-fifties. She was posed with a young couple whom Gena did not recognize. The couple leaned on golf clubs, but Grand-mère held hers perched on her strong shoulder. She stood holding the photo when she heard a voice behind her.

"Well, Ms. de Bienville. This is an unexpected pleasure." Mr. Crippett entered and, extending his hand, greeted his visitor.

With her free hand Gena shook his and apologized for the unexpected aspect of her visit. "I was walking on the Promenade and simply couldn't resist the temptation to see if you were at home."

"Very gratifying to an old man like me. Temptation, indeed!" Mr. Crippett laughed pleasantly and invited her to sit. He summoned Carroll to bring them some tea.

Gena, photo still in hand, took her place in the chair that he indicated. "Mr. Crippett, you knew my grandmother." She held out the picture to him.

"Yes. My parents knew Mrs. Jacqueline well. They often dined at LeMoyne and she, here at Stokely. I became, in a way, a protégé of hers, thanks to your father. I was friends with him even though he was a couple of years older. We ran around together when he was here in Manawassa. Mrs. Jacqueline saw my abilities as an engineer and set me on the course my life took. My father hoped I would follow in his steps as a businessman, but, well, sons often disappoint their fathers." He took the picture and pointed to the couple. "Believe it or not this is me...," he tapped the young man in the photo. "...and this is my late wife Stella. It was taken a couple of years before we were married. Your grandmother was very good to us both. Stella never lived at Stokely. My job took us all over the United States. Stokely was our retreat, our sanctuary. I only came back here permanently after I retired. By then my beautiful Stella had passed." He got up, gently set the photo in its rightful place and returned to his chair. He fell silent and strummed his fingers on the table next to him.

Gena gave him a moment to recover from his memories before she spoke. "It's funny I don't remember your parents or you at all. I was at LeMoyne off and on as a child and teen. But then children were to be seen and not heard and usually not seen for that matter. I disliked being here at the same time as my cousin Langlais. Perhaps that drove out all the other pleasant memories." She thought bitterly how she purposely had blotted out her memories of being at LeMoyne with Kayton when they were young. A wave of sadness passed over Gena as she recalled the luncheon. Why had she been so cold to him? Quickly she changed the subject. Neither her host nor she, it seemed, wished to discuss the past. "This is a very comfortable room."

"It's my favorite despite the fact that it isn't as grand as the other rooms here. I don't show it on tours since it is my inner sanctum. I feel very protective of it and, besides, the decor is a little shabby compared to the rest of Stokely."

"Then it's an honor to be invited here." Gena craned her head to take in the room. "Besides, I don't think it's shabby at all. I think it's charming. The furnishings look natural...as though the room were built for them and not the other way around."

Mr. Crippett glowed with satisfaction. Carroll knocked and entered. He set the tray next to Mr. Crippett and departed quietly. Her host poured out the tea and Gena took a cup.

"I like that little desk over there, the one in the corner that holds the photo of Grand-mère."

"I thought as much. You're here to reclaim your property."

"My property? Do you mean the photo? I have a number of pictures of Grand-mère. You're welcome to keep it."

"No, I mean the desk."

"The desk. I don't understand."

"That desk is over a hundred years old and belonged to your great-grandmother Léonie Mathilde."

"Really? I don't ever remember seeing it at LeMoyne." She sipped some tea and continued. "I didn't think you could possibly have known her."

"I didn't get it from her, but I did meet her once, not long before she died. She was very old, but still commanded a presence. In her lucid moments she could tell you every business dealing she had done in her lifetime. When not so lucid, she would prattle on about her deceased children- Henri, Aurélie and Liliane."

Gena decided to play dumb thinking she might garner some useful information about her family from her host. "Liliane? I don't remember her ever being mentioned by Grand-mère, not that she really spoke much of any of her siblings. I don't believe she ever knew them, you see."

"I believe that she was usually called or Lily or Calla Lily. Her full name was Liliane Aimée."

"Ah. I remember now," Gena tried to act casual. She did not want Mr. Crippett to suspect that she was trying to solve some irrational ghost mystery connected with LeMoyne, "from some family tree or other I once saw."

"Sometimes Léonie would get very agitated about her husband and the nurse."

"Really?" Gena faked ignorance about the pair. "Grand-mère said that my great-grandfather John and Léonie were separated. They couldn't divorce because she was Catholic. Anyway, he just disappeared out of the family picture so to speak. Although…" Gena paused briefly and debated mentioning the next bit of information. In the end she told Mr. Crippett since he might have some additional information. "…on my recent visit to an old man named Mr. Margiddy it was implied that my great-grandfather John ran off with the nurse. I suppose it doesn't matter.

"Either way Grand-mère said her mother didn't mind because Léonie… how did Grand-mère put it? "Mama wasn't that fond of her husband and thought him less than a man." I think that affected Grand-mère; I mean being raised by a woman with that attitude. Her own husband… I shouldn't say anything, but Grand-mère never really mentioned my grandfather and she never took his last name, Seton-Hayes. That would have been quite a name: Jacqueline Alexandrine LeMoyne de Bienville Seton-Hayes. I've seen him in photos and he was like a billboard model, cardboard and always posed with a smile. He died fairly young." Gena caught herself. She dropped her eyes and stared at her cup of tea. She hated that she lost control and revealed things about her family. She had no idea why she had let down her guard. She wanted to get information from Mr. Crippett, not the other way around. Her host respected her silence. She resumed conversation as naturally as she could.

"If you didn't get the desk from my great-grandmother Léonie, then how did you come to have it?"

"My temporary possession is due to your grandmother, Mrs. Jacqueline."

"Grand-mère?

"Yes. The desk sat somewhere in LeMoyne, though I couldn't tell you where. A hurricane in the 70's, Big Bertha, caused a lot of destruction here."

"I vaguely remember when I was in college Grand-mère saying something about having to fix LeMoyne after a hurricane. I didn't visit that summer and, when I did come back, there were a lot of the trees in the Lake Grove gone. Grand-mère said the hurricane had uprooted them."

"Oh yes, and unfortunately it afforded the opportunity for that damned restaurant to be built in the biggest gap left by the storm." He scowled in disgust. Gena was grateful she hadn't mentioned dining at *Hall's* just prior to her visit, much less that it was her favorite lunch spot.

It also damaged a number of homes," Mr. Crippett continued,

"especially on the Promenade. LeMoyne was one of them. Your grandmother had to clear out several rooms in the house while they were repaired. She stored most of the furniture in the garage, but a few things which she treasured most, she brought to Stokely for safe keeping. My parents were glad to accommodate her wishes. When the repairs were done she came back for her items, all except the desk. Years later, before he died, my father told me the story. After he and mother were both dead I asked Mrs. Jacqueline if she wanted it back. She gave me the oddest reply. She said something like, "Of course. It belongs to LeMoyne. It must return at the right time." I suppose that now is the right time."

"That is a strange thing to say." Gena refrained from relating to him that her grandmother often came out with odd comments that had no apparent point of reference. "What could she have meant?"

"As far as I'm concerned she meant that a de Bienville would retrieve it at some point and take it back to LeMoyne. Perhaps I ought to have sought you out before this, but it's been here so long I had quite forgotten about it."

"It is such a lovely little desk. I can't imagine Grand-mère not wanting it."

The old gentleman paused, then spoke gently. "I don't mean to disparage your family, Miss Gena, but I think Mrs. Jacqueline and her mother didn't get along particularly well. Perhaps the desk evoked bad memories."

Gena drank her tea pensively before replying. She reflected that Grand-mère had said very little about her mother Léonie Mathilde, none of it was good. Gena hadn't wondered why. Among the de Bienvilles there was never much conversation about family. She knew that Léonie had been beautiful, proud and not very personable. Perhaps that was due to the fact that her husband John had run off with another woman. She reflected that it was then Léonie had dropped Martin as her last name, whether legally or not, Gena couldn't say. At last she addressed the issue at hand.

"It doesn't hold any bad memories for me, Mr. Crippett. I would love to have it back at LeMoyne."

"Done and done. I will send it over. Is tomorrow afternoon, say 2 o'clock, suitable?"

"That sounds wonderful."

"So now that that's settled, what was the occasion for your visit? I didn't mean to sidetrack you. Is there anything specific you came for, other than the subconscious command to retrieve your property?"

Gena gave him her rehearsed excuse. "Actually, there is. I so enjoyed touring your gardens, especially the Japanese garden. Do you remember my telling you about my family's rooftop Japanese garden? I was wondering if you had any books on the subject. I think I would like to have a small Japanese garden as a reminder of that happy childhood place."

The rest of the visit was spent chatting about gardens and looking for Japanese gardening books. Gena left with a couple of tomes under her arm. Mr. Crippett escorted his guest to the door and called after her as she walked to the Promenade, "Tomorrow afternoon, delivery around 2."

***

A Happy Interlude in New Orleans

Marguerites was a famous French restaurant, famous at least to the natives of the Crescent City. Most tourists or businessmen had never heard of it, much less eaten there. But Steve ran in the restaurant circles so he knew where he wanted to eat this night of all nights. It had been a tiring day for him and that did not help his nervousness. As he dressed in front of the mirror he mouthed his speech a half dozen times. He wanted everything perfect.

Katie was late. They needed to leave in the next fifteen minutes and it took her that long, plus another fifteen minutes, to get ready to go out anywhere. He thought about his late wife Sherry. She had the same difficulty getting anywhere on time. It must be a woman thing. He smiled to himself and thought, "But when she was ready, she was beautiful and the same can be said for Katie."

Just then the door flew open and an apologetic Katie rushed in weighted down with packages.

"I'm so sorry. You know me and antique stores. Baubles." She held up her plunder expecting him to be annoyed. Instead, after she had deposited her baggage on the bed, he kissed her. She responded in kind then pushed him playfully away.

"More of that later, I hope. I need to get ready." He admired her shapely form as it retreated to the bathroom."

"I'm a lucky guy."

***

The couple settled into a cozy table on the balcony. They sipped their drinks and perused the menu. Katie was determined to have alligator as her entrée, but Steve advised against it.

"You wouldn't want to eat a relative of Tootsie's would you?" Katie was still upset about the disappointing trip to Margiddy's, Gena's frostiness and misconceptions. She had really hoped that the old sailor would open the door to some new clue.

"Speaking of Tootsie and her companion…I'm afraid we're no closer to figuring out the mystery than before. Her current wacky theory is just plain wrong. Margiddy wasn't much help at all. By the way, how did you come to know about a hundred year old retired sailor who lives at the edge of a swamp with an alligator? You never fully explained how that came about."

"Funny you should ask that. I happen to be in the Everglades and met this alligator…"

"Ha, ha. I'm serious."

"Mr. Crippett introduced us. They're very old acquaintances. Mr. Crippett and Margiddy, not Crippett and Tootsie."

"Margiddy and Mr. Crippett? That's an even odder friendship than Margiddy and Tootsie."

"It's a longstanding one from what I understand. Crippett's grandfather knew Margiddy's father."

"I'm confused. Mr. Crippett's family is from up north. Margiddy said his dad was from New Orleans. I'm pretty sure he said it was his mother who was from Manawassa, well, Blount Swamp."

"That doesn't mean his dad didn't live here. A person can live somewhere they weren't born, you know."

"Margiddy said his father was the son of a slave killed in the Civil War. I guess there was a lot of moving around for those who were left behind after the war. So how did Mr. Crippett's grandfather know the son of a slave?

"I have no idea. Maybe Margiddy's father was the butler before Carroll."

"I doubt that. Carroll is at least 200 years old."

"For whatever the reason, Crippett keeps tabs on old Margiddy's welfare. He's asked me to help check up on him from time to time."

"Admirable, but Mr. Crippett doesn't seem like the type to be so..."

"Kind-hearted and thoughtful?" Steve scowled.

Katie apologized and kept the rest of her thoughts on the strange friendship to herself.

Dinner arrived in four delicious courses. Katie was glad to have ordered the crawfish. The sauce was exquisite. As she took the last bite of the lightest chocolate mousse she had ever tasted, Katie was convinced that nothing could top the gastronomic pleasure she had just experienced. Then for some reason Steve moved his chair right next to hers. She wondered if she had spilled mousse on her dress and he was going to tidy her up like she was a messy baby. While she was checking for chocolate stains their server approached with a silver bucket of ice and a champagne bottle. Katie's eyebrows lifted and she stared at her companion. This was an unusual move on Steve's part. He hated champagne. The bubbly was poured, tasted and approved by Steve who was now looking very uncomfortable.

"Katie," Steve drew in a long breath, "This sounds so cliché now that I've come to the moment...I love you and want to spend the rest of my life with you. Will you marry me?" He pulled a small black velvet box from his jacket pocket and opened it.

Katie never was very comfortable with surprises, bad or good. She never knew what to say and usually something stupid escaped her lips at those moments. Tonight was no different.

"The rest of your life. Can't be too bad...there're more years behind than ahead, so if it isn't fun at least it won't be for very long."

Momentary hurt passed over Steve's face, but he knew Katie and he waited.

"That was a dumb thing to say. Are you sure you want to marry me, considering what a nitwit I am?" tears welled up in her eyes.

"Yes." Realizing how that must sound, Steve quickly acted to correct any misunderstanding. "You're not a nitwit. You're just quirky and funny." This was not going at all as he had planned. "Katie O'Neill you are a beautiful, intelligent and wonderful woman. I don't want a life without you. I want to be with you if you'll have me. You're the person who gives me... who keeps me on my toes and... "

"Yes. I will marry you." The tears escaped the borders of her eyes and her heart pounded. Steve reached over and put the ring on her finger. Then he kissed her. After much admiring of the ring on her part and expressions of satisfaction on his, they talked about wedding dates and telling the children. To any onlooker they appeared to be adolescent lovers whose only world consisted of themselves.

It grew late and Katie excused herself to go to the ladies room. She was on her way back to the table when she mis-stepped on her high heel and keeled over to one side. She bumped a man as he was coming towards her.

"Excuse me. Must be the champagne. I'm engaged." She showed her ring hoping to cover the embarrassment she felt.

The gentleman smiled as he steadied her and replied, "Congratulations."

She looked up at him and thanked him. He was a very handsome older African-American man with the greenest eyes she had ever seen. He reminded her of someone, but she couldn't think who.

***

PART IV
THE INVESTIGTION BEGINS

CHAPTER I
THE DESK

Mr. Crippett was true to his word and the desk arrived promptly at two o'clock the next day. Gena had cleared a space in her bedroom for the heirloom. She romantically envisioned using it as a non-business correspondence desk. Then she realized she had no real friends except the few here in Manawassa, and a desk was hardly necessary to communicate with them. Nevertheless, she felt the desk belonged in her room next to the huge fireplace.

It needed a good polishing so she went downstairs for some lemon oil and a rag. As she gently rubbed the mahogany wood the luster of the grain glowed brightly. Gena felt a kind of spiritual attachment to the thing. Grand-mère had apparently rejected it as an object necessary to adorn LeMoyne, but had still wanted it to return here. She sat back on the floor, rag and oil in hand, and pondered Mr. Crippett's words: "It belongs to LeMoyne. It must return at the right time."

"*Belongs to.*" It must be connected with the mystery here. Mr. Crippett could not have known that. He had totally forgotten about the little desk. If she hadn't stopped by unexpectedly, it may never have come into her hands. It wasn't like the Tiger Door. She didn't expect to have nightmares about it. It was a beautiful lady's desk. She opened the drop-leaf door to oil the pigeonholes and two little drawers inside. To her amazement when she opened the left drawer she found a small bundle of letters inside tied in a faded ribbon.

In her excitement she absentmindedly set the bottle of polish on the edge of the drop-leaf. It fell and rolled behind the desk. Gena couldn't be bothered. She scooped up the letters and settled herself into a nearby chair. Carefully opening the packet she noticed that there were only a few letters and all in French. They were from the great patriarch of the de Bienville family, Georges Henri, to his daughter Léonie.

They covered a two year span. Gena leafed through them to find the earliest letter and began to read. A command of the French language was a de Bienville educational requirement so she completed her task fairly easily despite the handwriting and quaint old fashioned phraseology. Twenty minutes later she had learned a little more about her family.

Most of the letters dealt with business matters, the father

instructing the daughter as to her dealings with the Martin side of things. A few of them disclosed a distasteful fact about her family: Jean Langlais de Bienville, Léonie's brother, was a serial womanizer. Apparently Gena's despised cousin Langlais wasn't the only degenerate de Bienville. The correspondence revealed that the females among the household staff at Maison Bienville were in constant danger from Jean Langlais. He didn't limit himself to Bienville staff, but meddled with other Mesdames and Mesdemoiselles of New Orleans, both rich and poor. His father was continually on his guard against his son's amorous behavior which posed a serious threat to Jean Langlais's upcoming marriage to a wealthy New Orleans debutante.

In the final letter Georges Henri refers to Léonie's plan to cover up his son's latest debacle. She undertakes the unenviable task of devising a plan to save her brother's, therefore the entire de Bienville family's, reputation. The missive was penned while he and his wife were on an extended honeymoon in Europe.

October 15, 1906

My Devoted Daughter, Léonie,

I did not wish to disturb you so close upon the heels of your recent loss of Liliane Aimée, but I wished to ask if the business of your brother's current flagrancy has been resolved. I have not heard from you as to any resolution. My illness which began when you were here recuperating this summer has now progressed to the point that I fear I may have little time left in my sojourn upon the earth. If this were not so, I would have taken the matter in hand myself this summer.

Jean Langlais wrote to me of your request that he and Antoinette remain in Europe some months beyond their original plans so that he might make the acquaintance of certain potential investors on the continent. Since he mentioned no other information I assume he is unaware of the result of his latest indiscretion. This is to your benefit and gives you a significant interval for making satisfactory arrangements before they return, if you have not already done so.

I fear that this burden, as was your recent one, is unavoidable. Any scandal which would besmirch the de Bienville name must be circumvented. I now offer my advice in this matter having based my opinion on the other harlots with whom I have dealt on Jean Langlais's behalf: money is a most effectual form of persuasion. If this is how you have addressed the situation, I will naturally reimburse your expense. If you have already undertaken other means, well and good. If not, then God guide you to the resolution, whatever course of action it may entail.

With Paternal Affection,
Georges Henri LeMoyne de Bienville

Gena scowled as she finished reading this last letter. How dare this patriarch, this fiend who had bartered off Léonie into an arranged marriage, have the gall to ask her to protect her brother Jean Langlais so that he could carry on as usual. How unfair it was that both then and now males were permitted different standards, moral and otherwise. They could do as they pleased and maintain a façade of benign ascendency in the public eye. Things have not changed that much in a hundred years. She sat for some time letting her anger subside.

The Bienville family name, Bienville Enterprises had been everything to Georges Henri, to Léonie, to Grand-mère and to her. What good had it done them? They had money, but there was no true familial bond. Léonie was chattel to her father. Jean Langlais was a playboy who cared nothing for the family name or his marital vows. Jacqueline was a hard core business woman married to a cardboard husband and she, Gena had an empire, but lost the man she loved.

"Damn. I can't do this anymore." She flung the letter on the floor and stalked out of the room. A cup of tea would help relax her, but she would have to wait for Katie to return to help her sort things out.

***

CHAPTER II
BAD NEWS

"It's always hard to get back from vacation." Katie sighed.

It was late afternoon when the happy couple returned from New Orleans. Steve pulled up to the back of the Belle. Katie hopped out and headed into the inn while he got her big bag to take up to her room. She checked in with Addie at the front desk then headed upstairs. She met Steve halfway on the steps to the fourth floor.

"Mr. Crippett just called me and asked if I could run over to Margiddy's and see how he's doing. Apparently a couple of days ago when Crippett was there he wasn't feeling well."

"So late in the afternoon? It'll be Tootsie's dinner time about now, I expect. I wouldn't want her having leg of Steve for supper." She threw her arms around his shoulders and kissed him. "After all we've only been engaged a few days."

He deposited the suitcase in her room and left. Katie unpacked. She took a very long relaxing bath, savoring a good book and a glass of white wine. Just as she was headed down for dinner Steve called.

"Katie, I've got sad news. Margiddy's in the hospital."

***

Gena called Katie early the next morning after she and Steve had returned from New Orleans. Although relieved that Gena sounded friendly again and wanted to get together, Katie explained that she couldn't meet right now, maybe later that day. Things had come up that she had to deal with. It had to do with Margiddy. He was in the hospital and she and Steve had been asked by Mr. Crippett to go out to *The High and Dry* today. It probably wouldn't take long. She was just about to go pick up Steve.

Gena briefed her on the desk and the letters she had found. They didn't seem to cast any new light on the mystery, but did tell Gena that her great-granduncle Jean Langlais was a jerk like his namesake.

"That gives me some comfort." Gena laughed.

"Mmm." Katie knew she needed to leave, but couldn't help getting caught up in the moment. "Can you read me that last letter? I have an idea, an outrageous one, but who knows?"

Gena got the letter and translated it over the phone to Katie.

"Okay. We know that Léonie's brother must have had gotten more than one lady pregnant. Right?"

"It seems so."

"Léonie was in New Orleans recovering from something and learns about it, from her father, I guess. She tells her brother to stay in Europe longer."

"I assume she does that because she's waiting for the child to be born."

"Not necessarily. The child might already have been born. When was the letter dated?"

"October."

"I think she may have paid off the woman and sent her away. Maybe she wanted things to settle down before her brother returned. At any rate she obviously didn't want to bother her father who was very sick."

"But that doesn't help us at all. Unless…" Gena was so excited she dropped her cell phone. Katie was hello-ing on the other end while Gena looked again at the letter. She picked up her phone and practically shouted, "Unless the child is born much later, say in January, 1907. My God! Don't you see what that means?"

"Not really." Katie was bewildered.

Once she was calmer Gena explained. "Grand-mère was born in January, 1907. Perhaps this illegitimate child factors into the mystery. What if Léonie was never pregnant? What if she simply took this child as her own? Then Grand-mère was not Léonie's daughter at all, but Jean Langlais's. Maybe the little girl I see isn't Calla Lily, but Grand-mère as a child.

"It would throw a monkey wrench into our previous theory, if that's the case, but it seems far-fetched."

Gena was grateful that Katie used the word "our" with regard to the theory. It showed that she was willing to accept Gena as an equal in the knowledge of ghostly things.

"Katie, it would make sense. Léonie lost all of her children young. She had no children to inherit her interest in Bienville. What a gratifying irony it would be if she raised the child of her despicable brother Jean Langlais as her own? He probably wouldn't care. No. He would never need to know. That's also why she never told her father about her solution. Another point in favor of this theory was that Léonie's other children had been sickly and weak and died young. Grand-mère Jacqueline was not at all like her *supposed* siblings. She was strong and lived to a ripe old age."

Katie seriously doubted that this was the case, but refrained from telling Gena. She recalled her own flights of fancy regarding the spirit of Belle Magnolia. She also noticed the time.

"Listen, Gena, this is something to think about, but I have to go pick up Steve. We're off to *The High and Dry*. Let's get together later today if it's not too late.

***

Katie was pleased that their brief conversation had gone smoothly. Since their parting had been bitter, she wanted any reunion to be pleasant. She thought about using her engagement as a reason to go over to LeMoyne to smooth things over, but it turned out she didn't need an excuse. Gena sounded eager to meet. Whatever bad blood there had been, it seemed to have dissipated. The disagreement they had had about the nature of ghosts remained moot for now.

As she drove to get Steve she reflected on the last couple of days. New Orleans had been amazingly wonderful. She arrived home at the Belle elated. Then came the news about Margiddy and her happiness deflated a little. Gena's crazy speculations didn't help her regain a joyful mood. Why couldn't things just stay nice and unsurprising?

Poor Margiddy. Steve had gone to check on him as Mr. Crippett asked. He found the old salt passed out in the middle of his living area. Steve had immediately gotten him to the local hospital, but they transported him to Pensacola. Anticipating the worst, Steve notified Mr. Crippett who knew the most about the old man. Crippett headed to Pensacola right away. Steve called Katie to let her know what had happened. Later that evening Mr. Crippett called Steve and said that Margiddy was in the ICU, but, considering his age, was not doing too badly. Mr. Crippett said he would take care of all the medical expenses up front, but the hospital needed Margiddy's identification papers. These were kept at Stokely. Carroll would know where they were and should bring them to the hospital as soon as he could. He further asked Steve to go over *The High and Dry* with a fine tooth comb in the hopes of locating a will. Crippett had never convinced the old sailor to make one, but recently

Margiddy had talked about writing one himself. Also while there Steve might see if he could locate what Margiddy referred to as his "treasure." Margiddy never specified what it was. Crippett doubted it resembled anything most would consider valuable, but Steve should give it a try. Katie told Steve she hoped Margiddy didn't mean Tootsie.

Now Katie and Steve were off to fulfil their mission. The old tug didn't have electricity. They made plans to search the tug beginning mid-morning in order to catch the light. Katie figured they would only need a couple of hours to find anything. Afterwards she hoped she and Gena could meet that afternoon. From what she recalled of her visit not much was there. Margiddy lived like a Spartan. She assumed that he had no real valuables and, if he did, they would be few and easily transported back for safekeeping at Belle Magnolia.

Katie was wrong on both counts. It had taken them all day to accomplish their mission. What they did find was so incredible that that the word "valuables" hardly covered what they discovered.

***

After Katie hung up to go pick up Steve Gena's brain began to race. Could it be that Grand-mère was not the daughter of John and Léonie, but the daughter of Jean Langlais and some unknown servant girl? That would mean Grand-mère was the child she was seeing in her dreams and Jean Langlais, the man. She had no clue to the woman's identity. But who was the dark, foreign man? Was he just the doorkeeper? Maybe he was symbolic for Léonie's father Georges Henri. What about the little girl Calla? Gena was so sure the little girl in white was Calla Lily and she had been murdered. All these new wild conjectures began to fall flat. Gena was far too practical to go off on irrational tangents. This kind of thinking was anathema to her logical self. She knew why she had conjured up a ridiculous theory about the dissolute Jean Langlais. It was from her hatred of her own cousin Langlais.

She read the letter again laying aside all fancifulness. The facts looked different this time. Jean Langlais had gotten a woman pregnant. Léonie and her father knew of it. Since her father was ill Léonie took care of it. She asked her brother to stay away. The safest thing to assume is that she bought off the girl and that was that. Maybe she forgot to tell her father her plan or was waiting until Jean Langlais returned so both she and her father could rake him over the coals. How this fit in with Calla Lily's death, the Nurse and John running away and her grandmother, she hadn't a clue. Her dream still haunted her. Gena mentally worked all the facts she knew in different ways until her head began to ache. It was like trying to put together a jigsaw puzzle where all the pieces were black.

***

CHAPTER III
THE NOT-QUITE-DEAD MAN'S CHEST

"Are you locked and loaded?" Katie smiled at Steve through the window of her SUV. She had just pulled up to *Triple-S Farm* as he was walking out of the door. "I'm not going anywhere near *The High and Dry* unless you're carrying some form of firearms. I have no desire to meet Tootsie, especially with her owner away."

"Legally owned and accounted for." Steve brandished his shotgun and set it carefully in the rear of the car, tossing in a backpack and a box along with it. "I'm ready for an adventure."

"Any word on how Margiddy is?" Katie pulled onto the road and headed for the middle of nowhere.

"He's doing pretty well. It looks like he'll pull through. Crippett says that there may have to be a change of venue for him. I imagine it won't be easy to separate him from *The High and Dry*."

"Or from Tootsie either."

"He talks a lot about her, but I've never seen her. I suspect Tootsie is a figment of his imagination."

"Let's hope so."

"The plan is to go through the place to see if there is anything he might want while he's staying at the hospital..."

"They won't let him have his pipe, if that's what you're thinking. Or Tootsie." Katie laughed.

"And, we need to find his treasure, Crippett says."

"What do think qualifies as treasure to Margiddy?"

"Tootsie." Steve leaned back and pulled his cowboy hat over his face.

"Very funny."

Eventually they reached the field and despite Steve's theory that Tootsie wasn't real, Katie made him take his shotgun. He grabbed the gun and the backpack. They headed cautiously for the tug. Having made it safely aboard, they began their search. After a couple of hours scouring every inch of the tug they were at a loss. There were a few old tattered shirts and shorts, an assortment of cookware, some plates and utensils. A few boxes of worthless odds and ends were stacked in a corner. A pack of dingy playing cards lay on a table set against a wall. It was covered with a rough canvas cloth that must have served for elegance aboard *The High and Dry*. There was no artwork, just a small section of wall above the table that showcased old mariner instruments and other items associated with a sea-faring life.

They assessed whether or not any of it needed to be taken to the Belle for safekeeping. The tug had no electricity, hence no refrigerator. Any food that would have needed refrigeration, Margiddy must have eaten, so there were no perishables to convey to the Belle. Everything else was canned or boxed and could remain there for now. His few extra clothes weren't worth taking. The items in the boxes were equally useless.

"I suppose these could be his treasure," Steve indicated the instruments on the wall.

"I expect they are – mementos of his time aboard various ships." Katie fingered a compass that was rusted into a frozen state. "He must have charted things with this at one time. It's funny how people end up, isn't it?" She tried to picture Margiddy as a virile young sailor alive with the salt air, balancing on the deck of a ship which tossed upon the waves. Instead all she could see in her mind's eye was the man she'd met: a rheumy-eyed codger, dressed in faded tatters, bent over and walking with halting steps. The sea had beaten a good deal out of Margiddy.

They resumed their task and found some papers stuffed in an old leather bag. Most were just receipts from thirty years ago. There were some battered magazines of equal vintage and a collection of post cards from a couple called "Squeeze and Maria". The receipts Katie paid little attention to. In case they had importance she set them next to Steve's backpack. Finally, exhausted, she plopped into the captain's chair and shrugged her shoulders. Steve hopped up on the canvas covered table. Both of them were dripping with sweat.

"I doubt there's a will or any real treasure other than those instruments. Let's call it a day." Steve rose from the table and in doing so hooked the canvas on the set of keys perpetually clipped to his belt loop. The canvas dragged behind him as he took a few paces towards the hatch.

"Shall I carry your train, your majesty?" Katie laughed.

Steve reached around to dislodge the offending cloth when Katie burst into song:

"Fifteen men on the dead man's chest…Yom-ho-ho, and a bottle of rum!"[4]

"What the…." Then Steve stopped and saw what Katie saw. Underneath the table was a battered old seaman's trunk.

***

---

[4] From *Treasure Island* by Robert Louis Stevenson.

CHAPTER IV
THE SECRET LOVER

The day seemed interminable to Gena. She accepted that she must wait until later or tomorrow to meet with Katie, but felt like she ought to be doing something in the meantime. She grabbed a fourth cup of coffee and settled onto the sofa in her bedroom. She propped her feet up and read the letter from Georges Henri to Léonie a dozen times, as if multiple readings would unlock a clue. It proved fruitless. She reached for her journal and pen that lay on the side table. Then she sketched out three basic scenarios:

The letter of Georges Henri has no bearing on the mystery.

• The original theory stands: Léonie murdered Calla Lily causing John and the nurse to run off. Calla is the ghost-child-guide in the dream. John and the nurse are the man and woman; Grand-mère is the baby. The man in robes is still unknown – the Tiger Door-Keeper? Grand-mère's parentage had nothing to do with theory. She is Léonie and John's daughter.

The letter of Georges Henri does have bearing on mystery.

• The ghost-girl of her dreams is Calla Lily who is the spirit guide leading Gena to discover Jacqueline's true parentage. That means that the man in the dream and father of the infant is Jean Langlais (Léonie's brother), the woman and mother of the baby is unknown; the baby is Grand-mère. The mystery to be solved is: Who is the woman, Grand-mère's real mother? The man in robes is still an unknown factor.

• The ghost-girl is Jacqueline, Grand-mère, who appears as a child. Since Gena is so fond of her grandmother, she comes as the child-guide in white. She is also the baby. Her parents are Jean Langlais who is the man and the unknown woman of the dream. Calla Lily isn't a part of the mystery. Robed man is not important.

None of the scenarios worked. They all left the man in robes unsatisfactorily accounted for, and two of them left the woman's identity a mystery. One left Calla Lily out altogether, and Gena believed the child was important. The other issue was whether the child in white was the ghost of a person or a "house-spirit" as Katie believed. Gena had her first dream at age ten and Grand-mère was still quite alive, certainly not a ghost. That might mean that Katie was right. And what in the world did the Tiger Door have to do with all this? Did she conjure up the tiger in her dreams because the door frightened her when she was a child?

The abundance of caffeine finally got to her. She was jittery. A walk around the lake would help. She looked over at the desk which had given up its secret so easily. She hadn't finished polishing it. That would be activity enough.

She grabbed the rag off the desk top, but the polish had rolled onto the floor and behind the desk. Squatting down behind the desk to retrieve the polish she said aloud to the desk, "I wish you had provided a little more to go on." She picked up the wayward polish and stared at the back of the desk. It looked odd for some reason. She walked around to the front of the desk and peered under the writing tray which was still down. You would have expected a drawer under it. There was certainly room for one, but there wasn't any. She tapped the floor of the desk. It sounded hollow. She tapped underneath. It must be a false bottom.

"Secret." She shouted out loud. "Of course. Many old desks have secret compartments. Why shouldn't this one!"

Gena threw herself into a thorough examination of the desk. She felt around inside it for buttons and knobs and sliding compartments, all to no avail. She controlled her desire to scream "open sesame" at it. Instead she went downstairs to her laptop. Perhaps the internet could yield information about secret compartments in old desks. Fifteen minutes later she was back up in her bedroom. She walked to the back of the desk and saw a thick strip of wood that ran the width of the desk back. She felt along the underside of the strip until she found a small metal latch-plate. With one press the secret drawer popped loose. In awe she pulled it slowly out holding her breath as she did so. She was afraid of being disappointed. She wasn't.

Lying there in neat bundles, and yellowed with age, were letters. It was such a reverent moment that Gena sat down on the floor and prayed for the first time in years.

"God, please let these letters help me solve the mystery. I want my peace of mind back." It was the best she could do.

Gena gingerly lifted the top bundle noticing the date as she did: March 10, 1913. She looked at the bundle underneath. The year on the top letter was 1912. She began removing the packets and laying them on the bed in order. One, two, three, four…seven altogether, one for each year from 1907 to 1913, all varying in thickness. She checked to see if the oldest letter in each bundle was on top or on the bottom. The bottom. No year seemed to have contained many letters, perhaps three of them in the thickest bundle. Neither were the letters very long, one or two pages at most. Some appeared to be just half page notes. She wondered where to start. She was eager to solve the mystery and thought that perhaps it was best to begin with the latest bundle. Then she wavered, thinking she was being too impatient.

She began with the bottom letter of the bundle with the earliest year, 1907. This ought to be the oldest letter. Suddenly she realized she hadn't looked to see who had written the letters. She withdrew the bottom letter from its brethren and read.

It was in French as was Georges Henri's, but was from a completely different person. It was signed Pierre. His French was not as refined as Georges Henri's making the translation more of a challenge than she expected. Gena originally hoped to meet Katie that afternoon, but with this discovery she now hoped they could postpone to the next day. She wanted time to translate all the letters. Should these contain the key to everything, she wanted to surprise her friend not only with their discovery but, perhaps, with the solution to her mystery.

Her efforts were hampered by the shaky penmanship and faded nature of the documents. The phraseology was awkward and reflected the lack of a refined education. Even allowing for the archaic nature of the French language at the turn of the twentieth century, this man wrote very bad French.

March 10, 1907
My Little Black Kitten,

To be sent away has damaged my soul. I have little to occupy myself here. In the days before your marriage when New Orleans was our world, I looked upon the city as though it were Heaven. Now it is Gahanna. I see none of its graces, merely all of its sins.

I still have old friends here and we have renewed our acquaintances. Yet while they revel I cannot amuse my spirits with drink and women as do they. I cannot remain idle. For to do this is to be plagued by memories. I have been to the docks and secured a position aboard a ship. I have a preference for a life at sea. Such an existence will remove me bodily farther from you, but my heart remains in Manawassa. Send your correspondence to Jerome. When I dock in New Orleans I will be there. I pray we shall meet again.

You're Pierre
An afterthought, my dear one,
I would have enlisted your aid in getting work aboard one of the Bienville ships, but I did not want to risk being recognized. P

Despite the irony of nomenclature, the "Little Black Kitten" must be Léonie Mathilde. Grand-mère told Gena that Léonie was wild, and it turns out that she had a lover, someone from New Orleans. Now the puzzle of Léonie was beginning to make sense. She had fallen in love with someone before her marriage to John was arranged. Her father must not have known about him or, perhaps did, but thought this Pierre was not good enough for her. Poor Léonie had wed John Martin. In those times what choice did a woman have?

After having read a few Gena felt she needed to reproduce these in English so that Katie could read them, too. Undertaking the laborious task of translation and transcription was the kind of industry she needed right now to distract herself from all the confusing theories, as well as her recent encounter with Kayton. She fetched her laptop from the downstairs office and seated herself at the little desk.

She could not bear for her translation to reflect its author's shaky education and she consequently took some license in her English renditions. This produced a more readable product. After long hours at the computer, broken only by a few occasions to snatch something to eat, she produced as complete a translation as the letters allowed. Some were terribly aged with the ink faded so badly she could not make out anything. The readable letters and portions of letters provided precious little information. Most were pretentious declarations of undying love and fidelity. She reviewed the ones which she felt offered the most potential clues to her mystery of LeMoyne.

May 4, 1907
My Black Kitten,

You say you have built a fountain. Do not grieve. You do well to think of it as a memorial to our love. Think of the waters of life that flow from the fountain as holy waters that cleanse all souls from wrong. It shall stand both as a memorial to our love and as a sepulcher to lost love.

I am finding life at sea bearable. The solitude suits my abandoned soul. When I gaze upon the vastness of the ocean, I know I am mere flotsam. I belong here. I could not be soothed so well had I remained ashore.

My soul is yours,
Pierre

This letter gave her a feeling of strange excitement. Pierre clearly refers to the fountain that still stood in the back yard of LeMoyne. The stone mason told her it was from the early twentieth century. She now had a year: 1907. It seems Léonie had built it as a tribute to her lover. Gena supposed that the unhappy sailor saw it as a way to cleanse their sin of adultery.

***

October 17, 1908
Chérie,

The excursion at sea lasted longer than I had expected. I had the chance to dock at many ports which presented to me new things. Yet, nothing could distract my attention from you. This will be my life and I have accepted that. You say in time we may meet in the City and I pray that is so. I received your last missive when I was in New Orleans. I have it now.

I am to return sometime after the New Year and will long for our meeting if it be your will.

Always your own,
Pierre

The rest of the letters waxed maudlin without saying much. It was obvious that Pierre worshiped Léonie. The seldom saw each other after he went to sea, and always in New Orleans. At this point Gena paused to deliberate. Léonie's husband had left her with no moral or legal recourse. She couldn't openly admit to a lover, and as a Catholic she couldn't divorce. She couldn't wed her lover because John wasn't dead. Poor Léonie.

October 10, 1912
My Lioness,

I dream of our last meeting. To part again was misery. When your word came to me that you were ill I became a man out of my mind. Until I hear from you I daily pray that you are not taken away to God. Should you die! I think of all the grand things that would be said of you, and nothing of faithful Pierre. Yet I do not resent it. Should I return to find you gone I will throw myself into the sea and join you in Eternity.

Your Devoted Pierre

***

January, 1913
My Beloved,

I raced to Jerome's when I returned praying for a word from you. I read the first lines of your letter with elation. You had restored my world to me. My love was alive and well. Then, but a few lines more, my world was turned into desolation. What ought to have been joy, you have made a curse to me! But as in all things I live to serve you. It will be made so, my dearest, my Black Kitten. I will do as you say. It is enough to know your love is as undying for me as mine for you.

I have one short voyage before I return.

Ever your servant,
Pierre

***

April 15, 1913
Chérie,

I have returned to fulfill my vow. To see you again is all I desire. Nothing more than that. My heart, which alone holds all my memories of you, will never desert you. I know what you ask of me is not what you truly want. It cannot be. I wanted to hear from your own lips that it is so. Abandoning that hope, I know that you will hide all we have shared deep within your memory room.

> *Obedient in my devotion,*
> *Pierre*

She was not sure what to make of the last two letters. Certainly the final one was pathetic. "Your memory room." Gena whispered softly to herself. "Léonie's heart." The romantic buried so deeply in Gena's mind was temporarily resurrected. True love does not fade and die. Her own heart, her memory room, had always held remembrances of Kayton. When she had seen him sitting there at *Hall's* her whole being was initially flooded with joy. How sad it was that this joy was quickly swallowed up by festering anger, anger against herself, not Kayton. She mentally shook herself to fling these thoughts far from her. She needed to concentrate on the task at hand.

Gena felt that now she really had something to go on. She glanced over the entries she had made in her journal before discovering the love letters. She added the new information to her theories. She composed the following list of facts from the letters:

1) Léonie had a lover whose name was Pierre.
2) They had known each other in New Orleans before she was married.
3) After the marriage he followed her to Manawassa.
4) Some incident in 1907 occurred to disrupt the lovers' affair.

5) Because of the incident, Léonie banished her lover from Manawassa.
6) He went to New Orleans and went to sea.
7) The pair saw each other seldom, but they corresponded by letter.
8) In 1912 they met, but something eventful occurred that changed their situation.
9) Pierre comes to New Orleans to fulfill some request of Léonie's that is not stated in the letter from April, 1913
10) There are no letters after April, 1913.

She looked at Pierre through Léonie's father's eyes. He must have been French, but the style and language of the letters pointed to a minimal education. The fact that he had to work indicated he hadn't come from money. That he went to sea meant he had no particular trade. All in all, it was not a suitable match for Georges Henri's daughter.

Gena wondered how Léonie, who was of the highest class, had met Pierre. She leaned back in her chair and thought about Léonie, this woman she knew so little about, except that she had been a cold, hard woman of business. There must be more to the story. Her great-grandmother could not have been born that way. Other than being separated from the man she loved and married off to a man she didn't love, was there anything else which had happened in her life to forge her personality of iron?

She had been someone's lover. Pierre obviously knew her in a whole other light: his Little Black Kitten, his Chérie. However, their acquaintance had happened, he followed her to Manawassa and presumably got some sort of employment. Gena wondered how they arranged their liaisons. They couldn't have held trysts in a house full of people. What was the Victorian version of a lover's motel? Léonie must have travelled to and from New Orleans on business. If so, why did Pierre come to Manawassa? They could have met on her trips to the city. He must really have wanted to be near her all the time. That was true love. Then came banishment.

Her mind drifted back to her own days with Kayton. It had been obvious that, at first, they both wanted to be near each other all the time. That is why he left New Orleans to complete his medical studies in New

York City. New York was where Gena needed to be in order to pursue her career. Then slowly they drifted apart. No. She drifted away. Even with his grueling and crazy schedule he had taken every free moment to be with her. It was she who consistently put him off. No wonder he left; she lived in her own world within New York, a world that excluded him. He was alone there.

In an instant the hardness that was Gena LeMoyne de Bienville's protection from herself dissolved into nothingness. Emotions held for years behind a dam of bitterness came bursting through the breach. Gena broke down and cried uninhibitedly. Her tears were for all the joys and sorrows; lives and deaths in her life. She allowed herself to rejoice or mourn properly for the first time. She remembered the few happy times as a child at LeMoyne. She grieved for the death of her childhood: the friendless little rich girl who was forced into adulthood too quickly. She lamented that her parents died so young. Tears of sadness flowed for her loss of Grand-mère. They mingled with tears of joy for all the good memories she had of her parents and grandmother. She cried bitterly for her choice of a career that had banished Kayton from her life. She mourned the death of their relationship, a death she caused by shutting out the man who loved her. At the same time she was glad he had found a wonderful woman who loved him, and that they raised a son together. Then she wept for Kayton and Joe who had lost a loving wife and mother. She marveled that LeMoyne was both blessing and curse to her; a source of fear and comfort. Slowly the cacophony of conflicting emotions resolved itself into a symphony of peace. Gena remained quiet for some time and nursed a warmth of joy in her heart.

Renewed by this unexpected gift of self-awareness, she resumed her deductions. She looked at her notes and the clues in the letters. The lover managed to write as often as he could while at sea. Since there were no letters beyond 1913 Gena assumed Pierre had died. Did he kill himself? Surely that was not the vow he promised to fulfil. Yet, if he still lived, why did he no longer write her? After reading his crude, but heartfelt, pledges of love it would be impossible to think he abandoned her, unless that was her request of him: excommunication.

A sudden thought struck her. John Martin and the nurse disappeared in 1907 never to be heard of again. If the law was at that time as it is today, perhaps Léonie had John declared legally dead. Seven years from some point in 1907 would fall in 1914. Sometime early in 1913 Léonie told Pierre it must be over for good. He writes the heart wrenching letter of April promising fidelity no matter what. She is spurred to action by his love and declares John dead. It would take several more months. She would have relayed the plan to Pierre. Perhaps he was to cease writing until she carried it out.

Gena set her journal down and frowned. That was far too dramatic. Her newly risen emotional side needed to be pushed down in favor of logic. If Léonie did wed Pierre, there was no family record of it. What if she had married him, but because of family disapproval, kept it a secret? By this time all objections had died with Georges Henri. Almost immediately she contradicted this idea. The reality was that John's disappearance wasn't connected to any sort of dangerous activity. He hadn't had a boating accident or some other mishap which could have resulted in his death, but not the recovery of his body. He had run off with another woman. That might be grounds for wishing him dead, but not for declaring him legally dead.

She tried a different tack. What if Léonie had grown tired of Pierre? Since Gena had no letters from Léonie to him, there was no evidence for how Léonie felt about Pierre. Pierre's letters assume the same fidelity and undying love that he felt for her. Perhaps the sexual relationship had been mutual, but the love was all one sided. What if he became a liability and a threat to her position? What occurred to make him write those anguished words in January of 1913? What did he mean by: "*What ought to have been joy, you have made a curse to me! But as in all things I live to serve you. It will be made so, my dearest, my Black Kitten. I will do as you say.*"

Gena sat up straight and arched her stiff back. Perhaps Léonie broke things off completely: no rendezvous or letters. Slave to her that he was, he obeyed at first. Love was too strong and he came back to Manawassa to hear from Léonie's own lips that their affair was over: "*It cannot be. I wanted to hear from your own lips that it is so.*" Not being welcome, maybe he became angry and left. Then Léonie having tired of this rough fellow had gotten rid of him. Léonie had resources to hire someone to kill her lover aboard ship or in New Orleans. She excommunicates him then sends an assassin to ensure its permanence.

Gena had no doubt that Léonie was a murderess, but it wasn't Calla Lily she had killed. It was Pierre. Perhaps it was both of them.

Without evidence to the contrary, everything pointed to Léonie being capable of murder. It was an appalling idea, yet she felt relieved of a burden. The rest of the mystery, whether the victim was Calla, Pierre or both, was only a matter of course. She would have great deal to share with Katie.

She didn't have long to mull over these new revelations. Her cell phone chimed and she answered it. It was Bear Mountain Stone Masons. They could start work on her fountain right away.

***

CHAPTER V
UNLOCKING A CHEST

The strong light of day was waning and making the interior of the tugboat murkier. Steve worked at the chest's lock which was pretty badly rusted. He grabbed some sort of metal object off a nearby shelf and began to hit the lock. It didn't budge.

"They really made things to stand up to abuse back in the old days." He struck it again with the same lack of results. It was getting harder to see so he shouted to Katie to get the flashlight out of his backpack. She went over and unzipped it.

"Phew! What's that smell?"

"Tootsie bait, just in case." He kept at the lock.

"I think your shotgun's a better idea."

"I didn't exactly load it."

"What! You jerk. In that case, I really do hope Tootsie is a figment of Margiddy's imagination. If she isn't, I hope she eats you, not me."

"Look, I hated the idea of killing her when the old salt was away, assuming she was real. I did bring ammunition; it's just in the car. Thanks." Katie handed him the flashlight and Steve began to examine the lock to see if there was a more effective way to bludgeon it. "It would help to pull it from under the bench. He made a calculated pull on the chest, but it wouldn't budge. Even with Katie's help it stayed put. A discouraged Steve settled back on the floor.

"Got it." Katie went to one end of the long bench and lifted it. Following her lead, Steve addressed the other end. It was heavy, too, but not nearly as heavy as the chest. Together they moved it out of the way.

Now that it was in the open they could get a better idea of its size. The old chest appeared to be about two feet by three feet and thirty inches high. It was studded with rivets and at one time must have had leather binding straps, only fragments of which remained. Nothing could say "treasure chest" better than what lay before their eyes. Steve leaned down once more to attack the lock.

Just then Katie noticed something hanging on the wall among the medley of navigational instruments. She reached up and plucked it from its peg. It was an old key.

"Try this."

Steve craned around and took it. "How long were you going to hold onto that before you let me have it?"

"Considering your cavalier attitude towards Tootsie, you're lucky I gave it to you at all. It's been fun watching you try to open the chest cavemen style. Here, let me hold the light for you." She took the flashlight and shone it on the lock.

Even with the key, the lock was hard to open given its rusted state. When he succeeded both he and Katie were stunned at what filled the battered old chest.

"Oh my God! How much do you think is there?"

Steve was picking up stack after stack of hundred dollar bills from the chest and laying them on the floor.

"Based on how many bills are in a stack, assuming they're all the same, and the other stacks…," he counted the remaining stacks lined up in the trunk, "I'd say at least a quarter of a million." He flipped through a stack of bills. "Scratch that. Could be a lot more. Some of these bills look pretty old and may be worth more than a hundred each. Hold on." He set the stack that was in his hand atop the others. He leaned over and with both hands scooped up something. He brought it up to the beam of the flashlight. It shone brilliantly.

"Holy…"

"Steve, Are those silver dollars?"

"Nope. Like the Christmas carol says, "Silver and Gold."

***

CHAPTER VI
CROSSED T'S AND DOTTED I'S

Never had Langlais de Bienville felt so good about crossing his T's and dotting his I's. Gena was a goner. He pushed back his chair and propped his feet up on his desk to read Dr. Franklin's bogus medical report. There was just enough truth in it to be convincing since many of the Board members had seen Gena in some of her moods before she left New York. Langlais had let the members know of his concern about Gena's mental health after his visit. He lied that during this recent visit to her in Manawassa Springs he'd persuaded her to see a doctor for an evaluation.

Langlais congratulated himself on his own brilliance. Langlais's old crony, the one who supplied him with whatever sporting drugs he wanted, was a Dr. John Franklin. It was sheer coincidence that there had been some Franklins who were old friends of Gena's parents. They had a son, John, who had become a doctor, but Langlais's Dr. John Franklin wasn't that old family friend. However, Langlais had fed his own Dr. John Franklin all the information he needed to be convincing in that role. According to the doctor Gena was pleasant during the interview, a little stiff, but didn't seem any the wiser. She was curious about why an old friend should show up right now, but he'd explained that. He also managed to sidestep the fact that he was a doctor by profession.

The visit Dr. Franklin made to Manawassa had paid off: to the Board it was in a professional capacity; to an unsuspecting Gena, a familial one. To reinforce the idea of a professional visit, Dr. Franklin had made a big show of arriving and checking into Belle Magnolia. He mentioned to the innkeeper Katie O'Neill that he was paying a call on Gena de Bienville. He had make a point of letting her know he was a doctor. She mentioned she was a friend of Gena's. Without giving away too much information or violating his supposed doctor-patient confidentiality he let Katie know he was Gena's doctor and had come there for a routine checkup. This was to ensure that Katie, who was rational, could counter anything an unbalanced Gena said about the purpose of Franklin's visit. Gena could protest all she wanted that it was just a friendly reconnection with an old family friend, but the innkeeper of Belle Magnolia could state otherwise. The fact that there were two actual Dr. John Franklins would prove that Gena's mental instability had led her to confuse the family friend with her medical doctor. She was completely incapable of handling the reins of Bienville. The ruse had worked.

Now that the face-to-face had taken place and could be attested by at least one non-partial witness, Dr. Franklin had created a phony medical report. The reliable old doc had managed to make Gena sound like a consummate threat to the Bienville. Her mental health was no longer a case of minor stress; it was approaching a full blown psychotic break. Langlais had already convened the board for Wednesday morning to address the issue. Meanwhile Cody had been alerted to deal with potentially less cooperative members using his own methods of persuasion.

"Coercion is a powerful tool when strategically applied." Cody pounded one fist into the palm of his other hand.

"True, my friend." Langlais spouted their favorite poem.

> *Blackmail is a handy tool.*
> *It very seldom fails you.*
> *But should it not work on a fool,*
> *I suggest you try the thumbscrew.*

The cronies had laughed and Cody departed for his business dealings. Langlais stretched and resumed a more productive posture. He composed the letter that he would send to Gena on behalf of the board. It would let her know that she was no longer majority shareholder and that he, Langlais LeMoyne de Bienville, was no longer her lackey. He was now in charge. The board regretted to hear of her health issues, but felt that they might compromise the future of Bienville, etc.

All in all, it was a great day.

***

CHAPTER VII
A CLOSE ENCOUNTER

"Unbelievable. This old guy lives on a dilapidated tugboat in a remote field on the edge of a swamp, with an alligator for a companion, and he's a millionaire." Katie stared at the stash.

"Multi, by the looks of it. The whole bottom is several inches deep in this." Steve let the coins sift through his fingers.

"What kind of coins are they? Spanish doubloons?"

"Look American to me. Though, wait a minute, this is foreign." He held up a large coin inscribed with an indeterminate language. "Still, it's made of gold."

"We've got to get this out of here and back to the Belle. Mr. Crippett is going to have a heart attack when he sees this, especially since there's no will. I mean when it was just the tugboat and its contents…"

"Don't forget Tootsie." Steve continued to pull out the paper money from the chest and line it up on the floor.

"… I wasn't concerned about finding a will, but someone is going to be very happy assuming Margiddy left one."

"It might be in here." Steve rummaged around the chest and drew out a smaller box. It appeared to be of a vintage equal to the chest. It was locked.

"Let's open it."

"Not now. If a will isn't in here, then there isn't any. We need to get this stuff," he swept his hand around the floor which was littered with stacks of hundreds, "and the coins back to the Belle. Daylight's going fast."

"You're right. We obviously can't lift the trunk and I don't see anything here to load…"

"Get my backpack."

She brought it over. Steve took out the parcel of fish that was to be Tootsie bait and tossed it over by the hatch. "Let's not forget to throw that out before we close up here."

They loaded the pack with as many of the hundreds as they could stuff in. Katie told Steve she had a number of sturdy canvas shopping bags in the car. "We can use them, too."

When they reached the car Katie was adamant that Steve literally ride shotgun. Grumbling he loaded his weapon from the box of shells he'd thrown in the backseat. Only then did they return to *The High and Dry* to begin conveying Margiddy's booty to the SUV. It took seven trips to clear out the trunk, and all went smoothly until they were returning to *The High and Dry* for the final load. Steve was a few paces behind Katie when she stopped suddenly.

"Steve." The inflection in her voice indicated fear. "Look."

Coming towards them was the thing they had joked about all day: Tootsie. Apparently she *was* real and a good nine feet long to boot. She was moving slowly on her on squatty legs, but both Steve and Katie knew how quickly she could traverse the space between them if she chose.

"Katie," Steve whispered as he stepped slowly in front of her, now glad that she had made him bring his gun, "Stay still and behind me." Steve was prepared to blast the hapless alligator when she altered her course and did the last thing they expected. She started up the gangplank into *The High and Dry*. As her tail disappeared into the door Steve told Katie to run for the car. She didn't need any encouragement.

"Be careful." She yelled as she slammed and locked the door.

Steve headed to the tugboat ready to shoot. Hopefully the old 'gator would come down the plank after she figured out that her friend wasn't there. He had no desire to meet his adversary in the confines of the boat. He had just gotten to the gangplank and was standing at a safe, but effective, shooting distance from it when Tootsie emerged from the interior. Steve raised his gun.

Meanwhile Katie waited nervously in the SUV. It had been parked in such a way that she had no view of Tootsie, the gangplank, or Steve. After what seemed a millennium she began to think she needed to do something. She didn't see Steve returning and hadn't heard a shot. Her fear was that Steve was now being served up, limb, by limb, as Tootsie's dinner. Prayer was the only weapon she had. She closed her eyes. When she opened them she saw Steve, limbs and all, almost at the car. He was grinning.

Without thinking she flung her door open and right into his stomach. Ignoring his exclamation of pain and warning to be careful of the shotgun, she threw her arms around him. He had to hold the gun away from himself for safety's sake since Katie seemed oblivious to the danger.

"What happened? I didn't hear anything. Is she dead?"

"Alive and well."

"You made friends with an alligator?" She was shaking with a mixture of fear and relief. Steve disentangled himself and set his shotgun down. Then he held her.

"I didn't have to. I was standing next to the gangplank ready to shoot. I aimed when she came out the hatch, but when I saw her I couldn't' make myself kill her."

"Why not?" Katie pushed herself away and stared at him as though he were crazy.

"She had the packet of fish in her mouth. She moseyed down, ignored me and headed towards the swamp. She was just hungry."

Katie couldn't help bursting into laughter. It dispelled whatever was left of her fear. "Margiddy told me that she didn't eat people, just fish. I guess he was right."

"Nah. She just knew I wouldn't taste as good as that red snapper."

"Connoisseur." Once again she threw her arms around him and gave him as passionate a kiss as circumstances allowed."

***

CHAPTER VIII
AN EXCHANGE OF NEWS AND A SUPRPRISE

Gena had been in readiness all morning for the knock on her door. Katie had not made it back in time yesterday to meet. She had been very mysterious as to why. For Gena's part, even though she was sleep deprived (the excitement of the letters had kept her awake for hours) she was fully alert and eager for her neighbor's arrival. Finally the knock came. She let Katie in, impatient to reveal that the mystery was on the brink of being solved, that she had found love letters.

Even though Katie knew Gena wasn't really mad at her anymore, she was unprepared for a welcome as warm as the one she got. Not only were Gena's initial words friendly, she did a very un-Gena thing and hugged Katie. Katie surmised that Gena must have turned into a pod-person while she was at *The High and Dry*.

"Welcome back. I hope New Orleans was wonderful."

"It was. As you know I really had intended to come over right away, but like I told you, Margiddy and all."

"No, problem. I've been very productive. You'll be proud of me. I made progress on the mystery here."

"Wonderful." Katie struggled to know what to say next: Margiddy, the treasure, the close encounter with Tootsie. Instead she blurted out her wonderful news. "Steve and I are engaged."

"That is, well, that's fantastic." The pod-Gena hugged Katie again and escorted her to the living room. She wanted Katie to get over with her news of the engagement, something which had been anticipated for some time by all Manawassans. Then she could amaze her with news of the secret love letters. First, Gena felt she ought to acknowledge Margiddy's troubles.

"I was sorry to learn that Margiddy is so ill. I know I wasn't nice to him and I'm sorrier for that."

"I don't think he thought you were unkind. I imagine he thought you were funny with all your formality; funny in a way that he liked.

"Thank you for making me feel better. I hope he makes a full recovery. I'd like to go chat with him again."

Katie tried and failed to picture the old man and Gena chatting. It was as odd a juxtaposition as Tootsie sharing her fish dinner with Steve.

Obligingly Katie narrated the events of the previous day at *The High and Dry*. Gena was shocked at their encounter with Tootsie and glad of a happy ending. She was even more amazed that Margiddy turned out to be a hoarder of wealth.

"I know a lot of people who went through the depression hoarded things, not just money. His life is a mystery. By the way, who's taking care of Tootsie?"

"I imagine she can take care of herself."

"Yes. You're right." Gena broke into the most beautiful smile that Katie had ever seen on her face. Something more than mystery solving had occurred while she was in New Orleans.

They both laughed and Gena continued, "Let me congratulate you on your engagement. Tell me everything."

She narrated the whole trip in her usual offhand manner. Katie's version related the proposal's unexpectedness (at least as far as she was concerned.) She showed off her ring in every possible light, all to Gena's "oohs and ahs".

"I was like a drunken sailor after it happened. Actually, I was a little tipsy. On the way back from the restroom I ran into a man, literally. I would have fallen down if he hadn't grabbed me. I showed him my ring, too." Katie paused a moment and became serious. "Have you ever met someone and you're sure you've seen them somewhere, but you know you can't possibly have? It was like that. He caught me. When I looked at his face, I knew him, but I had never met him. I had no idea who he was, but I'd talked with him. Does that make sense?"

"I've heard there are only six or seven shapes of faces. Our brains process features in such a way as to fool us into thinking we are seeing someone we know." The old Gena was back.

"Maybe he has a doppelgänger I've known."

Katie suggested they have a nice midmorning snack. A gift she had laid by on the coffee table she now proffered to her hostess. Gena was delighted to unwrap some beignets and chicory coffee. She immediately went off to the kitchen to prepare them. They had been intended by Katie as a peace offering, but as such, were not necessary. Gena was perfectly gracious, Katie mused, unless she was biding her time plotting some deep-seated revenge. The hostess returned with a tray laden with coffee, beignets and some additional goodies. The pair chatted amicably for a while. Gena controlled her desire to blurt out her news. Instead, she waited for the right opening.

"I wish the beignets were a little fresher." Katie eyed the last bite before popping it into her mouth. "But I'm being selfish. Enough about me. How have you been? You haven't had any more bad dreams I hope? Any more thoughts about Léonie's father's letter?"

"No, but something else came up. That is to say, some *things* came out of the desk. Love letters." Gena was clearly excited. "I can't tell you how I feel; you wouldn't understand. I believe it really is likely that my great-grandmother was a murderess. Actually, I suppose you would understand since you've been through it all."

"Maybe not, since I am pretty sure that my great-grandmother didn't murder anyone. So start at the beginning and catch me up."

Gena opened the floodgates about her discovery. She laid her story out excitedly, but logically. She ended with her conclusion that Léonie had murdered her lover Pierre and perhaps, even the child Calla Lily.

"It seems so sad. From his letters you would think that they had an undying love. In the last letter he tells her to keep all that they shared in her heart. I know my great-grandmother was considered a hard woman, but to have to admit she murdered someone…"

"Are you sure? I mean you have circumstantial evidence. I know when I was investigating Belle Magnolia, I leapt to some erroneous conclusions because I didn't have all the facts, or else I did, but was looking at them the wrong way." Katie bit her lip and hoped she had not mortally offended Gena.

"Mmm. I hadn't really thought about that. I was so excited to get any kind of clues. If I'm wrong, I'm not sure where to go from here. In your situation just finding out the truth resolved everything. Since I didn't walk into the Lake or anything, I assumed…"

"…that everything was fine now. A similar confidence happened to me…before I walked into the Lake. We need to be sure. Let's look at some different angles. Léonie continued to see Pierre once in a while after her husband disappeared. Then suddenly, after five or six whole years, decided to kill her lover. Why not before? Something crucial happened in 1912. Wait a minute. Wasn't that the year the *Titanic* sank or was it the *Lusitania*?"

"The Lusitania was long afterwards in 1915, World War I. It was torpedoed by a German U-boat." Encyclopedic Gena dished up the facts. "I doubt he was a deckhand on the Titanic. Besides it sank in April, 1912, a full year before Pierre wrote his final letter. He certainly wasn't writing after he was dead." Gena paused and gave a quirky smile. "Given my new acquaintance with the nature of ghosts, maybe he was." Katie burst into laughter. Gena joined her. "Besides I don't see how either one of those ships could have a bearing on our case. Maybe we should look at something closer to home."

The two women sat in thought. Katie broke the silence.

"Can you read me the letters, I mean the translations."

"I almost forgot. I translated them into English on my computer." Gena went to her study and printed up the documents. It took far less time for Katie to read them in English than it had taken Gena to translate them.

"Here's something. Did you notice this?" She read part of a letter aloud:

September 1, 1907

My Little Black Kitten

> *The child thrives and I am glad of it. So many parts of your soul were buried with the others. Yet this one is different. She will have her mother's strength and heart. I may be far away but I am her protector. I will never let anything happen to her.*

"I read it. I assume he's referring to Grand-mère. What's so unusual about that? She was born in January, 1907 and was a very sturdy woman. By the way, when I came to my senses I tossed out my crazy theory based on Georges Henri's letter... all that rubbish about Grand-mère being Jean Langlais's daughter, Léonie never being pregnant and taking the child as her own. My imagination ran away with me."

"I was pretty sure the letter was a red herring."

"You're right, but it wasn't worthless. In a roundabout way it led to the discovery of the secret drawer. If I hadn't dropped the polish in my excitement when I found it, I never would have gone to the back of the desk. That's when I noticed something funny about the desk."

"I'm glad we're agreed. Back to the letter. It isn't the reference to your grandmother when she was a baby that caught my eye. It's the tenderness. He feels protective of her. I don't mean to drop another bomb on you, but what if your grandmother is not the child of John Martin and Léonie, but of Pierre and Léonie? We both know Margiddy talked about how the other three children were like their father, weak and feckless. Yet, your grandmother was…"

"…anything but. You may be right. I think all theories are up for grabs and it doesn't pay to be shocked by any of them. This make the most sense yet." Gena had become excited again. "There was a lot of Bienville in Grand-mère's appearance, but, when you think about it, she looked nothing like my grandfather John. I know that from old photos, though like all old photos they're stilted. People had to sit there looking glum and unnatural. Katie, I think that's it. I am a descendant of a completely unknown man, my great-grandmother's lover Pierre something or other."

Kate shook her head. "That still doesn't answer two questions: Who was the woman Léonie's brother got pregnant, and does she figure into this; and who is Pierre, and what happened in 1912?"

"That's four questions, Katie." Gena smiled. "Seriously, I think we need to keep Jean Langlais's paternity suit in the red herring category. Pierre and 1912 need answers. Maybe Léonie wasn't a murderess. She just severed all contact with her lover to preserve the family name, the family pride. He loved her so much he gave her up. Maybe we need to find out who he was, his name. The mystery doesn't have to be about murder does it?"

"I don't know. In my case, or Belle Magnolia's case, it was. At least it was an attempted murder that went awry."

"The woman, the man and the baby must be Léonie, Pierre and Grand-mère, my real family. The little girl Calla Lily wanted me to know that. She's been the guide through all this. For whatever reason she felt a kinship with the tiger. He stirred me up. He was the… the vehicle for bringing me the resolution. I ought to have accepted her invitation to take a spin on the tiger all those years ago." She laughed and took Katie's hand. "Thank you. I think LeMoyne can be at peace and so can I."

"Not so fast. It sounds plausible, but what about the man with the robes in the dream. What about his identity. Don't you think we need to find that out, too?

A loud knock cut off Katie's protests. Gena found a very distraught looking Bear Mountain Stone Mason foreman standing on her front porch.

"Mam, I ordered the workers to stop. We've found something. We can't do anything more. I'm sorry."

"What? Is it something with the fountain's plumbing?"

"No, mam. You need to come see this."

By this time Katie had joined her friend and the two of them followed the foreman to the fountain. Along the way he explained that they were removing the huge stone pavers and excavating the subsoil when they found something underneath. They reached the spot and he indicated where they should look. A horrified Gena and Katie stared down into a hole. Lying at the bottom, and clearly distinct from the soil, were two human skeletons.

**

"This is horrible. I'm not sure what to make of it. I thought I had everything figured out. I thought Léonie was innocent." The women were back in the living room waiting for the police. Gena had lapsed back into a frightened nervous state. Katie was forced to take charge. She asked the crew to stay until the police came. She floundered around to think of something comforting to say.

"It might be nothing. It's probably an old Indian burial mound or something.

"Didn't you hear the workman say there was a gold chain and locket next to one of the skeletons? I doubt the ancient Native Americans had access to a jewelry store. This is frightening and it has to do with the trouble here at LeMoyne."

"You're right. Two dead people in your back yard isn't a good sign. I mean if it is something, something to do with the mystery here, you'll find it out. We'll find it out together." Her cheerful attitude was wasted on Gena.

"At what cost? Bad things come in threes. First Margiddy and now this. I wonder what's next."

**

CHAPTER IX
THE BOX, THE WILL AND MR. CRIPPETT

"We got all of it safely to the Belle. We cleared out Katie's fireproof file cabinet and stuffed it in. You know Katie. Now she's sure that lightning will strike the Belle and all her important papers will be burnt to a crisp. She's looking forward to your return to relieve her of Margiddy's treasure. Finding all that loot knocked the will out of my head, but there was a small chest inside the trunk. We haven't opened it. Thanks."

Steve addressed this last remark to a server who had brought him a glass of iced tea.

"Oh, not you. I'm having a quick lunch at *Hall's*. Promised to bring the ladies home some pecan pie. Speak of the devil." Another server brought two Styrofoam containers and set them in front of Steve while he listened to Mr. Crippett. "Good, I'll do that. I was just calling to make sure it's okay to open the little chest. If there's a will, it makes sense it would be in there. It sure wasn't anywhere else. I suppose Tootsie could have eaten it." Steve grinned. "You're right. I'm sure she preferred the snapper. I'll let you know if we find anything. By the way how's Margiddy doing?" Steve laughed so hard at Crippett's reply that he choked on his tea. Several irritated looking old women glared at him. Recovering his composure he shook his head. "Tell him Tootsie's fine, but I don't think the hospital permits alligators to visit."

Steve paid his tab, collected the pie and headed for Belle Magnolia. When he arrived he was told that the women had left to do some shopping. He was glad, not only because it meant Gena was feeling better after the discovery of the skeletons in her back yard, but also because he could get some work done at the farm. Treasure hunting had eaten into his time. Before heading to *Triple-S* he went to the Belle's back office, unlocked the file cabinet and drew out the box. After examining the lock he hazarded a guess that the same key that opened the trunk might open the box. He got the key from the plastic bag in the top file drawer. It worked. Inside were only two things. One was the will. He glanced at it: "The last will and testament of…." The other item was an old journal written in French. Steve assumed it was Margiddy's and wondered how the old seaman, who could barely navigate English, could compose a journal in French. It must belong to someone else.

Once back home Steve called Mr. Crippett to let him know he'd found the will. When he mentioned the journal Crippett suggested getting it translated. Although it was an odd suggestion Steve gave it to his daughter-in-law Selena who was fluent in the language.

Later that evening Steve called Katie to tell her about the will and journal. She was so consumed by the recent discovery of the skeletons that she didn't hear a word he said.

***

CHAPTER X
SKELETONS IN THE CLOSET

When human remains are found buried, not in cemeteries, but on private residential property, it requires all sorts of red tape for them to be removed. If the remains are determined to be less than 75 years old, it is a police matter; if over that number, it falls to the State Archaeologist. Frenzied activity followed the discovery. The local police were called that day, but were unable to determine the age of the bones without disturbing them. The medical examiner was called in. He stated that the bones were quite old, but could not say off hand that they were older than 75 years. Gena, hoping to speed up the process, reluctantly brought them Pierre's letter from 1907 that mentioned the construction of the fountain in that year. The Bear Mountain stonemasons verified that the type of stone and its condition pointed to the fountain having been set into place no later than 1915 and most likely prior to 1910. Since the bones lay undisturbed under a massive paver, it seemed logical to date the bones earlier or concurrent with the fountain's erection. Although it couldn't be stated positively that this was the same fountain, the authorities ceded that the bones were older than 75 years. Gena gave the go ahead and the site became the venue of activity by the State Archeologist. The bones lay there until his team carefully extracted them. Upon termination of this process another surprise awaited Gena.

While the initial stage was going Gena was tearing her hair out. Katie did her best to keep her friend focused. The archaeologist's preliminary guess was that the remains were of a man and a woman. The first thought that struck both women was that the skeletons had to be John Martin and the nurse. John Martin had not just been separated from Léonie, nor had he run off with the nurse as rumor had it. They had died. The women were further shocked by the archaeologist's statement that the skulls of both adults showed signs of trauma. Their heads had been bashed in. He would need to examine them more closely to determine if it was accidental or intentional.

Gena didn't need to examine anything further. They certainly didn't have an accident and bury themselves under the fountain. Her mind reeled at the thought the pair had been murdered in such a brutal fashion. She and Katie together reasoned the course of events. Gena reluctantly insisted that the murderer had to have been Léonie. Although it was possible she was a quadruple murderess, with the new evidence of the skeletons, Gena excluded Calla and Pierre as victims. She limited Léonie's crimes to John and the nurse. She must have discovered that her husband was running away with the nurse and killed them both. She was a tall, strong woman. No doubt she was not only willing to do the deed but capable of carrying it out herself.

Katie countered with the theory that Pierre did it. It made more sense. It was probably the reason he was sent away. Katie waxed romantic as she laid out her ideas.

"Léonie has just had their child, hers and Pierre's. Pierre is ecstatic because he knows the world believes it to be John's so the child is safe. While Léonie is recuperating, John and the nurse plan to run away together. Oh! Oh! I know. John has realized that this child doesn't look at all like him or he knows that Léonie has a lover. Whatever. He can take no more. He rushes to the nurse and begs her to run away with him. She consents. Pierre, who is sneaking to the house to see Léonie and to catch a glimpse of his child, comes upon them as they are preparing to leave. How dare John treat his wife with such disdain! He crushes their skulls and buries them.

"Then he rushes to tell Léonie. She is furious. She has been quite happy with the arrangement and couldn't care less that John is running away. If news of John's elopement gets around it would have tarnished her only slightly. If John and his lover are found murdered, people will assume she did it because they don't know anything about Pierre. Then the de Bienville name is destroyed. She has Pierre bury them and then she banishes him forever from Manawassa. Meanwhile, tormented by the sight of that spot where the lovers are buried, Léonie raises a fountain to cover it out of her sight. They see each other in New Orleans occasionally. Then in 1912 or 13 Léonie decides she never wants to see him again. "

Katie fell back into her chair apparently exhausted from her task while Gena stared at her with consternation. "Can't you just picture it, Gena?"

"Not really. It sounds more like the plot of a Russian novel than real life. Next you'll be telling me that Pierre, inspired by Anna Karenina, committed suicide by throwing himself under a train."

"Now *that* would not make sense. Probably he threw himself off his ship while at sea in 1913. Maybe Léonie had him killed."

Gena glared at her friend and resumed her own train of thought. "I don't think Pierre would risk coming to the house. Even if he did and saw John and the nurse escaping, I don't think he would have killed them. I think he would have been thrilled. I suspect that while Léonie was convalescing from childbirth, John and the nurse were having relations, maybe even long before. Léonie may have walked in on them, smashed their heads in and then sent word to Pierre to bury them."

"Then why send him away?"

"Because he knew what had happened. Léonie was practical, if nothing else, and I assume she felt it was enough to correspond with him and see him occasionally."

"It might have been practical, but not very romantic. I'm sorry that we keep going back to implicating your great-grandmother, but if it happened the way you said, it was a crime of passion, not premeditated. You've hinted that Léonie was not a very nice person. Maybe we've gotten her all wrong. She was in an arranged marriage. Her husband probably didn't want it any more than she did. He may, for all we know, have been a serial philanderer and have driven her into her former lover's arms. Having a husband that only pretends to love you, but really doesn't, can alter your personality in a very negative way..." There was a slight tone of regret in this last statement but it was quickly amended, "...only if you let it."

Gena nodded at her friend. She herself had made discoveries about behaviors and situations where love could be painful. She had only lately realized that in any relationship there were two people at fault, though one might bear the greater responsibility. In Katie's case it was her husband; in Gena's, it was she herself. Gena forgot all about Léonie and Pierre and quietly poured out her heart to Katie about Kayton. She told her about from the beginning to their latest encounter. She was sorry she had been so cold and forbidding. He was the same warm and generous Kayton. Her recent epiphany about herself compelled her to go to him and ask forgiveness. Her hope was that he would forgive her; she had no expectations beyond that. Humility was a new thing for Gena, but it gave her peace. Each woman had her own reasons for the quiet moments that followed.

"I believe we've accounted for all the people in my dream, even the man in the robes. It must be Pierre. Calla Lily is the girl in white, my guide which is why she is the one who appears to me outside of the dreams. The man and woman are John and the nurse. I think LeMoyne has been my savior. I've come to regret so many of my selfish actions. Not only did I hurt myself, but the one I loved. Perhaps, in a way, this self-realization will help atone for Léonie's sin. I wouldn't want anyone to pass judgment on me without knowing everything. It's unfair that I pass judgement on her. I think I have closure now. My great-grandmother Léonie de Bienville murdered her husband and his lover. It was a crime of passion. She paid for it by leading a cold and barren life. I can only hope that LeMoyne is at peace and my dreams will stop."

The two sat in silence again. Katie dispelled the solemnity of the occasion with her characteristic humor.

"I think it's over. Now you can quote Professor Henry Higgins, "By George, I really did it!"" Katie gave a smile to her friend and patted her back. Gena only replied glumly.

"I think Dr. Frankenstein probably said the same thing."

***

CHAPTER XI
THE KEY

That night Gena found she couldn't sleep. Whatever peace she felt earlier had evaporated. Whether it was the excitement of having solved the mystery or the annoyance of having an archaeological dig in her back yard, she wandered around the house reading a book in her living room, looking over some papers in her office, browsing a magazine in the small parlor. Finally she decided to take something to help her sleep and went up to her room.. She flicked on the chandelier, but before she reached the bathroom it went out.

She felt around the edge of the bed and reached the switch on her lamp, but nothing happened. "Damn storms." But there was no storm, not even the slightest breeze. It was pitch black. She ran her hand down the front of the nightstand and opened the drawer to retrieve the flashlight she kept there. She clicked it on expecting to see the wall in front of her illuminated, but nothing happened. Before a curse could escape her lips, the room was flooded with light. It wasn't a warm, friendly yellow that ought to have come from the beam of her flashlight or the lamp or the chandelier above. It was bluish green, bright as day, and came like a telescopic ray from behind her so that it cast distinct shadows on the wall she faced. Her heart leapt into her throat when she saw not one, but two shadowy outlines, her own and a much smaller one. She was shaking now and clutched the flashlight as if it could protect her from the unwanted guest behind her. Slowly she turned to face the origin of the second shadow. She knew who it would be.

Standing next to the fireplace was the little girl swathed all in white with skin as pale as milk. The light came directly from her so that everything next to and behind her was black. She spoke in French.

"Do not be alarmed. I have come to help. You must keep looking for the key. You have some things right, but so much else wrong. There is not much time. If you fail I cannot say what will happen."

Gena found her voice. "Are you threatening me?"

"No. No. But you have not found the key. You must find the key. The rock is the key. There is no other. The rock is the key." Her eyes danced with a green fire that struck to the core of Gena's soul.

With that the room went black. Then the lights flickered and electricity was restored. Her flashlight came on of its own accord. Gena sat on the edge of her bed, terribly frightened. She fell on her bed and began to sob a desperate prayer, "God help me. God help me. Somebody help me find the key." Exhausted she fell asleep at last.

***

The next morning Gena wasted no time in calling Katie and relating her experience from the night before.

"It wasn't a dream. It was like the other times. This spirit girl is becoming real and coming to me face to face. I'm afraid something is going to happen to me."

Katie recalled her own face to face meeting with one of her spirits. It had immediately preceded her near drowning in Lake Manawassa. Now Katie was frightened, too, but she didn't want to convey that fear to Gena.

"I don't think the spirit means you harm. I don't know what the hurry is but let's calm down, take a stroll around the lake and have an early lunch. *Blacksmiths* or *Hall's*?"

They followed Gena's suggestion of *Blacksmiths* and added a trip to Sugar Beach. By afternoon's end Gena was far more relaxed.

"I do feel better. Thanks, Katie. I have some ideas about locating the key. Did you know there is a small display case in the Library that has keys in it? They're from various buildings in town. I'm wondering if we could attack the Library tomorrow, preferably avoiding the Owl."

"No one can avoid the Owl. She's omnipresent, at least at the Library. I think that's a good idea though. We need some sort of new path to follow."

Fate helped them along their journey and it did not lead to the Owl.

***

"Mr. Crippett's back from Pensacola. He'll be relieving you of the pirate treasure." Steve tossed his hat on the chair next to him. He and Katie were having brunch as they often did before the frenzied activity of late. His early morning chores were done and the mid-morning sun was not yet too hot to enjoy the back garden of the Belle.

"Margiddy wasn't a pirate, but how in the world did he get all that loot?" She poured out his coffee.

"I have no idea. He may have just been saving it for a rainy day.

You saw how he lived…not exactly a New York penthouse. I don't think the old fellow had much need for money. Crippett says Margiddy will be coming home in a week or so."

"The question is: what home? Seriously, Steve, he can't go back to *The High and Dry.*"

"No, sadly, he can't. Crippett's had a hell of a time convincing him of that, but the old sailor finally caved in. Crippett says he's pretty frail and might not last much longer."

"I can't see Margiddy in a nursing home. That would be awful for him."

"That's why he's going to live at Stokely."

"What? Carroll will love that." Katie almost spilled her coffee all over herself.

"Carroll won't be responsible. He'll have a nurse to tend to him. Though I think Carroll will consider that an invasion, too."

"They'll have to turn one of those grand bedrooms into an imitation tugboat…complete with Tootsie."

"Carroll would really love that."

They ate and laughed for an hour when their tête-à-tête was interrupted by a pale Gena clutching a piece of paper in her hand.

"What now?" Katie noticed the look of concern on her neighbor's face.

Gena collapsed in a chair and handed Katie the letter. After reading it she passed it to Steve.

"What can it mean? Where in the world did a third skeleton come from?" Gena looked more nerve wracked than Katie had seen her yet, if that was possible.

"And an infant to boot-ie. Get it? A baby bootie." Steve glibly quipped. His humor was neither appropriate, nor appreciated at the moment. Katie glared at him. He got its meaning, cleared the table and left.

"I feel like we're back at the beginning. We now have two dead adults and a baby. Gena shook her head. "But who are they all?"

Katie screwed her face up. "I don't think we need to alter our theory much. The woman is the nurse. There's no one else it can be. Same for the man. It has to be John Martin. As for the baby. I think there's only one possibility. It's John Martin's and the nurse's."

"But how in the world did it get there?"

"We need to look at that those letters again – all of them."

Gena went to LeMoyne and retrieved the bundle. The women poured over them throughout the morning and discussed the facts. Once again they came to different conclusions. They agreed that the man and woman were John and the nurse, but their agreement ended there. Gena went back to the former theory that Léonie had done what her father asked. She had gotten rid of the child and its mother, who happened to be the nurse. She asked Pierre to bury the infant and its mother when John had stumbled upon the burial and had to be silenced. Then Pierre buried them. No one would have known about the infant. Instead, the staff must have assumed that John and the nurse ran off together. That's how the rumor started.

Katie countered that there was nothing more than a suggestion that Léonie ever did anything about her brother's illegitimate child. "Besides, how did the nurse know Jean Langlais? You have to know someone, in the biblical sense, to get pregnant with their child. And if the mother was from New Orleans it would be dumb for Léonie to bring the baby to Manawassa to kill it. I am about to switch on you again and absolve your great-grandmother Léonie of heinous crimes. This is what I think happened."

Katie firmly believed that Pierre was the father of Gena's Grand-mère Jacqueline. She reasoned this from the content of the letters and Pierre's longstanding relationship with Léonie. Even Gena acknowledged that three of Léonie's children were weak and died young, but Jacqueline was strong and died an old woman. This had to mean that she had a different father. She believed that Pierre killed John and the nurse because they knew he was the real father of Léonie's child. The nurse who must have been having relations with John was far along in a pregnancy of her own. The archaeologist said one reason they hadn't detected the remains of the infant earlier was because they were of an extremely young infant.

"So you see Gena, you can't automatically assume such harsh things about your great-grandmother. I know that somehow more evidence will come to light. We don't have to solve this today. We have time. Don't you remember what the little girl said: "The rock is the key?" We haven't found the key or the rock yet."

"Yes we have. That's why I'm worried that I've failed.

"I don't understand."

"Katie, don't you see? The fountain was all paved around in stone. We have three skeletons and they were buried under a *rock*. We have the rock and the key," She gave Katie a fierce look, "but we're no closer to a solution."

***

CHAPTER XII
IN THE SHARK'S JAWS

The last twenty-four hours had been awful. The remains of an infant had put her and Katie at odds once again. Even though Gena felt they knew what the rock and the key were, Katie insisted they still investigate the keys in the case at the Library. Gena was impatiently waiting for Katie so they could go together. She plucked the mail from the mailbox and bought it inside. She sorted the trash from the bills and then stopped. An envelope from Bienville Corporate was staring her in the face. She hadn't been expecting anything so she assumed it was an unpleasant missive from Langlais. She took it to the living room and hardened herself against it contents. She would remain calm at all costs. Unfolding the letter she read. As she did her face went from angry red to ghostly pale. She began to shake and all signs of composure fled.

Katie arrived and found her knock unanswered. She came in and hello-ed her neighbor. When there was still no response she headed towards the living room.

"Gena, you'll have your chance to talk to Dr. Landry and ask forgiveness. He's staying a little longer at the Belle. I'm sure it's fate…" Katie rushed to her friend who was prone on the sofa and convulsed with sobbing. "My God! What's wrong?"

Gena seemed oblivious. Katie raised her to a sitting position and noticed a crumpled piece of paper in her hand. She pried it from the clenched fist and read.

September 18, 2007

Geneviève LeMoyne de Bienville
Maison LeMoyne
Manawassa Springs, Florida

Dear Ms. LeMoyne de Bienville,

I write on behalf of the entire Board of Directors of Bienville Enterprises. Regrettably, you are relieved of your majority interest in the corporation. A contingent of shareholders has signed their shares over, giving me the necessary authority to take action against you. The recent medical exam conducted by Dr. John Franklin has confirmed what have been the concerns of the Board members for some time now. As long as your mental instability had not impacted the welfare of the company, Board members were willing to grant you further time for recuperation in Manawassa Springs. After reporting to them my recent and distressing visit to you, they requested a full health exam by Dr. Franklin to which you consented. The report is attached. You will note your signature agreeing to the examination.

The lapses in rationality that preceded your retreat to Manawassa Springs have grown worse according to the report. Dr. Franklin found you to be incoherent on a number of topics unrelated to business. The Board members might not have been forced to this action had your instability stopped there. Recent matters have shown that your current mental health poses a threat to necessary business affairs. A year ago when a proposed Creighton-Howard merger came before the Board you expressed exaggerated concerns, none of which was critical. At the time the Board was somewhat perplexed at your reluctance, assumed that the timing was off and acquiesced to your judgment. When the offer surfaced again recently, under circumstances even more favorable to Bienville, you gave no rational explanation for your vehement opposition.

An emergency meeting of the Board, of which you received ample notice, was convened. Your decision not to attend was an indication that either you are standing in defiance of the Board or you have no concerns for the corporate health of Bienville. Either way the results of the meeting I have stated above. In addition to being made Board chairman I am assigned the temporary position of Chief Executive Officer which I expect to be made permanent in the foreseeable future.

On behalf of the Board and all of the Bienville Family I wish to extend thanks to you for your long service. You retain, of course, a large number of shares in Bienville. However, should you wish to consider the sale of all or some portion of them, feel free to contact me.

Sincerely,

Langlais Bourgogne LeMoyne de Bienville
Chairman of the Board/CEO
Bienville Enterprises

Katie set the letter on the table and in doing so knocked the envelope to the floor. She picked it up and pulled out the medical report.

It was Greek to her, but Dr. Landry could figure it out. A small hand written sticky note was stuck to the report. It was carefully formed in block letters.

Gotcha. Payback for the coke bottle was a long time coming, but worth it. Revenge is a dish best served cold.

***

Steve had missed Katie at the Belle but was told she was over at Gena's. He became concerned as he came up the walk and noticed the front door wide open.

"Katie?"

"In here."

He came around to the living room where Katie was perched on the edge of the sofa stroking Gena's back. Gena was crying. "What the hell is going on?"

"This." She handed the letter to Steve. After he'd looked it over, she gave him the report and the sticky note.

"They can't do this can they?"

"I don't know, Steve," she looked up at him and lowered her voice to a whisper hoping Gena wouldn't overhear. "I'm concerned for her. There really was a man named Franklin who stayed at the Belle. He was a doctor. Gena has been acting a little strange."

"Strange, sure, but not like you when you saw ghosts." Katie blushed and Steve continued. "Gena's about as crazy as I am. It's this Langlais guy…"

"Her cousin."

"He's obviously engineered this to destroy her for some reason."

"Gena." A man's voice rang out from the front door.

"It's a friggin' convention." Katie indicated to Steve to go keep whoever was at the door away from the living room. Instead he returned with Dr. Landry. It only took Kayton a second to get to the sofa and lift Gena into his arms. She buried her face in her hands and continued to sob as he enfolded her.

"Whatever it is, it will be all right, Gena." Kayton rocked her gently back and forth until she stopped crying and leaned her head against his chest.

Steve addressed Katie with a shrug. "Sorry I couldn't perform my assigned task. He said he was an old friend and he needed to see Gena. I said she wasn't well and he said he was a doctor…"

Gena and Kayton sat down on the couch. She had calmed down considerably. He kept a strong arm around her and asked Steve and Katie for an explanation.

Katie first introduced Steve and then let him have the honor of explaining. When he had finished Kayton burst out in anger.

"Langlais de Bienville is one of the slimiest creatures on the face of the earth. He's always been a conniving liar. Whatever suits him is truth, whatever benefits him is his goal, and whatever he wants is his god. Everyone is expendable."

"You know him well, I gather." Katie asked.

"I've known him since I was a child in New Orleans. He's always been a shady character. When his grandmother was alive she barely managed to keep him out of prison. Since she died I guess he's had no watchdog. He's certainly been after Gena's power in Bienville for a long time. He's wheedled or blackmailed his way into the graces of some powerful men."

"Kayton," Gena looked with swollen red eyes at her former lover, "how do you know all this?"

"Do you remember my mentor, Dr. DuPont who left New Orleans for a practice in New York a little before we moved there?"

"A slight smile crossed Gena's face. "The handsome one with the green eyes? I do."

"Pierre's still in New York and," Dr. Landry cleared his throat, "he has connections. I would ask him from time to time how you were doing."

Nothing could have made Gena happier than hearing those words although she was too shy to express her feelings.

"Here's the medical report." Steve handed it to Dr. Landry.

"Franklin. You didn't tell me the doctor's name."

"You know about him, too?"

"He's a suitable comrade for Langlais. He's one of the biggest supplier of legal drugs, and illegal, to the wealthy classes in the City. Like your cousin, he's slippery. But this time I think we've got him."

"How?" Three voices chimed together.

"Leave it to me. DuPont will come in very handy. Look, I need to get to New York as fast as I can. Give me all the papers here." They were put into his hands. He stuffed them into the envelope and turned to Gena. Taking her hands in his he said in a most matter of fact manner:

"I came here today to apologize for being so stand-offish at lunch the other day. The fact is I never stopped loving you. It isn't that I didn't love Marla. I did; she was my wife, my friend and companion. I accepted that you had your own life to lead and so I found happiness with her. I probably thought of you more times than I should have. She knew about you, but she also knew that I loved her and I never would have done anything to hurt her or Joe. She was an amazing woman. I know I told you I came here to see Joe, but I really came to see you. I'll make this right. I promise. I don't expect you to feel the same way about me as I do about you. We're different people now, but I can and I will help you."

He stood and left without another word. Katie and Steve felt rather awkward at his speech even though he seemed perfectly comfortable making it in front of them. Throughout his declaration Gena sat with her head down looking at her hands which were entwined with Kayton's. After he left she lifted her head. Steve and Katie knew instantly from the look on her face that Kayton was wrong. Gena felt very much the same way as the good doctor.

***

Steve had to go, but Katie did not want to leave Gena alone. A timid knock came at the front door. She excused herself and told Gena she would get rid of whoever it was. She opened the door and there stood Reese with her arms straight at her side and a blank expression on her face.

"Hi, Reese. I'm sorry, but Gena isn't feeling well today."

The little girl looked up at Katie, stared right through her and said in a very deadpan manner, "I know. You need to call someone to help." She turned and left. Katie was covered with goose bumps. Then a thought struck her. She pulled out her cell and called Reese's mom, Rose Helper, who was a part-time nurse.

"Rose, you're not on duty or anything are you? Good. Gena has had a very upsetting day. I need to go to the Belle. Is there any way you can stay for a few hours with her? You can? Bless you. We're at Azalea Cottage in the living room right now, so just come on in the front door."

***

CHAPTER XIII
THE PACE QUICKENS

The Seaman's Journal

Rose agreed to stay with Gena, even overnight if necessary. Rose thought it best that Gena should try to rest and even sleep if possible. She suggested that Katie go back to the Belle for now. This left Katie free to catch up on her paperwork. She hoped it would distract her from ghosts and skeletons and slimy cousins. It didn't work out as she planned. Her mind kept going back to recent events.

She checked in on Gena mid-afternoon. Rose went home to see how Casey and Reese were doing and to get dinner ready for later. Meanwhile Gena and Katie had a light snack and tried to converse as normally as possible. Katie assured the distraught woman over and over that Kayton would make things right. Casey returned after a couple of hours and Katie went back to Belle Magnolia. It was a relief when Steve came over in the evening. He found her in her little office.

"I come bearing gifts." He handed Katie the old seaman's journal.

"What's this?"

"It's the journal…from the chest."

"What are you doing with it? When did you open the chest? I thought we locked it up in the fire safe?"

"Is this what married life is going to be like? I tell you things and you don't pay attention."

Katie punched his arm and put on a sulky face. How many times had she used the same line on him?

"I told you a couple of days ago that when I got the will for Mr. Crippett, I found the old journal. Doesn't ring a bell? It was in French so I gave it to Selena to translate and asked if she could get it done as soon as possible."

"In French. Oh, my God!"

"Is that important? I was pretty sure it couldn't be Margiddy's. Turns out it belonged to some man named Cephas."

Katie's head was spinning. She wasn't sure why she thought so, but she believed this journal was important for the mystery. "I can't read French. When will the translation be ready?"

"Oh, ye of little faith." Steve pulled a thumb drive from his pocket. "Selena was glad for a chance to practice her French. She says she deserves a medal for translating this at all, especially this quickly. The handwriting was awful and faded. The author was educated in basic French, which was also colloquial, Selena said. She is very proud of having turned it into very eloquent English."

Katie was not really listening. She plugged the thumb drive into the USB port of her computer and brought up the document. She threw herself into the journal.

"Thank you, Steve. Give my thanks to Selena, Steve. Tell her she's a peach, Steve. I love you, Steve. You will make a wonderful husband, Steve, you're the greatest…" Steve rambled on trying to get a response from Katie, but she was too absorbed. "Okay, you're busy. I understand. I'm going over to *Johnnie's Bar* to find a blond to hook up with. See you tomorrow."

"Make sure she's nice, but not possessive. Our wedding's not too far away." Katie replied glibly without turning her face from the computer monitor.

Steve grinned and distracted her long enough to give her a warm kiss. "Forget the blond. No one can compete with you.'

But Katie was once again immersed in the seaman's journal.

***

Selena had tried to format the translation as though it were the journal itself. This meant the first page had what appeared on the fly leaf of the volume, one word: CEPHAS. Katie barely took note as she plunged into her reading. The journal began on the next page as follows:

March 1907

> *I am cast away at sea and this is my only form of amusement in the few spare moments I have to myself. Life here is lonely and hard. I was used to a hard life as the son of a slave. My mother died giving me birth. She lives with the angels. My father died in the war of deliverance for slaves. He was a good man and now lives above with my mother. Slavery is ended, but a harsh life for the Negro did not. My own salvation came from a family in New Orleans. M. de Bienville took me in and restored me. I found pleasure in his service and gave my life in devotion to him and to his daughter. I tell my story.*

Katie looked up from the computer and complete understanding infused her face. Cephas. The Catholic in her told her that the name was from the Bible and it meant "Peter." Not only that, but Pierre was the French for "Peter" and they all meant one thing: rock. The rock is the key. Katie was about to read firsthand what was needed to solve the mystery of LeMoyne. She had the key in this journal and tomorrow she would lay all Gena's fears about LeMoyne to rest. If only Kayton could do the same with the debacle of Langlais's plot.

***

Steve called Katie very late that night with news from Kayton Landry. Before he left for New York Landry contacted his mentor Dr. DuPont and explained everything. He faxed the documents and said he was hand delivering the originals. All DuPont said was that there was a breakthrough and Gena was bound to be proven the victim of a conspiracy concocted by her cousin Langlais and Dr. Franklin and some other unsavory Bienville board members. Kayton was unable to relate the details, but apparently the FBI was instrumental in bringing them down. DuPont had already been working with the agency, but had not been at liberty to divulge anything to Kayton until now. The undercover operation which had been going on for some time had come to a head that day at corporate headquarters. The letter and medical report that Kayton brought DuPont was turned over to the Feds and, though not in themselves of critical importance, they provided icing on the cake. Kayton was taking a midnight flight and planned to be in Manawassa by morning. There was more Steve wanted to tell her, information from Mr. Crippett that, along with what Kayton had told him, might be crucial in sorting out the mystery at LeMoyne. He was too tired to pour it all out now.

Katie had a lot to tell Steve as well, but it was clear that both of them were tired. Since he had to rise at five am, she made the decision to spare him until tomorrow. She, too, would be up very early to go over to Azalea Cottage and check on Rose and Gena. The news she had would blow Gena away.

***

CHAPTER XIV
GENA IN THE DARK

When Gena woke up she was on the floor. She didn't know where. Her head ached. She gently touched the right side of her head and felt a large lump. Either she had been blinded when she fell and struck her head, or she was in a place of utter darkness. She opened and closed her eyes a few times hoping to determine whether it was blindness or darkness that shut her off from the world. It proved ineffective. She closed her eyes because for some irrational reason it made her feel safer and less vulnerable.

Gently she raised herself to a sitting position. This movement, easy though it was, made her head throb all the more. She began to feel around the area in which she sat. She was on a wood surface, not carpet. The wood was very roughhewn and splintery. That was all she could feel because wherever she reached around her there was only air. As high as she stretched overhead there was nothing. She decided to stand, but carefully. She put one leg, then the other, underneath her. With her hands above her head to prevent reinjuring her head she maneuvered onto her knees and then to a crouching position. She began to rise very slowly until she was fully upright. As high as she reached she could feel nothing. Her prison was at least high enough to stand comfortably in. She was clueless as to what to do next.

A bizarre collection of thoughts began to race though her mind. "I'm dead. I assumed Hell would be hot and fiery. Maybe this is Purgatory. The child-ghost is punishing me for failing. No, Langlais has kidnapped me and put me in a cellar. Maybe I am still asleep. I must wake up. If I don't I will die. I'm hungry and thirsty, so I can't be dead. "

She clenched her fists and stopped her racing thoughts. Gena knew she had to proceed logically. What was she doing before this happened? Rose gave her a sleep aid and she went to bed. Why was Rose at LeMoyne? That's right, she was upset and Rose and Katie wanted her to rest. She remembered that Katie and Steve and Kayton had been all around her to comfort her. Comfort her for what? The letter. She had been in hysterics because Langlais had driven her out of Bienville. He persuaded others that she was crazy. Maybe she was crazy. Maybe she was trapped in her mind. Maybe she was really in the psych wing of a hospital hallucinating. No! She refused to acknowledge that. She shouted to the darkness, "I am not crazy." The darkness answered.

"No, you are not crazy, Gena" came a soft voice.

Gena whirled around to face the Voice. Her eyes were still shut, but she knew whom she would see when she opened them. The Voice belonged to a child. The Child. Gena knew when she opened her eyes she would be looking into the deep green eyes of a curly headed ten year old girl, pale as the sand at Sugar Beach, dressed all in gauzy white and wearing a blue sash around her waist.

***

CHAPTER XV
VANISHED

"Where is she?" Katie was frantic.

She had come over two hours ago, early in the morning, to see how Gena was doing. She heard Rose in the kitchen and found her there making coffee. Katie greeted her and accepted a cup. The two sat down and the nurse let Katie know how things had been during the night. Katie offered Rose an explanation for Gena's condition, a fuller one than she had given her yesterday. Leaving out the whole ghost aspect, Katie explained the stress caused by the skeletons and now her cousin's letter, had shattered Gena's nerves.

"I'm sorry to hear that. We all like Gena lot, especially Reese. I hope she recovers quickly. She rested very well last night. She took some of her prescription sleep aid. I stayed with her chatting for a while. She grew calmer and in twenty minutes she was drifting off. I stayed until she was solidly asleep. I sat and read until I got tired and then I went to the other guest room. I set my watch for two hour intervals and checked on her throughout the night. Last check was a little over two hours ago and she was still resting quietly. I couldn't get back to sleep so I came down to get some coffee."

Rose wanted to get back home by seven thirty to help get Reese off to school so Katie ran upstairs to check on the patient. She tapped on the door, but there was no answer. Gently she pushed the door open and tiptoed in. The bed was made up. Katie assumed that Gena had wakened and was in the bathroom. The door was cracked so she called to her, but got no reply. A horrible thought rose up in her mind. What if something had happened to Gena? What if Gena had committed suicide? She hesitated to push the door open fearing that her friend would be dead on the floor. She worked up her courage, bit her lip and flung it open. Nothing.

In less than a minute she had bounded back down the stairs.

"Where is she?"

"What do you mean, "where is she?" Rose asked incredulously. She's in her room."

"No, she isn't. The bed is made, but no one is in the room or the bathroom."

"Are you sure?" Rose's look of concern quickly shifted. "You checked her regular bedroom, I assume. I apologize. I thought it would be better for her to sleep in one of the rooms across the hall. There's a Jack and Jill bathroom between the two bedrooms on that side. I told her I wanted to leave the doors open so I could hear her if she needed anything. She agreed."

Katie sighed with relief. "Thank God. I'll try again."

"I'll go with you."

The pair walked up the staircase. Katie repeated her previous procedure, tapping at the correct door, but again got no reply. The two went in and found to their dismay that this room was empty, too. The bed had been slept in, but Gena was not in this room, the bathroom or the adjoining room. They searched the house from top to bottom beginning with the second floor, then on to the third. They even grabbed some flashlights and looked in the old attic nursery. They scoured the first floor last. No bathroom, no closet, no niche was left unexamined. Their efforts ended on the sun porch.

"Where is she?" Katie looked around the sun porch. She shivered as her eyes rested on the huge painted wooden door. The tiger which crouched in the middle of it stared back at Katie, its burning green eyes mocking her as if only he knew the secret of Gena's disappearance.

***

CHAPTER XVI
THE MEMORY ROOM

An eerie light suffused the room. Gena now realized that there was a group of people. Four were standing and one was seated. The pale little girl with the blue sash stood in front, partially obscuring the seated figure. To the child's far right stood a woman wearing a blue dress with a white pinafore. Her hair, which was abundant and chestnut colored, would have been magnificent had it not been partially hidden by a white cap. She was quite attractive and you could tell from her face that she was not only kind, but capable. On her left stood a man in an old fashioned suit with a stiff collar. His hair, which was brown, was thinning on top and a droopy mustache veiled his upper lip. In contrast to the nurse he looked rather incompetent. At the opposite end on the child's left was a tall, powerfully built swarthy man with a pierced ear. He was magnetically handsome. He stood to the left and slightly behind the seated figure.

"Are you frightened? Please do not be." The little girl had the sweetest voice Gena had ever heard.

"Where am I?" Gena asked.

"You are in the Memory Room."

"What? Where is that?"

"It will come out in good time. I am Liliane Aimée Martin." She curtsied.

"Calla Lily."

"Yes. That is correct. All, but one, called me by that name. You, Gena, have summoned us here."

"I? I have summoned you?"

"Yes. I suppose it has been mutual, for we have been calling you for many, many years." Her green eyes grew wide.

"Since I was ten years old. I know that now."

"Let me introduce you."

Without turning she indicated with her right hand.

"This is Nurse Emily Sattherwhite. She cared for me until the end. She loved me very much. No one could have wished for a kinder or gentler nurse.

Emily inclined her head slightly and smiled a smile that lit her entire face. She was more than attractive, she was quite beautiful in a warm and comforting way.

"With her is my father, John Martin. He loved me, too. It was he, with Nurse Emily, who built a Kipling jungle for me and gave me my protector."

"Shere Khan, the tiger in the door."

"Yes."

The man bowed to Gena. She recognized him from the old photos. She could see that although he was weak, he was good. Yet in his goodness he was unable to withstand forces stronger than he. If he was a man that suffered, he did so due to his own inability to take action.

The little girl swept her left hand to the tall man behind her.

"This is Cephas. You may also know him as Pierre. He was a faithful servant to my mother. And last, my mother, Léonie Mathilde LeMoyne de Bienville."

She stepped aside to reveal the person seated. Gena gasped. A stately woman with luscious black hair piled atop her head sat bolt upright. Her countenance was unruffled, but not serene. It was imperceptibly haunted by something that Gena could not name. The general aspect of the lady was imposing enough, but then Gena saw her eyes. They were large burning green eyes; depths of fire that revealed unspoken sorrow. Gena was overwhelmed with sadness and felt like crying. Before she could inquire of her child-guide the meaning of all this Gena saw something which alarmed her horribly: the grand lady who sat, composed and austere, held a dead infant in her lap.

***

Steve got what could only be described as an incoherent call from Katie. Gena was missing. He dropped everything and rushed over to LeMoyne. He found Rose and Katie in the living room. She quickly caught him up on the events of the morning. Basically, Gena had vanished.

"It's my fault. She's probably walked into the Lake…only no one was there to save her." Katie burst into tears.

Steve put his arms around her. The memory of her own near death in the waters of Lake Manawassa were still with her. It hadn't been Steve who had saved her exactly, but she always felt that it was. Rose sat very quietly. She recalled the incident since she had been at the ER the night Katie was brought in. Her offer to bring them coffee and something to eat was accepted and she retreated to the kitchen in order to let the pair discuss the situation in private.

"Look, you don't know that she walked into the Lake."

"Where else could she be? We have to do something. Let's call the police."

Katie, unless she's been missing twenty four hours, they won't do anything."

Katie sniffed loudly and Steve pulled out a bandana for her to blow her nose. "Let me ask you this. When you arrived was the front door closed and locked?"

"Yes. I had to use the key I kept yesterday to unlock it."

"And when you and Rose checked the house were all the other doors and windows closed and locked?"

"They were."

"Her car is still here and her purse?"

"Yes. Steve. That's what's so weird. She can't have just vanished inside the house…unless the house has secret rooms in it."

"Did you ever hear her say there were?"

"She may not have known. Steve, I'm desperate, please, we have to do something."

"Let me make some calls. I'll get a bunch of people out looking for her in the area… people I can trust to keep it quiet."

"Thanks." She gave him a hug, happy that he always had a calming effect on her. A yawn replaced her tears. "I spent all last night reading the journal. It's the key to the mystery here at Azalea Cottage, I'm sure."

Steve made his calls. Rose entered with the coffee and some breakfast food. She asked if it were all right to head home. Sam had stayed a little late to get Reese off to school and now needed to go to work. Katie apologized for keeping her and she departed.

"Done." Steve pocketed his cellphone. "Some folks will be scouring the area. Let's eat then search the house together. Two heads are better than one, especially when one is so sleepy."

They ate fast and began a methodical search. Beginning with the first floor, they felt along stretches of walls, tapping here and there, but had nothing to show for their efforts. Gena's bedroom was next, then the rest of the second floor. That also proved futile. By this time Katie was discouraged and upset again. She trusted Steve so she controlled her urge to sit down and cry.

They went up to the third floor for the final attempt. The entire back of the third floor was an attic room which spanned the width of the house so that when you came to the landing, its door was straight ahead. There was a small bedroom to your right and one to your left. Neither had been used, Gena had once told Katie, since she and Langlais were children visiting LeMoyne. Both were sparsely furnished and would be easy to search. Steve started for the bedroom to the right, When Katie grabbed his arm.

"Did you hear that?"

"I didn't hear anything."

"Listen. I hear a voice. It's coming from ahead of us."

Steve strained his ears. The attic door lay in front of them. He walked to the door, Katie following cautiously behind. She had conjured up a vision from *Jane Eyre*: Mr. Rochester's crazy and murderous wife locked in the attic of *Thornfield Hall*. What if Gena had gone totally crazy? What if she always had been crazy? What if all this had been her imagination and she was in there wild-eyed, drooling and holding a knife?

Steve opened the door. It was pitch black.

"Gena. Are you in here?" No reply.

"Gena, it's Katie; we're here to help." Her voice echoed off the bare walls. "Dammit, Steve, I can't see anything."

As the words left her mouth Steve switched on the miniature flashlight he kept clipped to his belt. The beam was small and tight and offered a very small viewing range. He waved it around the room. It was empty. As hard as they tried to see a secret door or opening, they saw nothing. Then the voice came. It was faint, but it clearly said:

"I'm in here."

A light tapping began. Steve and Katie followed the noise to their left, but only saw a wall with no indication of a secret door.

"Gena, Gena. We're here, but we can't see a door. How do we get to you?"

"I don't know." Gena sounded tired.

"Katie, the entrance must be from the bedroom."

Steve and Katie rushed to the bedroom that abutted that side of the attic. Katie switched on the light and looked around the room. It was empty, but in front of her and to the right she could hear the tapping and voice, softer now than in the attic. Both she and Steve approached the wall ahead of them. It had a shallow fireplace bordered on either side by bookshelves sparsely populated with children's book. Katie began tapping and Steve looked for some sort of latch.

"We can hear that it's hollow, Gena, but we can't figure out how to get in. Where is the secret panel or whatever?" Then Katie spied it and her heart gave a leap. "The rock is the key." Perched above her head on a shelf was a geode. Its outer layer was a shiny malachite green. It was cut in half to expose a hollow black hole in the middle of whitish gray crystals. It looked eerily like a large green eye staring at you. Steve had seen it at the same time and, being the taller of the two, easily reached up and pulled. A loud click indicated that the bookcase had been freed from its frame. They lost no time in entering the secret room. Steve switched his light on and directed it to the wall on their right. Seeing a light switch in the wall he clicked it on. Now they could see they were in a very narrow passage or hallway. It turned to the right just ahead of them. They rounded the corner and stopped in amazement.

Gena sat with her back against a wall so that they were all facing the same direction. Ahead of them was a miniscule and simply furnished room. There was a single bed with a table next to it. On it stood an old fashioned lantern. There was a desk chair, but no desk. A small circular rug filled the space of the floor. Gena spoke like someone in a dream.

"This was her Memory Room, Léonie's Memory Room. In his letter I thought Pierre meant her heart, but he meant this secret room where the desk once stood. This was where my great-grandmother would write the man she loved, the man she had to send away. This is where his letters, their secrets were kept and now are revealed."

She turned to Katie and Steve and smiled. Then she collapsed in a faint.

***

"Is there anyone here?" Dr. Kayton Landry's voice boomed throughout LeMoyne. He was worried. When he arrived at De Luna Regional it was four in the morning. He had rented a car and driven to a motel fairly close to Manawassa. He managed a couple hours of sleep. When he got up he saw his phone had a message. It was from Steve. Gena was missing. He had people out looking for her. Whenever he

249

arrived he should come to LeMoyne.

Kayton had lost no time. He didn't even bother to shave and change. So when a bleary eyed Katie rushed down the stairs at LeMoyne she met a tousled, unshaven Dr. Kayton Landry. Quick as a wink she explained that Gena was okay, but Steve needed help to get her downstairs and to the hospital. Kayton disappeared up the staircase and Katie called the ambulance with Steve's cell.

The doctor rode with the EMT team to the hospital. Steve wouldn't let Katie go with them, but made her go back to Belle Magnolia. He came with her.

"Look, Kayton says she's fine. She didn't walk into the Lake and almost die. She just got lost in her house and was hungry and a little dehydrated. She'll be fine. Let's go sit in the garden, relax and you can tell me the story of the journal. It seems the spirits had two sleuths solving the crime, with two different keys.

***

CHAPTER XVII
CONCLUSIONS

As they drank their iced tea and lounged in the garden Katie related her discovery.

"You're not going to believe this, but the journal told me everything. It belonged to a man named Cephas. He was the son of a slave who was killed in the Civil war. Apparently life was tough for him until, and you won't believe this either, he entered the service of Georges Henri LeMoyne de Bienville — Léonie's father.

"She was only fifteen when he came to work there and he was almost thirty. He fell madly in love with Léonie and she with him, but they never consummated their relationship."

"Consummated. You mean they never had sex?"

"Consummated sounds more polite. First, she was too young, then she was forced to marry John. Anyway, I'm getting ahead of myself. Léonie was a great beauty and the staff at Maison Bienville began to gossip that she had a lover. It reached her father's ears. She didn't want him to find out that it was Cephas so she told him it was some blackguard named Marcel Dubois."

"Blackguard? Your word or his?"

Katie blushed. "I think Selena translated the French as "scoundrel," but you know me I have a flair for the romantic. "

"Really, I hadn't noticed."

"Now, hush. Let me finish. Dubois was a well-known lowlife in New Orleans, famous for wine, women and song. Only it wasn't song, it was gambling. This all happened about the time John Martin came to New Orleans for a business deal. On previous trips he had been with his father who died."

"He went on business trips with his dead father? Interesting."

"Steve, please shut up. Next thing you know Léonie has been given in marriage, as they say, to John Martin. She wasn't even eighteen years old. But here's the irony. They go off on a European honeymoon, something everybody did back then and…"

"Is that a hint?"

"No. A honeymoon in the Caribbean is just fine with me. Do I have to tape your mouth closed?"

Steve leaned over and kissed her. "There's a better way to keep me quiet."

"Where was I? Oh. So, John builds LeMoyne and takes Léonie there when they return. Now here's the irony part. Léonie's father sent some of his staff to work at LeMoyne to make sure Léonie doesn't have intrigues with her supposed lover…"

"Intrigues, lovers, you say. This is like listening to one of your Jane Austen movies."

A stony glare silenced him. "One of the staff was…"

"Let me guess. Cephas."

"You got it. You'd think Léonie and Cephas would get hot and heavy because, from what the journal says, John is a spineless wimp."

"Sounds reasonable."

"But that's not the way they did it back then."

"Who says?"

Ignoring him Katie rushed on. "He became her protector and confidant. She had a maid named Marthe DuPont, too, but it's Cephas she relied on. Marthe does become very important. I'll save that for later. Now I'm getting to the good part. Before Calla died Léonie went nuts. John had her carted her off to some mental hospital in New Orleans. Cephas went, too, and stayed at the family home in New Orleans while she recovered. I'm sure if they had let him stay with her in the asylum he would have. He was completely devoted to her.

"He was also devoted to her children, even if John was their father. He writes about her children, Henri, Aurélie and Calla Lily with affection. Gena has a grim picture of how Léonie felt about her own children, but Cephas says she loved them even if it was a stern kind of love. He says she showed her grief only to him. Cephas really had a tender heart. He writes a very pathetic passage about Calla's death, but from what I can tell there was nothing unusual about it, even though Margiddy said there was.

"The night Calla died the idiot maid who was supposed to watch her snuck out. While she was gone the poor little girl must have become delirious. She got out of bed and fell down the steps. Oh, I forgot. She was living on the sun porch at that time. Her father and the nurse, whose name is Emily Sattherwhite, took her to the porch to stay a month or two before she died. They decorated it like a jungle in India. The child loved

India. And that is why the porch has that big wooden door with the tiger and all the animals. Léonie refused to show her emotions to the household, but, like I said, to Cephas she was quite sorrowful. He carried the little girl up to her room and laid her out on her bed so everyone could come to say goodbye.

"All this time Léonie is pregnant with Gena's grandmother. And yes, the father is John, her husband."

"Because Léonie and Cephas haven't consummated. That was the way they…"

Katie pursed her lips and raised an eyebrow. Steve clammed up.

"She goes to have the baby in New Orleans. She takes Marthe, Cephas and Nurse Emily. After a month or two they return to Manawassa Springs. There has been a winter storm that knocked down a huge old oak in the back yard of the property. It was completely uprooted and left a hole in the ground. One night Cephas is looking out the window and near this oak he sees John Martin and Nurse Emily. John is strangling her. Cephas runs out to help. He breaks them apart, but the Nurse falls, already dead. Cephas now sees something on the ground. It's a baby wrapped in a blanket, also dead. The baby, not the blanket. Cephas suspects that Emily has murdered Léonie's baby so she and John can run off together. He assumes that John sees the murder and kills her. Cephas thinks that John may not have loved Léonie, but he loved their children. Cephas thinks John didn't know that Emily planned to kill Léonie's baby before they ran off. That is why he was strangling Emily. So Cephas grabs John to take him to Léonie, but John fights back. When John breaks away, he falls and hits his head on the downed oak and…"

"…is dead. The one time he chose to grow a pair and fight back. Not very good timing."

Katie leveled another one of her icy stares at Steve.

"Cephas is very remorseful since he didn't mean to harm John. He rushes to tell Léonie. So that is how three skeletons came to be under the fountain. Léonie banishes Cephas who goes to New Orleans and then to sea. Marthe becomes the baby's new nurse…."

"Wait a minute. Wait a minute." Steve raised his hand. "I have an essential question. If the baby is dead and buried, what baby is Marthe the nurse to?"

"That's right. I forgot some details."

"Important ones, I'd say."

"When Cephas goes to tell Léonie what he's done he hears a baby crying in the nursery and realizes that Léonie's baby is *not* dead. Léonie tells him that the dead child is John's and Nurse Emily's. She has known for months that Emily was pregnant by John."

"I guess they were busy consummating while Léonie was away at the looney bin."

"I give up. I can't turn you off." She scowled at Steve.

"Running commentary is my forte."

"More like ruining commentary. Now may I return to my story? Then Cephas realizes that John must have murdered the baby and Emily to get rid of evidence of his indiscretion, so he doesn't feel quite so bad that John is dead. He sees it as Providential. Léonie tells Cephas to bury all three of them in the hole. Later she erects the fountain over their grave."

"Problem solved." Steve nodded thoughtfully.

"Not exactly. The journal is sketchy after his banishment in 1907, but we have the letters he wrote Léonie. They didn't see each other much those five years. When they did meet they didn't…"

"…consummate?"

"Correct. Then in 1912 something unbelievable happened."

"I know this one. The unsinkable ship, the *Titanic*, sank. I saw the movie…all nine hours of it. Sherry insisted."

Katie was glad that Steve loved her enough that he could mention his late wife without wondering if Katie would take offense. She was so happy that the two of them were natural together. There was nothing forced because one was always keeping secrets from the other. She thought of her marriage to Dave which had been one long secret on his part. She thought of Léonie and John. Secrets killed love and marriages as slowly and as surely as a virulent cancer.

"You okay?"

Hoping he wouldn't mistakenly think she was upset about his mentioning Sherry she quipped. "Yes, I was just contemplating the last few hours of Leonardo DiCaprio floating in the water. Very sad, but I didn't mean the sinking of the *Titanic*. Léonie, who was well into her forties in 1912, becomes pregnant by Cephas."

Katie paused to see if Steve's face would reflect the amazement he ought to have felt, but she was disappointed.

"Pregnant. You know; she was going to have a baby."

"I know what pregnant means."

"Aren't you going to ask who this baby was?"

Steve furrowed his brow and screwed up his mouth. Then he said, "Marius Guillaume DuPont."

***

"Gena opened her eyes expecting darkness. What met them was daylight. She wasn't in the Memory Room anymore. She heard voices near the door.

"Doctor Landry, she's awake. I'll get Dr. Haskell."

"Thanks." Kayton crossed to the bed and took the patient's hand. "Good afternoon."

"Kayton. You're here." She began to stir restlessly and tried to sit up. The heart monitor picked up speed.

"Hold on." He gently eased her back onto the pillows. "Let's not give your doctor a cause for alarm."

"You're not my doctor?"

"No, but I'm the man who still loves you and who wants you to know that the twisted plan against you perpetrated by your cousin has been thwarted, by the FBI, no less. His downfall had been in the works for some time, something to do with an illegal merger among other things. You'll be back in charge of Bienville signing memos in no time."

"You may not believe me," she literally beamed at Kayton, "but I'm the Gena who still loves you and doesn't care whether she ever signs another thing for Bienville, unless it's her own severance pay."

He leaned over and kissed her forehead. The heart monitor reflected Kayton's action just as Dr. Haskell entered and addressed the tow of them.

"I can see my patient is doing just fine."

***

"How did you know that? Marius Guillaume DuPont isn't a common name." Katie gave Steve one of her looks. He spoiled her moment of revelation. "Come on. Tell me how you figured it out. I can see that I'm not the only one who has uncovered secrets. I suppose you know what we call him?"

"You may think me dense, but I can put two and two together.

My version is a lot shorter. The journal was in Margiddy's possession. It sure wasn't Margiddy writing in French. So it had to be someone close to him, like a father named Cephas – the name on the flyleaf of the journal. Cephas means Peter or Pierre in French. Pierre was Léonic's lover. Consummation was inevitable. A baby comes along. Men are men. Told you so."

"Good Lord. You know how to take the romance out of things. I remember the day Gena and I visited Margiddy he said his father was a sailor and that all he left Margiddy's mother was "his record." He was pointing to the wall where the sailors' instruments were so I assumed he meant them. But he meant his father's journal in the chest we found under the table by the wall. Pierre records the name of his son as Marius Guillaume DuPont in his journal, but you haven't answered my question. How did you find out Margiddy's real name was Marius Guillaume DuPont?"

"When I was getting the will for Mr. Crippett I saw his real name on it. I just figured that Mar-gi-ddy was his sailor's nickname, a corruption of the French"

"Well, it spoils the rest of my story."

"I doubt that. Besides I don't know where the surname DuPont comes from. I assume it Cephas' or Pierre's last name? You have a way with storytelling so go ahead." Steve played an invisible violin. "Finish the sad ballad of Cephas and Léonie."

"Gladly. Léonie went to New Orleans to have her baby which was fathered by Pierre or Cephas, whichever name you like. She brought Marthe DuPont with her. Remember I told you her maid Marthe would come into the story? After Margiddy's birth, Léonie leaves the baby with Marthe and orders Cephas to marry her and be the father to the child. Here's the catch. Cephas, the son of a slave, has never had a last name so..."

"He takes Marthe's last name which is DuPont."

"Who's telling the story?"

Steve bowed his head in mock shame.

"It all comes together, don't you see?"

Steve made a motion zipping his mouth.

"He no longer goes by Cephas after he is married. He uses the name he has used for all those years in his love letters to Léonie: Pierre.

The rock is the key. Any good Catholic ought to have figured it out immediately. Cephas is the name for Peter in the Gospels. Peter means rock... Pierre is French for Peter." She beamed at Steve.

"Any good Catholic did. I did. I just told you."

"Very funny. So Pierre DuPont, Margiddy's father, and his journal comprised the key to the mystery." Katie leaned back and looked very smug. As she sipped her tea her expression altered. It morphed into puzzlement, then to realization. She grabbed Steve's arm sloshing his tea everywhere.

"Steve, what was the name of Dr. Landry's doctor friend, his mentor who moved to New York...the one who was going to help him expose Langlais."

"I don't think he said."

"Yes, he did. He asked Gena if he remembered him: Dr. DuPont. That was it. I'm sure he called him Pierre. Steve, I have to talk to Dr. Landry. I think his friend figures into this..."

"I think it's a coincidence. Katie, there have to be hundreds of Pierre DuPonts especially from New Orleans. It's not an unusual name. The founder of DuPont Industries was Pierre DuPont." Steve smiled. "You need to sleep."

Katie heaved a sigh and agreed. She had a penchant for getting carried away. She ought to relax and bask in having solved the mystery. Steve escorted her up to her room and gave her a pleasant tucking in. As he was about to shut the door behind him he heard her call out.

"Don't forget to bring Dr. Landry to dinner. He can catch us up on how Gena's doing," She nestled under the covers and said to herself, "and tell us about his friend Dr. DuPont."

***

Steve was hungry so he headed to *Hall's* to eat. By coincidence Steve ran into Kayton there. They decided to lunch together. While looking over the menu they discovered both had received a summons from Mr. Crippett to come to Stokely Plantation at two o'clock. Mr. Crippett wanted to discuss some things with them.

"Do you any idea what he wants us for?" Kayton handed his menu back to the server.

"Not a clue. Speaking of clues." Steve strummed his fingers on the table nervously "Did Gena tell you anything about what happened to her?

"She told me everything about her dreams, her girl ghost and some mystery about LeMoyne, but she left out the part about her recent adventure until she could share it with all of us: you, Katie and me."

"So are you concerned about her mental health? I mean ghosts and dreams that come alive are not everyday occurrences." Even though Steve knew these things to be real he hoped he would be spared having to explain about Katie's experience and his own apparition sighting. It was a man thing. Kayton relieved his fears.

"You forget I spent most of my adult life in the third world. We often had witch doctors, shamans, voodoo practitioners in the villages. Black magic was at our doorstep. Sometimes there was only a brave priest to stand between us and some of these figures; sometimes no one at all. I've seen things you wouldn't believe. It told me there is a spiritual world that holds both good and evil, and that some people devote themselves to the dark side."

"Like Gena's cousin Langlais?"

"Unlike the witch doctors, he used more sophisticated methods, but he could match any black magic practitioner step for step for getting what he wanted."

Encouraged by this Steve told Kayton the story of the Belle. Afterward they walked to Stokely and arrived at the door on the broad front porch.

A knock on the door brought the stiff and proper Carroll to greet them. He escorted them into the small study in the recesses of the house. Mr. Crippett was standing with his back to the door sorting some papers at his desk. He turned, greeted the pair and asked them to sit. Carroll was sent to bring some refreshments while Mr. Crippett proceeded with the meeting.

Refreshments arrived and the three men spent the afternoon in serious conversation. After their business was completed Mr. Crippett offered Steve and Dr. Landry a tour of the house and gardens. Steve, who had already had that privilege, excused himself and left. As he walked to his truck which he had left at the Belle he sank deep into thought. When he came to, he realized that he had overshot his mark. He found himself standing on the sidewalk slightly beyond Belle Magnolia. His eyes swept the circle of the Promenade with houses just visible through the lush shrubbery, houses nearby and those across the Lake reflected in the blue mirror-like water. Then he gazed at Belle Magnolia, the Grand Lady of Manawassa Springs, and at the wrought iron railings of LeMoyne that peeped out just beyond her. He shook his head and spoke to a nearby magnolia.

"Who'd have thought?"

***

Katie felt wonderfully alive that evening. Addie and Zeph, outdid themselves by making a spectacular dinner. Katie tossed her hat into the ring and whipped up Steve's favorite dessert, caramel Bundt cake with fresh raspberries. Steve brought over some specially chosen wine from the *Triple-S Vineyards*. All Dr. Landry had to do was show up and enjoy.

Katie forgot all about Cephas and Léonie and John and the nurse. She just enjoyed the food and company. Dr. Landry said Gena was fine and would be coming home the next day. He also said that his friend Dr. DuPont would be arriving tomorrow. They had never caught up on things since Kayton's return to the states and DuPont hadn't seen Joe Landry since he was a child. Kayton still wanted full details about Langlais's fall from glory, at least as many as the FBI would allow DuPont to divulge. It seemed a good opportunity to do all three. DuPont had been under a lot of strain working with the ongoing FBI investigation and was looking forward to relaxing in Manawassa Springs. Katie had already booked him a room.

Steve offered to clean up and left the table balancing a load of dishes. He headed for the kitchen. Katie and Dr. Landry chatted over coffee.

"I've got a lot to tell Gena and I think she'll be thrilled."

"That's funny." The doctor looked at his hostess. "She said almost exactly the same thing about you."

***

It was a glorious day. If one could have ordered perfect weather this would have been it. It was almost spring-like instead of stifling hot. Steve and Katie had aired out LeMoyne. It was clean and ready to receive its owner home. Since Gena's release from the hospital coincided with late morning they planned to provide a brunch for her. Initially it was to be at LeMoyne, but Katie said that until she had the chance to pour out the truth to Gena, it was better to hold the celebration at the Belle. After all,

Gena had just been through a traumatic experience at LeMoyne. With that and the skeletons and the Tiger Door, she might want a transition period before going back home. No, the Belle was the place. *Hall's the Deck* did the honor of catering an array of tempting delights including, naturally, Southern Bourbon Pecan Pie. Casey had brought it all over earlier that morning.

Everything was set when Katie heard the car drive up. She ran to the front door and down the sidewalk. Gena emerged from the car and Katie threw her arms around her. Steve who had followed her outside chided her enthusiasm.

"Don't break her."

"I'm fine and, having gotten through the last seventy two hours, feel unbreakable." Gena laughed.

"Amen." Katie put her arm around her friend and escorted her to the back patio. The men followed suit. They had hardly begun to enjoy their meal when Katie plunged into relating her discovery to Gena. Gena sat quietly eating her omelet and sipping her coffee. She made no attempt to interrupt or ask questions. As Gena was finishing her pie Katie concluded her summary with the exclamation:

That's the truth, the whole truth and nothing but the truth."

Three pairs of eyes rested on Gena.

She smiled at her friends and said, "Not exactly."

***

CHAPTER XVIII
THE TRUTH, THE WHOLE TRUTH AND NOTHING BUT THE TRUTH

Katie was crushed. "How can that be?"

Gena wiped some crumbs from her lips. Katie then realized how serene Gena was. She looked like all the good queens must have looked in the stories Katie read as a child, or at least how Katie imagined they looked. She was truly regal: imposing and humble, joyful and sedate, wise and artless all at the same time. She was so beautiful.

"Katie you have most of it right, but I need to interject a few amendments. Your story, as it stands, as Cephas understands it, has my grandfather John to be a cold hearted murderer. He wasn't."

"I don't get it. Cephas saw everything. At least he exonerates Léonie. He…"

Steve laid a hand on Katie's arm. "You discovered the truth about Belle Magnolia somewhere between life and death. This is Gena's story to tell."

"Let me tell you what happened while I sojourned in the Memory Room. I don't know how I got there. I just woke up in darkness and there they were. It began to seem so natural, talking and asking questions of these house-spirits."

This hit home with Katie. She herself had met the Belle's spirits and conversed in a similar way. She closed her eyes and, as Gena spoke, pictured herself there watching.

***

Gena addressed the tall dark haired woman. "Who is the child on your lap? Is this the dead baby under the fountain? Is it your brother's child?"

"No." It took only one word for Gena to realize the power and magnetism of this woman. She commanded everything around her, like a lion. Yet, in her lap lay the still, white infant. She could not command death. "It is my child."

"And mine." It was not Cephas, that is, Pierre, who spoke. It was Léonie's husband John.

"You seem puzzled." The little girl cocked her head. "Tell her, Maman."

261

"That wretched night an infant did die – my daughter Jacqueline. Nurse Emily had been caring for the child and discovered her death."

"But Jacqueline, Grand-mère, she..." Gena interrupted.

"... was the daughter of Nurse Emily Sattherwhite and my brother John Langlais. The grandmother you knew was not my daughter. Let me explain the truth. I learned of Emily's pregnancy while Jean Langlais was on his honeymoon and I was in New Orleans recuperating from my breakdown."

"So the baby wasn't John and Emily's child. It was as your father's letter indicated. Jean Langlais had gotten Nurse Sattherwhite pregnant."

"My dear, we ought to begin before that don't you think?" The weak looking man with the flaccid handlebar mustache interrupted.

"Very well. I believe Nurse Emily should tell her story."

In obedience Nurse Emily straightened her cap and patted her uniform into place. She spoke with a firm, but kind, voice.

"Although I grew up in New Orleans I received my nurse's training in New York City. I tended to a man who fell ill there while on business. His name was Georges Henri LeMoyne de Bienville."

Gena nodded, "Léonie's father."

"That is correct. I nursed him back to health. I returned to my native city and M. de Bienville assisted me in pursuing a career at St. Mary's. Eventually I left St Mary's and offered my skills to private employers. In that capacity I was once again summoned by M. de Bienville, this time to nurse his son Jean Langlais. I fell in love with the young man though our ages and stations in life were disparate. I believed he loved me as well. His father suspected our relationship was tending beyond nurse and patient. I was turned out of the house. That spring, before I left, we had conceived a child, though neither of us knew it at the time. It was that very day, by chance, John Martin was in New Orleans and petitioned me to come to Manawassa Springs to nurse his daughter Calla Lily."

"That is I of whom she speaks: Liliane Aimée Martin. She caught up her gauzy white skirt and curtsied.

Léonie took up the story. "Not long after her arrival I found myself to be with child by my husband. My heart had been broken twice by the deaths of Henri and Aurélie. I knew it was to be broken again for

Liliane Aimée would soon die. Dr. Landry had told us this."

"Dr. Landry?" Gena gasped.

"Dr. Jefferson Landry." Calla wore a dreamy expression. "I so wanted to marry him when I got well…and older, of course."

Gena smiled at the Child. "I, too love a Dr. Landry." The knowledge that this forebear of Kayton's had shared the practice of medicine drew her more deeply into the unfolding story.

"Hush, Child." Léonie continued. "Life pursued its dreary course at LeMoyne until one day upon returning from a business trip I ventured onto the summer porch where the Child had been laid. Liliane Aimée was quite still and her breathing shallow. Yet she sat up and pointed to the door. It was…"

"The Tiger Door. I know it well." Gena said.

"I became witless and was conveyed to New Orleans for recuperation. Jean Langlais was still away on his honeymoon. In his absence…"

Nurse Emily broke in. "I had written him a letter informing him of my condition. I was prepared to give the child up. I cared little for myself in the matter. I asked only that the child be taken care of for life."

Léonie resumed. "In his absence I found this letter from Nurse Sattherwhite addressed to my brother. When I read it I was angry with Jean Langlais. When I returned to LeMoyne I confronted Nurse Sattherwhite with my knowledge. John and the staff were not to know. Marthe alone I trusted to keep my secret. I laid out the plan to the nurse, one that I had also revealed to my brother. To accommodate my plan, Jean Langlais and his wife were ordered to remain in Europe several months longer. Both my child and Nurse Sattherwhite's were to arrive within a month of each other. I informed John and the staff that I would give birth at Maison Bienville. This was to done to so that Nurse would travel with me to New Orleans in order to conceal the birth of her child. Her child would then be given into the care of Marthe my maid. Emily would continue as my child's nurse. When all were strong enough we would travel back to Manawassa under these conditions. Marthe would live among her relatives in Blount Swamp and Nurse Emily would visit them there to suckle her child.

"When Langlais and Antoinette arrived home I was to arrange for the infant to go to New Orleans in secret ahead of them, along with

Nurse Sattherwhite, the child's mother. The staff was to be told that my father was dying, as was in fact the case, and that he had requested Nurse Sattherwhite to care for him. Marthe would look after my infant until I could engage a proper nurse. In New Orleans it would be given out Antoinette gave birth in Europe and thus the delay in the pair's return. In this way the child would be raised as Langlais's and Antoinette's son, but the child's mother would always be near. I am not as heartless as my legacy would have it. As you know my scheme went horribly wrong. The others will explain." She looked down at the dead infant with an impassive face.

"I was both grieved and overjoyed by the plan: grieved that I would never be known as my daughter's mother and overjoyed that I would see my child grow up with every advantage in life. I named her Jeannette after her father Jean Langlais." Nurse Emily fell silent.

A suffocating oppression descended upon Gena like the pressure she always felt when a huge thunderstorm was about to roll over Manawassa. She knew it was not her place to interject anything so she waited until Nurse Emily continued.

"One night I had just returned from visiting my daughter Jeannette at Blount's swamp. I looked in on Madame who was already asleep. I went to Jacqueline's room…" She paused again. "She was still and white and cold. Another Martin child was gone. I wept for the agony that John would feel. I had barely dried my eyes when I conceived a dreadful plan. The two infants were girls and were of similar age and appearance. The only difference was that the dead child was the weaker of the two. My little Jeannette took her strength from me not her father Jean Langlais. I returned quickly to Blount Swamp and retrieved my daughter. Marthe and I had grown quite close. She had no great love for her mistress, even if she was loyal to her. I explained to her what I wanted to do. She gave me her blessing and I returned to LeMoyne. I wrapped the dead Jacqueline in Jeannette's blanket and placed my Jeannette in the dead child's cradle. She now became Jacqueline Alexandrine LeMoyne de Bienville. My hope would still be fulfilled. My little girl would grow up with all the advantages of a de Bienville. I would inform my mistress Léonie that my child died in the night and Marthe would confirm it. I would tell her that Marthe buried the infant at Blount Swamp."

Emily ceased speaking and John began. "That is a terrible night never to be forgotten, and yet it was. Only rumor, innuendo and accusations spewed forth until all of Azalea Cottage became sullied by filth. That is why we have been calling to those who could help. That night I made such a wretched error. I was restless and sat in my study. I looked outside and saw Emily carrying a bundle. She laid it down and left. I became curious and went out to see what she was doing. She had been to the gardener's shed and was bringing with her a shovel. I stooped down and uncovered the bundle. To my horror it was my daughter. Emily, I assumed, had murdered her. After she first came to Azalea Cottage we had grown quite close. There were implications of unhappiness in both our speeches to each other. Nothing resulted between us. Upon my wife's return from her recuperation, Emily withdrew herself from me. I did not know why. I knew nothing of her condition of being with child by Jean Langlais. As I looked at the dead child I grew furious. Although I had ceased to love Léonie, I loved my children. Emily was startled at seeing me, but before she could utter a word I shook her violently. I heard someone behind me call my name. I was grabbed from behind and I let go of her. She fell backward and hit her head upon the downed oak tree. The next thing I knew I was struggling with Cephas."

A deep masculine voice softened by humility spoke. Gena looked at Cephas.

"I knew only what I saw: the nurse lying dead, my beloved Léonie's child dead and a madman of a husband, a murderer standing over both. I could not control my rage and seized John to drag him to Léonie. I was amazed that one so useless and weak could fight back with such strength. He broke away from my grasp and fell. He struck his head and died. I blamed myself and cursed my anger. I rushed to my mistress to tell her what had happened, to tell her that her child was dead. As I passed the nursery I heard a child cry out. I looked in and saw a child I believed to be Léonie's baby. I told Léonie what John had done and what I had done. I was bewildered that there was a dead infant. She did not tell me the truth."

Cephas looked at the woman he loved as she sat with her dead child. You could hear the incredulity in his voice.

"She did not trust me. I believed the dead infant to be Master John's and Nurse Emily's as Léonie told me it was. I lived and died

265

believing that. I was sent away to New Orleans and went to sea. I wrote my beloved Léonie and she wrote to me for six years until…"

Léonie spoke. "We shall leave that for the end." She looked at Gena. "Ask. I know what is in your mind."

Gena blurted it out. "Did you know that the baby who lived was not your Jacqueline?"

"Not at first." She looked at the still form cradled on her knees. "As was my custom, I had little to do with the child after she was born. Then the third month went by and I saw she had a strength that my others did not. Before she was a half a year old I knew that the child was Jeannette, the daughter of Jean Langlais and Emily Sattherwhite."

"Did you hate her for it? Grand-mère, I mean." Gena blurted out. "She said you were a stern mother to her."

"On the contrary, I was glad to have sturdy de Bienville stock to mold after my fashion, even if it was from my brother."

"And you did fashion her to be strict, but not completely."

"No. There was a goodness about this Jacqueline, a gentleness I can only suspect came from her mother."

"Thank you." Emily bowed her head slightly towards Léonie.

"Two Jacquelines and both de Bienvilles: a weak one who died and a strong one who lived. There were two halves in my Grand-mère that warred with each other: her de Bienville side and her Sattherwhite side; a hard side and a soft side. I am like her: a part of me is all business and a part of me loves Kayton Landry. Two sides: formal and wild, like LeMoyne and Azalea Cottage."

Gena turned to Calla and then knelt on the floor to be on a level with the little girl.

"I now know the truth now. I know that you are the little girl of my dream; John and Nurse, the man and woman; and Cephas, the dark man. I don't understand the meaning of the Tiger Door, or why I mistook Reese to be you."

"Neither do you understand why, when you were ten years old, you also experienced odd behavior and dreams?

"What could be the connection?"

Calla broke into a delightful childish laugh. "Maman, let me tell her. Please, Maman, please."

"As you wish."

"I died when I was ten years old. It was an accident. I would have died soon enough anyway, had I not wandered out the door in a delirium. I was seeking the eternal Kipling world where I would be happy forever. So, you see, I died before all of these awful things happened. That means when I died Azalea Cottage, or LeMoyne as you call it, was still in its innocence. Azalea Cottage was sorrowed under her burden and so her plan was simple. Every ten year old girl among the de Bienvilles would experience her trauma through me until the truth was made known and she was cleansed. The Cottage would call for help until someone came to rescue her. I was allowed to choose the call and naturally it had to have Shere Khan and the jungle animals in it. That is why the Tiger Door was never allowed to be removed.

"So when I was ten I had those dreams and what my mother called 'the stares.' I remember now. It's been buried inside me for so long. I would think that I was seeing someone, but before I was sure she would disappear. My trances worried my parents a bit, but I grew out of it."

"By the time you turned eleven, I daresay. I imagine you ceased hurling objects at your cousin as well." Calla's impishness made Gena laugh.

"Did my grandmother experience any of this?"

"Please let the Child finish." Léonie commanded, though softly. All the same it was a command and Gena fell quiet.

"Jacqueline did indeed."

"So Grand-mère and my mother when each was ten years old…"

"No. No. Your mother was not a de Bienville, except by marriage."

"Oh. And it didn't affect the males?"

"No, only the young ladies and there were not many of us. Some were more easily called and never lost the pull of LeMoyne completely; others were weaker." The little girl paused as if to permit Gena another question.

"That means Grand-mère would have received the call at age ten, yes?"

"She did indeed, but in vain. She struggled with the dreams and messages. It was Maman, her supposed mother…," Calla looked at Léonie with beseeching eyes. The lady nodded and the child continued.

267

"...her supposed mother who quashed them. I am sorry to say so, but Maman did not want the truth revealed. Jacqueline, for of course she now had the dead child's name, never forgot us. She knew about the trio buried under the fountain, but she did not know the whole story. What she suspected she buried deep within her. She believed that her mother Léonie had done a dreadful thing and she did not want to admit it. She put us off and would not help us. I believe she wanted you to be our helper. It was not until many years after Jacqueline abandoned us that another young girl heard me speak to her and saw the Tiger in her dreams.

"You mean me."

"That *is* true. You did." Calla cocked her head to one side and her ringlets quivered in the eerie light. "You were ten years when you were called, but there was another before you and two others after you."

Gena rose to her feet and stared down at the Child. "Who could they possibly be?" Gena asked. "Grand-mère had only one child – a son – my father; and on my cousin Langlais's side, there have only been sons. Other than Langlais and myself there are no other de Bienvilles left. I am the only female de Bienville left. Where did these two young de Bienville girls come from?"

"Liliane Aimée, you must let me continue."

"*Oui, Maman.*" The little girl stood in an attentive pose.

Léonie resumed the narrative. "You forget the letter that my father wrote to me not long after Liliane Aimée's death." Léonie stared deeply into Gena's eyes.

"I remember it. The letter referred to an illegitimate child your brother Jean Langlais had fathered by Nurse Emily. The child was Grand-mère who was substituted for the dead Jacqueline."

"The letter never specified who the mother was." Léonie glanced at the nurse who bowed her head.

"No, it didn't, now that you mention it." Gena looked puzzled. "I just assumed...and just now you revealed that Nurse Sattherwhite was pregnant with your brother's child...and you found a letter from her to him..."

"I was deceived in Jean Langlais's love for me. I was not the only one to whom he confessed his love." Nurse Sattherwhite kept her head bowed. John Martin brought his arm gently around her and indicated for Léonie to proceed.

"My brother had many women," Léonie picked up the story, "one of whom was the daughter of a well-to-do tradesman in New Orleans. Her name was Serendipity Frasier. Upon learning of her condition, her father confronted Georges Henri about his son's reprehensible behavior. This was at the same time I learned of Nurse Sattherwhite's condition from the letter she sent Jean Langlais. My father suspected a liaison between Nurse Sattherwhite and Jean Langlais, which is why he sent her away, but he was never told about the child she carried. I wished to spare him; his health was poor. He, along with all of New Orleans, was supposed to believe that Nurse Sattherwhite's child was Antoinette's and Jean Langlais's, but, as I have said, that did not happen. My father did ask me to facilitate the matter of Miss Frasier's condition. So I dealt with both situations. I relocated Miss Frasier to Manawassa Springs where she had a son named John. I saw to it that she entered service at one of the wealthy residents on the Promenade. John grew up and went into service as well. He later married a woman from here. They had a daughter, Amaryllis."

Gena gasped. "Reese's grandmother!" Léonie ignored her and continued.

"John and his wife moved into Quarter House, the house where all Lemoyne servants lived, and became my servants."

"That is an amazing coincidence." Gena cried involuntarily.

"No. It was LeMoyne who drew John here where Amaryllis needed to be raised. When this Amaryllis, who is, as you have guessed, Reese's grandmother, was ten years old we came to her. She was very receptive, but by then another world war raged. John went to war and was killed. Her mother attributed little Amaryllis's mental woes to this. The girl was sent away and no longer could help us. LeMoyne waited another twenty years for you, Geneviève. Your Grand-mère knew you would come of age when you were ten. That is why she hosted your birthday at LeMoyne. Sadly you spent too little time here as a child to be of use to LeMoyne.

When Amaryllis grew up she married and had a child named Rose. By the time Rose was ten she lived far from Manawassa Springs and LeMoyne. Her experience of our calling was quite weak. Yet her own daughter…"

"Reese."

"The family was drawn back to Quarter House and Reese had strong abilities to perceive us. Your defenses against the call of LeMoyne had been weakened by the stress of your business affairs. You had begun to lapse into the dreams of your youth. After you moved here they only strengthened. Then Reese came of age. The combination was for LeMoyne…"

"Azalea Cottage, Maman."

"She is known by both, Child." Léonie smiled at Calla. It was a grave smile, but a smile, nonetheless. "The convergence of your two powers brought about the circumstances by which the truth would be made known. Now you know almost all of it. There remains one last tale to be told. Then you will be reunited with all of your family."

Gena shrank back. "I'm going to die."

"Don't be a silly goose. It is as I told Father not long before I left this world: "All will be well, Shere Khan will take care of everything. I have told him to be vigilant. He will not let go until everything is set to right. There will be no secrets. We will be a real family one day, all of us together." You must now meet the last members of your family."

"I have more family? There are more de Bienvilles than Rose and Reese?"

The man Cephas spoke again in his strong, but sad voice. He reminded her of the man who sang "Old Man River" in the movie *Showboat*. He was weary. You could see that even death had not abated the power of grief over him.

"Yes. I will pick up from the awful night I was banished. I lived mostly at sea. In the next six years I saw Léonie a few times in New Orleans, but we were unable to engage as lovers. Finally, I could stand it no more. My ship put into Pensacola and I slipped away. I went to LeMoyne. The house was dark and silent. I found my beloved. We went to our Memory Room and I had her. She did not resist. At last we enjoyed our love as we ought to have done all those years. It was the only time we did. I left somehow knowing I would never see her again. Some months later she wrote that she was with child. She laid out the course my life was to take.

She left LeMoyne for New Orleans before her condition could be discovered. She took Marthe DuPont with her. When I returned from the sea I married Marthe and became Pierre DuPont. Our son was Marius

Guillaume DuPont. You know him as Margiddy."

"I can't believe it and, yet, I do believe it. There was something in Margiddy's face that haunted me. His eyes were thick with cataracts, but they were de Bienville eyes. We share de Bienville blood. I have a new family, one far better than Langlais: Rose and Reese and Margiddy."

"And my grandson."

"What grandson?"

"Margiddy had a son – Dr. Pierre DuPont. You already know him."

***

As Gena watched the forms of the spirits began to oscillate. They melted into colors which swirled round and round like little tornadoes which then melded into one. A tall figure now appeared before her garbed in a flaming yellow-orange robe with a magenta sash. Black hair tumbled down her back and her dark face glowed with joy. Fiery green eyes looked down on Gena. She was captivatingly beautiful. She was LeMoyne and Azalea Cottage coalesced into one spirit. She gave a grateful and triumphant smile as she dissolved out of sight. Gena knew she would never see her again.

***

Gena finished painting her scene. Katie was stunned and didn't know what to say. She had only been a little off, she thought defensively. She had figured out Cephas was Pierre and that Margiddy was the son of Léonie and Cephas, but she was shocked that the dead baby wasn't John's and Emily's. Cephas had thought so because that was what Léonie told him. That was what his journal said. Even more shocking was the fact that the dead baby was Léonie's and John's – the true Jacqueline de Bienville; the baby that had lived was Jean Langlais's and Nurse Emily's. This was more convoluted than a Russian novel. Gena was a de Bienville, not through Léonie, but through her jerk of a brother Jean Langlais. In the end it didn't matter because there were other, nicer people in her family and now Gena knew it. Katie snapped out of her reverie and noticed that Steve and Kayton were throwing guilty glances at each other.

"What's going on? Is there something you aren't telling us women?"

"Guilty as charged." Steve held out his hands as if for handcuffs. "Mr. Crippett let Kayton and me in on the fact that DuPont was

271

Margiddy's son. Margiddy, for all his fine qualities, had left his wife and son Pierre for a life at sea. He never came back to them. They assumed he was dead. If the sea hadn't killed him, age ought to have. The man is around ninety-five years old. DuPont never imagined his father was alive. Crippett has been working on the old salt to meet his son. I think it's going to happen, by the way."

"Wait a minute. You don't get off as easy as that. I was right, Steve. Say it." She turned to the doctor. "Kayton, your friend Dr. Pierre DuPont is a long lost relative of Gena's and I thought he factored into all this even before you and Steve met with Mr. Crippett. So there. By the way, what does he look like?"

"Look like? He's in his sixties, African-American…"

"Green eyes?"

"Bienville eyes." Gena said. "I can't believe I never noticed."

"He lives in New York now, but is from New Orleans?" Katie pushed on.

"Yes. He still comes down quite a bit." Kayton and the others were looking quite puzzled.

Katie satisfied their curiosity. "I'm sure I ran into him when Steve and I were in New Orleans." She looked at Steve. "He's the nice looking man who kept me from falling down the night we got engaged. I knew I had seen those eyes and that face before. If Margiddy were younger, they'd look just alike. I don't suppose I'm a long lost cousin or anything, am I?"

Gena laughed. "A best friend is sufficient for me."

***

CHAPTER XIX
THE NEW FAMILY

Several Weeks Later

"Fall finally got here." Gena brushed aside an annoying bug from her face. "And a whole new set of insects came with it."

"Let's go inside." Katie laughed. The two women headed into the sun porch of LeMoyne to enjoy the day without the annoyance of bugs.

"I am glad to be reunited with my other family." Gena set her tea down on the glass table. "I enjoyed our get together at Stokely the other day. Thanks for coming. Think of it: my distant cousins Kayton, Rose, Reese, Dr. DuPont and Margiddy all in the same room with me. It was strange to see Margiddy at a manor house instead of the old tugboat, but he seems to be adapting."

"Indeed he has." Katie laughed. "Mr. Crippett says the old sailor's ordering around Carroll as if he'd been doing it all his life."

"Good for him." Gena smiled. She had been smiling a lot lately. Between cleansing LeMoyne and reuniting with Kayton, she had a lot to be happy about. "I think it's wonderful that Rose will be his nurse. Imagine, finding out that they are long lost cousins whatever times removed, as am I. It's funny, though. Rose didn't seem all that surprised. If she had known about all this she never said anything. Maybe one day we can talk and get to know each other better, the way family members should. Speaking of family reunions, Dr. DuPont was genuinely happy to find his father again. It melted my heart to see old Margiddy hug his son. I love my new family."

They sat enjoying their chicory laden coffee and beignets, compliments of Kayton who had just arrived again from New Orleans. Soon they would be joined by the man himself as well as Steve. The pair had been off doing man things. Katie had not really had an opportunity to broach the subject of Langlais's downfall with Gena. Needless to say their focus had been on recent events. Gena was more inclined to elaborate on her experience with her beloved house.

"I call it the 'Ten Year Old Syndrome.' Calla died at age ten, as we now know, by accidentally stepping off the porch in the last delirium of her illness. She was a sad, but inspirational, little girl and I'm glad LeMoyne, I mean Azalea Cottage, took her as form in which to appear first. Each of us de Bienville women, whether we knew we were de Bienvilles or not, channeled the spirit of Azalea Cottage when we turned ten: Jacqueline, Amaryllis, Rose, Reese and me. The house called each of us to solve the mystery and cleanse the stain on her spirit. Jacqueline and I knew we were de Bienvilles, not that it helped us, or at least not Grand-mère. The other women supposedly had no idea of their family connection, but it didn't stop the spirit from in possessing them. I shouldn't really call it possessing."

"That sounds spooky." Katie said. "Let's call it "inhabiting.""

Gena paused and laughed. "How ironic. A house inhabiting a person instead of the other way around. But it really isn't even that strong. It was more of a visitation in order to issue a personal invitation: You are invited to solve the mystery that has plagued the house of LeMoyne. I mean Azalea Cottage."

Katie couldn't get over the change in Gena. She had become practically light hearted. After so many years of being burdened by her work at Bienville Enterprises, by her loss of Kayton, by the incessant, but subconscious, nagging of Maison LeMoyne, she was set free to be the Gena of her youth.

"You know, Gena, there's no need to correct yourself. Maison LeMoyne and Azalea Cottage are reconciled. LeMoyne represents not just the bad or sad things that happened here, but the good, too."

"Do you think so? I feel like the colloquial designation of Azalea Cottage honors little Calla Lily and her father better. They both loved azaleas, which by the way I intend to plant in abundance. I want to recreate the garden in honor of them and Nurse Emily. I'll rip out the cursed fountain and…"

"Wait, wait." Katie laid her hand gently on the arm of her animated friend. "To be reconciled doesn't mean that one has triumphed or destroyed the other. It wasn't a war where the good guys had to defeat the bad guys. Think of it as a quarrel between family members. Léonie, Cephas, John, Emily, Calla all wanted to be loved. As is so often the case in this world, things got all mixed up and sometimes that leads people to do things that are not very nice. Things happen that aren't intended. I'm not asking that you excuse anyone's behavior, just that you forgive them so the Le Moyne de Bienville and the Martin halves of the house can live together in peace. Azalea Cottage was built by John Martin out of love for his bride. Léonie, poor wounded soul, imposed the name LeMoyne on the house out of discontent, but that doesn't mean the name isn't important. It tells a part of the story, too. All of the components, the azaleas, the old oak, the swing, the fountain and…"

"…the Tiger Door. I'm not afraid of it anymore. I think it's beautiful. I look at it now and see all the wonder that little Calla must have felt about going home to a new world. In her pain and suffering the innocent child was given a gift to help her imagine what Heaven would be like, or her understanding of it. Her father and Nurse Emily must have had some joy along with the bitterness of Calla's illness. I even think about Léonie, torn between her duty and her love. No wonder life was sour for her. It was only at her death that she knew love and forgiveness. The Tiger Door has a calming effect on me. It's funny. Now that I know I am perfectly sane, Mr. Pearse thinks I am a complete lunatic because I plan to restore the door and keep it in place." A quiet hush stole over Gena. Both women sat without conversation for a time, just sipping their drinks. Gena broke the silence.

"You're right, Katie. The last thing I saw before you found me was the one spirit that embodied both halves of the house. She was breathtaking. I will honor this Gemini of a house. A twinned soul, so to speak, like my own and Grand-mère's and…even Léonie's. It has given me a family I never knew about, one with members as dissimilar as the components of LeMoyne herself. Who would compose a family of the steadfast cousin Dr. Jefferson Landry and the tormented Léonie, of salty old Margiddy and his polished son Dr. DuPont, of shy Rose and her raucous little Reese, of…"

"…gracious and saintly Gena and soon to be convicted slimy felon, Langlais?"

Both women laughed.

"I shouldn't laugh at my cousin's misfortune."

"He deserved what he got. Dr. Franklin and Snake-man, too. Perhaps prison will do them good."

"I daresay Langlais will be running it before he gets out since he couldn't get control of Bienville. At least he'll have plenty of time to work on it."

"Speaking of which. Who is going to run the thing? Bienville, I mean." Katie bit her lip. Despite Gena's liberation from the mystery of

LeMoyne and a return to the gentleness of her childhood, she still had a business head and Katie assumed she intended to use it.

"Glad you asked. I am in the process of disposing of my predominant interest, much to my financial benefit and peace of mind, by the way. It will be put into trustworthy hands, I assure you. The FBI has been a real help in that regard. May hat is off to them for weeding out the tares. It's sad in a way. Other than Langlais and myself there are no more de Bienvilles to run the business, unless you think Margiddy wants the job." Gena and Katie both laughed. "I don't feel any attachment to it anymore – one of the gifts of the spirit of LeMoyne for cleansing her, to use your expression. The one stipulation that I did make was that the name Bienville be kept and that was to honor Grand-mère's memory."

"A worthy name it is, too." Kayton Landry quipped as he and Steve stepped through the door of the porch. Both men planted kisses on the cheeks of their respective loves. "She hasn't told all." Kayton said as he settled into the chair next to Gena.

"I was waiting for you." She reached out her hand to his. As more coffee was poured out the pair unfolded their plan to Katie and Steve.

"A charitable foundation for medical services to the third world. I don't know what to say. That's great. Wonderful. Amazing. Fabulous. Perfect." Katie flailed her hands around in excitement and would have swept her mug and plate off the table if she had continued with her list. Steve intervened by catching her hands, thus saving the crockery from sure destruction.

"She can't talk without moving them." He smiled at his fiancé.

"Very funny…," She gave Steve his hands back then leaned over and pecked him on the cheek to let him know his tease was forgiven. "…but unfortunately it's true enough when I get excited. Now that I've regained my voice without the need of my hands, my rationality has returned. Your plan makes perfect sense. One has the medical know-how and experience in third world countries and one has the business acumen."

"I tend to let my ideas run away with me. I need Gena to keep me grounded." He looked at her and gave her hand a squeeze.

"They are always good and selfless ideas, though."

"Where will you live?"

"We'll travel I suppose," said Gena, "but Azalea Cottage will always be our home."

"Definitely so if Joe has anything to say about it. He is thoroughly smitten with Talia Pearse, but medical school is first." Kayton beamed with pride. "Oh, and Pierre DuPont has agreed to be a part of the new organization."

Katie looked at the happy couple and knew that it might take a while, but inevitably Gena and Kayton would marry. Their long lost love would be fulfilled after years of separation. She always tended to wax romantic in these situations. It wouldn't matter if she were twenty years old or seventy. It was her nature. She pondered her own future as Mrs. Steve Mallory and felt a joy rush through her.

As if reading her thoughts Gena directed a question to her and Steve.

"Getting entirely off subject, I know, but I wanted to ask the two of you if the date has been set?"

"We're looking at Christmastime." Katie fingered her engagement ring. "I'm not a very patient person and I'd do it tomorrow, but that would be selfish."

"We want all the children and grandchildren here," Steve explained. "That makes the holidays the best time."

"If we had some champagne I'd offer a toast." Kayton raised his mug in a mock toast.

"Just a sec." Gena rushed off the porch and returned with a bottle of fine champagne and four glasses. She handed it to Kayton to open.

"Do you always keep a bottle in readiness?" Kayton pried off the wrapper and popped the cork. "I guess I have a lot of things to learn about you after all these years."

"I always appreciated the Boy Scout Motto: Be Prepared. A lingering part of my business mentality." Gena laughed and passed Katie a glass of bubbly.

"A useful part that we can all appreciate." Kayton poured the rest of the round.

When they had received their glasses Gena lifted hers and toasted.

"To my best friend Katie and her wonderful fiancé Steve. May they live happily ever after."

"Here, here! To Steve and Katie. A long, happy marriage," a unison of voices proclaimed.

Gena raised her glass again and turned to face the massive carved wooden door where the burning tiger prowled amid the frolicking animals.

"And to the Tiger Door which saved my life. May it ever watch over LeMoyne, known also as Azalea Cottage, and protect all who dwell within her."

"To the Tiger Door."

***

EPILOGUE
THINGS TO COME

Wedding plans were in full swing and Gena made every excuse she could to be of help to Katie. The two had just returned from extensive and expensive shopping. They were at LeMoyne looking over Katie's latest additions to her wedding trousseau.

"I thought you were immune to weddings, but since you offered." Katie was holding up two distinctly different outfits in order to get Gena's opinion. "Which for the reception? The sexy secretary or Marian the Librarian?"

"Marian. You don't want to shock Manawassa society."

Katie looked at one, then the other and tossed both on Gena's bed. "I'm really hungry and the guys should be here any time now."

The friends headed downstairs to the kitchen to get things ready. Steve and Kayton had gone to fetch some pizza. Things had gotten sidetracked when Steve was called to the farm about one of the calves. Kayton tagged along. His years as a doctor in some of the remotest areas of civilization had also taught him a thing or two about impromptu veterinary science. Once the crisis was resolved they rang the women to let them know they were on their way.

"We might as well put our feet up in the living room in case "on the way" is code for "haven't even ordered the pizza yet."" Gena led the way to the living room and the pair chatted about the upcoming wedding. Both of them jumped when a loud knock came at the door.

"Must be the food. Did you lock Kayton and Steve out for some reason?" Katie grinned as she headed for door. Opening it she was completely surprised.

From the living room she heard Gena shout, "It's about time."

"It's not them. It's Miss Minnie." Katie stood stomach to face with the tiny, shriveled old woman. Miss Minnie as she was known in Manawassa was an octogenarian who lived in a small, but quaint, gingerbready Victorian that she herself, and everyone else as well, called the Dollhouse. It was obvious that the old lady was distressed. She was mumbling and ringing her hands.

"What's wrong, Miss Minnie?" Katie escorted the elderly woman into the foyer.

"Can I use your phone? They're everywhere, all over now. Such pests. I can't stand it anymore. I'm being driven to distraction. It gets particularly bad this time of year. I had to get out of the house."

Katie who hated roaches with a passion shuddered involuntarily at the thought of these vile insects. "Do you need the name of a good exterminator, Miss Minnie? Because if you do, I've got one."

"What?"

"For the roaches. I have the name of a good exterminator."

"What roaches?"

"You said your house was full of pests, so I assumed you meant roaches."

"No, no, no, no, no. It's the ghosts my dear. They've taken over the Dollhouse."

ANOTHER BEGINNING

Characters from *The Lady With The Lantern*[5]
Characters from the turn of the twentieth century

Aloysius Bellingham: English ex-patriot who founded the Stoa, an intellectual center in Manawassa Springs, around the turn of the twentieth century. He built "The Grand Lady" of Manawassa Springs: Belle Magnolia. The house harbored a dark secret. Bellingham died in 1943.

Lulu Magnolia Brock Bellingham: Aloysius's second wife and his junior by 22 years. She was a great benefactress and beloved by Manawassa Springs. She died at a very young age.

Victoria Bellingham: Aloysius's cousin who came to assist in the household duties after the death of his first wife Susan in 1896. She eventually became Aloysius' third wife in 1912 She was cool and efficient.

Eudora Bellingham: One of Aloysius' and Susan's children. She inherited Belle Magnolia in 1943 and lived there until her death. She was always flighty and in her old age became very strange.

Dr. Harold Caldwell: Physician and childhood friend of Lulu Brock Bellingham. He tended her in her last illness.

Modern Characters
Anna Wilkes: An owner of Belle Magnolia who purchased it in the 1970s after the death of Eudora Bellingham. She was the first to realize that the house held a dark secret.

Katie O'Neill: The current owner of Belle Magnolia and the woman who solved its mystery. She turned the house into a Bed & Breakfast. She also appears in *The Tiger Door*.

Steve Mallory: Retired Naval officer and Katie's love interest. He is a partner in an organic farm/vineyard with his son and daughter-in-law. He also appears in *The Tiger Door*.

Bethlehem Bradley: The librarian of Manawassa Springs called "The Owl" by Katie. She also appears in *The Tiger Door*.

---

[5] The Lady With The Lantern takes place in different time periods. One set of characters are from the turn of the twentieth century. Some of them live into the middle and late twentieth century. Anna Wilkes' story is set in the 1970s. Katie, Steve and Bethlehem Bradley are characters from the early 21st century.

Made in the USA
Charleston, SC
19 June 2015